Praise for

THE

Foreign Student

"Choi's descriptions are strange and powerful.... *The Foreign Student*'s plot is carefully orchestrated and camera-ready. It takes a war, an epistolary betrayal, and a natural disaster to effect a kiss."
—*New York* magazine

"First novelist Susan Choi writes in clear, unburnished prose."
—*Washington Post Book World*

"It is in Choi's beautifully detailed evocation of the rich, albeit scarred emotional landscapes of her characters that she is at her best—grave, clear-eyed and artless." —*Publishers Weekly*

"An accomplished, perceptive novel, which invites rereading and lingers in the reader's memory." —*Booklist*

"So many first novelists write books full of saved-up images and earnest performance, but Choi seems to have put self-interest aside and make a pact with the story about how it wanted to be told. Her allegiance to it is absolute, her prose elegant and self-assured." —*Arizona Republic*

"Choi tells her story with meticulous attention to detail and unfailing self-confidence." —*Miami Herald*

© 1998 by Marion Ettlinger

SUSAN CHOI was born in Indiana and grew up in Texas. Her first novel, *The Foreign Student*, won the Asian-American Literary Award for Fiction and was a finalist for the Discover Great New Writers Award at Barnes & Noble. With David Remnick, she edited an anthology of fiction titled *Wonderful Town: New York Stories from "The New Yorker."* Her second novel, *American Woman*, was a finalist for the Pulitzer Prize. In 2004 Susan Choi was awarded a Guggenheim Fellowship. She lives in Brooklyn, New York.

THE
Foreign Student

a novel

SUSAN CHOI

Perennial
An Imprint of HarperCollinsPublishers

A hardcover edition of this book was published in 1998 by HarperFlamingo, an imprint of HarperCollins Publishers.

First HarperPerennial edition published in 1999.
Reprinted in Perennial 2004.

Designed by Elina D. Nudelman

Library of Congress Cataloging-in-Publication Data

Choi, Susan, 1969–
    The foreign student : a novel / Susan Choi. — 1st. ed.
      p. cm.
   ISBN 0-06-019149-X
   I. Title.
   PS3553.H584F6 1998
   813'.54—dc21   98-11919

ISBN 0-06-092927-8 (pbk.)

04 05 06 07 08 ❖/RRD 12 11 10 9 8 7

Acknowledgments

I'm grateful to the Fine Arts Work Center in Provincetown for its generous support.

I'm also deeply indebted to the following people: the Lee family, Hilary Liftin, Cindy Klein Roche, Steven Stern, Peter Wellington, and, most particularly, Semi Chellas and Peter Wells.

1950   Before the war his family spent their summers at the country estate they had once lived on all year around, before his father's appointment to the university and their move to the city. Each May, as the sharp stench of the city emerged, he would see his mother roused from her long winter of homesickness and catapulted into action by the nearness of the day they would finally leave for the country. Their house in the city was violently cleaned. The furniture was hauled into the corridors and each room scoured until nothing remained but the sunlight entering the wide, high windows to point out the damp streaks on the floors. During this time the usual order of the house was suspended. His mother vanished into an apron and became indistinguishable from the servants, who shouted at her and at each other as much as his mother usually shouted at them. He became one of the anonymous children, evicted outdoors with the perishable food and told that they had to eat everything. And his father would be magically transformed, appearing with a feather duster bobbing in his hand, gliding toward the library end of the house. His father cleaned those rooms himself. Hidden behind doors that were generally closed upon rigorous silence he could be heard, if the doors were approached: a tender *slap, slap* of books removed from their shelves to the desk, a murmur of pleasure, turning leaves for a long interval, then finally the cover closed again and the nearly inaudible sound of a feather duster moving across wood. The scouring of the house took days but his father's languid progress through the library rooms often proceeded, its ardor disguised by a dignified lack of speed, for weeks. It began long before the other cleaning began and often ended well after the rest of the house had been transformed into a furniture morgue, phantom lumps in the center of every room, skirted by the immaculate floor.

For the last few nights before their departure, mats were spread for sleeping in the small foyer, and the rest of the house was sealed as if against a plague. Messengers bearing the annual and ineffectual suicide threats from his father's students were blocked by a wall of packed trunks, stacked three deep, on the porch. He remembered the packing of the house and the leaving of the city as the most exhilarating occasions of his childhood. He would sit between his parents, each of them resting one hand idly on one of his knees, a traveling bag cramping his feet, his skin itching with longing to be exposed to the warm air it sensed through his jacket. Half a day's travel to the north, the other house was being roused from sleep, its servants rehearsing the gestures of servants, its furniture being rediscovered beneath sheets.

Now, leaving the city, he was headed south. By the time he ascended the steps from the basement office into the street a bruised color in the sky was all that was left of the sunset. The card in his breast pocket made a stiff place in the front of his shirt, a shirt that was otherwise depleted, soft from wear and stained with sweat beneath the arms and in an oval above his sternum. He had stolen everything in the office that he could lay his hands on bearing the emblem or a recognizable mark of the United States government: a regulation T-shirt, USIS letterhead, several pieces of official correspondence that were addressed to Peterfield, and a sheet of old news off the wire. At the last minute, he went back and took Peterfield's Underwood. The black case banged rhythmically against the outside of his knee.

He walked in the street, in the slim margin between the gutter and the slow-moving traffic. His glasses were sliding down his nose. He didn't stop them. He saw no one else walking. A ROKA soldier hanging by one hand off the side of an open-backed truck dropped the butt of a rifle before his face, and the truck, which had been barely moving, stopped. The soldier rode alone on the running board. He was wearing American-issue boots, which were far too large, and Republic of Korea Army fatigues.

"Where are you going, to study hall?" the soldier asked. He didn't answer. They watched each other expectantly. He wondered, the thought brief but terrorizing, if they could have been schoolmates. The truck's bed held two benches, both full. The floor of the bed was also full. The twin rows of boys were seated so close together that their shoulders were forced to twist to one side. They sat facing each other over the heads of those packed between their feet. The soldier said, "Can you hear me?" Balancing the butt of his rifle, he made a light jab and knocked off Chuck's glasses. In Chuck's vision the road swam. Laughing, the soldier looked toward the driver, who was cleaning his nails. The faces in the bed were impossible to see.

"I have ID," he said. "I work for the wire service."

"You have papers?"

"ID." He shifted the Underwood to his left hand, casually, but he did not yet reach for his card. He squinted hard at the soldier. Could they have been schoolmates? "I translate. I have Special Status."

The soldier turned again toward the driver with a look of mock amazement. The driver was not watching them.

"Then where are you going?" the soldier resumed. He yanked

3

the black case from Chuck's hand. Without turning the case on its side, he snapped open the clasp and the Underwood crashed to the street. The bright black carapace cracked open, spilling the carriage and throwing forward a cluster of type bars. The soldier had leaped away from the falling machine in panic, barely saving his shoes. One reel of the ribbon was dislodged and the inked strip of cloth unfurled into the street, the bright reel bouncing over the stones and then stopping abruptly when the whole had unspooled. Peterfield's mail, the old sheet of news, and the blank letterhead all fluttered to the ground. The soldier stood waiting for him to gather the papers together. The driver had looked up in annoyance at the sound, and he spoke to the soldier now.

"Put him in, we have to go."

The soldier looked at Chuck. "Get in," he said. "You're drafted."

"I have ID," said Chuck.

The soldier lifted his rifle and punched the muzzle into the center of Chuck's sternum. He felt his lungs collapsing, and a seal closing over his throat. He fell against the curb. The driver slapped the side of his door and it made a large, hollow sound. "We have to go now," he said.

The soldier hesitated. He lifted the rifle and thoughtfully looked down its length. Chuck tasted blood, the champ of a bit. He gasped and then vomited. The soldier drew back, smirking, and kicked the typewriter. The platen flew free and rolled to the gutter. When the truck began to move he caught hold and jumped onto the running board.

After the truck had passed Chuck rolled to his stomach, and reached across the ground for his glasses. Then he sat wiping the lenses free of dust with the tails of his shirt. The acrid stain down his chest was pale pink on the gray cloth. His chin was wet, and the skin there burned. He pulled the T-shirt from its hidden place in the waist of his pants and filled his mouth with the taste of its cotton, biting down on the soft mass, soothing the terrible itch that the acid had made on his tongue and in the back of his throat. When the cotton was wet he sucked the cloth, and swallowed the liquid. He hadn't eaten all day. He stood up again, wobbling.

The car was waiting for him where his uncle had said it would be. A single pair of eyes, probably a child's, blinked from a doorway.

"I'm Lee's nephew," he told the driver. He knew he hadn't been followed but he squatted next to the car nervously, pressing against its dark flank.

"I knew who you were," the driver said. "Come on. Let's go."

The car's backseat held fur coats, fine rugs, goosedown bedding. He burrowed into these things. "Careful," said the driver. "Lie flat." The driver came and unrolled a carpet over him. Darkness closed in, and then a soft crushing weight as the driver methodically buried him. He closed his eyes and fought for breath.

When the car began to move he tried to imagine the streets as they drove, to visualize each building as it passed. He often did this when he couldn't go to sleep. Choosing one street, he'd try to reconstruct it from the pavement to the rooftops. It was always surprising how little of the city he remembered, although he'd lived here all his life. He often wound up with just the litter around his feet, a storefront, the shape of the road.

o n e

1955   The mountain at night was pitch dark. The twin beams from the headlamps would advance a few feet and be annihilated, and only the motion of the bus striving upward indicated that you were not at sea, and only the dispersion of stars in the sky marked off what lay around you as a mass and not an infinite void. His first time up this road from Nashville the bus had put him off in the middle of nowhere and nothing and its tail lights winked out around a bend before the driver thought twice and backed up. The small lights reappeared. When the bus was alongside again the door swung open and the driver pointed into the featureless blackness. "That way," he said. Chuck had still been standing at the side of the road with his suitcase hanging from one hand and his overcoat over one arm, and this was the petrified figure that Mrs. Reston, the vice chancellor's housekeeper, found at the door to the vice chancellor's house forty-five minutes later. You would not have known that the motionless person had just walked two miles straight uphill with a steady and terrified step and only the slight paleness of the gravel reflecting the stars to direct him. To Mrs. Reston he seemed to have dropped into the pool of porch light from outer space. She showed him inside and unclamped the hand from the suitcase's handle and unbent the arm from beneath the drape of the overcoat, and gave him some tea in the kitchen.

Mrs. Reston was annoyed with the bus driver for not having explained things more clearly. It would seem like a failure of hospitality, in her opinion, unless a person knew that the gravel drive up to the vice chancellor's was too steep and shifty a purchase for the lumbering bus and even most cars. They'd go skittering right off the edge. As far as hospitality went, *she* was ready. She had been ready for his arrival for days and had been waiting with a pot of tea and her embroidery basket and a pile of *Silver Screen* back issues for hours.

She gave him his tea in the kitchen, in order to impart the idea that he was not a guest, but a boy being welcomed home. This tactic, based on years of experience with free-floating, frightened young men, fell securely within the realm of which she was the mistress, and she would have done it even if the vice chancellor had not been away for the weekend. But she was glad that he was. "You must be tired after such a long trip," she said. "I'm going to keep you down here a quick minute because I've been so anxious to meet you, but then I'll take you right up to the guest room. There's the one nice thing about the vice chancellor's being away. You can sleep late. Otherwise I'm very sorry he's gone. Oh, my goodness, you look so tired! Are you going to perish?"

He shook his head and smiled. He was somehow not capable of speech.

"How many hours was your trip?"

He took a long time to answer this question, so long that although she was never quick to judge, and so unflaggingly optimistic in all situations that the vice chancellor had once complained to her about it, the horrible thought crossed her mind that he didn't speak English at all, that he had faked his letters the way some boys faked their grades. And then he said, in a voice that snagged on its own exhaustion, "Eighteen hours and—" He wanted to add something, to answer her kindness as well as her question. "And we stop to take fuel in Alaska."

"Alaska! First time in this country and you've already been to Alaska. I don't think I will ever see Alaska in my life. Was it beautiful?"

This did not seem the word. It had been a gloaming, purple and vast. Past the end of the world. But he didn't have these words, either. He nodded, and nodded again when she said, "You poor thing. Let me put you to bed."

It was a tidy but comfortable room, with a high bed and a lamp on the table that was already lit. Mrs. Reston turned the bed down and patted it briskly. He stood helplessly by. All the distance he'd plowed through, and her one simple gesture disabled him. He followed her back to the door.

"Sleep *late*," she said, turning away.

He shut the door after her, and looked down at the knob. Then he opened and shut and reopened it. She was already far down the hall.

"Excuse," he called.

"Yes dear?"

"If I have to lock." He twisted the knob.

"But you don't. It's all right. We don't lock our doors here."

"Ah. Thank you."

He shut the door again and sat on the bed. Then he lay back on top of the covers, and pushed off his shoes with his toes. The shoes were too large, like the suit and the coat.

After a while he sat up, undid the knots in his shoelaces, and set the shoes beside each other on the floor. He lay down again and tried to find sleep. The thought of the door filled him with shame, because he could not accept the lack of precaution as a sign that he was safe.

꧁✿꧂

After a breakfast of poached eggs, fried ham, grits with butter, a half grapefruit, and a short stack of buttermilk pancakes, of which he ate only the grapefruit, he was sitting alone on the porch. The day was clear but the air was full of mist, and the broad clear slope in front of the house was slick with dew. It was so quiet he heard every sound: the faint scraping of pine boughs against each other, the creaking of top-heavy trees, birds calling, and from deep within the house the murmur of Mrs. Reston's kitchen radio and the hiss of the tap as she cleared up the dishes. Then a roaring rose from nowhere and gained quickly in volume, and a tiny cream-colored convertible shot up the road and stopped dead right in front of the house. After a moment's hesitation the sounds of the morning began to make themselves heard again. The car's door opened and slammed shut and the car's driver came striding up the walk with her gloves in one hand.

Mrs. Reston had heard the engine and she came outside, drying her hands. "Oh, that *car*," she said. "But it does handle well up this road. I imagine Katherine could drive it right up the side of a cliff." Katherine came up the steps and put out her hand and Chuck found himself standing and shaking it. From a distance he had thought she was a very young woman, even a teenager, but as she approached he realized she was at least his own age, if not older. Katherine shifted her gloves from hand to hand. "Is that really your name?" she said. "Chuck?"

"No." When she nodded impatiently, interrogatively, he added, "Chang. Is my name."

"Somebody's changed your name from *Chang* to *Chuck*? Was the idea to make it easier to remember? Correct me if I'm wrong," she said to Mrs. Reston, "but you're not going to save any syllables going from 'Chang' to 'Chuck.' You're not even going to save any letters, unless you transliterate the name as the French would. And I don't see why you would want to do that. Have you fed him, Mrs. Reston?"

"I tried," said Mrs. Reston.

"I guess our traditional Southern breakfasts are too austere even for a Buddhist. What did you give him? A ham-and-egg sandwich with strawberry jam and a side dish of hollandaise sauce?" Mrs. Reston laughed and wiped her eyes on her dish towel. Katherine laughed with her, but as she turned away he could see her expression reverting to one of angry watchfulness, as if she were waiting for a signal that she didn't expect to receive.

She had been enlisted to drive him to Strake House, where he was going to room for the year. Katherine was often to be found performing odd errands around Sewanee, driving faculty widows to shops or retrieving drunken young scholars from police stations, although nothing about her except perhaps her car, her idleness, and her failure to outright refuse seemed to qualify her for these missions. Among year-round residents her solitary peculiarity neither escaped notice nor was talked about much, anymore. She was twenty-eight years old, and unmarried.

After they had left Mrs. Reston and were driving away he said, after several false starts, "I am not a Buddhist."

"I didn't think you were. I'm glad to see you're not a mute, either. You talk very little."

"I am sorry."

"Are you worried about your English? You probably read and write just as well as any of our home-grown scholars. They're geniuses. Little Shakespeares. You'll be quite amazed."

"Shakespeare," he began.

"It's the talking that stumps you. Don't worry. It's the same way with everyone. Speaking English is far more difficult than reading it or writing it. One must be spontaneous, witty, and charming *sans cesse*. It's a tall order even for those of us who were raised to do nothing but."

By the time Strake House came into view they had lapsed into what he hoped was a mutually comfortable silence, destroyed the instant she cut off the engine. He had barely managed to unfold himself from the car before she seized his suitcase and overcoat and was making her way up the walk, calling over her shoulder that the housemother was very kind, and that his room was very large, and that he would not have to share it with anyone, although she had to wonder, she continued aloud, to whom this was in deference. He knew that the warm stone façade just ahead was the end of the dream as he'd dreamed it. Dreams were place markers, waiting rooms, dead time. In dreams you rehearsed— but none of his dreams had achieved the refined complication of the actual moment. A presemester hush lay everywhere, the perfect peace of a place that is utterly empty, but knows it will soon be filled up again. There were petunia beds edging the walk. The pale brown gravel resolved into hundreds of colors and shades when you looked at it closely. And her feet, swiftly scissoring, mounting the steps, and his suitcase appearing beside them.

"I have a piece of advice for you. If you really like Shakespeare, you must take Charles Addison's lecture. It's a little like going to the theater. It doesn't matter if you don't get all the words." Then she bade him good luck and shook hands once again, and was gone.

Mrs. Wade, the Strake House mother, asked if he knew how to ride a bicycle, and when he said yes she presented him with a blue three-speed Schwinn. It had been left behind in the basement one year. On the first day of classes he rode it to the quad with the tails of his jacket flapping behind and his hair sticking up off his head in the wind like a cock's comb. If you had asked him one month earlier whether or not he could imagine himself arriving for his first actual day as an American student with twin sweat stains under his arms, and the cuffs of his pants crumpled up where he'd had them stuffed into his socks, and his notebooks tied onto the rack of a rattly blue bicycle, he would have been dumbfounded. But for that past month he had been alone, and exploratory. He took an English grammar with him but he never really opened it. Instead he watched the mist from the sprinklers scattering small rainbows over the quad, or the groundskeepers trundling wheelbarrows. He learned the layout of buildings by heart. There was always the whine of a lawnmower coming from somewhere on campus. Wandering through the woods where they were wild he would just start to think himself lost when the faint lawnmower sound would be carried to him like a beacon. A deserted university in August can feel like paradise. He grew tired of anticipating his various arrivals and dating his life from a moment that would not stop receding further into the future. And so by the time the term finally began he had acquired an odd proprietary arrogance. He was dirty and in love with everything and in possession of secrets, and when he came up the flagstone walk pushing his Schwinn he did not care what anyone thought of him.

Only the very beginning of the semester was placid, and perilous. That first day the flagstone walk had been lined with pale, tailored, spit-shined bodies completely absorbed in themselves until Chuck grew near. He seemed to be pushing a ripple of silence ahead of himself. Everyone swiveled, and smiled, and stuck out a hand, and the hysterical idea occurred to him that he was a general inspecting his troops. This idea carried him along but it wasn't able to prevent the incessant bobbing of his head and the hand he was using to shake, and the ceremony could have absorbed the rest of the day had someone not offered to show him the bicycle rack. Although he could have found that bicycle rack in his sleep, he allowed himself to be led to it, and then into the lecture hall, where he was stood up in front of the throng, and made the occasion of a speech about America's duty.

But Sewanee soon achieved its own characteristic atmosphere of perpetual crisis, and from then on, although he was still noticed, he was no longer closely observed. He did what he'd done at the wire service: put his head down and looked diligent constantly, and was diligent most of the time. This was the only attempt he made at concealing himself. He never tried to fit in, and eventually found that not having strived for some particular niche had settled him into a niche of his own. He was kept company more than made sense to him by a freshman from Georgia named Crane, whose father was in paper—not newspapers, all of which Crane held in contempt, but the actual stuff they were printed on—and also the Klan, in the capacity of Grand Dragon of the brotherhood of Atlanta. Crane announced this to Chuck on the occasion of their first meeting, in the hallway, introducing himself by way of a lengthy recitation of his family connections. Chuck discovered his own particular charm—he had an infinite patience for listening. So he listened, and spoke very little. He listened to Crane's lengthy discourses, generally delivered to him without warning, while he was trying to study, and from his own doorway, which Crane liked to violently seize by its frame as he spoke. He listened to the conversation roiling around him in the dining hall, where he ate alone if he did not eat with Crane. (He didn't have to eat alone. He would have been welcomed anywhere, nodded to, smiled at. These were well-bred and, they liked to think, worldly southern young gentlemen, and they had heard a rumor that Chuck worked for army intelligence during the war, and many of them secretly wanted to know him but never knew how to extend themselves, and he certainly didn't extend himself.) And he listened to Charles Addison's great Shakespeare lectures.

Addison lectured once a week, on Wednesday evenings, in the

middle of the supper hour. "To discourage attendance," he told them, surveying his audience, which spilled into the center and side aisles, with a standing-room crowd at the back. The tactic to discourage attendance was so unsuccessful that the dining-hall staff had instead reduced the quantity of Wednesday-night cooking by half, substituting bins of cold sandwiches, which were left outside the dining-hall doors along with apples and cartons of milk. Eating during lecture was forbidden, on the principle that blood from the brain would be diverted to the stomach for the ignoble work of digestion, and so going hungry became part of Chuck's sense of eventfulness, along with the noisy journey across the quad afterwards, as everyone made for the sandwiches, destroying the nine p.m. hush. Chuck arrived early each week to find his seat in the middle, near enough to miss nothing, far enough away to feel hidden, but at midterm his happy anonymity dissolved. Instead of an exam there would be recitations. Each recitation had to be a monologue, but beyond this constraint they were free to choose anything. They were reminded that in Shakespeare's time, men had played women. They were urged to be bold.

He lay awake sweating the whole night before, the collection of noises that made up the speech jabbering away through his brain, and by morning was so nervous he seriously considered staying in bed and dropping out of the class. At last he was overwhelmed with shame and got dressed. Waiting his turn, he sat folded up on the floor of the dim corridor outside Addison's office, his forehead planted on his knees, whispering the speech into his lap as if it were a mantra. *Yee elb sov hills brook stan ding lake.* The corridor had been transformed by the sort of festivity that often results from collective hardship. Around him students paced and hissed and waved their arms, absorbed in their own mnemonic battles. His sense of condemnation was vivid. He felt he knew exactly what awaited him, and by the time his name was called and he had stepped into Professor Addison's office everything was adequate to his worst expectations. He began, woodenly, to recite. *Make mid night mu shrump that re joice.* Relieved from every possibility apart from that of absolute failure, his memory kept on unfurling. *I have be dimm the noon tide sun.* When he reached *'twixt the green sea and the azured vault*, Addison stopped him.

"'Vault,'" said Addison.

"'Balt,'" he answered.

Addison sighed and made a tent with his fingers. After a moment Chuck's mouth opened again tentatively, and Addison's hand flew up, stopping him. He clamped his mouth shut and gulped.

At last Addison said, "I was going to ask you why you chose such a difficult speech. It's one of my favorites—unfortunately, one of the ones I'm least able to endure hearing butchered."

He stared at the floor.

"Now it occurs to me that any speech of Shakespeare's is likely to contain the letter 'V.' It would have been conniving of you to locate the one speech that doesn't, if such a one exists. Instead you've been bold, as instructed, and lumbered all over the alphabet. Do you have trouble memorizing English?"

"I think so," he whispered.

"For twice the trouble I would suggest four times the effort."

He nodded mutely.

"You may go," Addison said.

The next day at lunch Addison found him in the dining hall. "Are you free to take a walk?" he asked. Chuck set down his silverware and followed without protest. Once they were outside he continued to trail the professor at a cautious distance. He had never walked casually with a professor as if that man were his friend. Social protocol at Sewanee confounded him. In his first week he'd shaken hands with the colored table servant at formal Friday dinner. This man, who he had learned was named Louis, had been stationed at the end of Chuck's table in a brass-buttoned jacket and snow-white felt gloves, and when Chuck found that the evening's seating arrangement had him at the end of the table where Louis stood, he had greeted Louis and shaken his hand. Louis's grave demeanor and immaculate dress seemed to dictate this, but later Crane told him that his gesture had been inappropriate. "You can't be casual with them," Crane said. Walking with Charles Addison, Chuck kept his silence and watched the ground. The sun was high and Addison's shadow was compact, but Chuck still lagged behind. "I intend to teach you to pronounce the letter 'V' and the fricative 'th' by the end of this term, as a matter of preserving my sanity," Addison said. He stopped and turned around. "What the hell are you doing?"

Chuck hesitated. "When I'm growing up, if you walk with a great man, a professor, you got to walk behind. To not step on the shadow."

Addison burst out laughing. "I'm not a great man."

"You're my professor."

Addison studied him, amused. "I'd prefer that you walked alongside me."

Chuck nodded acquiescence. After a further hesitation he stepped forward, and then they continued.

This became their habit. Most days, Charles Addison came and found him in the dining hall, and then they walked together for about half an hour, repeating words or sounds back and forth. Sometimes they discussed the broadest generalities, but mostly their conversations went like this: "Thistle." "Thithle." "Thistle!" "Thithle!" *"Thistle!"*

His spoken English may have actually grown worse during this time. He was called upon to demonstrate it far less often than he had been at USIS, and there was also the effect of his listening, and the things that he listened to. Communication at USIS had always been a brusque, economical affair: the same few sentiments expressed and reexpressed, and the same few phrases used to express them. One day he had sliced open his fingertip on a piece of paper and found himself cursing in English with surprising extravagance. Peterfield and Langston had roared their approval, but later that night Chuck sat down to the Webster's with renewed determination and impatience: if all of that could settle into his throat in the normal course of things, to billow forth without warning, then where were the words that he needed? He studied in all his free moments, but the rate at which he fed himself words was so slow that they weakened and died before having a chance to accumulate, and now, at Sewanee, the rate was too fast. The few words he had were overpowered and swept away. His limited English was mistaken, as it so often is by people who have never been outside their own country, for a limited knowledge of things. But he didn't bother to dispel this impression. He liked having a hidden advantage.

Sometimes he was reminded of Katherine. She was an established figure at Sewanee, and although she was not often seen, she was of long endurance, and this was enough to ensure she was frequently mentioned. He heard that her family was rich, and that somehow she had broken with them. That their ties couldn't have been very strong in the first place, he assumed and admired. She seemed particularly American to him, not in spite of her isolation but because of it. Obligation or dependence would never have entered her realm. Brushing near her he had sensed the shape of possibility, but he didn't know what it contained. Eventually his idea of her grew so elaborate and sufficient and remote from the actual woman that it was a shock, one morning in early November, to find her standing in the lobby of Strake with her gloves in her hand.

"I've been waiting for you to form an impression of good ol' Sewanee," she said, "and assuming you've formed it, I've come to extract it by force. A stranger's perspective is terribly valuable. But

I've had to do a tricky calculation: to hit on the precise moment at which you had formed your impression, but not yet ceased being a stranger. Does this seem like the time? Would you like to go for a drive with me?" The leaves were at the height of their brilliance, that feverish climax that just precedes death. He said Yes.

t w o

The autumn brought an end to accidental encounters and unexpected distractions, all the things that Katherine welcomed but that were not any part of her life. The semester was no longer beginning, and the restless way in which everyone watched what the others were doing, and the exuberance with which they threw themselves into the novelty of hard work with one foot still stuck in the summertime, were all over. The air was pristine now, monastic and preoccupied. There was the subterranean hum of activity folding in on itself. It was a pattern she was accustomed to, one she even felt she thrived within, as her orbit grew increasingly far flung from Sewanee and she was more and more often alone. This time of year reduced life to the pith. In July she had met the vice chancellor's wife on a path in the flower gardens, each of them walking alone, with the racket of insects around them, and they had greeted each other warmly and talked a long time, but in the way that two strangers might if they met in a country that was foreign to them both and discovered they spoke the same language. The summer was a place apart from the normal course of things. The vice chancellor's wife was not her friend. If they saw each other now they would smile and ncd, and keep moving. In the autumn Katherine stayed in her car more than ever, and when she left it she carried her keys in her hand, like a talisman.

Even her friendships with the hired women, the housemothers and housekeepers, were now brisk and pragmatic. Sometimes she still did stand at Mrs. Reston's kitchen door, trading gossip that verged on the ribald, and laughing with her until it seemed that they were weeping. But mostly she moved between them, each domicile a solitary island, ferrying their occasional news back and forth, once in a long while driving them to the good stores in town, and on holidays to the bus stop, when they set out on their pilgrimages, to a sister somewhere, or a nephew. She tried to take their example, and stiffen her spine. Although she felt they must be lonely, they never betrayed it. Nor did they voice discontentment or speak harshly of people, although Katherine often felt there was something they all shared and all took for granted, a placid assertion they made, that they were glad to have staked out their lives on the unobserved edges of things, and that they had their attention half elsewhere. At other times she thought this might be an illusion. Mrs. Reston's whole world did consist of the vice chancellor, and Mrs. Wade couldn't sleep if a boy in her house missed his curfew. Even Katherine would feel faithfulness well up unbidden, at the sight of the dogwoods in bloom on the quad, or the chapel's pale stone turning gold in the late afternoon, or one of the nameless, unowned, cosmopolitan dogs angling eagerly toward her, ears pricked, while her frightening love for this place pinioned her where she stood.

She took care to do things that could only be done at that time of the year. She ventured into her attic, too stifling in the summer to set foot in, and chased away the squirrels with a broom. She picked up turned leaves and stuck them in her heavy books, with leaves from other years, now brittle and forgotten. She attended evening lectures sometimes, feeling that if only she approached the lecturer—on Gothic architecture, on the poetry of Ireland, always an elderly, sage visitor who came a great distance to stay just one night—and posed a question like the questions she saw them ruminate with care, they would be able to speak easily to each other. But she only attended the lectures, and jotted things down on the program, her thoughts recorded as they burst forth in the stillness of the lecture hall, the lecturer's voice like a single, rich note tolling over and over, and her mind, stirred by something, shooting silent fireworks within her skull.

More than anything she drove, watching the leaves turn, and the changes the season made. She was always shocked by the way in which autumn, after dropping constant hints of its nearness, still managed an ambush. She would come out from her house one cold morning and stop dead in her tracks. It was like striking a match to a kerosene lamp and then turning the key: the hills were suffused, with a light from within blasting forth. Looking along the ridge, after every trace of green was gone, she would realize how many shades there had been, each one now a slightly different red, the hill a single thing on the very point of falling to pieces, the trees flinging their dead branches to the ground where they broke explosively underfoot, and the air turning chill and carrying those noises, of tree death and the chattering of creatures, over miles and miles, unaltered. She would sense the shearing away of yet another year from beneath her feet. The passing of time somehow made itself felt the most powerfully during the autumn, in the way the season precisely repeated itself, and the years in between disappeared, each night the clouds lying black against an orange sky, and every autumn linked to the next to make one endless autumn through which her life shot, like an arrow.

Driving, she watched the low sun flashing through the trees. Or coming out into cleared land, one hill swung away while behind it another revolved, the crown of trees on its crest turning a new side to her, and in the gap of sky that widened in their midst a shred of cloud scooting across like a toy on a string. She would drive as far as Alabama, and turn around. She would wend her way north, and duck under the Kentucky border, but she never simply went up to Chicago, or St. Louis, or down to Birmingham. She was always driving back, in the evening, with the western light blinding her out of her rearview. The road that found Sewanee from the west passed down the center of a vast agricultural plain, so level it looked machine-made, lacking even slight dimples or humps where a tree might survive. The red dirt always seemed freshly turned. From here the mountains spanned the horizon ahead like a modest green hedge. Sewanee's own mountain was hidden within this. One would never think, coming toward the place this way, that Sewanee's mountain was a singular thing, circumscribed by what seemed from within like an impassable horizon. She often left town from the north and made a great, aimless loop west and back, one hundred miles without the least reason, finding the farm roads that lay along surveyors' lines until she was here again, splitting the red waste and watching the green take on texture and depth, as the mountain closed in, and the road, as it always had, started to climb.

Katherine's father had been at Sewanee—no one ever seemed to "go" or "attend," it was someplace you always just were—and he liked to return for the summers. The mountains were full of grand yet squat, low-eaved, stone-floored summer houses, as cool as iceboxes. The houses were mostly full of well-heeled old women, faculty widows or society dames who went to the mountains in June because the weather was cool and the company good. Sewanee had always been a summertime retreat. No one remembered which had come first: the well-heeled old women or the striped picnic tents on the quad; a dance orchestra in the evenings sometimes, all the way down from Nashville; and good meals every day, barbecue at least every week, and cocktails all afternoon on the broad patio of the faculty club overlooking the gorge, with the boys from the kitchen tricked out in white jackets and gloves. It had been this way forever. Many of the houses now belonged to successful alumni whose affection for Sewanee, or sense of indebtedness to it, made them want to return every year. It was also true that Sewanee men lived in the South, where they had been born, and so Sewanee was a summer refuge from Birmingham, or Atlanta, or Jackson, that was not someplace like Provincetown, or Maine.

Joe Monroe was one of this group, but he also had other incentives. It gave him great pleasure each year to affect casual ostentation at what always, even in the absence of classmates, felt like a reunion. He wanted to demonstrate the extent of his worldly accomplishment in the setting most likely to emphasize it. At Sewanee he had been a charming but talentless student. Although he worked hard he was only ever average, and even that was largely because he'd had the good sense to cultivate the best-friendship of his first roommate, and to keep him as a roommate all four years. This arrangement had made Monroe secretly miserable. The roommate was famously brilliant, academically careless, slight, unathletic, pseudo-aristocratic, and strangely devastating to the girls. His name was Charles Addison, of Nashville, although once he'd arrived at Sewanee he never really left there again. After graduation he went to Princeton for his doctorate but returned to accept a position from his alma mater, which felt lucky to get him. They never changed their minds about this, and so Addison continued to be lionized at Sewanee long after the larger world of his profession had come to see him as a man who failed to live up to his potential, out of laziness, or arrogance, or both.

In the beginning there had also been a wife from up north, but her failure to adapt had earned her the indifference of everyone, including, it seemed, her husband, and when she vanished from the Sewanee social hothouse she wasn't really missed. This development would have been disastrous for the careers and reputations of most men, but in Addison's case it seemed attractively inevitable. Everyone assumed that he had driven her crazy with neglect and justifiable contempt. Addison had visited Katherine's family on the odd holiday throughout her whole childhood, but it was years before she learned that he had ever been married. And he didn't strike her as a man who thought he'd botched up his life. On the contrary, he seemed to enjoy his own company more than anyone else's. He agreed with Katherine's father's view of him. Joe Monroe dated his own emergence as a possibility, as someone who might amount to something, from the moment at which he found himself accepted by Addison as a good enough companion and foil. In many ways the return to Sewanee was for the sake of seeing Addison, because Joe could continually assert the depth and longevity of the friendship, as well as his triumph. The way he saw it, he had gone forth into the world and made a lot of money, while Addison had lingered in the past. But it was this past against which Joe defined himself, and which in Katherine's family set the standard for everything.

Katherine's own attachment to Sewanee when she was a girl had only been slight, and the acquisition of a summer boyfriend in the year she turned fourteen—a chemistry professor's son who went to college up East but came home for vacations—did not really increase it. The existence of the boyfriend had effected a much more noticeable change in Katherine's mother, who began treating Katherine with a strange sort of prodding dissuasion, warning her not to play hard-to-get, or to cheapen herself. Glee began to say things like, "You're too young to be serious," but Katherine didn't feel serious at all. It seemed to her that Glee was saying she was too old *not* to be serious. The truth was that Katherine spent most of her time with the boy doing nothing. Their options for physical transgression were never quite clear. While Katherine dwelt morbidly on the possibilities, the boy seemed content to go swimming. Sewanee had a river that cut a deep cleft through the grade of the mountainside, sometimes pausing to spread at the base of a steep waterfall. They both had the same favorite swimming place, a coincidence that might have been the sole cause of their courtship. They would walk there together, on a narrow path that was lumpy with tree roots, holding hands. They both wore sneakers and shorts with their suits underneath, and limp towels tossed over their shoulders. Sometimes the path grew so narrow they rotated sideways, still yoked, and then rotated back. But when they reached there she left him, and went off by herself. The riverbed at the head of the falls was a jutting stone shelf, and the water slid over its edge in an unbroken sheet. The falls were so constant they seemed motionless as they disappeared under the surface. When Katherine stretched out and let her ears fill with water the roaring of the falls turned into a noiseless vibration. She liked to pretend she was lying in bed, and tried to untrain her body from floating. She would feel her legs sinking and towing her hips along with them, until she was just an archipelago of new breasts and shoulders and face. She kept her eyes closed. Somewhere near the base of the waterfall the boy was scaling the rocks, or squinting at the prospects for fishing. In the afternoon, when the high cliffs cut off the sun and threw the pool into shadow, he would come to the bank nearest her, holding open a towel. There was an odd, delicate formality to their companionship. They had little to say to each other and little real desire to sneak off alone. The only thing she had to conceal from her mother was the very lack of something to conceal.

One day she came downstairs to the living room and found Charles Addison sitting there alone. "I'm waiting for your father," he said. He looked her very frankly up and down. She was wearing a fitted gingham sundress, with spaghetti straps and darts. It was the sort of thing her mother insisted on putting her in for evening dates with the boy, and not the sort of thing she wore much otherwise, but she was wearing it now, and the womanly cut of its little-girl fabric suddenly struck her as lewd. She lowered herself onto the wicker ottoman across the room from Addison and looked around vaguely. She could feel her initial flush growing cool on her skin, and that strange, delayed bodily acuteness, as if she'd been running. Self-conscious, she raised an arm and scratched at her back between her shoulder blades. She knew it looked gawky and crude. "The bugs have been awful this summer," she said. "Much worse than they usually are."

"It was a rainy year. The ground is still marshy in spots. Pleasant breeding holes for bugs."

"That's revolting," said Katherine, unconvincingly.

"Don't be babyish."

"I'm not."

"You are," Addison remarked calmly. "I've noticed this about you. At a distance you're unnervingly old for your age. I watch you when you don't realize I'm watching, and you're as old as the hills. Then I say the first word and you're babyish."

Katherine cast about for a reply but she could not find one.

"I suppose that's the way your mother has taught you to act. The only girl in a bevy of boys. Have you had terrors from all of your brothers? I'll bet you have." He was smiling pleasantly. "My God, they must terrorize you."

"No." Katherine laughed. She liked her brothers, but they were a different breed. She liked the idea of being terrorized by them; it made her wish they had. But no, they had never done that.

"If I had a babyish baby sister of your description I would give her hell on earth. I would make her regret every breath that she took."

"Oh, would you?" Katherine felt her nerve sharpening, growing alive to the challenge of him. "I'll bet you would. You're enough to make someone regret being born." She had never had this sort of conversation. Suddenly uncertain, she reached again for the elusive itch, but it was not there. She deeply preoccupied herself with an imaginary discomfort, one arm hooked awkwardly over her head, and realized suddenly, with horror, the nervous prickling beneath her arms that was soft hair there, gathering sweat. Her mother had bought her a woman's razor for her birthday, a heavy stainless-steel thing with an elaborately worked handle and tightly shingled blades, but its habitual use seemed absurd and she had put it away and forgotten it. The arm dropped.

"Come here," Addison said.

Crossing the room, she had known; he had only taken her by the shoulders and turned her, and seated her on the edge of the sofa before him, and scratched her carefully between the thin gingham straps. Her hair hung thick and loose, an upper boundary, and below was the snug upper seam of her dress. It was a small compass. Her skin beneath her hair teemed unbearably, but his hand would not move there. "Where is it," he said, searching slowly. Then his fingers paused. It was not a bite; it might have been no more than a slight interruption in the color of her skin, a mark that she would never see, or his attention gathering and disabled by its own weight. He suddenly pushed his hand up, raking over the teeming skin, into her hair. They heard the motor of a car and a door blithely slam, and she had risen and moved, like a sleepwalker, out of the room.

*I*nevitably, after the packing in New Orleans and then the driving and arriving and unpacking were accomplished, and the annual inventory of new symptoms of the house's collapse had excited everybody, they would sink into listlessness. There was nothing to do in Sewanee. Every summer was a ritual of marking off great chunks of time: the time between breakfast and lunch, and from lunchtime to cocktails, the days between tea at the Struthers' and that weekend's barbecue, the number of hours between dinner and when it seemed all right to get into bed. There was something defeated and even unseemly about getting into bed while it was still light outside, but Katherine often did it anyway; unless her parents weren't out on the porch, and then she would sit there with a candle, listening to night-bugs hurl themselves against the screens. For several years it had just been herself and her parents. All her brothers were now married or gone off to school, and although one had to spend one's summer somewhere—she would hear her mother say this on the phone, in a tone of flirty wheedling that made Katherine cringe—none of them seemed to want to spend it in Sewanee. That she could not gather all four of her children beneath the same roof for the space of three months was sometimes regarded by Katherine's mother as a personal failing, and sometimes as an affront. The remaining presence of her daughter did not seem to offer much solace. For ten years Glee had had nothing but boys, and her supposed incompetence with rambunctious boy babies was a topic she discussed enthusiastically and constantly. But when she finally got the daughter she'd often despaired for, she seemed slightly baffled. Katherine became the sole student of the commentary on How Things Were and How Katherine Should Be that Glee felt compelled to produce, and so Katherine grew up in the unflagging glare of her mother's opinions. Glee's vigilance widened the distance between them, and although each probably saw the other more than any other person, both felt only growing unease. They moved through the house trying not to cross paths, and when they did, sought to arrive swiftly at some minor topic of conversation, like the weather, or the right thing to wear to a party, or the weather's effect on the party or even their clothing's effect on the weather: "If you wear that it will rain," Glee announced, as her daughter came lagging downstairs.

It never did, but it threatened to all afternoon. The party had decided to keep to the broad flagstone deck that pushed off from the rear of the president's house, hanging over his fine sloping lawn. It seemed risky to venture much further. Everyone in the party was, for the most part, old, and for the most part female. Many of them were clustered around Charles Addison, laughing with what they seemed to feel was dangerous abandon. They were gasping and fanning themselves. Katherine watched her mother move across the flagstones, one hand regally proffered, and Addison seize it and pull her toward him through the crowd. He kissed her briskly on the mouth and then, making a mock show of recalling himself, on the hand. They laughed hard and exchanged witticisms. Katherine could not hear what they were saying but it didn't matter, it always looked the same, that infuriatingly smug show-offiness of adults. Her father was back in New Orleans for a few days on business. Her mother didn't take advantage of his absence so much as flaunt it, as if the very fact of her continued existence under such circumstances deserved special praise.

Katherine went to watch the kitchen boys husking sweet corn, ripping away at the tight layered leaves, and then fastidiously going to work on the squeaky silk threads. Eventually she found herself at the head of the flight of stone stairs that swept from the deck to the lawn. She began climbing down. The sky glowered and grumbled, noisily shifting its great weight like heavenly furniture. The rain was all around them. It only needed a catalyst, some first effort to give a stir to the air and send everything tumbling. She came off the steps onto the lawn and strode into its center. She imagined herself to be the unacknowledged focus of a collective, multifaceted attention: matronly disapproval, or maternal annoyance, or some other keen, distant disinterest. The weather was attending on her, too. Looking back she saw heads up there, bobbing eagerly, but from this distance she could not make out their eyes. For a while she trailed conspicuously to and fro on the otherwise empty lawn, like a lightning rod. Her dress was a yellow silk sheath. Her mother claimed that even water would stain it. She was still on the grass, hoping for telltale droplets, when shrieks and leaping flames from the deck drew her reluctantly back there.

The air was so pregnant with moisture that the coals wouldn't light. The kitchen boys were dousing them with straight gasoline and throwing lit matches. A wall of fire would spring up with a *whump,* burn a minute or two, and then seem to evaporate. An acrid combat stench had filled the air. "You're just burning off the gas you pour on. You've got to light the coals from underneath," Addison was saying. He was ripping up the *Chattanooga Tribune* and stuffing crumpled balls of it between the coals. Several women cried out that he might burn himself. Louis, the head cook, tried batting Addison away with a pair of tongs. "Mister Charles," he said. "Please." It was another well-known eccentricity of Addison's that he was friendly with the colored help. He often made an irritating display of shaking hands with the table-servers at university functions. He asked President Clate whether he didn't have kindling in his house, and when the boy Clate sent in reemerged with an armload of logs Addison threw his paper in the air and sat back, to the delighted titters and remonstrances of his blue-haired attendants. "None of you people have the first idea how to start a fire. We need *kindling.* Don't you know what that is?"

Louis said, "I'll send some boys down, Mister Charles."

"No, no, no. I'll get it myself. I'll need an able-bodied assistant, though. Someone who's not afraid of rain."

"I'll go," Katherine heard herself saying.

"Your dress, Katherine," said her mother.

"You could let her pick up a twig every now and then. It might keep her from getting more spoiled. Hard labor?" he inquired of Katherine. "Do you think some hard labor might save you from becoming a thoroughly sickly and disagreeable young woman?"

Glee was still laughing, happy to be doing so, as she thought, at her daughter's expense, as they made their way across the open lawn.

"I'm not 'spoiled' or 'sickly,'" Katherine said as they walked.

"My God. I know you're not."

"I bet I could outrun you right now."

"Even in the little dress and sandals?"

"Yes."

"I'll bet you could. I'll bet you could beat me senseless as well."

"I might," she began.

"You look lovely," he said. Before she could reply he added, "You dress beautifully. In spite of what your mother says."

"She likes the dress. It's that she's worried I'll ruin it."

"I'm sure you will."

When the screen of trees behind them had grown thick and they no longer saw the house, she turned—she had been for so long, it seemed then, fourteen whole tedious years, moving within narrow grooves, over familiar surfaces, testing the very few things she had power to do and the very few ways she could do them. Even when she was alone she felt as if she was measuring up. But this had blown her off her small planet into a void and she couldn't touch ground, she couldn't do anything but what she was doing and so she turned to him, suddenly, leaning with her hands as if she were leaning for support against a tree, and he pushed her away. "Not now, we haven't got time," he said. He was on the ground, looking for twigs.

"Then why?" She fought against a sudden rush of tears. "Why did you bring me here?"

"I wanted to see what you'd do, darling. I wanted to see if you'd do what you did."

When they had gathered enough they went back through the trees without speaking. As they drew near the house her mother came down to meet them, laughing again, her glittering gaze fixed on Addison. Katherine's dress had twigs and leaves stuck all over its front and it might have been snagged. "Charles Addison," Glee chided, "*look* what you've done to my daughter. . . . "

three

They sped past the base of the drive to the vice chancellor's house and he thought of the night he'd come up, able to grasp only motion, not a sense of the distance, and then standing still to feel space reexplode all around him. He tried to make conversation, telling Katherine about walking up that first night, and about the lamp Mrs. Reston had put in the living-room window. He had walked for twenty, maybe thirty minutes with only thin moonlight sifted onto the gravel, scared out of his mind, before he'd seen that small promising glow. Mrs. Reston hadn't turned on the porch light in advance, not wanting to greet him with a big cloud of bugs, and so he had been greeted instead by that sudden shock of a spotlight on him, and when his sight came back, Mrs. Reston there smiling for all she was worth. He had been extremely grateful, he carefully explained, for the confidence of the promptly opened door, and the lack of locks. The windows were open to the night air, his bedroom door was open to the hallway, and although this had made sleep impossible for a long time it had also reached back to encompass his terrified toil up the hill, and now this trial seemed like a transforming and deliberate arrival. It was wonderful, he concluded, that it had never occurred to Americans to keep their doors locked.

"Not so wonderful," she said. "People trust too much here. It's not like this everywhere."

"I like to learn to trust in outside," he said.

She found this mistake evocative. "In outside?"

"Where I am living, before this, it is no any safe to walk." He gestured outside the car. "Outside, in a countryside. I can't do this there."

"Because of the war?"

"Yes," he said. His voice rose slightly at the end of the word, as if he meant to continue, but he didn't say anything else. Just like that, he had remembered his dream. He could never understand what it was in the full light of day that lay across his path like a trip wire, waiting for the slightest touch to recall the night to him. He'd been having the dreams ever since he left Korea. All that had been needed was for that life to withdraw itself slightly, to give his mind space to restage things. The dreams were so frequent he'd begun to realize when he was inside them, and then he would fight to get out, the dream a clingy web that withstood every effort to tear it, every flinging of his limbs only sealing it more closely to him. Sometimes he woke with the disturbing sense that his own voice had just finished a long ricochet through the room. The dream flickered past his sights and was gone.

Katherine was saying, apologetically, "I don't know anything about the war."

He shook his head, a gesture that reminded her of someone flinging water from his ears. "There is not much to know."

"I'm sure there must be."

"No."

After a moment she said, "I've always wondered what a war really looks like. There's no way to tell, reading the papers."

He shrugged, but said nothing. She was a little pleased at his brushing her off. "Perhaps it's not too much trust," she corrected herself. "Perhaps it's more a sort of thoughtlessness. Sewanee is an island. Nothing new ever washes up here, and that makes people dull. They stop noticing things. You're the first new thing here in a while."

"I know islands," he said. "This is no any island."

"An island of the mind. Or an island of the soul." She laughed briefly. "You'll see."

That fall he'd often walked in the woods. In some places white pine trees grew so tall that their trunks had lost their branches to a height of twenty, thirty, forty feet or more because they didn't get light. The stumps descended down the trunks like thorns, and between the pines nothing else grew. The dim air seemed full of fine, plum-colored dust. He would feel as if he were homing in, the thick mat of needles crackling beneath his feet, toward a place where stillness was accumulating, and then suddenly the trees would give way and he was standing at the edge of a cliff, facing a bright void, looking down over farmland that stretched away into haze. People spoke of living on the mountain, but he saw they lived in it. There were many places like that, where the view was unutterably lovely, and at the best of these the university had erected a huge white crucifix. It was the first thing that anyone saw, coming up the long gradual road through the lesser mountains, that indicated the nearness of the mountain itself, in the same way that Mrs. Reston's lamp had been the first thing Chuck saw as he climbed. Katherine always noticed the cross making its first appearance like a pale stitch in the green mountainside, even when she tried not to. It would vanish behind turns and then reappear, growing steadily larger. And when she was leaving she watched it in spite of herself, nearly running off the road, as it slowly diminished backwards in the frame of her rearview.

He spoke very little after they came down out of the mountains into open farmland. She watched him watching the road.

"Do you drive?" she asked.

"No."

"I'll teach you if you like."

"Yes." He nodded. "Yes I would."

It occurred to her that she was taking him someplace specific, a place that had no significance apart from what pointless repeat visits can eventually bestow anywhere. This was the penultimate landmark in the drive up to Sewanee, a tiny oasis with a gas pump and a Coke machine where she habitually pulled over, even if she didn't need anything, just for the sake of stopping short. She didn't know why she did this. She always grew frustrated and impatient with the people who ran the place. As soon as she had turned off the engine she would suspect that the boy who pumped the gas was sullen, or even sadistic, in the way he slowly loped out to her car. The woman soda jerk in the cafe seemed reluctant to lift her arm, and the arm itself seemed to be made of lead. By the end of three minutes Katherine would be mad with impatience, and she would hop back into her car and gun the engine, and swear to herself, and scream her wheels in the dust. But she always inserted this hiatus into her drive. She couldn't seem to do without it. Going in the other direction, away from Sewanee, she never thought to stop there. It was on the far side, and too near the foot of the mountains to be separate from her blurry sense of prologue, when she felt she wasn't quite on the road. She would rarely perceive it had passed, and if she did, she would hardly think of it. Looking for it now, she nearly missed it.

There was a filling station and a café, yoked together because the town they were attached to—the town itself was nowhere in sight, and must have lain far inland from the road, tucked between sheets of farmland—was too sparsely populated to spare more than a few sets of hands to run both places: the boy, and the woman, and an occasional old man who fixed strangers' cars that washed up. The three didn't seem to be related. There were always other people hanging around in the café, or leaning against the front of the garage, and as she and Chuck came out of the car and walked to the café together, these began to emerge. They must have known her as well as they knew the distant streamer of smoke from the train or the mud puddle that formed in the dust every time that it rained—she was an unremarkable, semiregular feature of the landscape, something which excited little speculation and which vanished from memory the moment it vanished from sight. But now they noticed her. She bought Chuck and herself a pair of sodas and as they stood wordlessly drinking them, in front of the café doorway, and watching the boy slowly, with many looks over his shoulder, handle the gas pump into the tank's mouth, the people, all ten or twelve of them, gathered to watch, also—to watch her and Chuck, standing there, watching her car.

She was afraid for a moment, and sensed that he was also. They slurped their drinks, staring ahead. The boy looked back at her uncertainly, and she nodded, and so he looked down at the nozzle again until a spurt of gas leaked down the side of the car and then he snatched the nozzle out. As the boy wiped down the side of the car and washed the windscreen, lifting each wiper blade with an excess of care and restrained admiration—it was a very nice car—there was a waiting that they all shared in, and the mass of it gathered around them. But it did not tip or tremble; it kept steady. They might have been watching a ship come in, Katherine thought. For a moment she could feel it. The arrival in a strange land, and stepping onto the gangplank as the whole harbor paused in its work and turned a single gaze toward you. She stood there with him in a half circle of constant, unshy observation until she had paid the boy and they had emptied their glasses and slowly walked back to her car.

"They don't know what to make me," Chuck said, as they were driving away.

"Don't know what to make of you."

"Yes. Sorry."

"Don't apologize. Your English is much better than I'd thought. It's much better than you led me to believe, the first time we met."

He didn't think he had led her to believe this at all. "I read, write—fine. Speaking, it takes slower."

"You mean it takes longer, or that you are slow."

"Yes. I'm sorry."

"I wish you wouldn't apologize. Please don't." When he was silent she said, "Does Bill Crane treat you well? Does he make conversation with you? That's very important if you're going to learn."

He was surprised that she knew who Crane was. "He is very good."

"A good friend? A good conversationalist?"

"Both."

"He's a fine example of his type, that's certain. I'm glad he's nice to you."

"Everyone is kind here. It really is. You are," he added shyly. "To take me to drive."

"I wanted you to see the country around here, before the leaves went away. You've been up on the mountain ever since you arrived."

"I have been to places. Last month I go to Mobile, Laurel, and Augusta," he said, enunciating each name with great precision.

"Really?" she exclaimed. She had hoped she was taking him on his first exploration of America. "What for?"

"There is something, the Episcopal Church Council. I go to churches belonging in this, and talk on Korea."

"Just for your own amusement?"

"No, I do it for the council, when they ask me. But I like to give a talk. I have a projector, and I show some slide."

"Of the war?"

"Not so many." Most of his pictures were from a set of National Archive photographs of Korea, in which it looked dim, impoverished, and unredeemable, in contrast with his presentation, which sought to be generic and not surprising or unpleasant. He generally explained that Koreans were farmers, that they enjoyed celebrating their holidays clad in bright costumes, that they were fond of flowers and children—that they were unremarkable, hardly worth the trouble of a lecture. The slides were never quite appropriate. Like his remarks, he kept them as generic as he could, and changed them often. He understood that people liked something to look at, and that even the least seasoned audience eventually lost interest in looking at him. He also gave a potted history of the war, and answered questions. "What kind?" said Katherine. "You must have found it annoying, when I asked you to describe what a war looked like."

"No. This isn't annoying."

"I didn't realize you had to answer people's stupid questions all the time."

"Your questions is not stupid. Nothing you say would be stupid."

She looked at him, surprised.

He blushed. "I tell you a very, really stupid one."

"All right."

"In Mobile, a man asks me if Koreans live in trees."

"Like monkeys!"

"In a tree house," he clarified.

"Like monkeys in tree houses! What did you say?"

"I say no, but maybe he's thinking of the kind of a house we do have, near the water. The kind of a house up on legs, like this."

"On stilts. You were too polite."

He smiled. "That was okay."

"You're polite to say yes to the church council."

"I don't mind it. They give Sewanee, for my tuition."

Katherine was embarrassed. The arrangement embarrassed her, but also the fact that it hadn't occurred to her that such an arrangement must exist. She was silent a moment.

"How do you get there?" she asked finally. "How do you reach these little towns?"

"I take Grey-Hound bus."

"That's terrible!"

He actually enjoyed it a great deal, but instead he said, non-committally, "No."

"I'll drive you the next time you go. How far in advance do you get your marching orders?"

"It depends. Sometimes a lot of time, sometimes just a few, one or two days. I like this bus, though. It's a very quiet time."

"I won't hear of it."

"I do really," he laughed. "I sit, I watch this go by. Like going to the movies."

"Do you like the movies?"

"Yes. Very much."

"We must go sometime."

"Okay."

"But I still won't hear of your taking the bus. I'm going to drive you the next time. That's settled," she said, holding up a hand. He watched her eyes calmly scanning the road, until she glanced at him. "Do you give up?"

"I do," he said.

"You'll call me when you have a new assignment?"

"You make it sound like—you make it sound like I'm a spy," he said, smiling.

After she'd dropped him off he went upstairs to his room and sat on his bed. It was late. He'd missed supper. He wondered if Mrs. Wade had set aside something for him, but he couldn't get up.

Crane must have heard him come in. He came and hung off the door frame, the frame groaning in protest. Crane seemed morose and self-absorbed, as usual. After some time he said, "You want to come home for Thanksgiving with me? Where the hell are you going to go, right? I guess that you'll have to." Crane said this gloomily, as if it were a judgment on himself.

"Thank you. I think so."

Crane did a pull-up, and thrust his legs into the room. He hung there like a pendulum. "My folks don't know you're an Oriental," he puffed, swinging hard back and forth. "My folks are cracked." It was clear that the two statements had nothing to do with each other.

"Okay." He was not paying much more attention to Crane than Crane was paying to him. He no longer wondered at Crane's unlikely, unflagging attachment. He knew that for Crane he was an easy and dependable possession, as if at any time Crane might announce to someone, "My man Chuck." But he liked Crane. Crane was his only real friend, his only possible confidant.

"Where'd you say you were all day?" Crane asked. Without any hesitation whatsoever he lied, "At the library."

*H*e was used to the constant pressure of the future, a dark hive of possibility that he had never learned how to ignore, until now. Now he ignored it completely. The outer limit of his vision sprang up right before his face and he refocused. He didn't think about his next church council lecture, or how he would arrive there, hoping the event, when it came, would escape his attention. It had taken days for him to realize that Katherine had offered to drive him in the way that he heard people say, when they met by accident, "We must see each other soon!" Hearing these exchanges it was never any problem for him to understand that the insistence was insincere, but talking with her, sitting right alongside her—he'd had difficulty judging her meaning. He would walk the paths of the campus with his head bowed, his algebra equations radiating in every direction, his latest dictionary words floating past like bits of floss on a fine summer day, lost in the landscape of his thoughts, but with the problem of her looming throughout, like a hill in the distance. It became clear that her offer of a ride had been no more than kind conversation. He blushed slightly to think it. He was embarrassed not only by his mistake, but by his sudden disappointment.

Dean Bower sent him a note saying that he had been invited to speak to the congregation of St. Paul's Episcopal Church in Jackson, Tennessee. He accepted ten dollars' pocket money for a round-trip bus ticket, a lunch, and some small improvement for himself he was left to decide on, like a new pair of socks. The first move was made, and nothing intervened to correct him, and so he went on, each elapsed day eroding the likelihood of his conversation with Katherine a little more, until he might have actually forgotten, because there no longer seemed to be anything to remember. Then she called him, on the telephone that sat on a glossy round vase-table out in the hall of Strake House. "I don't think I gave you my phone number," she began. "I'm sorry about that. I don't even think I gave you my name. My last name is Monroe." Hearing nothing but silence from him, she felt newly uncertain. But she said aloud, soldiering forth, "Of course, Mrs. Reston knows how to find me. Almost anyone does. But I should have made that simpler. In any case, I hear you're invited to give your talk in Jackson. That's lucky for me. It's a place I'd like to know." She listened carefully for possible signs. Until now she'd assumed he was afraid of imposing on her, but now it seemed she was imposing on him. When she hadn't heard anything from him for days she'd given way to curiosity and gone to ask the dean's secretary about the foreign student's lecture. "I thought that I might send my aunt to see him. Is he asked to speak anywhere lately? I have an aunt almost everywhere."

"He's going to go down to Jackson, Tennessee, next week," the secretary had said. "Have you got an aunt there?"

"No, I haven't."

"That's too bad. Have you met Mr. Ahn?"

"I met him with Mrs. Reston when he had just gotten here."

"He's a long way from home." She sounded vaguely critical saying it. "If you tell me where your aunt lives I'll let you know if he's going there, Katherine."

"That's all right," she'd said. She'd decided to wait and see if he would phone. But then he hadn't.

He had managed to locate his voice. "I just find out myself."

"You just found out."

"Yes. I just found out myself."

"I just heard, too, I'm sure not long after you did. In any case, I'd still like to drive you. I like to drive. I'd still teach you, if you still want to learn."

"I go Thursday. Not this one, the next one."

"If I teach you to drive, you won't need a ride anymore."

"I have no any car."

"Perhaps someone will give you one."

"Yeah!" he said, laughing.

"That would be fine, wouldn't it?" Her voice sounded so reduced. He was standing hunched over because the dried-out rubber coil of the phone cord refused to stretch straight, and his face brushed near the bush of fake flowers sticking out of the vase. He smelled dust.

In the week before their appointment she went to the library and looked for a book on Korea. All she found was a copy of Terry on the Japanese Empire, thirty years out of date. She remembered her father having Terry on everything, when she was a girl. All the flawlessly knife-scored, fragile colored maps, and ads for ancient travelers in the back: Nippon Cruise Lines, Bank of Taiwan, Southern Manchuria Railway. The Yamatoya Shirt

Manufacturers, specializing in *silk, linen, and cotton crape.* Grimy photos of thin rigged canoes, with a sail like a sheet of notepaper impaled on a stick. She flipped to the part on Korea: *Korean ideas of hygiene are almost as negligible as those of a Hottentot. The average Korean well is little short of a pest-hole. The average Korean man is 5 ft. 4 in. tall, of good physique, well formed, with not unhandsome Mongoloid features, oblique dark-brown eyes, high cheek-bones, and non-curling hair that shades from a russet to a sloe black. The olive bronze complexions in certain instances show a tint as light as that of a quadroon,* and under "Seoul Entertainments," *Korean Dances (insipid and wearisome)*—

"Christ!" she burst out, tossing it aside.

Katherine came to pick him up early in the morning, with the giddy whirr of the engine floating far ahead through the still air and her scarf and a ribbon of car exhaust streaming behind. It was unusually warm for November in the mountains, and she was driving with the top down and no hat. When she arrived at Strake House he was waiting for her on the front steps in a thin-looking suit. He was holding a cardboard box that had the slide projector in it, with a brown bag on top. Mrs. Wade had made him a lunch, which saved him some money. Added to what he had saved in not buying a bus ticket and in deciding to stick with old socks, he had the whole ten dollars left over, the bill still folded in half in the envelope that had come from Dean Bower. It was in his power to make some kind of gesture. He wasn't nervous anymore when she pulled up.

They slid down off the mountain and found the road that would carry them west to Jackson, which lay five hours away on the highway from Nashville to Memphis. Autumn had left the hills not so much bare as rubbed dull, like an old sofa's cushions.

The road surged and stuttered, unrolling with growing momentum and then braking hard against towns where a post office and drugstore would spring up across from each other, with one traffic light strung between them. The wind roared too loudly to talk. At first they worried that perhaps they should shout to each other, but eventually this worry was gone, as if the wind peeled it away. One hour passed, and then another, until their wordless cocoon of loud wind in the midst of dull hills pouring past seemed ancient and permanent, and not requiring anything more. Around noon they had to change roads and he leaned toward her with a finger on the map. She hardly glanced at it, taking the sharp right without slowing down, and they slammed hard together against her door, and then slowly came upright again as the car headed north.

Jackson was a considerable small city of six churches, but they were all close together on the neat grid of main street and side streets that made up downtown. They wound through these, their eyes trained together on steeples and signs. Now, in the drowsy noontime hush that they moved through, the silence between them seemed huge. They found St. Paul's and pulled into the white gravel lot alongside it. They had arrived very early. Katherine turned off the engine and they sat listening to its reluctant rattles and clunks as it spun to a halt, and when these were finished, they listened to the birds.

"You must want lunch," she said at last. "You'd better have eaten before you give your talk."

He understood now that he had been expecting the drive to transport him to a place in which he would find himself very calmly buying Katherine lunch with his ten-dollar bill. The simple and absolute logic of such a plan almost guaranteed that it would take place. He fingered the envelope in his pocket.

"Maybe we go find something," he said, accidentally sounding reluctant.

"Mrs. Wade is too good a friend of mine for me to let you waste your lunch. It would break my heart. And I'm not hungry."

"But it must be."

"I'm not." She took her case from her pocketbook and lit herself a cigarette. "I'm going to stretch my legs and take a look around. That's what I need most." She got out of the car, lifted her arms above her head for a moment, and then strode away.

He watched her recede. She crossed the lawn to the front steps, craned her head to look up at the steeple, and then vanished around the side of the building. She had left a thin ghost of smoke near the car. He got the lunch bag from between his feet and unrolled it. The crackling of the paper seemed deafening. He glanced around, but there was no one outside on this street, which was lined with old spreading oaks, stripped bare, reaching sideways for each other. Then he peered into the bag and caught his breath. It held two sandwiches carefully folded in wax paper, two red pears, two slices of cake, and a thermos of water.

They ate sitting together in the small churchyard. "Mrs. Wade is an artist of sandwiches," Katherine said. The churchyard was only half full of grave markers, most of them of the sturdy, prosperous-looking kind, shaped like fat slices of bread, although some were badly leaning and no longer legible. "I never used to notice a church," she went on, balling up the wax paper that had contained her sandwich. She produced a pocket knife from her bag and cut up her pear; if there was a seed she nicked it out and sent it flying. "Churches used to seem like part of the landscape, like rocks or trees. It never occurred to me that there was any difference between them. Not just differences in appearance, but differences in faith. I never gave it any thought at all."

"You do now?"

"I guess I give it a little more thought. For example, this is a plain white shingled church and there's nothing very surprising about the proportions of the steeple. And it's Episcopal, but I don't know what that means from Methodist, or Baptist, or any of the others."

"My mother," he said, surprised to hear himself saying it, "becomes Episcopal some years ago."

"My father was a Catholic. That meant he didn't want any religion in the house at all. I think my mother might have been a Lutheran, but she had to please my father, which was wonderful for her because I'm sure she never wanted to bother with religion in the first place. When I was twelve years old I had a great longing for God. I prayed and mooned about the house and threatened to become a nun. I thought my situation was very tragic. But I outgrew that. You know, when you're a child you want so badly to set yourself apart, and you imagine you're something you're not. Other things came along that I was better at."

"What things?"

"It sounds like you don't think I'm good at anything."

"No!" He flushed. "No."

"I don't know. Other things. In any case, I was thinking that it's strange, because now I'm older and I seem to have come full circle, and started noticing churches. Why did your mother become an Episcopalian?"

"A missionary."

"Are there many Episcopal missionaries in Korea?"

"And Catholic."

"And she didn't want to be Catholic? Or did the Episcopals get to her first?"

"I don't know."

When he didn't elaborate she said, "And your father?"

"No."

"And you?"

"No." She had handed him part of the pear and its scent filled his nostrils. Flowers' perfume, he remembered, is their prayer to God. Where had he read that? He prayed sometimes, but mostly as a reflex. He might be struck, and then it would fly out of him: *please God.*

They saw the priest coming across the yard, frowning and nodding in welcome. "I'm Katherine Monroe," she announced when he'd drawn near, rising to offer her hand. He was looking at Chuck as he groped for it. "I didn't realize Mr. Ahn would be accompanied."

"I'm Sewanee's most famous idler, Father, so I'm always trying to be useful. I thought it would be nice if Mr. Ahn didn't have to take the bus. Shall we get your machine from the car?" she asked, turning back to him.

He followed them, half hearing Katherine's elaborate replies to the priest's inquiries about Sewanee. The hem of her skirt snapped around her knees as she walked. At the car she lifted his box to him and set about raising the top; the priest helped her. "Can you suggest any interesting places in town, Father? I thought I'd take a walk. I've never been in Jackson before."

"You're not going to listen to Mr. Ahn's talk?"

"I don't want to make him nervous. I think it's easier to speak in front of people you don't know. That's all right, isn't it, Chuck?"

He didn't know whether he was relieved or disappointed. He and the priest stood watching as she resecured her scarf around her neck and stowed her gloves in the glove box. Neither of them seemed able to proceed while she was still there. She popped open a compact and glanced at herself, and as quickly shut it again.

"I'm all set. Did you think of anything I should see, Father?"

"Our town hall is a pretty impressive building. If you follow this street to the corner and go left, you'll find some shopping."

"That would be lethal," she laughed.

"If you were a southerner I could think you'd take an interest in our monument square, but you might find it interesting anyway."

Katherine laughed again. "I am a southerner, Father."

"I'm sorry. I wouldn't have guessed it."

"What would you have guessed?"

"Oh, no. It was my mistake to assume in the first place."

"I lived up East awhile. I think I must have lost my accent there."

"My goodness," said the priest. She knew they were watching her all the way to the corner, where she turned left as he had suggested. Then she'd moved out of sight.

Inside the church the priest showed him a screen he had brought from the Sunday-school room, and together they dragged out a table to set the projector on. Chuck brought an extension cord out of the box and the priest complimented him on how prepared he was. Until now his compact self-sufficiency on these journeys was the one thing that he could rely on to steady his nerves. He liked to board the bus, in his thin suit, with his round-trip ticket, directions he'd made for himself from the library's atlas, a sum of money too small to seem unearned in his pocket, and the box in his arms that contained the projector and all of its needs: extension cord, slides, a spare bulb. All he required was electricity and a blank wall. He was an itinerant, as solitary as a country doctor, or the missionary who had converted his mother. He hadn't realized how much it gratified him to be independent this way until today.

He turned the projector on and a weak square of light swung around the room and fell short of the screen. He pushed a psalm book under the projector's front and glanced apologetically at the priest, but the priest was nodding and waving a hand. "That's just fine. I can tell that you've done this before."

"A few, two-three times." He put the slides in order and dropped them one by one into the carousel, checking that each had gone in right side up. Number one was the map: Korea After 1945. Number two was The U.S. Infantry Coming out of the Seoul Railway Station. He put his thumb on the slide-changer button and fired the carousel through the full rotation. Then he fiddled for a while with the focus. His palms were sweating. He asked the priest to show him to the men's room and once alone rinsed his face and scrubbed it dry with a coarse paper towel. He bent over to touch his toes, and dragged his knuckles back and forth on the floor. Then the door swung open and he sprang upright in embarrassment.

"We're ready for you," the priest said.

The audience was mostly older, charity and book-circle women, and a few intent men. "Hi," he croaked, and they all smiled at once, in response. "I am Chang Ahn. I study at Sewanee, University of the South, but before this I live in Korea."

"How old are you?" a woman interrupted.

"Now I am twenty-five years old."

"You look so young," she said sadly.

He usually began his address by saying that his presence before them was the direct result of MacArthur's Inchon landing. "I'm not here, if this doesn't happen," he said, feeling melancholy suddenly. The faces in the audience blinked at him. He turned on the projector and Korea After 1945 appeared on the wall. He ducked through the beam apologetically. "Here it is," he said, letting the shadow from his forearm mar the picture. "I am sorry the map is not more big."

He explained the positions of Japan, China, and the Soviet Union, around the edges of the fuzzy square of light. "This is makes the fate of Korea. The Japanese colonize, at the beginning of this twentieth century, so when the Second World War is beginning, they are already there."

He paused and looked around. "Okay?" he asked anxiously. A few people nodded.

"You remember," he went on, "in the Second World War it is United States and Soviets together, Japanese with the Italians and Germans. The Japanese are in Korea, this is a terrible time," he sighed. "Okay. The Soviets, in the Second World War, fight against the Japanese, and they fight in Korea." He threw his arms wide.

When the Japanese surrendered at the end of the war, the Soviets and the Americans split the job of overseeing the Japanese withdrawal from the Korean peninsula. A line was drawn at the thirty-eighth parallel, which split the country roughly in half. The Soviet military would administer the northern half, the Americans the southern. This was, in theory, a temporary arrangement. Provisional governments were set up on each side for the duration of Korea's reconstruction. The Soviets, on their side, enabled the return from exile of a great people's hero, a revolutionary who had fought the Japanese throughout the thirties. Chuck cut himself short. "This man become the leader of Communist North Korea," he concluded. The Americans, for their part, imported a committed anti-Communist expatriate named Syngman Rhee, who had graduated Princeton and lived in the U.S. for the preceding forty years. Rhee was put in charge of South Korea. Over time the rival governments dug in, and in June of 1950, went to war.

He always felt hopeless, called upon to deliver a clear explanation of the war. It defied explanation. Sometimes he simply skipped over causes, and began, "Korea is a shape just like Florida. Yes? The top half is a Communist state, and the bottom half are fighting for democracy!" He would groundlessly compare the parallel to the Mason-Dixon line, and see every head nod excitedly. "In June 1950, the Communist army comes over the parallel and invades the South. They come by surprise, and get almost all to the sea." His hands swept: an amazing advance. The UN made a force to fight back, of the South's Republic of Korea army, ROKA, and the United States army, and some other armies, like Britain's.

The particularities of the UN force never interested anyone, and he quickly skipped ahead. "The Communists go fast, until the UN force is crowded into a very little space at the bottom of Korea, around the city Pusan." He pronounced it for them loudly: *Poos-ahn.* "This is like, if the war is all over Florida, and our side are trapped in Miami." Now MacArthur's genius showed itself: instead of trying to push back, over the land, he took his army to the sea, and sailed up the coast, to Inchon. He landed there and cut the Communists in half, off from themselves. Seoul was liberated, and the tide turned around.

He genuinely liked talking about the landing, and MacArthur. It all made for such an exciting, simple minded, morally unambiguous story. Each time he told it, the plot was reduced and the number of details increased, and the whole claimed more of his memory for itself and left less room for everything else. He punched the slide-changer now, and Korea After 1945 was replaced by The U.S. Infantry Coming out of the Seoul Railway Station, a soap-scrubbed and smiling platoon marching into the clean, level street. This image made a much better illustration of the idea of MacArthur than any actual picture of the Korean war could have. People were often surprised by the vaulted dome of the train station, and the European-looking avenue of trees. "That's Seoul?" a woman asked, vaguely disappointed. The file of troops looked confident and happy, because the picture had not been taken during the Korean conflict at all, but in September 1945, after the Japanese defeat. The photo's original caption had read, "Liberation feels fine! U.S. and their Soviet allies arrive to clean house in Korea." No one was dreaming there would be a civil war.

He followed the U.S. Infantry slide with Water Buffalo in a Rice Paddy, and then Village Farmers Squatting Down to Smoke, which satisfied the skepticism of the woman who had asked about the Seoul railway station. Everyone murmured with pleasure at the image of the farmers, in their year-round pajamas and inscrutable Eskimos' faces, and then the double doors at the back of the sanctuary creaked loudly and Katherine was standing there, with her pocketbook held to her chin, looking lost.

Each of the twelve or so heads clustered in the front pews turned to look at her. She let the door fall shut and slipped into the rearmost pew. "I'm sorry," she said. A flush appeared on her cheeks to match his.

He couldn't remember where he'd left off. The awareness that he was blushing made him blush even more deeply. He wondered if anyone could see it. Often the darkness of his skin seemed to guard his emotions from notice, as if the fact of the color blotted out all that happened within it. He fingered the slide-changer nervously, and the carousel shot ahead, throwing a new picture onto the screen. For a terrifying eternity he stared at this without recognizing what it was. The rough grain of the image, fine rubble, a burial mound. . . . His gaze crisscrossed it wildly, searching for something that might help him locate himself.

When he remembered why the image was there, it was like remembering the plot of a childhood fable. Although the remembrance was deeply familiar, it wasn't convincing, because it didn't seem to make sense. The priest was in the front row, his eyebrows straining upward with encouragement. Chuck took a deep breath, and began again. "You maybe don't believe it, but Korea, the land, looks very much like Tennessee." He gestured at the picture of hills. So much, sometimes he woke in the morning and just for an instant was sure he was home. The mist coming out from the mountains. The soft shapes of hills. His hands formed them. At last he stopped seeing her.

Afterward, as everyone moved in awkward clusters to the yard, he said, "I thought you aren't coming."

"I didn't think I was. I was nervous for you. I thought my coming would make things worse." When they had gotten a good distance from the church building she lit a cigarette. "I didn't want to throw you."

He looked back. They were all conversing in small groups now, slightly exaggerating their gestures and their absorption in each other. He knew that they were watching him and Katherine. He shook his head at her. "Throw me," he repeated.

"Startle you. I didn't want to make you falter."

"But you throw me," he said at last, simply.

"I'm sorry. You did very well."

"Yes?"

"Yes, you did. Come on," and she turned back, cheerfully calling out, "Father! Did you see, I wasn't tempted by the shopping at all."

They were invited back to the priest's home, with some of the most interested women parishioners. He was relieved that they all seemed too old to have had sons drafted into the war. They were only fascinated by Oriental things. For him this was the easiest sort of conversation, with people who knew nothing and liked everything. He was asked, with much embarrassed laughter, to describe a Korean wedding dress. He stood up to do this, his hands palm down, shelving briskly against his ribs to emphasize the high waist, then flying apart and returning, as if he were outlining a heart in the air: a very—how do you say it? he pointed at someone's waist. This here. Waist? the woman suggested. "*Sash*," Katherine called out. "Yes. A very"—his hands outlined capaciousness—"sash," and as he did this he saw Katherine watching, suppressing a smile.

It was nearly five o'clock before they left, full of coffee and chocolate-caramels and a subtle, unremitting scrutiny, disguised as politeness. It followed him everywhere in America, varying in tone or intensity but always bringing with it the same slight electrification, as if he weren't just caught in a narrow beam of light but somehow animated by it. The priest took both of his hands. "I'm so pleased you could come. I wish you the best of luck, the very best of luck," and then, "Well, Miss Monroe! I hope you enjoyed your visit with us, because I know that we did. You're going to disappoint a whole bunch of people if you don't come back." She laughed. Chuck thought the priest kept her hands for too long.

They returned to the silence of the car. The sun was low as they left Jackson, and by the time they reached the open highway it was pulling the last, strangely attenuated fraction of itself beneath the western line of hills, and the shadow from the hills was spreading across the road and already fading as dusk set in. It had grown much too cold to take the top down again. Katherine turned on the headlights and all the mysterious, iridescent jewels of the dashboard appeared. The night turned black fast. Clouds had sealed off the sky that afternoon and so there were no stars, only the nebulous light that the car pushed in front of them. He could see her face in the dashboard's glow, lunar and remote.

After some time she said, "I almost always drive alone. I used to drive to be alone, and then later I just was alone, so I drove. To solace myself. It feels very private. I'm only trying to say that sometimes I don't talk when I'm driving."

"You don't have to talk."

"I don't want you to think I mind having you here. I like it. It isn't an intrusion."

"I don't think, I mean, I'm glad you don't feel no any trouble—"

"It's no trouble at all for me. I find it easy to be quiet with you. If I was uncomfortable I wouldn't feel I could have any privacy in front of you and I'd talk all the time. If I'm quiet it's a friendly kind of quiet. Does that make sense?"

"Yes. I like this idea."

"That's good. You can go to sleep if you want. Don't worry about me, I'm used to long drives."

Because he thought it would make her more comfortable he

closed his eyes, but he never slept. Hours later, as they began the slow climb up the mountain, straining around the turns, sometimes gliding on a brief level patch, and then straining again, he kept them closed, playing the old game, gathering what he could remember of the landscape into his mind. The nearer they grew, the more there was—he was surprised by how much there was—until he felt the slight dip, and knew they'd reached the last turn, and then his eyes were open, and she left him at his door.

*T*hat day marked the outermost limit of autumn. The fallen leaves shriveled and faded to a uniform dull shade of brown and lay everywhere, many inches deep, washing back and forth despondently. The daylight was a dead shade of gray too weak to cast a shadow, and although it never grew severely cold, the wind bit. He wished for a bright snowfall to transform the landscape, but even this high in the mountains snow was rare, and if it came it would come late and be thin. The winter mostly made itself felt as a yearning for the nearing holiday.

His trip home with Crane was approaching. The nearer it grew, the more Crane deprecated his family. Finally Crane declared he didn't want to go home at all. "You're a fool for agreeing to this," he told Chuck. "Oh boy, you wait." Crane began talking incessantly about his family's bigotedness, their old-fashionedness, and the overall, staggering impossibilities posed by his mother. He made alarming predictions about his parents' probable behavior toward Chuck which would have seemed cruel, if it hadn't been obvious that Crane needed a companion in dread. "They don't hang Orientals," Crane now said, coming into the room. Crane never knocked. "There aren't any down there to hang. I don't think they'd know one if they saw him. I wonder if they would hang him. They might mistake him for a nigger and hang him, or have the sense to see he's not a nigger and *not* hang him just because of that." If Crane had shown concern for Chuck, or indications of some noble aim like the creation of peace and understanding between a Grand Dragon of the Klan and a young Oriental, Chuck might have been frightened or angry, but Crane's only aim was to further a general atmosphere of crisis, and Chuck grew calmer in proportion to Crane's efforts. He wouldn't give Crane the comfort of unnerving him.

By the time they were finally in the car, though, Crane was quiet and content. The anticipation of going home was what he found upsetting: the promising, and the arranging, but mostly the continued possibility of *not* going home. So long as that option remained he felt cornered and panicky. Then he got on the road, and the space between himself and his home began diminishing. His driving was reckless, and they made quick time. It was only ten o'clock in the morning when the occasional shack or motel began to give way to legitimate-looking buildings assembling themselves by the side of the road. Atlanta was a big, flat, poorly organized city and it gave very little warning before suddenly enfolding them and extending in every direction.

They were met at the door by a butler who must have heard them drive up, because he was already there, smile unfurling, as they mounted the steps. "Well, well," he intoned. "We never do believe it till we see it. Your mama's going to feel more restful now, I hope. I guess I'll go and tell her you're arrived."

"This is Chuck, all the way from the South Seas," Crane said. Chuck didn't correct him. Crane gave him a slap between the shoulder blades, pushing him closer to the butler, who stepped back and smiled icily. "This is Driggsie, Chuck. Don't listen to him because he doesn't know anything." The butler laughed a long time at this observation, making clear his appreciation for its depth and originality, as they followed him down the front hall.

In the parlor Crane stood at the window, staring out at the

damp Atlanta winter. Chuck walked along the bookshelves, hands held carefully behind him, reading the spines. Now that Crane was placid, he felt his own nervousness stirring. Then he heard a woman saying, "Billy, there, sweetheart," and Crane's mother had run into the room and taken Crane by the shoulders, bent him to her, and pressed her lips to his cheek. An ecstatic stillness came over her face. When Crane tried to introduce Chuck she looked briefly confused. Then she disengaged herself and held out an arm to him, smiling.

The three of them sat together in the front room and had coffee. "Do you know what Chuck used to do in Korea, before he came to Sewanee? Can you even guess? Of course not. He translated the American papers into Korean, so that the Koreans could read them. Isn't that something else?"

"Not all papers, just some stories I choose for putting in Seoul papers," he began, before Crane cut him off.

"What they did, Mother, is they had an outfit for getting American stuff out to the Koreans, you know, who've never even seen a movie or drunk a soda pop, and part of it is getting the news from America into the Korean papers, so they know what's going on. And Chuck knew English, better than anyone there, anyway."

"How did you learn English, Chuck?" Crane's mother asked. She was holding one of Crane's hands, and beaming quietly at him. Crane shifted and huffed in his chair, inconveniencing her. Although he was careful to look beleaguered in her presence, it was clear that her absorption in him was something he not only enjoyed but expected. Crane and his mother were tranquilized now, not by the fact of being together so much as by the end of the period of waiting.

"My father," Chuck started to tell her, leaning forward slightly. She was a beautiful woman, with a coil of blond hair at the nape of her neck that showed no signs of gray.

"He learned it in school, Mother," Crane burst out impatiently.

For the rest of the afternoon Crane was an expert on Chuck's history, relating it with a mixture of pride and incredulity, only occasionally referring to Chuck for confirmation. "Isn't that right? You see, Mother, it's complicated. You can't even half understand." In the early evening the three of them went for a wet, chilly walk through the neighborhood. Prosperity in Atlanta seemed to find privacy undesirable, as if exposure were a necessary component of success. The houses were tremendous and too close together. Each might have concealed another wing extending as far back as the façade went across. Crane's mother had a shawl around her shoulders and held Crane's arm tightly in both her own, squeezing confidentially. Chuck kept falling back a few paces, but each time he drifted completely from her orbit Crane's mother would pause, to point out something to him, or ask him a question, so that he would be drawn close again. He would have been more comfortable had she neglected him. He was surprised by her kindness, and more touched by it than he wanted to be. He couldn't help valuing kindness more, the less it was expected. When they got back they had drinks, and Chuck told Mrs. Crane about his father's library. Something in her excessively attentive listening posture made him feel that she didn't believe him.

Crane's father came home and they dined. The senior Crane was regal and suspicious. His suspicion extended to his wife and seemed to find its culmination in his son. "What have you brought us?" he said, shaking out his coat, and then shifting his examination to Chuck, "Mr. Ahn," he said. "Welcome to my home." He had the air of a man accustomed to, but not necessarily interested in, frightening people. "You are an emissary from a distant land. I hope we can make you feel welcome."

At the table he carved and interrogated simultaneously. "You've been at Sewanee three months?"

"Yes, sir."

"I see you haven't starved to death in that time."

"No, sir."

"But you have never had turkey. I see from your eyes you have not. That we can claim. When you look back, Mr. Ahn, on your first years in America, on your first lessons in things American, you will think of the Cranes. I am giving you white meat and dark. You will develop a preference in time. You may develop a preference right away. If you do, exercise it." The plate made its way down the table to him.

"I do eat a bird like this once," he said. He had been on the plane from Seattle. Seoul to Tokyo, Tokyo to Juneau. All the way across the ocean he had kept his cheek pressed to the porthole until he finally glimpsed, straining his eyes forward, in the plane's direction, the outer edge of the sunrise. They were flying straight into the dawn, cheating the advancing cusp of it. The light had run first in a line along the horizon, like water sluicing through a groove, tracing a slight curve, less pronounced than the surface of a lens, and he had realized that it was not something wrong in the glass of the window or an optical illusion but the shape of the world he saw. It had thrilled and desolated him. He had wanted someone's sleeve to catch, someone to show. He had felt then that he was as far away as he could ever be from anywhere. Landing in Alaska, and then continuing his journey, was in some way a return, after where he had been.

But he didn't tell them this. He told them about the chicken. The plane had refueled in Juneau and gone on to Seattle, where he changed planes for the third time. On this plane a lunch had been served, of fried chicken and a scoop of mashed potatoes, with a well of melted butter in the center. He hadn't known how to eat the chicken. It sat tensely on his plate, like a bundle of elbows, wobbling with the movements of the plane. He barely recognized that it was chicken. He sat staring at it in dismay, lifting his knife and fork several times before finally deciding to steal a glance at the other passengers, to see what they did, and then he saw they were all watching him. For a long moment no one moved. No one gave him their example. He braced the chicken between his knife and fork and pressed down, and the chicken scooted to the left, off the plate. His knife struck porcelain.

"You are trying to make us ashamed of our countrymen," Mr. Crane declared.

"No," Chuck said. This was a compliment, a lengthy one. He wasn't being clear. There had been a man sitting across the aisle from him, a large man in a beige and white suit. And when he had tried to cut the chicken with his knife, this man had burst out laughing. "No, boy," he had said. "You eat it like this." And he picked the chicken up in his hands, and tore at it with his teeth, still laughing to himself, never giving Chuck a second glance. Everyone else picked up their chicken then, and Chuck picked up his, and a buzz of voices and activity rose in which he was ignored. The chicken became a strange, private pleasure. He ate it savagely. The man had been southern. When he'd started to speak Chuck had only meant to say something, to make a friendly remark, but the longer the story grew the more it seemed to lash about on its own, in unintended directions. He went silent and there was an uncertain pause. He thought, *Someone pick up their chicken. Someone—*

"I know what it's like to get out of a scrape. I was figuring on failing algebra," Crane began. Then they talked about other things, and the buzz between parents and son rose and covered him over.

They were going to stay the night there, and drive back the next morning. "Early," Crane told his mother. He was being severe—distinctly, recognizably severe. Chuck thought Crane had transformed in his father's presence, striving to evoke his father in his manner, but the manner was strained, and when his mother came to embrace him, Crane's head tilted back slightly as if he was enduring pain. He closed his eyes.

At the door to the room where Chuck would sleep, Crane

stopped him. The hallway had been lit when they came up, but Crane put the lights out as they walked. Now there was only the light that filtered up from the staircase, and the indistinct voices of Crane's mother, instructing the maids, and the maids' brief assents. "Was it all right?" Crane asked. He spoke softly, out of caution, or tiredness. "The old man isn't so bad, really. He's got a bum heart. It will give out one day. That makes my mother nervous all the time. I think she'd like me to come home and live forever. You could tell she was nervous, I guess."

"Yes," he said. A loneliness, seeming to dictate no response, to contain no possibility of removal, had opened within him. "Your mother is kind. Gentle."

"She's a good old girl. The old man, that thing with the Klan, it's just like a club, really. A brotherhood. It's all wound up in the politics here. He liked you, don't you think? I think he did."

"I hope so," he heard himself saying. He did not want Crane to know what he thought of his father.

After Crane left him he sank down on the bed, gazing blankly at the room, and then he got up and began moving through it, with silent caution but voracious, like a thief. He wanted to find something that made an intimate disclosure: a personal object, or the trace of a private decision, but the room was for guests, like a room in a hotel. The drawers were empty. There was nothing stored under the bed. He pulled the curtains aside and stared across the lawn at the great dark mass of a neighboring house, its windows gleaming gold through the trees. Everything here was an obstacle, showing him what he wanted by keeping him from it.

four

In September 1945 John Hodge arrived in Korea with the Twenty-fourth Corps, to oversee the Japanese surrender. He expected to be going home soon. The Americans and Soviets were splitting the job, by splitting the peninsula in half. A few American commanders, a map snapped out over a table, the heels of their hands planted on it. With two atom bombs days before having leveled Japan, the problem of how to administer Japan's former possession was not the most absorbing, and the time at the table was brief. They chose the thirty-eighth parallel, latitude north. It was on everybody's map, and it fell just halfway, with the largest city, Seoul, on the south side. Because the Soviets were already on the peninsula, while the Americans would ship out from Japan, the Americans suggested that the Soviets administer the North. The Soviets didn't object.

It took Hodge a week to move his men from Okinawa to southern Korea, and by the time he was there, the Soviets were finished. They had accepted the surrender of the Japanese forces in the country's northern half and pulled themselves up to the parallel, following their American allies' orders to the letter, stopping there as if they'd hit a wall, but their obedience to that neutral, invisible line had already removed it from the phantasmal realm of the geometry of solids. The thirty-eighth parallel ceased to be a set of points sharing an angular distance from the equator, and manifested itself as a thing. It was well on its way to becoming a political border. Even then, in September 1945, when it was still thought of as denoting nothing beyond its own coordinates, as if its former affiliation with the system of meridians and minutes could exempt it from history.

By the end of 1946, postwar Korea's two principal stewards had irreparably fallen out. The project of establishing a new Korean government, to replace that of the departed Japanese, foundered when the two powers disagreed on the legitimacy of the Communist party in Korea. The U.S. rejected it entirely, while the Soviets recognized it solely. When each nation set about establishing a Korean government under its own auspices, on its own terms, and in its own zone, the thirty-eighth parallel ceased to be a line and became a border, and soon was not only a border, but one made of mirrors. Each Korean government claimed sole legitimacy. Each noted that it was sovereign over the entire peninsula, and that its borders coincided with those that had always been Korea's. Being made to disappear in this way, the line revealed itself as entrenched. Rival radio broadcasts aimed themselves at each other across the divide, emitting the usual Imperialist, Communist, American-pig-fucking pig, everything, every name you'd ever heard and then plenty you hadn't, but there you were, stuck in Korea. Hodge couldn't go home.

With the role of the Americans transformed, by 1948 Hodge found himself in the position of military governor, with all the misery attendant on that office. Only after installing Rhee as the Republic of Korea's president did the Americans realize he was unmanageable: bellicose, paranoid, and so undiscouragably determined to declare war on the Communist North that the United States deliberately underequipped his security forces.

Rhee's government was repressive, incompetent, and stupen-
dously unpopular. Peasant uprisings throughout the South took
the food supply hostage. The trains didn't run. Hodge needed
platoons to make order, but all he had, the only security outfit
that was intact and had all its equipment, was the National Police,
who had been assembled by the Japanese. Dismantling them
wasn't an option, but using them, as Hodge did, irritatingly created the need for even more security. South Korea was a logistical
disaster, crowded with junk and angry people who were unem-
ployed at best, but generally homeless and starving. They committed crimes, intended and inadvertent, thefts and arsons,
unpremeditated murders and antigovernment, proleftist insurrec-
tions. And so Hodge used the National Police, and his situation
grew even worse. 1948 turned into 1949. Opposition to the par-
titioning of Korea, then to the stewardship of the U.S. and the
USSR, now to the Rhee government, mostly maintained by leftist
farmers' unions, had been constant since the Americans' arrival,
but now, enraged by the increased power of the National Police,
this opposition solidified into an armed guerrilla movement, with
cells scattered all over the south. Hodge tried to create a constabulary which was not as militaristic as the National Police, but this
force was equally despised, and completely ineffectual. Hodge
needed more soldiers, not fewer.

*H*odge's American force at the time was embarrassingly small.
Most of the Americans in Korea in 1949 had been passed over for
more important duty elsewhere. They were demoralized, flaccid,
and lazy. They hated Korea. Hodge had difficulty blaming them,
although their disdain arose more out of a sense of overwhelming
inconvenience than discriminating taste. The roads were terrible
and the countryside stank. Their equipment was rusted-up,

broken-down stuff from all over the Pacific that MacArthur, the Far East commander in chief, had to recycle because Washington wasn't giving him money to spend in Korea. They weren't giving him men, either. MacArthur was glad to be holed up in Tokyo. When Hodge called MacArthur from Seoul to complain, MacArthur told Hodge to use his best judgment. This drove Hodge crazy. It was MacArthur's cavalier dismissiveness more than Washington's terse, firm refusal that convinced Hodge he had no hope of money and men from America and that he'd have to do things by himself, the only way he knew how.

And so Hodge decided to build the Republic of Korea its own army. Almost immediately he ran into a problem with words. Korea had its own language for weapons and warfare and soldiers, but the words were attached to Korean ideas, and these were of no use to Hodge. He wanted only the American idea of expedient slaughter, the American idea of order. He didn't know any Korean. Working this sort of thing out meant more negotiation and more time and he didn't want to negotiate, he didn't want to spend time, he wanted to go home and retire. He went to the Rhee government's new Ministry of Public Information and discovered that it was a shabby little room with peeling linoleum tiles, two desks, one typewriter, one ashtray, and three employees. The third employee was standing at the window, hunched over the typewriter, which was propped on the sill, along with the ashtray and a Korean-English dictionary. He was the only one working. The other two sat at their desks, reading newspapers and uncomplainingly ashing their cigarettes onto the floor, their only acknowledgment of the third one's solitary labors. The third one looked, to Hodge, about fourteen years old. He could never tell how old these people were.

When Hodge found out that the third one was a high-school graduate of one week's standing, that he had been working at the ministry the same length of time, and that the dictionary was his personal possession, Hodge commandeered him.

"His English is best good," the other two protested.

"Exactly," Hodge said.

Hodge told Chang not to bother him with nuance. Hodge only wanted the Korean soldiers to be taught to give and receive orders, as if they were really American. "Make it work and don't tell me about it," he said. In the end it was probably wise. Chang had done enough translation already to know that there weren't ever even exchanges. You wanted one thing to equal another, to slide neatly into its place, but somehow this very desire made the project impossible. In the end there was always a third thing, that hadn't existed before. For Hodge there could never be third things.

Hodge meant to imagine an American-style army out of the materials at hand, and what did not fit would be altered by force. In this spirit, Chang didn't adjust things to the names that existed, but adjusted new names to the things. The result was that Hodge's Republic of Korea Army was inarguably American apart from the fact that it consisted entirely of Koreans in oversized uniforms running around yelling things like, "Grab your mechanical-gun-that-shoots-fast and get into the car-with-no-top!" Hodge's ROKA soldiers were no more corrupt and no less battle-ready than his Americans, and on the whole they had much more commitment. It wasn't conviction so much as the feeling of power that accounted for this, although they had no equipment that hadn't already been old when it was used to fight World War II, no tanks, no antitank weaponry, no more than a handful of planes. Chang had never imagined himself in an army, but when he saw this one he realized that nothing, no categorical boundary, no threshold of qualification, stood between him and that destiny. His aversion to the idea of serving this government as a soldier was so intense it had left little room in his thoughts for the chance he might one day be drafted. Now he was afraid that not even his poor health and good English would be enough for exemption.

And so the things he had done for John Hodge, the small ways he had helped, had to be. At the end of it Chang wanted something certain. Some kind of lasting guarantee.

"What are you talking about?" Hodge said. This was coming at him from all sides. Everybody wanted it in stone, they wanted signatures and seals and sacred promises, because in conditions of total uncertainty, where nothing was more impossible than a promise, nothing else would suffice. Chang wanted it in stone. Even if he could trust Hodge, he couldn't trust it would always be Hodge. No one hoped this more than Hodge himself did.

"I want," Chang began. It wasn't a language problem. It was a vision problem. Hodge did not really see him. For the most part this was good. He wanted no one to see him. But now he needed to appear, and prevail. "A guarantee. For not being enlisted."

"You? Enlisted?" Hodge thought that this was hilarious. He didn't know, couldn't have known, even then, with his shortage of men and machines. Things were bad, but they would never be desperate.

When the Americans had first arrived, with their loudness, their larger-than-lifeness, their prodigality and their devotion to leisure, the idea that Chang would soon be subsumed by that force was as incomprehensible to him as everything about the force itself. Even so, he promptly fell under its influence. He was fifteen in the fall of 1945. He became a restless, disobedient son. He won his school's poorest student as a best friend, and together they addicted themselves to the American traveling movies, more for the sheer pleasure of attending than for the feature, which they barely perceived. The film was always an almost soundless square of shadow and light thrown against the wall of a building beneath a sky that never got dark enough. He and Kim would drink Budweiser beer and sail the cans at the flickering wall, and each can made a quick flash of light as it struck before clattering onto the ground. Overhead they could see the military's search-lights moving agitatedly across the clouds. They watched the sky more than the film, waiting for the bright reflection from an enemy plane getting caught, like their cans, in the beam. They were disappointed that it never happened. They'd been bored and disgusted with everything.

The fall of 1945, with its surreal flood of American things, had been their first term of secondary school. If the Japanese hadn't lost the war Chang would have been sent to Tokyo to do his studies, and would have never met Kim. But they did lose it. Everywhere the Japanese disappeared from their buildings. Coca-Cola arrived, and Budweiser, and American trash became the stuff that held the city together. You'd see oil lamps made out of Budweiser cans. Chang's half-uncle, Lee, walked into an abandoned Japanese textile factory on the outskirts of the city in the spring of 1946 and claimed it was his. By 1948 he was rich, and a congressman. The new South Korea was hungry for brash enterprisers without previous distinctions to shed. They gave substance to the lie of the country's rebirth, and they were needed to offset the decimation of elitists. No one who had done well before could continue to thrive. In the same month that Lee conquered the textile factory, government intelligence agents visited Chang's home and arrested his father in a second-floor library. Chang's father had been one of the small class of Koreans selected for the Japanese Imperial University in the 1920s, and one of a handful taken up by Japanese mentors and groomed for a teaching position. By the time Chang was a boy, his father had become the only Korean appointed to a university chair. From that point onward he was denoted by other Koreans in the same manner that had always been used by his wife, who simply called him the Doctor. That the Doctor was a source of pride to Koreans during the occupation made little difference when the occupation ended. He was declared a collaborator, and charged with national treason. The Doctor went to jail an aging man, recited poetry in the daytime to keep his mind busy, and in the nighttime, to lull it to sleep, put the books his family brought him on the floor of his cell to keep the cold from his feet, and was soon very ill. Eventually he would be tried, acquitted, and released. The American-supported government was characterized as much by a short attention span as it was by shortsightedness. Destroy colonialism, destroy elitists, destroy poverty; suddenly, the imported American enthusiasm for the idea of uplifting the oppressed, if not for its actual practice, would intervene. The American missionaries who had been attempting to do work in Seoul all along seized their mandate and instituted full scholarships in the schools, and in this way Kim entered Chang's life, Kim newly elevated, and Chang newly impoverished, his sense of order disordered and his resentment of his father's absence so intense that he had set to work destroying what little remained of his father's authority.

Although Kim was always dressed in the wash-worn, respectable clothing the nuns issued to him as part of his scholarship benefits, he moved in a cloud of acrid cigarette smoke that soon closed around Chang, the atmosphere of their shared world, the night excursions Chang took to meet Kim in the city park or on the steps of the National Library. "Hello, Comrade," Kim would say gravely. He knew Kim had a home of his own somewhere, a mother, a sister, no father, but they never went to Kim's home, and he often wondered whether Kim ever went there. He seemed more content roaming the streets of the city by night, dozing on benches as the dew slowly descended, his strange face serene. That face—reminiscent of a bat's, the small chin, the small, determined mouth, the great ears and the broad forehead beneath which his unusually large eyes were both opaque and penetrating, like those of any creature that can see in the dark. Kim rolled himself cigarettes and taught Chang to roll as well, and to smoke, and to stand tough and be a credit to their partnership. Chang relished their vagabond stench. But, for all his feelings of rebellion, he kept these ventures of his secret and kept Kim apart from his parents. Letting the two realms collide would have spoken too bluntly of the extent to which his family's life had become a nostalgic mirage that would soon evaporate, if not violently ignite.

Whether it was an inevitable effect of those times or the actual result of their friendship, Kim's entrance into his life marked a turn toward the clandestine that he would never feel truly reversed. Chang's unique contributions to their criminality were slight—a bag of crackers to eat with their beer, the hiding places his house's grounds afforded—but measured against his past self, he had changed. And yet he often sensed that he was only moving with the earth beneath his feet, as it gathered speed. He had conversations with Kim he had never had with anyone, had never even known how to have. They talked about how best to live their own lives, and whether there were absolute standards, or relative measures of rightness. They hatched plans to overthrow the new government. Getting drunk on a park bench one night they were approached by a member of the Seoul Constabulary. Kim leaped to his feet, slapped Chang's shoulder hard the way he might have urged a horse, and they were running. After this they retreated to the sanctuary of a white pine halfway down the slope of the private hill on which Chang's house sat. Its lower boughs had sagged under their own weight, forming a prickly bower around the trunk, and opening great holes in the foliage. They could keep up their watch on the searchlights. At night Kim waited here while Chang dined with his mother, and then read to his father until his mother retired. Coming down the hill across the damp, fragrant grass in the dark, with the lights overhead making a thick golden haze of the mist, he was already aware of the transience of these nights, although they repeated themselves with little variation. He and Kim acted of one mind, with no need to translate their intentions. He would come down the slippery hillside at eleven-thirty, feeling the rain on his shins where it angled beneath his umbrella. He would be carrying a bottle of sake and a bag of sweet rolls. When he finally got away from the house Kim often greeted him like a castaway greeting a rescuing ship, but tonight Kim was flat on his back, fast asleep, his face unperturbed even though there was rain falling on it. He could sleep anywhere, and through anything.

"Wake up," Chang said, touching his shoulder. "It's starting to rain."

Kim blinked several times, and then saw him. The rain was hissing through the holes in the tree. "Hi, Comrade." He smiled sleepily. "I dreamed something wonderful."

"What was that?"

"I can't remember." He closed his eyes again, reaching for it. At last he sat up and raked a hand through his wet hair. "I can't remember."

"It'll come back to you."

"I doubt it. What have you got there?"

Chang uncorked the bottle. Without seeking permission, or even bothering to worry about seeking it, he had begun to quietly pillage the wine cellar. The ground was damp from the rain, and growing cold now that night was approaching.

They drank for a while in silence. In the springtime they were constantly reminded of the provisional nature of the peninsula, the uncertain compromise it had struck with the sea. It had been raining for days. Either rain fell or the hills exhaled cold, clinging fog. The land might fold in half and sink beneath the waves. Chang lay back, letting the wet ground seep into his shirt. They passed the bottle slowly between them, and watched the searchlights. At the beginning of that night the sky was livid, a low bank of clouds that caught every beam pointed toward it, but by the time they had finished the bottle, and fallen asleep, and Chang had woken again, briefly frightened, then stiff from the cold, all the clouds had dispersed. Now he saw only shimmering, motionless depth, as if nothing could ever disturb it.

*H*e would always look back on his friendship with Kim as the most important of his life, and on that summer as their exemplary time. He had been an isolated boy, an only child whose inadvertent ability to seem without needs only further cemented his solitude. His easy comradeship with Kim was a miracle to him, even more so because Kim never seemed to sense the strangeness of their situation, or the tremendous significance with which Chang endowed it. Kim was presumptuous in the best of ways; a deep familiarity grew up between them because Kim presumed it already existed. Chang's discomfort at the extreme difference in their situations was consistently offset by Kim's lighthearted greed. "Can we have some jelly?" Kim would wonder. "Have you still got that purple American jelly?" Chang's hospitality was happily excessive. He would return with a whole meal on trays, assisted by the scowling hired girl. After she served them Miki would loiter, eavesdropping on their self-important arguments, about what made a great man great, about how to reform tenant farming, until Chang stared her out of the tree's perimeter and she stalked sullenly back to the house.

When the summer ended he felt a pang of irretrievability, and along with it a wave of annoyance at himself. His sentimentality seemed to be that of a young, inexperienced person. Although this was what he was, he did not find it forgivable. Only a very young person with an overdeveloped sense of his own importance, of the uniqueness of his own life, would imbue a single summer with such singularity and mark its passing with such grief. Only an alarmist would see in it a freedom that would not come again. But then, as the term wore on and he and Kim both found themselves overtaken by a somberness that seemed to press down from without but that may have been welling up from within, he felt the link between his life of the summer and his life at that moment grow thinner and more delicate, like the single spit of sand still connecting a promontory to the mainland, until at last the connection was destroyed and the summer moved away from him forever, a bright island in his memory that he wouldn't revisit in life. With the onset of winter he grew ill. His health had always been uncertain, less a fragile entity than a willful and unpredictable force. Now it filled him with cataclysms of coughing, with quantities of green phlegm that made rubbery seals over his throat, with an expansion of the invisible blooms within his lungs into overripe tumors. He was diagnosed with tuberculosis and confined in an asylum. "They should just kill me," he rasped to Kim when Kim came to visit. At first Kim visited often, sat on his bed recounting the recent atrocities of their teachers at school, waited out visiting hours until dinner was served and then picked over the tray with raised eyebrows and an inexhaustible appreciation for the nuances of hospital food. Chang was never hungry. Finally, after twice being caught sitting on the end of Chang's bed with his knees bent and his terrible shoes resting squarely on the covers, smoking, Kim was evicted by the nurses. His visits grew increasingly infrequent, but Chang knew Kim was not staying away because of the displeasure he incurred. Kim was beginning to list toward some other center of gravity. Even when they were together, Chang sensed his ear tuned elsewhere. "Just cover me with the dirty linens and let me suffocate to death," he finished. Kim laughed and shook his head, his eyes straying to the far side of the room. Kim understood the joke. When the Doctor had been released from jail he remarked that he would have rather been shot. The Doctor's pride was demolished twice over: he was no longer even esteemed as a threat. The collaborator had turned out to be an old man, self-absorbed, melancholy.

"Has he been here?" Kim asked.

"No. He doesn't leave his bed."

"Your mother?"

"She comes sometimes."

"From bedside to bedside."

"She doesn't come as often as you do," he said, and he felt his ravaged, exhausted, phlegm-lined throat tightening suddenly.

Kim looked straight through the glitter of tears that were threatening to spill. "Your father is a great man," he remarked, as if resuming a debate they'd been having all day. He found his pouch in the front of his shirt and began rolling a cigarette. "But he took the wrong position. He burned up all his greatness fighting an unavoidable obstacle. You have to take the position that makes use of the obstacle. You could be a great man because this country's gone to pieces. Not in spite of it. Because of it."

"I don't think I'll be a great man."

"You will. You won't be able to avoid it."

"The disease of greatness."

"That's right."

"Not in this country."

"Oh," Kim said, "there are opportunities buried everywhere in the rubble," and at that moment Chang's nurse stormed in, drawn by the pungent smoke. "Out!" she cried, pointing. "Out! Out!"

He emerged from the asylum late in the spring. In his asylum room his only view of the outdoors had been a single small window high in the wall that gave him a view of the changing sky: solid blue, solid gray, sometimes alive with the fluttering motion of snow. Now, after two months, he saw his meager piece of the world rejoin the whole. The spring annuals had finally bloomed, and the garden of his home was full of those flowers, crocuses and narcissi, whose short lives gave them a certain intensity and restraint that was absent from the exuberant summer flowers. His taste for the outdoors was insatiable. He would sit in the garden with a blanket around his shoulders, at a small table he'd had moved there, steadily catching up on his schoolwork. Yet the beauty of the season and his joy at being out were undercut by irreversible drift. Kim joined the Communist party. He appeared at school less and less, and was threatened with the loss of his scholarship. He would say nothing about how he spent his time. He had taken a job as a train dispatcher with the Seoul railroad station, but this job didn't account for his prolonged absences from school, and from Seoul.

Chang spent the summer alone, recuperating. When the school year resumed he began doing all Kim's work for him. He felt it might be the only way to keep Kim in his life. Kim would climb the two walls separating Chang's house's grounds from the street and the house from its grounds, break into the house itself and appear in Chang's room in the middle of the night; then they would sit up on either side of the weak pool of light cast by a candle, and smoke and drink in near silence while Kim copied the work into his own writing. Sometimes Chang talked about joining the party himself. It was a desire he wished he felt ardently, with no reservations, but every course of action gave him pause. Since his father's imprisonment he'd felt vengeful toward the new government, but it seemed immune to all potential intervention, especially his own. And so, when he talked about Communism, he was not expressing his unshakable convictions, but hoping such convictions would evolve as he talked. He wanted Kim to help him, to be his companion in the party until its workings felt not just familiar but crucial, yet Kim dismissed all these thoughts as wrongheaded. "Politics aren't for you. Don't you remember what I've said? You're destined to be a philosopher. Perhaps a mathematician. In another time, you might have been a theologian, but that's not a viable pursuit anymore."

"Philosophy isn't a viable pursuit," Chang said irritably.

But Kim would dip his pen, push his hair out of his eyes, and continue writing tranquilly. "You're a thinker," he'd conclude. "Not an activist."

In the spring of 1948 the rural stations of the Korean Constabulary repeatedly fell under night attacks. Their buildings were burned, their officers bludgeoned or stabbed with sharp sticks, their guns stolen. When two northbound trains on the Suwon-Seoul line were derailed, Chang finally asked Kim what he did. Kim handed him a leaflet. UNITE! it said.

"What do you *do*," he repeated.

"It's better the less that you know," Kim said.

Chang stared at him. The distance between them was unbridgeable, suddenly.

"It's better for you," Kim said.

One night he awakened to see Kim leaning over him, covered with blood. His mouth was split and blown up to the size of a plum. One eye had swelled shut, and the flesh around it was black and pus-gold. Chang gasped for breath when he saw him. "It's all right," Kim whispered. He rubbed at the scales of dried blood on one arm. "Look here—it's not mine. I'm all right." Chang woke Miki and she washed Kim carefully with warm water. Beneath the crusted gore there were wounds after all, and she dressed these expertly, dipping her first two fingers into a pot of balm she kept for kitchen burns, and swiftly stroking it on. Chang sat in the doorway as she worked, smoking, his eyes watering uncontrollably, feeling the hard fist of misery rise from his stomach and be vanquished at the back of his throat, again and again. "You need new clothes," he murmured finally, rising. In his room he assembled a full outfit, wool trousers, a barely

worn shirt, a tailored wool jacket with pockets. After some digging he came up with his second-best pair of shoes. When Kim
saw the shoes he shook his head vehemently. "They're too fine.
Give me something less fine."

"You need a fine pair of shoes. For your travels."

They were embarrassed suddenly, by this accidental reference
to how much they'd grown apart. They gazed away from each
other, at the floor, and at Kim's feet in their wrecked shoes. "All
right," Kim said at last, taking them.

"Is someone after you?"

"NPs."

"Then stay. They'd never think to look for you here."

That night Miki bedded Kim down in her own room. Soon
Chang realized that on the nights Kim materialized—always at an
hour between midnight and dawn, sometimes seated on the end
of Chang's bed, one hand resting easily on Chang's foot—he was
coming from her, or going to her. Chang was run through with
loneliness, although often he followed Kim down the back stairs,
and sat talking with the two of them, in the dark, in Miki's small
half-detached room, a room that had never existed in his consciousness before. During the days, when he passed Miki in the
corridor, they never acknowledged the nocturnal life they shared.

*H*odge thought things would never be desperate, but the truth
was that things were disastrous. It was a disaster that had Public
Information, though, and this was something new for Korea. At
the Ministry of Public Information Chang read the *New York Times*
and *Time* magazine, and ignored the Seoul papers. Reading the
Times was his ritual. Snapping open the unwieldy sheets, he would
secretly travel. But the greater the distance he gained, the more
Seoul bore down. The city and the way it was described were

becoming unhinged from each other. The widening breach that they formed was a place where disaster could flourish. Either no one saw this or no one admitted to seeing it. He wondered if his grasp of the situation was firmer than Hodge's. Hodge didn't want to know, and relied on his language problem to shield him, and his vision problem where his language problem failed. Hodge was intelligent beyond his own desires, and he was starting to pick up Korean, like lint. He couldn't shake it. Lucky for him, at the end of that year Washington decided that the military command in South Korea was out of proportion to both the country's immediate needs and its ultimate value. They gave the country to the State Department, along with its green, eager army and America's own, surly one. They told Hodge he could roll up his tent.

Chang went back to working full time for the Ministry, but he found that his stint with Hodge had earned him credibility and contempt in equal measures: he was deferred to, and disliked. He was now nineteen years old. He began to wonder what else he could do, and to unhappily examine his talents. From Kim he'd gotten smoking, and their awkward but effective tough-guy stance, the vicious self-protectiveness of the physical weakling. From Hodge he'd gotten American, to add to his good English. The English had come from his father, who beat it into him from an early age, putting things like Gibbon's *Decline and Fall* into his hands and then sighing with disgust while Chang struggled along. His father had been a translator, too, and when he was around nine or ten, his father had enlisted him. He had absorbed the minutiae of his tasks with a mixture of terror and childish pomposity, and it would later occur to him that this was the time his father liked him best: when he unthinkingly aped his father's grim arrogance without really possessing it.

His father was a fastidious man with inflexible habits he had cultivated more for their rigor than their capacity to comfort. There was nothing comfortable in their home; comfort seemed to threaten stagnation. They had never worked in the same place. There were bare, austere desks everywhere, and his father would choose one, usually for its relative lack of accumulation. Then Chang would collect the books. These might be anywhere in the house, on other desks, or secreted in drawers, or slyly camouflaging themselves in between other books. He had been an ungainly boy, with flat feet and a tendency to shove his chin ahead as he walked. He did not know if this peculiarity resulted from his dangerous habit of balancing tall piles of books with his chin, or if the chin was a natural gift that had then spawned the habit. While he harvested books in wordless self-importance from room after room, his father would sit on the edge of his chair, the chair shoved away from the table, holding the book in question fallen open in one hand, that arm propped tensely on one knee. He read the passage in question again and again, until the cadence of its words was as familiar to him as the walk that he obsessively repeated through the garden. The books that Chang gathered for him were not all dictionaries, although there were many of these: at least two in the language from which he was translating; two in Korean, one of which was for quick flipping, one of which was gigantic, an archaeological last resort; one in Latin; and one in Japanese, for sideways reference. Japanese was always the privileged arbiter. There were almost as many thesauri. But the rest of the books, tens of them, were simply used to help him think—other translations of the same work, other works by the same writer, favorite novels and poems, histories. He called them escape routes. He had a tendency to grow involuted, to lose the ability to see out, and often to hear. Sometimes a false rhythm would hypnotize him, and when he sensed that this had happened, he elected for the last resort of all, and made Chang read the passage out loud. This had been Chang's first success with English: in providing the tonic of mispronunciation that always shook his father loose from his stalled reverie by the sheer force of being unbearable.

While his father worked, he would sit on a stool in perfect silence, awaiting orders to look up certain words, often the words nested in the definitions of other words, then thesaurus synonyms for each of these. Every equivalence of terms was arrived at by taking an indirect route, as if by shooting slightly wide of the mark they could compensate for the inevitable shifting of meaning, the drift of a thought from its mooring once the word that had housed it was gone. When he was not leafing cautiously through dictionaries—he was taught to keep his eye at the top of one column as the pages went by, not to let it stray wildly trying to locate itself, and to use two hands, to smooth each new page he uncovered, to avoid making creases or dog-earing corners—he sat sharpening pencils with his pocketknife, letting the shavings fall into a bowl. Every once in a while he took the bowl to the fire and emptied it, and watched the sudden flurry of sparks snap up into the flue.

They made lists of possibilities: possible words, clauses, and finally lines. All the possible lines were retained, even as they pushed forward. Sometimes, a line that seemed fine would begin to grow lumpy and poor as more lines accreted beneath it. Sometimes, like a cheaply built house, the whole would have to be completed before it unexpectedly started to sag. Then they would go back and look at the parts they'd discarded before. But often there was no need for this. The thing would emerge and begin to grow buoyant, as if it could read only just as it was. This was what his father wanted: for the original to vanish. Then you knew it was actually there, bled in, letter by letter.

He had understood very little of his father's gloomy, elaborate ruminations, but he'd enjoyed the final flourish: his father would read the complete lines to him, would deliver these arduous gifts, made real only because he received them. He never knew whether he loved his father, but he had been in love with this, would thrill to think of it, was stricken and lost each time it ended—perhaps because these were the moments that *he* was there, suddenly bodied forth into the room, the only possible listener.

In the late fall of 1949 Police Chief Ho called a press conference to celebrate the unqualified success of his extermination campaign against the leftist uprising on the island of Cheju, and Chang was sent from the ministry to translate. After the Japanese withdrawal four years before, leftist guerrillas had found the labyrinth of caves and underground bunkers the Japanese had left behind, and the caches of small arms abandoned in them. In the space of a few months the rebels had taken control of the entire island, commandeering village grain supplies, dismantling bridges, felling trees to make roads impassable. Cheju was a mountainous island. At some points on its coast it seemed to rise straight from the sea, in steep cliffs and black, fragrant forests. Its cleared land was minimal and easily located, but its natural caves and the man-made bunkers attached to them were almost impossible to ferret out, their mouths hidden behind sheets of water where a thin creek fell over a rock ledge, or beneath the undergrowth in the ancient, vaulted woods, the opening sometimes only slightly wider than a man.

From the outset many of the villagers had mingled with the insurgents, and many more joined the uprising after an army of anti-Communist youth volunteers was deposited on the island by Ho's police, armed with semiautomatic rifles and bayonets made from bamboo. "Like a little war," Ho explained cheerfully. Those villagers who weren't eventually killed in the battles for the interior or arrested and interned in camps had now been relocated to the narrow coastline, where they perched between the choppy tide in front and the uncultivatable hills that rose steeply behind. The remaining guerrillas, encircled and deprived of the settlements from which they'd stolen food, would inevitably starve. "Periodically, now, these rebels emerge if they are hungry," Ho said, "and then we have some skirmishing, like yesterday." At the end of every utterance Ho smiled brightly, as if he'd been surprised by an outburst of applause, and held the smile while Chang gave the translation.

The conference was attended by more American and international news-wire journalists than actual Koreans, which meant that all was as it should have been. The state-run Seoul papers were expected to take their news from the Western-world wires and the *Times,* a method of newsmaking that didn't require much in the way of investigative journalism. Later that year, when a dozen Korean reporters came jostling their way into a news conference with blank notepads and sharpened pencils, they were promptly arrested. Seated on the platform beside Ho, Chang was startlingly young and thin by comparison. Ho was an obsequious holdover from the Japanese occupation, and little liked. Chang felt the weight of attention increasingly resting on himself. After the conference was over he stepped off the platform rather than leave through the side door with Ho, and was promptly waylaid by a reporter from the *New York Times* itself. This realization made him giddy. He tried to give the reporter a bored look.

"Is it true?" the reporter, Richards, asked. "No police casualties at all? This was four hundred armed guerrillas."

"The guerrillas arm with sticks." He shrugged, as if regretting that the guerrillas did not present a more worthy adversary. "To speak honest, the chief exaggerate the number of dead guerrilla, not underestimate the number of police. Mostly guerrillas give up when they face with resistance."

"How can that be? From what we're seeing out there, every day?"

"They have no any strength of conviction. You see, they get an order from the Soviet Union. They are poor, and with no any education. They love their country really very much. When they see police, they see they are wrong and they most times surrender."

"You've got to be kidding," said Richards.

"No," he said, taking a cigarette out of his case. Richards lit it for him.

"Docile, misled peasants. Is that my story?"

"Yes," Chang said.

With the arrival of the State Department as the presiding agency in South Korea had come the United States Information Service, overseas purveyor of American news and American culture, Gershwin and *Time* and democracy, and after the press conference with Ho, he applied for work there. The prospect of selling the U.S. to South Korea suddenly seemed much more attractive than that of selling South Korea to the U.S. He crossed over. He knew he couldn't get out of the loop. He thrived there, in the zone of intentional misinformation, the way the disaster throve in the breach. He had already sensed that, like his father, he had no real place in South Korea. He was the third thing, that people like Hodge both despised and required. Translation's unnatural by-product. He continued to translate, creating his place and becoming increasingly trapped there. Translation was a sure thing in American Seoul; neither side understood the other, but the constant racket of translation gave off an impression of good understanding, or at least of good faith. And USIS had the reputation for being a joke agency. He wanted to be part of a joke. He wanted to take refuge there, where wholly irrelevant information was made urgently relevant, rather than the other way around.

It was Peterfield who interviewed him. "You worked on the ROKA translations?" he said. "Jesus Christ. It takes one of those guys ten minutes to tell another one to mop the latrine. It's lucky they don't have to do anything really complicated, like fight a war. I can just see it now. What a mess."

Chang shrugged. "I do what they say," he said.

Peterfield gave him a sort of translation test. *Sense* and *sound,* his father had always instructed him. Now, *speed* as well. THOUSANDS GATHER IN CHICAGO TO SEE POPE. Luckily, the item was brief, and he was used to the newspaper style. He read newspapers constantly. While his father was devoted to weighing things down, drawing them into greater permanence, like building an extra leg for a table so that it can plant itself even more firmly, Chang felt he was practicing dispersal. The more the slight information was propagated, into language after language, the less it seemed to say. He enabled frivolity. He sat, pulled the dictionary near him with the curve of one arm, then thought better and left the book closed. The translation took him less than five minutes. He blocked it out in his careful print, on every other line of the long legal pad Peterfield had pushed across the table. When he was done he pushed the page of writing back.

"I can't read this stuff," said Peterfield. "That's your problem. I hope it says all the right things."

"It does. Says them well." *Sense, sound.* The sense sounded very well, he thought, pleased with himself.

"That's nice. But that sort of nicety doesn't matter much in this line of work. Just so it says it." *Nicety.* He would forever associate this word, in all its brave facetiousness, with Peterfield. If it mattered little now, it would soon matter less. It would soon cease to be an ornament, and become an obstacle.

He was hired on the spot. By the end of the day Peterfield had decided that he couldn't deal with Korean names, either. "We'll call you Chuck."

"Okay," Chuck said.

*H*e never told his father what he did. In the evenings, when he wasn't working late, he climbed the three flights of stairs to where his father lay, to see if he was sleeping. If he wasn't, Chuck would sit with him awhile. He often sat down even if his father was asleep, and listened to his breath rise and fall. The room was bare and renunciatory, but it felt less like a cell than a space without walls, a room that tried not to exist.

When his father was awake, he read to him from the Seoul papers. He knew his father would have preferred not to see him at all, but this preference, like Chuck's presence itself, referred to all the things they didn't talk about, and it, too, went unstated. Reading from the newspapers, he kept to the light foreign items, what his father called, placidly, garbage. His father claimed to have no interest in politics. His disdain for them was undemonstrative and constant, the attitude of a proud man who had been ruined by political misjudgment.

Chuck spent his days producing that garbage: culling and embroidering and shaping it. The decision of what to translate and pass on to Seoul's Korean newspapers became largely his, and in assuming this responsibility he also assumed a certain proprietorship over the information itself. Because he always had far more than he could use and because he was the arbiter, the censor, he seemed to have the raw material of a world at his disposal. The piecemeal views of it that he afforded, distorted by massive omission, kept it that much more in his control. Peterfield was happy to saddle Chuck with the generation of Korean press releases, which he considered mechanical drudgery; Peterfield was more interested in unambiguously powerful modes of transformation, like baseball teams and permanent cinemas. USIS was glutted with portable Americana, new recordings of American symphony orchestras playing American musical scores, new American fashions and stage plays and actual stories of small-town American heroes, and scattered across the tops of programs or at the bottoms of newspaper stories there were often schools mentioned, by name and location: Dartmouth—Hanover, New

Hampshire; Muskingum—New Concord, Ohio. His father's libraries were full of papers from American schools, but these revealed nothing but the name, while in the enthusiastic excess of information at USIS the school name sometimes emerged with some residual detail still sticking to it, half the curve of a hill or a bell in a tower or a row of identical shutters in a wall of red brick. These were slight, but suggestive, and he only ever needed a toehold. His mind did the rest. He circled his target, locating points of entry and cautiously probing them. He imagined letters, slight variations on a request that seemed by turns perfectly fair and completely insane. *If you please,* they began, or just *Please.*

He left work one evening and found Kim leaning on the building, waiting for him. "I need a favor. I need money," Kim blurted out. He took one of Kim's cigarettes and they walked together through the streets, kicking a rock back and forth. This was May 1950: they had been out of school one year. This year seemed like an epoch, a boundless continent of time across which each of them had struck out, propelled by innocent and arrogant ideas of adulthood, on his own. Since that time they had seen each other very rarely. They had not merely drifted apart but abruptly emerged somewhere lacking any confirmation of their friendship. At first, after their sense of mutual strangeness set in, they were made uncomfortable by each other, and kept their distance. Then such a quantity of time piled up, airless and isolating, like a cocoon, that they finally missed each other with disproportionate sadness and resignation. At least, Chuck did, looking out from where he found himself, with some bewilderment, in the world of the Americans. He wasn't yet used to the incremental changes in his life that took him distances he'd never meant to travel.

When they came to the gate of his house Kim squatted down in the street and lit a cigarette. "I'll wait for you here," he said.

"Don't you want to come and say hello to Miki?"

"No. Not today." When Chuck looked questioning, Kim averted his eyes.

At the Banto, Chuck examined Kim closely. Kim's clothes were threadbare. Not a stitch differed from the outfit Chuck had given him. But the shoes were incongruously cared-for; they looked newly polished, although their soles were worn to wafers. When he gave Kim the money Kim quickly folded the wad and pushed it into his pocket. "Thank you," he said, flushing. The flush surprised Chuck. He had never known Kim to have scruples about something as unimportant as money. "I don't like borrowing money from you," Kim added, after a moment.

"That's nonsense. I'm glad to help you."

"It's not for me. I'm going away for a while. I want to leave it for my mother and sister."

"Tell them if they ever need anything more, they must come to me. I make a lot of money now."

He could see Kim resisting this idea, and then finding a way to justify it. "All right. That's good."

"Where are you going?"

"Just out of Seoul."

"You don't want to tell me where, do you?"

"No." Kim grinned suddenly. "Do you remember how I used to call you Comrade? If I called you that now, you'd be arrested." Without meaning to they both burst out laughing. When their laughter subsided they sat smiling at each other, relieved. Kim rattled the ice in his drink. "It's not so safe for me here at the moment." He shrugged. "I'll be more comfortable elsewhere, that's all."

"I'd like to go with you. I mean, I wish that I could."

"No." Kim shook his head, as if this desire was silly. "You know, I joined the party because of you. Because of your freedom. You've never had to worry about money. It's left your mind so free. I admire it. When I joined I was thinking, Everyone should have that."

"It's not admirable."

"All I mean to say is, hang on to your freedom. You don't need to affiliate yourself with the party or anything else. Keep clear of that, whatever happens."

"Don't talk to me that way."

"What way?"

"As if you're saying good-bye."

"I'm not." Kim's edginess returned. He looked down at the table and then around, for a clock. "I'll be back soon. I'll try to send word in the meantime. All right?"

"All right," Chuck said, not sure what he was agreeing to, but before he said anything else Kim had grabbed his hand briefly and left.

The spring of 1950 wore on. In the Cholla and Kyongsang provinces the police lost control of cities and towns. The country-side was denuded; every tree within fifty feet of a road was cut down in an attempt to stop guerrillas from ambushing. Night travel was banned. Organized guerrilla warfare in the southern interior was diverting almost every ROKA division from the parallel. He read these stories off the foreign news wire, from the UP, the AP, from Reuters, in *Time* magazine, looking for signals from Kim as if Kim might burn a message in the earth, or build words from the trunks of felled trees. Not knowing what exactly he sought, he never found anything. He felt he had to keep his eyes trained for the most minute glimpses, but this vigilance exhuasted him and eventually it slackened.

*O*n a Saturday in June he was sitting cross-legged on top of his desk, reading the previous day's *New York Times;* on top of his desk because that morning Peterfield had leaned back in his own chair and broken it, then commandeered Chuck's chair while soberly swearing to have the broken chair fixed. His subsequent failure to do this had already inspired him to several jokes about the difficulty of translating *screw* into Korean. It was a slow day for them. When a reporter friend of Peterfield's from London named Jim Langston turned up unexpectedly, around three, Peterfield decided to call it a day.

"These Orientals," said Langston, glancing at Chuck. "Everywhere you go, they're squatting or sitting all folded up like collapsible music stands. They won't sit down in chairs."

"They won't wear shoes, either. Isn't that so, Chuck?" Chuck displayed a bare foot and kept reading.

"He understands English?" said Langston.

"No, he just sits there staring at the *Times* because I think it's cute. He does translating for me. For Christ's sake, Chuck, say something for yourself."

"Hi," he said shyly.

"Is your name really Chuck?"

"No, I am Chang," he said. He stuck out his hand and Langston shook it.

"American imperialism is nothing if not redundant," Langston said, turning back to Peterfield. "Here you've got a young man in possession of one of the very few single-syllable names his nation has to offer—I believe even my photographer could say it—and you're not content until you've renamed him 'Chuck.' It's the same with your absurd agency. Everyone in this country already wants to go to America, and now here you come promoting Judy Garland and baseball. You're going to give them all second thoughts."

"Chuck wants to go to the States so bad he's offered to come back as my butler."

"That's terribly sad. We ought to at least take him for a drink."

"Someone should stay here and watch the office."

"There's nothing happening anywhere, believe me, and there's nothing going to happen while we go and have a drink."

Peterfield and Langston had met in London during the previous war; since in Seoul they had gotten to like knocking off to the bar in the Banto for what they called political arguments. Langston bought the first round and told them that he had come down the previous night from the parallel, at the point where it neatly truncated the Ongjin peninsula. He was working on a story for the British news service in which he meant to make a great joke of the recent *Life* article that had called the new U.S.-ROK allied forces "the most formidable army in Asia!" "The most obvious plant piece I have ever seen," he remarked, over Peterfield's strenuous objections. At Ongjin, Langston and his photographer had watched an expedition of UN military overseers conduct a survey of parallel security, elbowing each other while squinting through binoculars at the impenetrable north-lying jumble of hills. Of course there was nothing to see. To Langston, and each other, they were making declarations to the effect that "the army has secured the parallel and not a gnat could get through it." "Our pictures are even more damning than their words, if you can believe that," he said, although he had found that the American readership, when confronted with images confirming their leaders' stupidity, somehow failed to get the point. But he was writing for Britain, and glad of it. "No embarrassing cheerleading," he said. "'The most formidable army in Asia'! My God! That is bloody surreal!"

The best picture from Ongjin by far, in Langston's opinion, had turned out to be a candid taken with Chief UN Field Observer Coverly's own camera, which he couldn't even point. After having a regiment soldier snap it he'd asked Langston and his photographer if they'd help him develop the film. It showed Coverly posing with a group of round-faced, adolescent South Korean Hospitality Scouts, wearing short pleated skirts and crisp sailor-style blouses with bright flopping neckties. Coverly was beaming with gratification, and holding tightly to the shoulders of one kneeling scout, as if he was planning to sit down on top of her. When Langston saw it he'd asked for a copy immediately. At first Coverly was flattered, but then Langston made the mistake of matching Coverly's effusions with fresh praise of his own, and Coverly grew suspicious. He decided not to let Langston have the photo after all. He feared it might be misinterpreted as frivolous, and so have bad implications. He'd actually said "intonations." "He said, 'I'm afraid it has bad intonations,'" Langston crowed. "A gorgeously apt malapropism. Just the same point I made when I first arrived here. I said, 'Well, this strikes a false note!'" Langston had left his photographer up at Ongjin, in the hopes that the UN observers would commit some fresh absurdity before leaving the peninsula for Seoul early Friday. They were probably back in the city by now, although Langston's photographer was a stick-to-it renegade type very hungry to capture a shot of what the Americans referred to, contemptuously, as the KPA's "saber-shaking." He'd missed every skirmish so far because they went intentionally unreported by the army news service, and so it was hard to predict where they'd happen. "He's probably sprinting up and down the parallel right now," Langston said. "God, he's lovely. He gets all my stories. I would lose my job to him except that he's verbally stunted. He speaks the worst English I've ever heard, and he was born and raised in London."

Twelve hours later, the bar staff at the Banto threw them out. The three of them had become unable to imagine a world in which one might be absent. After staggering back to the USIS offices with arms linked around each other's waists—any misstep of one brought them all down, and this must have happened repeatedly, because Chuck found himself covered with scrapes the next morning—they fell asleep on the cold tile floor, their heads pillowed on newspapers. Langston's photographer phoned late that morning; the furious rings finally woke them up just after ten.

He often wondered what would have happened if he hadn't been with them. That warning only made a difference of about half a day, not a great interval, nothing that would crucially place him, not like the slight touch that shifts the first stone on a crumbling hillside. Only time enough to think enough to hesitate. He could not refer to the gap and say, *Here was a turning point.* He did not know if there were other fates at all, only that his own seemed to date from that night, in the Banto Hotel, with Lucas Peterfield of Durham, N.C., and Jim Langston of London, and that he was drunk when the war started.

When the fighting broke out, at four o'clock Sunday morning, the only American officer posted on the parallel was an undistinguished military adviser named Leo d'Addario who had not been granted weekend leave. D'Addario was awakened by the sound of artillery fire, but couldn't tell whose it was. Later on everyone would agree that it must have been the North, firing on the South; why would ROKA units open fire when their American advisers had repeatedly instructed them against it? D'Addario leaped into his jeep, in his pajamas, and drove with his houseboy to Kaesong in the eerie dawn twilight to figure out what on earth all the firing was about, and on arriving ran smack into the North Korean army gliding into the center of town *on a train.* When they saw him, they shot at him. Driving away, d'Addario's jeep blew a tire and, bouncing along on the rim, he bit off the end of his tongue. By the time d'Addario had wired to Seoul in a panic, Langston's photographer had already called. The fighting quickly spread across the length of the parallel and began to move south toward Uijongbu, twenty miles north of Seoul. So far, the ROKA units caught in the fray had not maintained a single position. They were tumbling backwards.

At ten that morning the artillery was not yet audible from Seoul, and its nearness was dreamed of by no one. The streets were full of vendors who had pushed their carts into position hours before, to avoid the rising heat, and were now already asleep on their feet in the narrowing margins of shadow cast by the buildings. Women towing lagging children behind them or humping loads of vegetables and infants on their backs were out doing their shopping. Young boys squatted on the sidewalks, arms propped on the points of their knees, motionless with boredom. Chuck tried to keep to back alleys, jogging laboriously, touching buildings as he rounded their corners to help keep his balance. When he came into a street or square he forced himself to walk. Although he did this to avoid being questioned, he knew it was unnecessary. People glanced after him without interest.

The inadvertent effect of his hangover was a false air of calm. He felt electrified, in the grip of a state that was neither excitement nor terror, but identical to both. Peterfield had said, "They'll never make it to Seoul, but I would get your folks out, anyway. There might be a mess for a couple of days."

"But you don't think evacuation."

Peterfield snorted. "The United States military didn't come all the way here to hand this shit hole to the KPA the minute they came knocking. Are you kidding me? You're paranoid, Chuck."

He came into the house and said, calmly, that there was fighting on the parallel. "I'm sure it will be all right, but let's be on the safe side. Let's go to Pusan." He had found his mother sitting in the interior courtyard, eating a peach. She stared at him, the hand with the fruit in it stalled halfway to her mouth. She noticed it, and let the hand drop. "I don't want to move your father. Your father is sick."

"Let's be on the safe side," he said again. He spoke gently, because his head throbbed. "Pack a small bag," he told her. "I'll get him." He returned her uncertain gaze until she finally stood.

In the attic room his father was sleeping. He spoke his name, and then spoke it again. When his father's eyes blinked open he said, "We have to go. It's not safe here."

His father looked at him a moment and then turned his face to the ceiling and listened. "I don't hear anything."

"We have time, but we have to go now."

"I can't. I haven't walked in a year."

"If you won't walk, you'll be carried."

"If it's necessary." His father calmly reached for his glasses. "I carried you once. Do you remember?"

"No," he snapped. He'd begun to pace the small room impatiently.

"It was at the country place. We had gone out to the orchard because you wanted to pick pears. I took you out there and you wandered off, looking for ripe ones. Nothing was ripe yet but you kept going from tree to tree, sure you'd find something, and when you had gone too far for me to see you I heard you cry. You'd been bitten by a snake."

He remembered the orchard, of perfectly uniform, intricate trees. Moving among them he would play games of disappearance and reappearance. Coming even with one row its length was eclipsed, and then as he moved forward into the cleared avenue, his head turned alertly, it lengthened again, broke apart, tilting slowly to meet the next row even as that row slid into line and resolved and he stood between stacked trees again. The regularity of the orchard disguised its great size, and he often got lost and had to be retrieved and carried back to the house, crying with frustration.

"I picked you up and ran," his father said. He laughed briefly. "My God, I was frightened. But you were all right. In the end you were all right."

After some time he said, "Show me how you carried me."

His father gestured and he bent over the bed, working the

sheet loose and then carefully turning it back, like the leaf of a book, and finding his father there, diminished and lost. But he didn't really know this, only felt that he must be diminished, or felt this was what he should feel. That his father had now grown so small. He could not remember touching him before. When he straightened with a huge effort, hefting his father's body, he nearly fell over backwards. His father weighed nothing. In that movement of lurching with all his strength and finding no resistance, like falling upward, he suddenly remembered being snatched that way, right off his feet, and then the endless alternation of dark trees and corridors of light flashing past as they ran.

They remained that way, examining the room as if it were a place they'd just arrived in. His father's arms hung loosely behind him. Then he said, his voice abruptly compact with annoyance, "You'll have to take me on your back. I want to see in front of me. I don't want to look up in the air."

The trip to the station was maddeningly slow. He plowed ahead, feeling his father's groin bumping the base of his spine. His mother trailed behind them, holding the small parcel he'd had to assemble for her. As they inched their way through the back streets of the city he registered their progress as a diminishment of that motionless time in which nothing had yet happened, and no decision had been finally made. Inside the station passengers shoved each other violently or squatted and smoked. Small children hawked dented fruit, trailing clouds of flies. The train twitched and expelled a cloud of steam. He experienced the normalness surrounding him as a kind of insanity, either his or the world's. He wasn't sure which one he hoped for. On board the train he found a pair of seats. His mother sat shrinkingly, attempting not to touch things. It was eleven-fifteen. He tried to hear past the clamor around them, to tune his ear behind it, or below it. He stood in the aisle with one hand clamped on the back of his father's seat. Passengers jostled roughly by him, flinging bundles and birdcages and cardboard suitcases into the racks, oblivious and foul-tempered from the heat. There was no panic anywhere. He almost wished for a general fear that would siphon off his own and relieve him a little. His father raised his chin at him and he knelt down in the aisle beside his father's seat, and was ruthlessly kicked at and cursed as the train kept on filling.

"I don't think they'll reach Seoul," his father said.

"I don't think so either."

"It's very hot on this train."

"I know it is. We'll be all right." He stood up again quickly. The train had given a roused huff and whistle. "You must stay on the train all the way to Pusan," he said. "If there's confusion in the station don't stay looking for me. Go to Aunt's house and I'll meet you there."

"Where are you going?" His mother caught hold of his hand.

"I have to find myself a seat. It's all right."

"Where are you going?" she repeated.

"I have to go and sit down." He loosened her fingers and she looked at his father accusingly. His father nodded at him, the professorial cue of dismissal. "We'll meet at Aunt's house," his father said. "See you there."

The conductor was shouting. His father suddenly lifted one hand and he reached out and took it. "We'll all travel very comfortably," his father said. He was wearing a worn, baggy pair of pajamas, the gardener's. When he lifted his arm the cuff fell back, all the way past his elbow, and the too-large sleeve piled there, making the arm seem impossibly fragile. It trembled, not letting Chuck support its weight. "See you there," his father repeated. The hand dropped.

He jogged down the length of the car, into the car behind. The train was moving as he jumped off.

All that afternoon on the train, as it pulled out of Seoul, slid over the Han River Bridge, and chugged south toward the first stop, Suwon; and on the station platform, where he stood for what seemed like hours, suddenly afraid that he'd done the wrong thing; and in the streets of Seoul, where it was now so much hotter than it had been one hour before that the desperate craving for rain circumvented reason and perception and the hot, feeble breeze seemed to carry the smell of wet earth, they heard thunder. In the summers in Seoul there were thunderstorms most afternoons. Although the downpours always left behind a steamy heat even worse than before, the memory of this disappointment dispersed as quickly as the cool of each storm, so that they were always, in Seoul, dreaming ardently of rain. They heard the sound of thunder in the North and were happy about it, although the clouding of the sky and that hush, when the leaves seem to hiss, didn't come. By that evening it would be clear that the sound lacked the delicious, uneven undulation that makes children run outside, chests thrust forward and arms trailing, into the street. Its bursts were sporadic, but the growth of its volume unnaturally steady.

He went home that day, and was afraid of the house. Nothing had been said in front of Miki, but he wasn't surprised to find her and the few things she owned gone. It was impossible to allow himself the noises a body alone in a house makes. His own footfalls seemed too loud. He would stop short, frightened, on the stairs or in the center of a room, and each time the silence of the house came and stood all around him. He retreated to the tree and curled up there with a blanket, in the damp half-darkness, smoking incessantly. Perhaps Kim would meet him here. His desire for this to happen was so intense it became indistinguishable from a sort of intuition he decided to believe in. He imagined Kim had lied to him about leaving town as part of a ruse to outwit the police. He had nothing but the tutelage of movies with which to form his expectations of the crisis, and so he stayed where he was, awaiting the dramatic reunion with Kim and eventually, because he had gotten so little real rest, fell over asleep and was roused by the boomerang yowl of a plane flying low, sometime just before dawn.

News of the fighting had finally reached civilian Seoul at around suppertime the night before, and when he entered the streets below the hill on which his family lived they were crowded, although not choked, with people attempting to leave. A Soviet-made fighter had briefly strafed one of the boulevards— this was the sound he had heard—and although the incident was isolated and somewhat inexplicable, it had the effect of keeping most people in their homes, under the assumption that the army would concentrate its efforts on defending Seoul and not the open countryside. This was his assumption, too. He hurried through the streets to the USIS office, elevated by vicarious importance and by the tremendous relief he felt at having his objectless fear replaced at last with a clearly defined and univer- sally acknowledged threat, and when he arrived he found the office stripped and empty. The teletype, telephones, typewriter. He ran back into the street and into a column of pedestrian traf- fic, hand-drawn two-wheeled carts, old men leaning on sticks, women with the lumps of infants bound onto their bodies like gigantic tumors, small children trotting in overalls, and no young men his age anywhere. The sound of artillery in the distance was distinct and regular. He could feel it in the soles of his feet.

He thought of those days as an obliterating avalanche, swift, focused, and inevitable, but he had actually stumbled in circles, finding the landscape inscrutable, trying to grasp the possibilities and to form a plan accordingly, and failing. As many people as were trying to leave Seoul were arriving there to take refuge, and the streets seethed with travelers thwarting each other. He returned to the office again, standing in disbelief and then yank- ing out drawers and flinging open cabinets, looking for some- thing that could help him or something he could steal to make a feeble gesture of revenge, and finding nothing but blank paper, yellowed clip files, dead pens. Eventually he made his way back through the streets to his house. Beneath the tree he found nothing but his blanket, soiled—no message from Kim scratched in the dirt, cut on the trunk of the tree, made from the scatter of cigarette butts he had left there. He had forgotten to eat for a day. In the kitchen he ransacked shelves and pantries and spilled a jar of dried beans that he left where they fell. He found a stash of tinned fishes from Europe that were kept to tempt his father and ate the whole of it, tossing the oily tins behind him as he emptied them.

He wandered from room to room, and floor to floor, trailing the dirty blanket. Miki's room had surprised him, that time; now he crept through the house trying to flush out its hidden spaces. He plunged suicidally into dark closets, stretching his arms forward until he felt the walls. He jumped and flailed once, catching sight of his reflection in a mirror. When there was nowhere left to go he climbed the stairs to the attic. His father's bed stood there, shaped to the moment his father had left it. He crawled into it and closed his eyes.

When the bridges blew up he didn't know what it was, but he heard it and felt it—*BBBMM*. The surge seemed to press on his heart, as if the impact had spread out and permeated everything, the river, the city, the hill that his house sat upon, the house, the mattress beneath him. The house absorbed the blow easily, shifting slightly and then settling down, the force shaking but failing to topple it. And then he felt safe; it coursed through him like alcohol. Curling onto his side he managed to push his shoes off before twitching once, hard, but by then he had fallen asleep.

Miki found him there that evening. In the fading gray light he couldn't see her face, but he knew she was crying. He waded toward her from his dream. For some time she couldn't compose herself. She could barely breathe. She had exclaimed in dismay when she saw him. At first he assumed she was frightened for him, and then he realized that her agitation stemmed from his having caught her in the act of desertion. She had run away after he left for the station; first she had robbed his home, then she had gone to find her sister, and failing, had tried to leave the city alone but coming within sight of the river she saw its three bridges blow up, one, two, three, people raining down into the water. Those three bridges were the only way south. There were chunks, she said, gasping. Chunks of people came down. There had been so many people crawling over the bridges, like ants swarming out of an anthill. She told him again that she had robbed his house, harping on the triviality of the confession. Just one day before this would have ruined her life. She seemed angry that this was no longer true, and angry at his slowness. He was sitting cross-legged on the bed, in the twilight, watching her become a silhouette against the window. He remembered walking home in the rising heat of the clear, late morning, taking huge unsteady strides, balancing his hangover on his shoulders, feeling as disregarded as a prophet whose intimacy with the future makes coexistence with the present impossible. That day had been yesterday. Now events had overtaken him. "What happened to the things that you stole?" he asked, knowing it was a ridiculous question. But she said, to explain, "I fell down in the street." She lit the lamp and showed him her face. It was damaged; he reached to touch her and she ducked away. "You'll have to hide," she said.

When she showed him the wedge-shaped space beneath the stairs, too short to lie down in and barely tall enough for him to kneel, he was as disturbed as if he'd found a stranger lurking there. A panel pulled away, and there was the black, airless hole. "Your mother hid some money and precious things here, in boxes," Miki said. It was empty now.

He assumed she stayed with him in the hopes Kim might come. He had the same hope, but he could no longer deny to himself that they would both be disappointed. He wondered when Miki would realize this, and leave him, or betray him. Within a few days of entering the city the KPA took possession of the house. It was off by itself on a high hill, with an unobstructed view of the horizon and sky. The desecration of the house in this way might have been seen by the visiting soldiers as an inevitable form of justice, although later the house's remoteness and its expansive grounds would spare it, when Seoul fell again. The room where his father had lain became an occupation headquarters and the rest of the house was used and abused by turns as need and sentiment arose. He lay curled in his hole, listening. He lived in the hole for three months, from the twenty-ninth of June to liberation, in the last week of September. For at least one full month he was delirious with fever. The hole was unventilated, hot, and rank. Sometimes several days would pass before the house was entirely empty of soldiers and Miki could come to him, and his chamber pot would fill and overflow, or he would overturn it accidentally, shifting and curling as he tried to relieve the pain that was first in his muscles and then in his bones, as he lost weight and his spine and hips and joints protruded more and more sharply. He was covered with bruises; he compulsively pressed on them. He was so claustrophobic he thought he was going insane. His panic at the confinement would rise to an intolerable pitch and have nowhere to go; it slammed desperately within him the way he longed to slam against the close walls. He tried to dream of space. He tried to use the utter darkness to imagine a great space around himself, but any way he moved he touched a wall.

He smoked insatiably, further befouling his hole. Miki fed him, tried to clean him, supplied him with cigarettes, emptied the sickening pot, whenever she was left alone, but she was never alone for long. He hung his head out of the square aperture, gasping, his eyes rolling in his head from the glare. At first he would climb out and walk in the hall but he was soon so weak from the fever and the atrophying of his muscles that Miki wouldn't let him out at all. She was afraid that if the soldiers returned he wouldn't be able to move fast enough to conceal himself. At the height of his fever he must have urinated onto himself for days, until there was no more liquid in his body to be expelled. He stopped having bowel movements, and was grateful. Squatting on the terrible pot, its rim had pressed into his sore flesh like a blade. Never drawing breath that wasn't smoke, he felt the old tuberculosis crushing his lungs again, as if it had been dormant all this time in his chest. He coughed up material and caught it in the cup of his hand. When his expectation of Miki's betrayal faded he was bereft. He wanted to die through no fault of his own.

On September sixteenth MacArthur made his famous landing at Inchon and nine days later he announced the liberation of Seoul, so that this event would coincide exactly with the three-month anniversary of North Korea's invasion. The street fighting that was leveling the city at a snail's pace, house by house, block by block, actually lasted for several more days. Chuck didn't know any of this when the panel was yanked away and a terrible square of white light fell on him, marking the beginning of a fresh agony as his body fought the alternation of light and dark and shrank in terror from the open space where nothing touched against him. He'd grown used to his hole. When the panel fell away he squeezed his eyes shut and waited to die, but it was only Miki. She shook as she helped him through the aperture, like someone with palsy.

Slowly, civilian Seoul began to reemerge. ROKA patrols moved through the streets, on foot or in jeeps, examining the survivors. Often, they shot them. Being alive was considered a fair indication of having cooperated with the enemy. Although the

SUSAN CHOI

American forces refused to authorize these so-called retaliations,
they tended only to prevent those they actually stumbled upon.
While the new occupation settled back into the city he settled
back into his house. It was filthy and disordered—there was no
better description than to say it looked as if an army had been
there—but it was not, he was surprised to find, substantially
damaged. Piles of books had been pulled from the bookshelves,
but that was all. They spilled across the floor. The first time he'd
tried walking he simply toppled over, like a felled tree. Then Miki
came and lifted his arm over her shoulders, and they limped
around the room, exercising him.

He left the house at dawn, October 6, 1950. He would learn
the date once he arrived where he was headed. Leaving the
house, he thought, *If*—but the streets were quiet, the air was
damp and chill, and the patrols were audible from great distances. He leaned on a cane. He crept down the steep lane from
his gate, one shoulder scraping along the retaining wall. Barnyard
animals roamed in the streets. He saw a magazine photo of Stalin
in a cheap metal frame, hanging cockeyed off the side of a building. Drifts of ash had washed up in the gutters and there was rubble from broken KPA barricades strewn everywhere: rough
chunks of concrete, boulders, old tires, burnt streetcars and
pieces of track. The dirt-chemical smell of exploded, burnt, and
dampened wood was overpowering. Almost every building he
saw was a charred ruin, even the National Library, although later
he would learn that it had been preserved throughout the duration of the Communist occupation and only set on fire by the
Americans after they returned, to make a dramatic backdrop for
MacArthur's ceremony of restoring to Rhee the city keys. The ritual had been lavishly filmed and photographed by the world's
press. So the world's press, too, had returned.

He waited in the office for Peterfield, with the resurrected telephone, teletype, and typewriter. A terrible square of white light

fell through the window and began its day-long trek over the floor. He knew he was repulsively thin, yellow, and pestilential-smelling. His cheeks were sockets. His back was hunched. His muscles had grown shorter, and there was nothing vital enough in them to let them stretch again. When Peterfield came in and saw him he lit a cigarette, and sat down, and kept looking.

"You may be too sick for the draft," he finally said, "but that sort of nicety doesn't matter much now. If they try to draft you I can't go to bat for you."

"I know," he said.

"And I can't credential you anymore. I can't credential a god-damned Korean civilian. There are too many spies worming into this place. If I credential you I'm fired. No Special Status. No exemption."

"I know," he repeated.

They opened the office again, without discussing what Chuck thought of as Peterfield's abandonment of him. They never would. But seeing Peterfield that first day, undamaged and unre-pentant, struck at him as powerfully as heartbreak. Sometimes his stomach would seem to drop away and there in the void was the realization he had been discarded. Peterfield must have been affected as well, for their friendship was over. It seemed to have been corrupted by guilt, and the resentment that a guilty man feels toward the source of his discomfort. Chuck recognized that Peterfield hated him, and why, but the recognition couldn't do him any good.

five

At first nothing happened. The boy—his name was Courtlin, which had been his mother's mother's maiden name, or something, she did not know or care—came to visit her and they sat on the screened-in porch drinking iced tea and eating oatmeal cookies her mother had brought on a tray. This tray had also conveyed to them a pair of daisies bobbing in a bud vase, the sort of bright touch that made Katherine think of a hospital room, but she was so uninterested in Courtlin she couldn't even be embarrassed in front of him. She had considered telling him that she didn't want to see him anymore, but her best idea for an explanation involved her summer reading list. It had also occurred to her that she might have a need for him. Still, Courtlin bored her so much it made her furious, and this wasn't safe. She would be rude, he would be puzzled, he would ask stupid questions, and eventually her mother would notice. Katherine could never gracefully deflect her mother's attention, once it was roused. When her mother challenged her she always made things as bad as she could, declaring herself guilty of every crime, even ones she hadn't been accused of. "Courtlin, I've got to talk to you about something," she murmured when she heard her mother's footsteps mounting the staircase and moving down the second-story corridor. The radio was mooning away in the kitchen. They had an oscillating fan trained on them, nodding and rattling unsteadily. Each time it rotated as far as it could left or right it clicked loudly and stuck there, shaking with increased desperation, and just when she was sure it was finally broken, it unstuck and began turning back. It was driving her crazy. "Courtlin." He leaned forward and looked intently at her hands, which were permanently wrapped around her sweating glass of tea. "I'm worried and I want to tell you about it. I have all this summer reading for school and I can't get it done."

"Is it hard for you to concentrate, Katherine?"

"No, it's not that. I love to read." She not only couldn't concentrate, she couldn't sleep. And hadn't had an appetite in days. She cast her eyes dubiously toward the second floor. "My mother thinks I read too much. She's always shooing me out of the house."

"But you should read."

"I know. I want to go to college, like you." Here she managed to look at him, but he seemed so sincerely interested in what she was saying that she had to look away again. "That sort of thing isn't so important to my mother. She wants me to go out with boys and have fun. I mean she wants me to go out with you. She likes you. Don't talk to her about this."

"Of course I wouldn't. I like your mother, too." Here he glanced, dubiously, in the direction of the second floor. She often noticed him unconsciously mimicking her mannerisms. He was that dull. She loathed him. "But it's wrong that she discourages your reading," he went on. "She ought to encourage it. You're so smart, Katherine. Now, I mean it"—she was shrugging irritably— "and you will go to college, and you'll be a standout. I've always just assumed that you would." Courtlin was the sort of student whose good grades were thanks to his solemn conviction in the sanctity of education. His intelligence was thoroughly average, but he was a diligent, undoubting workhorse. His father was a Sewanee professor, after all. There would have been great shame in not doing well. He was taking the whole issue far more seriously than she'd anticipated. Now it looked as though they were going to have to talk about it all day.

"I guess what it means," she said, feeling cruel, "is that I won't be able to see you as much. I can't let myself. I've gotten so far behind."

"That makes sense." He looked miserably at her inaccessible hands, still fiercely guarding her tea glass. After a moment he added, as if he'd managed to convince himself, "We sure have been lollygagging around this summer. I've got to get cracking on an engineering project my prof up at school suggested I do. I've been moved into honors engineering for the fall, did I tell you? I almost didn't want to do it, it's going to be so much more work. So I think you're absolutely right. And we can help each other out, and keep each other in line." This speech was so unbearably pathetic that she was forced to reply, "I was hoping you'd say that. We should still have as much fun as we can, when I'm not reading."

Courtlin now seemed cheered by this new, shared seriousness in their relationship. "I should have insisted on it. I noticed you're still carrying *Mansfield Park* around. It seems like you've been slogging away at that one since May."

"It's boring," she snapped.

"I'm sure there's something worthwhile about it, or your teacher wouldn't have assigned it. I've never read it myself. I'll bet I've read other books on your list, though. I'm an engineering major but I'm sure I could help you out some. We have to take a lot of English classes at school no matter what field we're in. I think that's one of the really fine things about my school, that they won't let you take too narrow a focus." By God, she was bored. "What do you figure you'll major in, Katherine? You must have something in mind."

"English," she said.

She pretended to read Shakespeare, carrying a volume of something or other everywhere like a totem of seriousness, the way she had carried a diary when she was nine or ten years old, in a great ostentation of secrecy. Courtlin would drop by, just to say hello, just to see how she was getting along, at obviously regular intervals meant to seem casual—every three days, every four days—and when he did she was always prepared, clutching one of her father's slim, pale blue Penguin volumes as if she yearned to be left alone with it. She watched him watching her hands. She began to notice things about his body that repulsed her. She had never noticed his body before, not when they had walked hand in hand to the swimming hole, brushing bare limbs, modestly stripping to suits. Not even when he had kissed her. Then she only noticed the slight milky taste of his mouth, and accepted it. She had never kissed anyone else. But now her attention was riveted and unforgiving, and although Courtlin was serviceably handsome in all the usual ways he seemed unfinished, incompetent, afflicted with possible spasms. His hands fidgeted together. His limbs threatened to cease coordinated movement. His skin gave off an eager, oily sheen. He had become nothing but an oppressive, embarrassing body, and her impatience was equally physical. She wanted to pummel him. She would feel her angry flush surging up and steaming off her ears.

This prickliness was more than Glee could take. "That sour face will stick," she told Katherine, when they were alone. She was taking the tactic of criticizing Katherine very generally. Glee knew better than to tell Katherine precisely how she was wrong. That would only determine her further. "Miss Mood," she said, at the stubborn little wall Katherine's book made in front of her face. When this produced no results, Glee told rambling stories about the grown unmarried daughters of old friends. "I was actually stunned when I saw her. She used to be such a striking girl, and so sharp and fun, and now she's gotten—well, stocky. That's the only word for it. Ever since that boy she liked went and married someone else. Do you remember that, Kitty?" Katherine flinched here but kept her calm silence, chewing a straw as she read. "He was a cute boy, but she was standoffish. She thought she had him in the bag. I guess she didn't." Glee was exasperated with Katherine's coldness toward Courtlin. She wasn't going to have him scared off by moody vanity and selfishness.

Finally she said, one day, "Charles Addison's coming to dinner."

Katherine lay her book down and took it up again quickly.

"It's just family dinner as usual. I asked Courtlin, too. He's practically a member of this family. And I just adore his mother."

"Why don't you ask his mother, then," Katherine said.

Glee bristled. "I wish you would behave with a little bit of dignity. You're a fourteen-year-old girl and you act like a six-year-old brat. Your behavior humiliates me."

"I don't see why you'd be humiliated."

"I don't see how I couldn't be. The way you run hot and cold with him. I taught you to act better than that."

"At least I'm not leading him on."

"What in the world is that supposed to mean? You're toying with him. You act superior and it's ugly, if you'd like to know the truth."

"I'm not toying with him, I'm doing the opposite. He won't let me alone."

"Katherine. *You are going steady with Courtlin.*" She said it as if it were an accusation, or a criminal sentence.

"I am not."

"You're not! Then what exactly has been going on all summer?"

"Am I in trouble for not being nice enough to him, or for being too nice?"

"I expect you to act appropriately."

"Oh, appropriately!" Katherine shouted. "Appropriately!"

"Are you going with Courtlin or not?"

"I don't know."

"If I'm letting you run around with this boy doing just what you please, you'd better know."

"All right," she said, looking away.

"All right, what?"

"All right I'm going with him."

"Then act like it."

There was glacial silence between them for the rest of the week, but on Friday afternoon, the day of the dinner, Glee met Katherine coming downstairs, freshly bathed. Katherine had retrieved the silver razor and shaved carefully beneath her arms and from her ankles to the tops of her knees. She had sat in the bath so long that her fingers were pruned, but she was pink from the steam and smelled of soap and pressed cotton and orange-blossom water. She had pulled her damp hair down in front of her eyes between two scissored fingers, and cut bangs. She was wearing the gingham sundress. When Katherine saw her mother she paused warily, two steps up, and they studied each other. Glee gave her a rueful smile.

"Baby," she said. "You look sweet." She went and lay a hand against Katherine's cheek.

"I'm sorry, Mommy," Katherine whispered.

"No, no. Don't you dare cry." Glee pecked her forehead and stood back, looking her up and down. "You've gotten so pretty for him, don't you spoil it and cry."

By the time Charles Addison arrived, Katherine and Courtlin were locked to their usual seats on the porch, in the agitated blast of the oscillating fan. She saw him bound up and go rippling past the dense mesh of the porch screen, raising an arm to wave, and then he was in the foyer shouting cleverly with her parents, being made a cocktail, talking about why he was late. Katherine felt a dewy moustache on her upper lip. She lay one finger against it, cautiously. She had powdered her face. When she put the finger into her mouth she tasted talcum and salt. "I used to mow Professor Addison's lawn," Courtlin was musing. "I wonder if he remembers me. That was ages ago." Courtlin had interpreted the dinner invitation as reconfirming his importance to Katherine. She listened to the talk from the front room—". . . ran into LaMont on the way up and he had a court . . . " ". . . well we're privileged . . . " ". . . don't let her Charlie she'll murder—"

Then the screen door slammed back on its hinges and Addison stepped onto the porch with an old-fashioned held out in front of him, as if he meant to make a toast. He took a sip from it and smiled at them, benevolently and vaguely, and then his eyebrows shot up in a show of great surprise. "Is that Courtlin Jones?"

Courtlin was already on his feet, grinning. "Hi, Professor Addison." They shook hands vigorously and Courtlin dipped his head up and down like a dim-witted bird. "I didn't think you would recognize me."

"Nonsense! Well met, sir." Courtlin basked in this mocking attention. "And how is your father? When is he going to emerge from his learned seclusion?"

The two men sat down together to discuss Courtlin's father's recent experiments, and Courtlin's inevitable triumph in the engineering field, and the wisdom of studying the sciences versus the absurdity of studying the arts. Addison sat with his feet apart, leaning forward on his knees, jangling his drink emphatically in his hands, and soon Courtlin's feet were planted firmly apart and he was leaning with his elbows on his knees and his chin sticking out and a furrow of absorption on his forehead. Katherine's father came out with a drink for Courtlin, which he took with abashed ceremony, as if he were unworthy of it. He held it, as Addison did, out in the heroic expanse between his knees. Katherine hoped he would get drunk and do something stupid, but he hardly touched his lips to the glass. The drink seemed to have increased his anxiety about acting properly. At one point Addison said, "I'm more and more convinced that Katherine will ignore our best advice and study literature," and a snort of laughter burst forth from Courtlin and left him looking helpless and frightened. A few minutes later Katherine rose, as if she meant to be inconspicuous, and resolutely walked off the porch. Courtlin's eyes followed her, but Addison did not seem to notice.

In the kitchen she slouched against the door to the pantry and watched her mother and Mrs. Jackson, the colored woman who sometimes came to clean their house or assist with a dinner, zigzag anxiously around each other. She had to be asked to move several times before her mother told her to go back to the porch. "Be my hostess, sweet pea," Glee snapped. "You're underfoot."

"I want a drink."

"Save it, Katherine." Glee yanked open the oven door and Katherine barely had time to hop out of the way. As she retreated Mrs. Jackson gave her a sympathetic smile she made a point of ignoring.

She went upstairs to the washroom and locked the door behind her. Fortressed there, she turned on the tap and the light and put her face close to the mirror. When she reached up to fluff her bangs her hand trembled. Glaring into her own eyes, she felt a terrible pang of self-consciousness suddenly, of being "Katherine," and the more acute the awareness grew, the more distant and estranged she felt from it. She couldn't feel like herself. She thought of the ghostly filaments that sometimes drifted through her vision; whenever she looked straight at one it would leap out of sight.

Then she turned off the tap and snapped off the light and stood there in the soap-and-laundry-scented dusk of the washroom. Once the strangeness of not promptly leaving the room had dissipated she felt as though she could stand there forever, with an empty mind, not doing anything. At last she pulled the door open, unfurling her free arm extravagantly above her head. The second-story hallway was dim and attentive. She stalked down the stairs and made a grand entrance into the empty dining room. She leaned knowingly against the sideboard and lifted her chin at various angles. Then the kitchen door swung open and her mother told her to bring everyone to the table.

During supper she tried not to look at him. He was seated to her right, her mother to her left at one end facing her father at the other; Courtlin was alone on the opposite side. The table was not very large—Glee had left the leaves out—but in spite of this Courtlin looked lost. Glee had put him there after a long consideration of arrangements, and given that she and Joe always sat at opposite ends, the seating question had essentially amounted to deciding who would sit beside Katherine, and who would face her. Glee's sole purpose was to cultivate Katherine and Courtlin. Charles Addison had always been a frequent dinner guest, and although Glee relied on him to be her partner in flirtation, to arouse and gratify her and make her undiminished attractiveness meaningful, she took his comfort for granted and wasn't overly concerned with his needs. Her first thought had been to seat Katherine and Courtlin beside each other, leaving Charles on the other side alone. In recent years, with Katherine the only child left at home, they obviously sat one on each side when Charles came to dinner, and the addition of Courtlin to Katherine's side would underscore his role with her, both current and presumed. Soon enough, though, Glee realized that the seating of Katherine and Courtlin next to each other required a preexisting sympathy between them that for the time being didn't exist. It would be more to the point to have them looking at each other, with the space of the table between them. There was nothing like a little obstacle to make a boy newly appealing. Courtlin's affections seemed assured, but Glee wanted to keep him in place and patient while she ironed out Katherine's moods, and the sight of Katherine on the stairs that afternoon, looking so tentative and so pretty—she was startlingly pretty, Glee thought, and this thought had a biting edge to it she shook off impatiently—had seemed to reconfirm her decision.

Now she regretted it. Courtlin was foundering. It was her annoyance with him as much as her sympathy that roused her to action. She began to lavish him with attention and affectionate teasing. "You'd better get to work, Mr. Jones. I only invited you here for your appetite. These two selfish men always have too many cocktails before supper and then they don't eat. I get no appreciation at all from them."

"You're only saying that because the attention I pay to your cooking is so ardent it verges on the improper," Charles said, and Glee abandoned Courtlin for just long enough to laugh beautifully at her husband's best friend. She caught an unpleasant glimpse of her daughter staring down at her plate, looking stupid.

It was a terrible supper for Katherine. The unmoored feeling that had struck her in the washroom emerged again, unbidden. She desperately willed it away. Beginning to wonder what it meant that she was behind her eyes, within her skin, feeling the fall of her hair on her cheek, seemed like an irreversible disaster. Even at the age of fourteen she saw no glamour in going insane. Charles Addison was sitting beside her. Once, she knocked elbows with him, and submitted to the blush spreading over her face with suicidal resignation. She didn't care how thorough her humiliation was, as long as it was gotten over with. But instead of attacking her with ridicule, or being snared by the force field of her agitation, he only briefly apologized, and returned to his conversation.

After dinner they decided to have dessert on the porch, to catch the rising evening cool. It was just before eight. Like everyone who lived in Sewanee, they had the advantage of the mountainside. Set into a slope, the house and its porch looked through the tops of trees toward the west, where the sun was beginning to set. A breeze stirred, and the light flashed unevenly through the leaves. The light was distilled and intense, and beneath it the white siding of the house turned gold, and every face seemed rarefied and flawless. Glee had taken Courtlin's arm to lead him outside, but there she stopped short. "I've let Mrs. Jackson go home," she remarked.

"Let me serve dessert," Charles said, standing up again. "I won't ruin it. Go on and sit down, Glee."

"Let Katherine do it," Glee said. She squeezed Courtlin's arm confidentially.

"She refuses to be parted from you, Jones!" As Katherine went back inside she could hear her father continuing to tease Courtlin about his success with the two Monroe women. This was his favorite way of showing off to men. He inevitably claimed that Charles Addison and his wife wanted to be alone. "I can tell when I'm not wanted," he'd say, pretending to leave the room permanently. He considered it a testament to his self-confidence that he relished this joke. "I don't envy you, Courtlin," he was saying. "These Monroe women are pretty exacting. I'd be sorry to unload one on you if I wasn't so glad to get rid of her."

Addison had followed her into the kitchen. She reached for an apron and tied it too tightly around her waist before turning to face him, as if she were arming herself. "I'm all right," she said. "You don't need to help me."

"I'm not interested in helping you. I'm animated by selfishness. I have been smelling this pie since I got here—" He took the pie server and slit a vent in the pie's crust. A weak ribbon of steam issued out.

"Don't," Katherine said, batting a hand through the air at him. "I think it needs more time to set. It'll run if you cut it now."

"I haven't got time."

"We have time," he said.

She had taken up and put down the pie knife repeatedly, and now when she tried to extract it again from a jumble of cooking tools in the drawer they flew up in a mass and crashed everywhere. A spoon skittered across the floor. Addison bent for it, and handed it to her, and she threw it into the sink and turned away again. But she didn't cut the pie. She simply stared at it. She felt his gaze on her back, calm and amused and unswerving.

"I had no idea that you were enjoying the attentions of Courtlin Jones," he said. "That's brave of him. You must be exhausting."

"I don't 'enjoy' his 'attentions.'"

"Are they unenjoyable? Or isn't he attentive enough?"

"Both," she said, and then angrily, feeling tricked, "I don't want them to be any more. I mean, any more than they are."

"You don't enjoy them."

"No."

"I'm surprised."

"Why?" she demanded.

"He seems very devoted to you. And you require devotion."

"I don't know what that means."

"Don't you?"

"No."

She still faced the pie, which sat steaming, innocently, with decreasing strength, out of the small rupture in its crust. "Look what you've done," she said. "You've ruined the pie." Her hands were fumble-thumbed, the way they always were first thing in the morning, when she could hardly wrap her fist around a cup, or when she laughed so hard that her limbs became helpless and numb. Why was that? she wondered irrelevantly. Why was it your hands got so clumsy? She had the impulse to ask him. She took up the knife again, nearly flipping it into her face. He sprang up behind to help her, and was reaching around as the knife clat-

tered into the drawer. His body just grazed hers. She looked at his
hands holding on to the counter on either side of her. The baking
had filled the kitchen with heat. Her hair clung to her cheek, but
she did not have room to move and brush it away. The ends of
her bangs caught in her lashes, and she regretted them fiercely.
They were obviously fresh, and uneven. She had cut them for the
sake of doing something to her hair, but she should have let it
alone, and bound it back from her face like a sober, self-possessed
woman would have.

His hand guided hers back to the knife and together they
pressed it cautiously through the pie's crust and cut a slice. Then
he set the knife and her hand down and performed the delicate
maneuver of easing the slice out and onto a plate. He settled it
skillfully. The filling ran a little, and they watched to see how far
it would go.

"We ought to get married," he said. "We'll be terrific when it
comes to the cake-cutting. Shall we do another?"

"Yes," she said. They cut another slice, and then another; he
rotated the tin with his left hand as they cut, and kept her right
hand lightly cradled in his, as her body was cradled in his body.
She could feel his whole length, almost too warm, and the slight,
calm pressure of his knee at the backs of her thighs, and when
she unclenched them he moved tightly against her. The mumble
of voices from the porch unbraided and she heard each one sepa-
rately: her mother's sharp banter and her father's large, unselfcon-
scious laugh and Courtlin's nervous one. No one seemed to miss
them.

He said, "But you must want to marry Courtlin." He set the
knife down again, and her hand with it. "I hadn't thought of that.
Perhaps you're already engaged."

She laughed sharply. "No."

"There are unofficial engagements. Sometimes a girl engages
herself without realizing."

"No. I haven't."

"Are you sure?" He stepped away from her and when she turned he looked almost shy. She took heart.

"I'm sure," she said.

She waited: a night, a day, another night, another day. That evening she dropped into bed without thinking of anything, her mind's voice struck dumb with exhaustion, and the next morning rose just after dawn, as if summoned to a sober duty. She bathed out of the sink from the thinnest, quietest stream of water the tap could emit. She put her wet hair in a braid and curled the tail to lie against her shoulder. Every action presented another opportunity for hush. She didn't think of it as stealth. Stealth was a guilty word. She took her breakfast onto the porch and looked over her reading list, as the sun climbed and the wet, fragrant cool of early morning burned away. A hiss of insects filled the air. She heard her mother stirring upstairs and was in the kitchen rinsing her breakfast things when her mother came down. "I'm going to the library," she announced. Her mother did not seem interested in the reading list which Katherine was holding up as proof of her intentions. Glee had a hangover, and had only gotten up out of fear that Joe might get up first and bang things in the kitchen. In a better frame of mind she might have found it strange that Katherine was already dressed, but at the moment she was only irritated that Katherine, having gotten up, hadn't thought to make coffee. She pushed past her daughter and stood bleakly contemplating the icebox. In her robe and stocking feet Glee was a diminished, disorderly figure. Katherine gazed at her a moment before recovering herself and hurrying out of the house.

The walk was familiar. She had been to Charles Addison's home countless times at every conscious age of her life, just as she had been over the lines of his face and the patterns of his clothes with the same thorough, impassive attention that she had applied to everything as a child. Now she found herself in possession of a wealth of information. There was the round pink stone by the road that she used to balance on. Here was the walkway. She could anticipate the flagstone that would wobble. She had never taken any interest in these things before, which made them seem that much more meaningful: the imaginary houndstooth jigsaw puzzles in his jacket, sulky hopscotch on the flagstones while her parents took too long to say good-bye. It was a complicated inheritance that had devolved on her by degrees, unperceived. When she rang his bell she knew how it would sound, buried deep in the house.

He greeted her very politely, with a facile remark about pleasant surprises, but she was prepared for this. She breezed past him, waving her reading list, on her way to his sitting room. She knew he had a pile of books there, and she was going to see if he had any she needed, and then she was going to borrow them.

"Aren't the library copies sufficient?" he wondered, following her.

"I'd like to use yours."

"Why?"

"Because I'll bet you write things in your books when you read them. My father's always saying you're a brilliant man, so I figure if I have your copies with all your scribblings explaining everything I'll be ahead of everybody when I get back to school."

"Oh, yes. Well armed to meet the challenges of, what must it be? Seventh grade?"

"Ninth grade. My first year of high school." She was looking up and down his bookshelves now, her body awash in nervous sweat. Her hands were held calmly behind her.

"God help me," he said. Perhaps he meant her to hear him. "I'm very sorry to tell you that I never write in my books. Books are by definition complete and inviolable. I would never dream of maculating one."

"What does that mean?"

"Immaculate: spotless. *Macula:* mark. *Maculare:* to mark, stain, dirty. It's a word of which the Catholic church is very fond. Don't they teach you any Latin in the seventh grade?"

"French," she said. *"Je ne te crois pas du tout."* Her heart was pounding as she pulled a volume off the shelf. He came and peered over her shoulder at her selection. One of her hands still hovered at her back and as he hooked a finger into it she turned around and let the book fall open, exposing a random page, completely scrawled over. He wrote in every book he touched, on almost every page; there was not a volume in his home that wasn't covered by his marks.

"You lied," she said, as he bent down to kiss her. He didn't lift her up in his arms. His hands didn't touch her. His lips seemed decisive and dry, and then his tongue darted suspiciously into her mouth and she felt the shock between her legs, and tasted tobacco. Her neck began to cramp, straining to reach him. When she faltered he drew away.

She said, helplessly, "You taste like tobacco."

"You've been watching me smoke all your life," he replied, as if he were tired of her childish objections.

She continued dating Courtlin, but there was a change. She was warmer toward him, more sympathetic. Glee noticed a reassuring tenderness: when the couple sat murmuring together on the porch, when Katherine walked Courtlin to the foot of her front steps to say good-bye for the night. She had always just sat on the porch staring vaguely ahead of her while Courtlin had to let himself out, as if she were some kind of rajah, Glee thought bitterly, as if she were an arrogant prince. Now she was gentle, and interested. She questioned Courtlin about his engineering project, and remembered his responses, so that over time she was able to make meaningful comments about his progress, and offer solid advice when he ran into obstacles. She seemed alert and solicitous. She began to incorporate information about Courtlin into her dinner conversation with her parents: Courtlin's father's plan to take a sabbatical, Courtlin's efforts to get a new roommate. The old one was slovenly. Glee found herself in the unfamiliar position of seeing her criticisms heeded instead of ignored, and it unbalanced her, leaving her afflicted with the objectless annoyance that had previously been her daughter's prerogative.

Katherine now took the initiative in arranging dates with Courtlin, and she would inform Glee of the results with a guilelessness Glee found unnerving. We are going to walk up to Cross Point and have sandwiches, Katherine would singsong, or, We are going to study together in the library. She seemed slightly tousled and unguarded at all times, and as if her compulsion to report even the most mundane details—cold turkey and mayonnaise on white bread, the lovely stained glass in the reading room—were the effect of having been roused from a satiating sleep.

About half of these dates did exist; and when on them she was, as under the watchful eyes of her mother when home, gently forthcoming and rosily chaste. The other half of the time she had not made arrangements with Courtlin at all, and on these occasions she went to Addison's house and spent her afternoon having sex in his bed, on his floor, folded over his furniture, whatever way that he wanted, in adherence to his dictates. Her relationship with Courtlin, though it appeared newly placid, and pleasing to her, was no more physical than it had ever been. Courtlin neither touched her body nor saw it, because they did not go swimming anymore. She did not want to tan, she said.

Does he touch you here? Addison would ask, placing a finger

in the hollow of her collarbone; and when she said no, What about here? and Here? until the finger had wetly slipped into her. Then he would murmur, You sucked me up, didn't you, hungry girl. And she would say, Yes.

She became an elaborate liar. They were speeding toward the end of the summer, and although two weeks remained, there was no way to make any of those fourteen days contain anything other than the lengthening shadow of Labor Day. She refused a promise ring from Courtlin, on the grounds that even a seemingly harmless token might put a constraint on their mutual trust. "And besides that, I'm awfully young," she said. She suggested they keep taking things slowly; taking things slowly had worked well so far. Courtlin couldn't deny this. But he was starting to think it would be very hard, going back up to school. He declared that he might really miss her. He wanted a photograph of her. When she chided him for being melancholy he claimed, in a rare moment of wicked humor, that he only wanted it to show off to the guys. Of course this wasn't true. He would share the precious photograph with no one, or perhaps just one very good buddy. He imagined the photograph safeguarded in a silver gilt frame, perched on his desk, and softly communing with him during long, loyal hours of study. The uncharacteristic joke was an indication of how acutely he wanted this picture, for he feared she would sense his abject condition and respond as the old, irritable Katherine would have. But no such photograph as Courtlin had in mind, of the hazy, head-and-shoulders, string-of-pearls variety, that gets made when a girl graduates high school, yet existed, and she was able to refuse him this, too. She couldn't stomach his mooning over a picture of her. Her rudeness nearly reared up again, but she quelled it with the thought that Courtlin's corniness was always as laughable as it was maddening. What emerged from this internal struggle was an understanding chuckle and a pat on the hand. "You can write me," she said.

She might have been sorry for her treatment of Courtlin if it wasn't being repaid twice over. With Charles Addison she was the supplicant, and the more ground she lost the more desperate her methods became. She made reckless and dishonest declarations. They had a joke about the approaching interval of autumn, winter, and spring: they called it the Dark Ages. She had thought up the name, but it was Charles who had made it a joke. It was no joke to Katherine. She didn't worry about missing him. She had become too used to thinking of her life as a stormy passage of suffering and forbearance, and within this scheme a separation from him was inevitable and perhaps necessary. But the prospect of losing his interest entirely was incapacitating. She had no loss in her life to compare it to. Like any incomprehensible possibility, this one sabotaged even what was assured. When he came to undress her she flinched, and when he tried to console her she flared at him. She was contrary and unreasonable, and would persist in this way as if it were her only hope of self-preservation, until he exploded. "What have I got here?" he shouted one day. "A sniveling baby! A sticky, ugly crybaby!"

"I am ugly!" she shrieked in return. Because the fundamental disparity between them could not be discussed, their arguments lacked substance and logic, and could only escalate in absurdity until both of them were exhausted. The idea of striking a woman disgusted Addison, but at times like this he longed to strike her. He would wonder aloud whether they wouldn't both be happier "not doing this," although he realized that she was spurred to fury solely by the fear he would abandon her. "You wanted to be treated like a woman, didn't you," he said. "I've tried to give you what you wanted." She thought of her mother's recriminations: *Whose fault is that. Act your age.*

As the slope of late August grew steeper, the air became full of contention. One night her parents got drunk and fought viciously. Katherine balled up and wrapped her head in a pillow.

The next morning she went downstairs very late, full of resentment and fear, but her mother was all bustle: she and Joe were going to go to Chattanooga for dinner and dancing, and they were going to spend the night in a hotel. Katherine could take care of herself, couldn't she? Katherine took this as a gift of fate, a chance to redeem the doomed remnant of summer, and she determined to extract something memorable. Like Courtlin, she wanted reassurances and keepsakes. But Addison didn't greet the opportunity with the gratitude she had. The liberties of spending the night lay on the far side of a line he did not want to cross. A furtive, sweaty afternoon, one ear always kept cocked for the outside chance of the doorbell, was one thing; there was nothing essentially good about it, but it was what he was comfortable with. Having a freshly shampooed, cotton-nightie-clad girl sprawling under his covers, undoubtedly anticipating intertwined sleep, morning sunshine, and lingering breakfast, was quite another. His annoyance was not lost on her. When he finally quit his desk, where he had grimly remained in a pool of lamplight until almost one in the morning, she was sleepless and rigid. They tried to make love and failed. It was without a hint of disappointment or disturbance that he suggested they might be more comfortable sleeping apart, and as he made up his bed on the library sofa her helpless, vengeful crying only made him angrier, and he went and closed the two doors between them.

The next morning he was bothered by the memory. He stole upstairs and found her sleeping peacefully, a fistful of blanket pulled up to her cheek. He undressed and slipped into the bed beside her, pressing his erection against her hot, oblivious thigh, and when she began to stir he pushed her nightdress up past her breasts and forced himself into her. Even asleep she was wet, and in his excitement he thrust at her viciously, and rubbed his chest back and forth over her small breasts as if he wanted to erase them; her eyes had flown open and she gasped raggedly as he started to come. He yanked himself out and the burst of semen scattered over her stomach and along the shallow cleft of her sternum. One droplet landed on her cheek. "Darling," he said. He wet his fingers and smeared the come onto a nipple; then he pinched it, hard. She sighed deeply and closed her eyes, turning her face away from him. He pulled the nightdress down again, flattening it against her wet skin with his palms.

When she thought about the end of the summer she tried to imagine that his desire for her would be sharpened by absence, but even then, she knew this wouldn't be true. She began lying to him out of fear. She said she felt sick with guilt, which was true. And she said she was thinking of telling her mother. This was not true, but her longing to confess and to be reassured was visible, and he believed the threat, and threatened in return. She only grew more vague about her plans for disclosure. He tried solicitude. My sweetie, he said. My darling. Please. He scooped her up in his arms; it felt like holding a wet cat. His heart burst briefly within him, like the hollow, disconnected report of a gun. Her tears were always just below the surface, like her rudeness when she was with Courtlin. She was endlessly fighting these things. You'll forget me, she managed, and he laughed at her. I won't, he said. On her second-to-last day she finally asked him to write her. She had put it off because the question carried a weight of finality she didn't feel equal to, but now it could no longer wait. They had made love that afternoon without tears or accusations and he was in an expansive mood. It struck him as very sweet that she wanted him to write, and he thought it would amuse him, as well. He did not see the prospective correspondence as a crucial condition of life, any more than he saw the liaison as one, but he submitted to her restrictions: that he must type his envelopes, and make the return address Courtlin's address, in Sewanee. That a Sewanee postmark from Courtlin in the middle of the college term might be suspicious couldn't be helped. There was an element of risk in everything, she concluded, and at that moment he adored her for the great solemnity with which she had thought out her postal deception. Of course I'll write, sweetheart, he said.

She returned to New Orleans and began high school, hardly seeing what she did. She made occasional, oracular utterances in class that were never quite appropriate. She received three letters from Courtlin, each of which she read thoroughly, answered, and then threw away. She didn't remember what they said, or what she replied. Then at last she got a letter from Addison, in response to her voluminous two: it was a single sheet of notepaper. "Semester well underway . . . students who think that they don't need to read . . . hope you all are well, got a call from your dad trying to lure me down with tantalizing news of refurbished golf courses, he forgets that I can't stand the game. Best — C." She was stunned, and her answer, written as it was from a distance, and with nothing to lose, was raw. She mailed it more out of a desire to do damage to herself than to him.

His reply was chastened, angry, and swift, covering two tightly packed sheets, front and back. In spite of its greater length it still arrived in the same small, elegant, heavy-stock sort of envelope as the first letter had. Both the envelope and the typewriting on it had the look of adult writing things, completely different from the handwritten drugstore envelopes that were also arriving from Courtlin, and after a moment of hesitation Glee opened it. "*I took you seriously and perhaps I was taken in. We agreed you're not a child. Didn't we? I took you seriously when I took you into my house and took you into my bed. If you think I habitually find myself making love to exacting fourteen-year-old girls you are pitifully wrong. You exhaust me, you make me furious and you exhaust me. I'm sorry—*"

When Katherine tried to speak Glee cut her off. "Oh, Katherine," she wailed. "What can you tell me?" It was not a question. Watching her mother's despair Katherine felt her own begin to rise around her. She was left alone with her disaster. She sat on the floor and sobbed. She tried to curl against Glee's legs and Glee took her by the shoulder and shoved her away. *What can you tell me?* Katherine couldn't tell her anything. But later, when she was alone, she dismantled the razor—it had accumulated the melancholy, reproachful air of an object left by someone who had died—and sliced experimentally into the flesh below her wrist. Her attempts were half-hearted. She cut against the direction of the veins, and blood beaded up slowly. She wanted Glee to burst in on her, horrified, but Glee was shut in her own room, and that end of the house made a quiet, impregnable island. Katherine wore long sleeves until the thin wounds healed, although it was too warm, but this went unremarked. She lived out the rest of that year in her parents' home like a barely tolerated guest. She couldn't comfort herself with a sense of being persecuted. Her awareness of having been wrong, and worse, of having been stupid, was far too acute. She could have answered the fatal letter but she didn't. She understood now that she did not have a confederate in Charles. He answered her silence with silence. If her father suspected what lay at the root of the estrangement between his wife and his daughter, he chose not to pursue it. He considered it a crisis between women, and kept his distance.

The following spring Glee made a series of emergency phone calls to the girls' camp Katherine had attended from the ages of six until ten. At ten she had refused to return, citing as her reasons the camp's corniness, the enforcement of the group sensibility, and the grating immaturity of all her fellow campers. Glee had considered herself lucky enough to have kept Katherine at the camp those four summers. She had attended the same camp—it had gone from being a society fad, in her mother's time, to being a sentimental tradition in her own—until the age of eight, when she had also rebelled against the almost vatic preoccupation of Camp Cumberland with ponies and wildflower chains and Sir Walter Scott. Very little about the camp had changed since that time, which was the source of its appeal for women like Glee, who had felt it stultifying as children and now found it indispensable as mothers. Glee secured a place for Katherine and Katherine wordlessly embroidered her name scores of times into blouses and culottes and panties and even her socks. Once she had begun measuring off an arm's length of silk yarn at a time and stitching awkward, blocky K MONROES, she couldn't stop. After sitting a week hunched over increasingly precise and small labelings, nothing remained to be done, and she packed her suitcase and was put on a bus.

Returning to Cumberland at the age of fifteen, she had to ingratiate herself with girls of her age who had been together there every summer without interruption: devout lifetime campers who were now torn between the heady anticipation of graduation to counselor in the following year and the melancholy of bidding their childhoods good-bye. Katherine could not convincingly participate in the camp's frothy rituals of truth-or-dare and secret-sharing and sylvan moonlit swims, although she tried hard, out of bottomless loneliness and the humiliation of being disliked. But she was disliked. She was accused, groundlessly, of stealing, and although her furious denial frightened off all future accusers, it also deepened the aversion to her that both the campers of her age and the counselors, one year above but a universe away, seemed to share. A few of the very little girls idolized her because she was pretty, but their loyalty further embarrassed her. "Do you have a boyfriend, Katherine?" they would ask shyly. There were always two or three of them together, little girls who were frightened of water and trees, with legs like fragile stalks, smears of sunburn on their cheeks. They often asked to brush her hair, or practice braids on it. One of them was fumbling in her hair now, while she was trying to read. "No," she said. "You're all supposed to be canoeing."

"Do you have a crush on a boy?" they wondered, hoping the answer was no, that she was all theirs.

"No," she said sternly. And back in high school that fall she found that sternness had settled into her face, the way that sharpness settles into a girl's features or depth into her eyes, maturing her suddenly. Katherine became a beautiful, conspicuous girl who was subtly avoided, for no clear reason thought of in the same way as the boy whose father's suicide had been in the papers, or the girl who was going to be a nun, all of them anachronistically in high school, too old, too traveled, too private. A cool space hung around Katherine, and nobody entered it. Her attention seemed absorbed by a distant, ambiguous scene.

The following summer was better. In spite of her stormy reentry into camp life she was graduated to counselor along with the rest of the sixteen-year-olds. She carried the weight of responsibility more gracefully than she had the imperative to think things were fun. She gained a modest share of privacy. She was put into the littlest girls' cabin along with another girl who had been one of her principal tormentors. Katherine felt a pang of misery but said nothing. The other girl took her cue, and they divided the duties of the cabin fairly between themselves. They did not become friends. Katherine never made good friends with anyone, but the status of counselor could better accommodate friendlessness. A counselor was a grown-up, and a grown-up might be friendless by choice. Katherine was seen as a bookish girl. She took charge of the camp mailroom, a role that everyone agreed suited her. She became deeply attached to the paraphernalia of her small postal shack, with its great screenless window and a splintering plank for a counter, and these were the things she remembered for years: the damp, crumbling sponge in its cup to wet stamps, and the worn blue inkpad, like a moth-eaten theater seat. And the faraway shrieking of girls, and the sweat on her arm making stains when she leaned on her notebook.

She did not see Charles Addison. He no longer visited her family in New Orleans, and she no longer spent her summers in

Sewanee. Her parents didn't go themselves, her last two years of high school. A great deal was changing. Her father was sporadically ill, and her mother had the tired, harassed look of a woman who was fighting off fear. But in her role as camp postmistress, and out of the poverty of her long days looking after homesick little girls, Katherine tentatively initiated another correspondence. She felt inured to further heartbreak. If he did not respond, this would complicate her unhappiness, but it wasn't likely to increase it. And then he did respond. "Dear Katherine," it stated simply. "I have thought of you, and missed you."

After that she regularly sent him long letters, about camp life, about her family, about the social mechanics of high school, and the more time that passed the funnier, the less stilted and groping, her letters became. She had turned out to be a skilled correspondent. "You can really set a scene," he wrote once. "I float out of my chair. I don't even remember, for a time, that I'm here in drear old Sewanee. You almost make me embarrassed to try and write back." But he always did, and they began to be friends, in the delicately courteous way that she now understood would not have been possible if their affair had continued. Sometimes she felt too old, that she had suffered final disappointments and lowered expectations too soon. When she had first been separated from him she had missed him physically, with an ache in her stomach that left her sleepless and unable to eat. All that time her mind had been dead. It wasn't until later, when her body in some measure recovered, that she began to miss him with a philosophical fury and despair that she eventually recognized as having been borrowed from books. By the time she realized this, she no longer missed him. Now she couldn't recover the unsuspecting eagerness that had yielded so much pain. She was afraid she might never be that girl again. This didn't mean she no longer loved him. It was a question she would never satisfactorily resolve. If it was love, it was a calmer, deeper, less desperate emo-

tion than she had previously thought love should be. It could recognize ambiguity. She did not know if he loved her, but she knew
he had set her apart, and that he allowed certain quiet impulses of
his to speak to her. He often said he loved things about her; he
never uttered the shorter, more elemental phrase.

When she left home for college her father drove her to the New
Orleans airport and mutely embraced her, then pushed her away,
as if he thought the display wasn't pleasant for her and shouldn't
be long endured. His eyes were wet as he walked back to his car,
and he looked oddly stunned, holding them wide open so that he
wouldn't shed tears. He had never been particularly affectionate
toward his only daughter. Now she felt a great stroke of pain for
betraying him. She wondered if he knew what she had done. Her
mother had stopped speaking to her with such finality that
Katherine imagined Glee wouldn't waste words discussing her,
either. When she arrived at Smith she was the only girl without
bed linens, pillows, or towels. Every other girl's mother had
packed her the equivalent of a hope chest, marrying her daughter
off to college.

She tried to marry college too, but she couldn't, and after one
year she left it. She did not go home. Her father continued to
send her money, and—although she treated each instance as an
anomaly, an impulsive, inappropriate gift that would not be
repeated—Charles sent her cash as well. She had moved even further east, following the purposeful tide of the girls who had graduated that spring, to Boston. "I like to think of you tearing all over
the town," he wrote once. There would be a fifty-dollar bill
dropped into the envelope like an afterthought, not even concealed in the folds of the letter. She couldn't vent her fury by ripping it to pieces or crumpling it up—it was always stiff and
new—and so she would stand clutching it, trembling, and then
she would go and spend it quickly and vengefully on something
she did not need. She did not tear all over the town, and that flip-

pant phrase came to ache like a reproach. Boston was as esoteric and forbidding as the church of a religion she knew nothing about, and although she waited with her own beating faith for some change to be worked within her as she walked along its river, or sat in its park, she only felt less and less able to pass as a Bostonian. Charles never came to see her. He easily could have, and she harbored elaborate daydreams of the freedom they would have together if he did, the freedom of strangers in a strange place, like invisibility. But she didn't ask him to visit, and because she never asked, there was never a clear disappointment, and she couldn't frame a grievance.

She had two jobs in Boston. First she worked as a coat girl in a posh supper club. She mastered the complexities of the art easily but could not keep an open, agreeable look on her face and was fired. Next she worked in the typing pool of a venerable law firm, a mind-numbing, frightening job that made her long to be fired, but she was never even noticed, no matter how unproductive she was, and she finally quit. She couldn't afford to stay in Boston and live the way she wanted to, which was alone. That May, a girl she'd met at her boardinghouse took her along on a job hunt through a string of hotels on the coast, and she discovered the world of summer work.

Then her father wrote, asking if she would ever be able to drop by Sewanee, and do a few things to the house. It had stood empty for almost five years. The note contained only that request, but the impracticality of the request suggested something more, and her desire to interpret it as a kind gesture, an invitation, made her response skittish and unintentionally cold. She could not travel at all before September: she would be working. She did say, "I'm not sure where I'll be in the fall." And then another careful note from her father: "September's soon enough. It would be a load off my mind if you went and looked after that place. Get the squirrels out of the attic, and have the foundation checked for settling," and then a long list of other things he insisted she do, to save the house from dereliction, and his accountant's address, for the bills. "Do it as a favor to your old man. I don't get around very well anymore," he concluded, releasing her from having to thank him. The house was a gift.

The next four months passed with an easy, well-oiled inevitability that was the closest thing she had known to routine in a very long time. The extent of her gratitude surprised her. For all her terror of boredom it turned out that she was a creature of habit, and that she craved the familiar and secure. While her life had been a turmoil of uncertain rent and packing boxes and diffuse, constant panic she hadn't realized how lonely she was. She bought a car and drove to Sewanee, arriving in the middle of September. The key was underneath the mat, where it had always been, where keys always are, corroded by rust. It still worked. After throwing all the windows open she went upstairs to her old room and lay awkwardly across the bed, as if it were a bed in a motel and might be full of pestilence or strangeness. Then she cried herself to sleep. In the morning she decided to spend the winter.

He was taking his afternoon walk when he spotted the car. Although he didn't admit it to himself at that moment, he knew it was hers. The walk involved a similar self-deception. He always passed that house, on his rambling circuits along the deeply shadowed roads. Most of the homes on the mountain were just barely betrayed by a drive winding into the trees, but the Monroe house stood past a deep bend, at the top of a cleared slope, with its drive curving up the hill toward it. As he strode by he would glance at the house long enough to register that its windows were unbroken, its lawn mowed by a boy he paid himself. Just looking after it, as anyone would. Not awaiting anything. He rounded the bend and stopped. The car was sitting there in the drive, its top down. It seemed to hum with recent activity. He stood a long time, admiring it. The day was clear and hot but when the breeze picked up he could feel the coolness of autumn. Looking to the house he saw the main door standing open, behind the screen.

"My God," he said, when she came padding down the dusky hall, barefoot, in a worn-out cotton dress he recognized. "There you are." She was brown as a nut from the summer, her hair cropped. A dusting rag hung from one hand. She stopped short of the door and stood uncertainly, gazing at him through the screen.

"I was going to come and see you," she said. Her voice was hoarse. She coughed, and wiped the back of a grimy hand across her forehead. "I've been cleaning. It's dusty as a tomb in here. For goodness' sake, come in." He pushed the door open just as she came moving toward it, and they bumped each other and laughed, and in his confusion he caught her by the waist, meaning only to brush her cheek with his lips, but she seemed to have grown so thin, and his arms closed around her. Beneath the dress her skin was damp from working. She slid an arm behind his neck, bringing his face close to hers with the back of her wrist, because her hands were dirty. The rag dropped to the floor. When they lurched into the wall she struck it hard, bruising her spine, looped her legs around his hips as he lifted and pinned her in place with his weight. She wanted to consume him, force him open with her tongue and remake him, the way her body felt reshaped by his pressure. The door still stood open beside them. "Wait," she gasped, but she was gathered so tensely, unbearably craving the moment he punctured that pressure, and she wasn't able to let go of him to close it.

*B*ecause she couldn't decide she didn't need him, she did the second-best thing and decided to proceed on the assumption she didn't need him. Perhaps this was what kept him with her.

Perhaps it was the idea that while he still had her, he had something of life. He was bitter. He felt unappreciated by his profession, and he drank too much. While she was becoming an adult he had reached the far side of middle age, and could no longer reason himself out of the sense he was a failure. And so he both cherished her for her youth and resented her. He would lash out at her without warning. "What is it?" he snapped. "That look of infinite, aggrieved dissatisfaction?" and if she claimed that there was nothing there, nothing, "It's a source of endless shock and reassurance to me that you're incapable of hiding your feelings."

His dependence had never been like hers. He had begun their affair a finished person, fully formed and as incapable of self-doubt as he was of guilt. He could have died alone. He did not think she could ever become crucial to him, or decisive, as he had been to her. And yet she was a pleasure, sometimes badly needed. He knew he enjoyed her, and that when he saw something, or read something, or remembered something that was lovely or funny, he wanted to tell her. He had never felt the impulse to share anything with anyone. And so he did love her, in his way. He had always said he would treat her as if she were a woman and not a girl, in part because to him, this was a sign of his esteem for her. The trouble was she hadn't known what being treated like a woman meant. It seemed to involve being tested, needled, provoked. Once she really was a grown woman she would feel him in her own arrogant gait and in the dismissiveness of her speech and wonder, as she had after he had made love to her for the first time, that everyone else didn't see it as well, blazing on her like a rash. She always felt indebted to him, although she knew he'd exacted a price. He had worn her down, and what remained had grown hard. Her mind seemed to abbreviate itself. Her body was minimal, as if any flesh beyond the requisite betrayed indulgence. She was still thin and small-breasted. Her bones seemed too evident, as if to provoke the thought of breaking them, so that the thought would be admitted impossible. She was uninjurable. He went to fasten her dress and the expanse of skin diminished as the zipper's V sealed shut beneath his hands; they arrived at her neck, and the tiny hook there, which he married to its mate. Now the small collar encircling her neck seemed unbroken. Her back was concealed, her shoulders bare, her arms poised in a temporary diamond as she held her hair out of his way. When his hands left her neck the hair fell. She crossed the room for her coat.

six

When he had first arrived at Sewanee, Bower took him into his office and asked whether or not he could anticipate his emotions, come Christmastime. "Will you go home, my boy? We don't have the funds to send you. I wish that we did." He told Bower he wouldn't want to be sent, even if there were funds. He wanted Bower to understand that his loyalties had been transposed whole. "Of course we will all be here," Bower went on. "Mrs. Bower and myself." He could hear Crane banging through his suite across the hall, shouting imploringly to Mrs. Wade about his laundry, and periodically resuming what seemed to be an afternoon-long argument but was actually a series of phone calls to and from his mother. Crane had not invited him home for the holiday. He would certainly have declined if Crane had. This was nothing like Thanksgiving: the Christmas holidays were almost a month long, and he would never have considered spending such a length of time as an indigent guest. And yet the absence of the invitation bothered him. He wondered if Crane had considered, and decided against it.

He had trouble sleeping that night. A momentum of departure was building, and the coming emptiness of Strake House seemed real enough to be felt. The thought idly occurred to him, as he lay examining the murk of the ceiling and hearing the last sporadic noises of Crane's packing, that perhaps it was just as well not to sleep, because some dream might be lurking in wait for him. The instant the thought registered itself, sleep became doubly impossible. He swore in a whisper. Everyone would be gone tomorrow, and then he would do nothing but frighten himself. He tried to remember his late-summer happiness, when Sewanee had eclipsed all other possible worlds, and he'd been utterly, contentedly alone. He hadn't yet seen the way in which people were tied to things beyond this place, and as he'd stood watching the endless stream of students hurry past him on their ways home for the holiday, he'd felt unbearably conspicuous. As a corrective he thought about Crane, mired in his family life like a wheel in mud. He cast his eyes outside. The unbroken darkness there was only the effect of the mountain's topographic complications. Lives persisted all around him, settled in houses like ships, lacking nothing they needed. He would see their lights through the trees, if he went for a walk. Outside, the pitch of the wind rose and fell. With each renewed gust a draft would puff in. He rolled himself more tightly in the blankets, and then thrashed them away as it occurred to him that the window was unlatched. It was not. He climbed back into the bed, feeling the comfort of the warmth he'd left behind there. He must have fallen asleep. The next thing he knew was the squeak of the door coming open. He sat up quickly, and saw the whole room revealed in the white morning light.

It was only Crane. No sooner had Chuck noticed the sun than it went dull, obscured by a cloud. The air outside his covers was bitterly cold. He had been expecting this for some days, but his heart sank. The heat was being turned off now that everyone, or almost everyone, was gone.

Crane was grinning. "Good-bye, Scout. Now you've got the run of the place."

He swung his legs out of bed, but the instant his feet touched the floor they sprang back up again. Instead he pulled the blankets around his raised knees in what he hoped was a businesslike way. He didn't like having been woken by Crane, although he wasn't sure why. He only felt a sense of disadvantage. "You go to Atlanta."

"Hell, yes. I'm green, looking at you. I want to go home about as much as I want my toenails pulled off." It was hours earlier than Crane usually rose. He was standing with a suitcase handle tight in each hand, looking brightly scrubbed and a little breathless. "My mother's about set to drive me insane. I envy you, I'm serious. What're you going to do?"

"I don't know."

"I'd kick back and watch Mrs. Wade's television and drink beer twenty-four hours a day." Crane's eyes had been darting all over the room, as they always did, quickly hitting every corner as if expecting to find something in particular, and now they lit on the desk, covered with sheets of algebra, some completed and laid out neatly for reference, some halfway worked. A pair of textbooks lay open, the stiff new one pinned flat with a rock Chuck had brought from the driveway to use as a paperweight. That had been at the beginning of the term, when he would let the warm breeze flow in through his windows. It was strange to think of that gentle breeze now, in this large, chilly room. "Is this math?" Crane burst out, horrified. "What the hell are you studying for?"

"Just," he shrugged and looked at the papers, as if he wasn't sure how they had gotten there.

"Exams are over, boy!" He heard Crane whistling all the way down the stairs, then pounding back up to the telephone table. "I'm leaving this minute. For God's sake, I don't know! I'll get there when I get there," and then whistling back down again.

After Crane was gone he went to his desk and sat absently erasing an unsuccessful equation. The muted light seemed to threaten a storm. Outside his window the huge pines on the opposite side of the drive were lashing back and forth, and leaves skittered over the gravel. He rubbed out the rest of the page and blew the grimy tide of eraser rubber onto the floor. When the telephone rang he thought it would be Crane's mother, looking for him, and tried to remember what time Crane had left. "Hello?" he asked tentatively.

"This is Katherine. Monroe. Of course, you don't know another Katherine, do you?"

"No!" He fought with the telephone cord and finally stretched it out so that he could sit on the floor. "No, no, hello!"

"It's a scary day, isn't it? Very foreboding. I'm having a good time, though. I've just been sitting in my house poking away at a fire and I've finally got it lit, so I'm ready to fight off the forces of darkness. You've never been to my house, have you?"

"No. It sound nice."

"Oh, it's a creaky old place. It's a summer house. Right now it's ready to blow over. But it's nicer than Strake. You haven't left for the holiday." She pulled the telephone across the room and snapped open the curtains, peering out narrowly. She wanted to detect some sign of recent movement there, a haze of dust hanging over the drive or the like, but there was nothing. Any sort of evidence would have been more satisfying than no trace whatsoever.

"No, I don't go. I stay here."

"I stay here, too." She pulled the curtains shut again and dropped into a chair. "I wouldn't recommend it. I've done it for years and it's grim. I thought you might be staying and I decided to call, to let you know that there's a fellow-sufferer. I can tell you everything there is to do."

"What is there?"

"Well, nothing. But I knew you'd be at loose ends. With nothing to do you can go a little mad here. I haven't been a very good friend to you. We never went to the movies." She kicked at the ottoman. She was irritated with everything about herself today, absolutely everything. "I never took you to another church lecture."

"I don't have it. Coming to the holiday, I think there's no any time for it."

"They're all wrapped up in their holiday fuss."

"Yes."

"Well, I'm not. And you're not. Of course you wouldn't be going home. It's a long way to travel, isn't it? To Korea."

"Yes, it's a very long—"

"Would you like to have dinner with me?"

After a moment he stammered, "I—yes."

"You would? Well, good. That makes it much better. I was going to go up to Nashville, and it occurred to me that you'd be here over the holiday with nothing to do. Well," she said again. "All right. That's good."

"Nashville?"

"It's a much nicer city than Chattanooga. I can barely stand to say 'Chattanooga.' Nashville's very old-fashioned-southern genteel, it's very charming. Would you like that? Would you like to go there?"

For a time, after the call was done, he paced. When his room grew too small for this he ventured into the hall, and echoed up and down its length. He was all alone now. Even Mrs. Wade had left, to visit her sister in Mobile. Eventually he became alarmed by the conviction that hours had passed, and returned to his room to check the clock. It was still very early, but the scare had been enough to launch him into action. He found Mrs. Wade's ironing board collapsed near the washer and spent the rest of the morning ironing his single suit, the one he wore for the church lectures. He ironed it so thoroughly he almost burned through it. This task took a remarkably long time. When he was finished he went to the kitchen and fixed himself a sandwich using up most of the odds and ends of food Mrs. Wade had left behind in the icebox. He decided to solve the problem of having a minuscule amount of pocket money stored up by eating very little that night. After his lunch he tried to read in the library but the silence annoyed him. He went outside without a jacket and walked back and forth on the drive. It seemed unsafe to stray far from the building. He might lose track of time, and have to rush to dress, and be late. When he went inside again he looked critically at his suit, hung on the back of his door. It seemed to shine slightly. A cheap suit. He dreaded the moment he would have to put it on. When just an hour and a half remained he shaved, with the same nervous, self-defeating care he'd applied to the ironing, and cut himself twice. His face in the mirror looked haggard and alarmed, the two bloody flowers of tissue stuck to it.

By four o'clock he was standing on her porch with his wet hair combed flat on his head and his hands stuffed in his pockets. She met him wearing such a heavy, elaborate, floor-length robe that he thought at first she was already dressed. Her hair was floating when she pulled the door open, as if she'd been violently brushing it. "You're on time and I'm late, I'm always late," she said. She meant to say more, but then her pause hung in the air and grew longer. She had spent most of this day stopping in her tracks at the centers of rooms, as all the ways in which she might have expressed herself to Charles that morning finally occurred to her in solitude, throughout the afternoon. And then it was suddenly four o'clock and she was flinging the door open and finding him there, looking so grave, and so careful, and wearing his suit. His gravity startled her. She felt in the presence of something intricate which she might damage. In the morning she had seen a newly empty and maddening day stretching forth which she'd tried to redeem, but now she pulled up short, apprehensive, with the sensation, devoid of reference points but too distinct to be ignored, that she'd done something wrong. But she hadn't done anything wrong. She was treating the student to dinner, something she should have done long before this. Her only fault was in making him wait.

She retreated back into the house and he followed her. He could imagine her sailing through the most miserable hour of Seoul's worst marketplace without pausing to choose her direction. She led him to the library. "Do you mind waiting here? There are a lot of things, books. I'm so sorry. Please, look around. I'll be fast."

He eased a book out from its place and carefully transferred his gaze to it. "It's no hurry. You have a many beautiful books here."

"Thank you. Do you want a cup of tea? Or there's a bar, in that cabinet. You can make yourself a drink if you want to."

"I might. Okay," he said. She watched him move to a bookcase at the far end of the room, with his delicate courtesy, averting his attention from her until it was asked for.

Upstairs she was so clumsy she couldn't get her dress fastened. She groped blindly behind her back and waved an arm around her head before losing her balance and landing softly on the bed. It was spending whole days by herself, she thought as she lay there. Spending whole days alone, and forgetting how to simply be with people. He was still bent toward the bookcase when she came down again, reaching awkwardly to hold her dress closed at her neck and at the small of her back. When he saw her he immediately laid his book down. As he closed the zipper he said, "Lift up your hair," and she lifted it out of his way.

Before they left the house she gave him a book. She searched the lower shelves, where the books were crowded into double rows, one pushed behind the other, until she found it in its hiding place. "You must believe that I bought this for you," she said. "I found it not long after we drove out to Jackson. I didn't bother to wrap it, but it is a gift. You can tell I'm not just handing you a book that's been lying here forever because it's brand-new. I was browsing the campus bookstore not expecting to find anything new because they never stock an author unless he has died and been canonized. But here this was, like a message in a bottle washing up on a desert island. I hope you like it."

He had never been given a novel in English before, as if it was a matter of course that he could read it easily, for pleasure. It was called *Band of Angels*. He paged through it gently.

"What do you mean, *browse*?"

"It's what you do when you look at my books," she said.

As they walked to the car, he tried making different weddings for the word, but he could come up with only one match. "I browse the shelves," he said. It had a languid, elongated shape in his mouth. The limitation made the word seem luxurious.

*T*he days ended just before five now, and it was a frosty night. Katherine turned on the car's heater and shrugged off her wrap as soon as the car grew warm. He could see her bare arms without turning his head, and the chain that hung from her wrist like a ceremonial object, marking off the current moment from the normal continuity of time on either side. He longed for a costume of his own that would be equally exceptional. As they drove he contemplated his nervousness. He felt safe on the mountain because it was a point of pride for the people there that he would prefer Sewanee to his home. They thought of him as a romantic castaway, whose presence among them confirmed everything that was best about themselves. In this way they were like Crane's father, who had viewed his hospitality toward the stranger as the prerogative of a prosperous man. Chuck understood this line of thinking very well, and he understood what was required of him. At Sewanee he embarrassed no one with excessive gratitude, and so each act of charity toward him became an isolated instance of good manners. He didn't know how it would be in a city. He had never been in any big southern city apart from the bus station, and bus stations everywhere harbored only dispossession and deviance. They didn't belong to the cities they were found in. He looked at Katherine, but she didn't seem in the mood to talk. They were whipping along through the dark. Sometimes a bird would plunge through the headlights or a stunned deer appear at the side of the road, its eyes glowing, and Katherine would catch her breath and slowly let it out.

When they arrived at the restaurant they were swept past the heavy velvet skirts of the entrance into what felt like a private club for the very rich during a war. The room was broad, low, and plush, its thick amber light growing more intense the smaller the object it touched: the hangings on the walls loomed vaguely, the tables glowed, the waiters shone, and then the silver settings and the glasses blazed. A placid hum filled the room, undifferentiated, musical, and dense. The captain bowed at their table and left them, and a negro busboy came and poured water into their glasses, and deposited a basket of rolls, and lit a small candle in a hurricane globe. The deftness with which Chuck was received made him feel that his apprehension had been foolish and unjust. "Hello," he said to the busboy. He greeted the busboy as if they were both guests at a surprising and solemn affair. Whenever Charles did this, although Katherine knew he was trying to be kind, the gesture seemed boastful. The colored man could never have addressed Charles first. The busboy bowed and calmly strode off. Katherine looked around her, and met the gaze of a woman who stared at her frankly for a beat before turning away.

She didn't want him to notice the attention being paid them, but he already had. He had noticed it as soon as they had been at their table long enough for his jangling senses to settle, and begin reaching tentatively to measure the depth of the room and its contents. There was the tension of careful indifference from the tables nearest them, and steady observation from those farther away. And yet within the excess and complexity of this room he felt anonymity spreading through him like dye. When the wine arrived he took up his glass and looked around more boldly. The fumes from the wine filled his nostrils. He breathed deeply and his eyes watered. He saw faces glancing away from him, and each time he did he watched that person, fortressed as he was behind his glass, at his table, within the tightly circumscribed space of Katherine's attention, and no one looked a second time. Katherine wondered if they thought he was handsome. She did. The conviction sprang upon her unexpectedly, shearing through all her ideas of what a handsome man should look like, and then, as abruptly as it had come, it was gone again. She felt slightly unsteady. She remembered the first time she had ever dreamed in French. She had woken up thinking in it, and for a long moment her disorientation was intense, until English reasserted itself. Later, when she tried to recapture that unconscious fluency, she always failed. Looking at him was like this. She'd found him beautiful; then something intervened. She rested the edge of her glass against the tip of her nose and gazed across the small bright surface at him. They played the game of staring each other down, and he saw laughter flash back and forth across her face, but she never flinched. They both began to be a little drunk. When Katherine saw their waiter crossing the room with their plates in the air she said, "Don't look." They kept the thread of their gaze intact through the waiter's meticulous ceremony, and when he was gone she said, "Tell me something."

"What will I tell?"

"Something you've never told anyone."

"A secret?"

"No." The fine thread that had linked them seemed to drift away. "Come back," she said. He looked at her. "Not a secret. Something mundane you never thought was important enough to tell anyone."

"Some trivia."

"Yes."

"I love Worcestershire sauce." He pronounced it with strenuous accuracy. *WHOOS-ter-sher.*

"How did that come to be?"

"In Korea, American-style food is no any good. So I put soy sauce, and this is very bad. Then I find Worcestershire sauce." He thought of the Banto Hotel with sudden nostalgia. That had been his introduction, in the first year of the war, to American food. Or at least, the idea of American food. The Banto's restaurant, like every other dining room in Korea, even the American officers' club, could offer only pale indications: gray steaks, waferlike hamburgers, powdered potatoes. He'd drowned everything in Worcestershire sauce. "I don't need it now, this food is so good."

"Is it?" She'd hardly touched hers. "Are you glad we came here? Is it better than Sewanee to be here?"

"I wish you should eat."

"I can't. I'm not hungry at all. Do you know how easily you dodge questions? As if questioning were a pressure that drove you straight backwards. When people ask me questions I feel as if I'm being pulled forward into a spotlight. I can't resist it. I try to and can't."

"You shouldn't."

"Why?"

"Because I like to listen. I like to watch you talk."

"You like to watch *and* listen. How lucky I am."

"Yes."

"People are watching us, you know."

"I know," he said.

She felt the slight ripple of renewed alertness when they left at the end of their meal, like sensing the shape of a river's current in the shirring on its surface. From the street they saw the capitol building glowing white-hot on top of its hill. She slipped her arm through his. "I'm tight," she said. Her cheeks were flushed. The valet brought the car to the curb and mistakenly handed Chuck the keys. He thought, laughingly, *This is a dream!* When they had left the city far behind he suddenly asked her, with tender-seeming ceremoniousness, where she was from. It surprised him to realize how little information they had ever exchanged. "Miss Monroe," he said. "Where you come from? You come from Nashville?" He pronounced the town, musically, *Nash-a-ville.*

"Oh, no. No. I was born in New Orleans."

"Ah!" he said. He knew that New Orleans was a port city, and the imagination of this made him unaccountably homesick. "Tell me about New Orleans."

"I haven't lived there in a very long time. It's a nice place in a rotten sort of way. The weeds taking over the garden. I never decided to leave, I just never went back."

"For how long?"

"Nearly three years. I left a long time ago and went back just one time, and that was three years ago. I spent the winter."

"When do you leave the first time?"

"Oh, no. I won't tell you that. You'll do the math."

"Why, then?"

"I don't get along very well with my mother."

"And your daddy?"

She smiled at his use of the word. "My father and I got along all right. He's dead."

He was mortified. "I am sorry."

"Don't apologize. It's a long time ago now. The reason I went home that winter was because he was dying, and he died in March, I think. Three years this spring. It's not at all difficult to think about him. We were never very close. But I liked him. I just always felt remote from him. I'd gotten used to the idea I'd never see him again long before he got sick, so returning to see the sick man was like seeing yet another strange person. And I was there for so long, the whole winter. It was terrible." She pushed her hair behind her ears. "Not terrible. But you have all your familiar arrangements, and then you leave them behind, and the new set of arrangements are so strained. I was staying with my aunt, my father's sister, and she never liked my mother, so here was a declaration of war already. In my family you never could move a muscle without it being a declaration of loyalty to somebody and war to somebody else. Whose satisfaction do you think it's for, to be with someone when they die? Is it for them or for yourself?"

"I don't know. People will say it's for the one who is dying."

"I think it's the other way around. It's a purely selfish way of comforting yourself. My father didn't want us there mooning and weeping. He liked to have a good time and there he was, ringed around by all these anxious faces." She blinked sternly at the road. "In any case, he died. They promised it hadn't hurt but they can't really know that, can they?" She hadn't even been there. At the precise moment her father died she had been sitting in the front seat of her oldest brother's car being driven back to her aunt's in Thibodeaux, and her brother had been saying, "It's time you grew up, Kitty." She couldn't tell if he'd used the obsolete nickname out of malice or forgetfulness. She had insisted on leaving the hospital because she knew that her mother was coming. Her brother pretended this was a vicious whim of her own but it had really been a courtesy she and her mother practiced for each other. And although she had envisioned the funeral as an occasion for a reconciliation, when the day arrived, full of hush and exhaustion, she hung back behind her brothers, each with his wife, and watched her mother from that distance. She knew the burden of grief fell most heavily on the two of them. Her father had been her only ally. As they left the cemetery she had approached her mother as a distant acquaintance might, and they'd embraced in that way. "Do you know why I have money?" she said suddenly. "My father set it up. I tried to get him to undo it and he sent me a letter that said, 'Never argue with your dad.' It was easiest for him that way. Taking care I wouldn't—compromise myself. Those were his words." She felt unhappily promiscuous. Her voice seemed to possess a momentum toward self-exposure that reminded her of the nightmare in which she found herself in public, stark naked. "I can't hush up and I can't make you talk."

"You can."

"Can I? What about your father?"

"He is alive."

"And your mother?"

"She is also alive."

"Is that all?"

"I—no," he said uncertainly. They were turning onto the narrow, steep road that led up to her house, and he didn't say anything more. She had the idea that you might reach behind moments. She wanted to reach behind this one and say, Listen: give me whatever you're holding apart from me, just so I know there's a rift. I don't want the secret itself, only the fact of the secret, so that I can measure the depth of the rift—but she wanted the secret as well. One had to reach swiftly or the hidden, real thing dodged aside and you were left grasping air. She'd been thinking she felt sober. The car fitting around her like a shell always induced utter sobriety, although once she stepped out of it she often found that her drunkenness had simply been waiting for the drive to be over. She parked and they climbed out of the car, both feeling vaguer and more unbalanced than they had while in motion. She hesitated on the lawn a moment and he waited for her, seeing but not really comprehending the lights pouring forth from the house, and then he followed her inside and down the hall to the library, where Charles Addison rose from the sofa and came toward them smiling. "Hello, Chuck," he said. "Katherine. I dropped by and thought I'd wait a little while. Have you gone to town for dinner?"

She dropped into a chair near the door, with her coat in her lap, and stared at it. Addison studied her pleasantly. "I'm glad you finally had a chance to wear that dress. It looks lovely. Chuck," he said, "I'll see you when the semester resumes, unless you come to me sooner to complain about your grade." He retrieved a cup and saucer from the end table. "I've made tea. You ought to have a cup, darling. You look faded. I'm sure it's still hot."

"Go to hell," she said.

"I'll let you alone, then."

"Please," Chuck said. He hadn't taken a step in any direction since stopping in the doorway. "Please. Good night." He turned and strode out the front door, feeling freshly drunk, and the cold of the night hit him full in the face and shot down his collar. He'd forgotten his scarf in her car. The windows were bright and still, as if he'd left the house in a state of suspension. He let himself into her car as quietly as he could. It was still warm inside, like a just-abandoned bed.

He was a great believer in the capacity of struggles to be ironed out, by an almost geological process, majestic and imperceptible and absolutely uninfluenceable by persons. But after a few moments in which he saw no prospect of relief, he said, sounding more nasty than he meant to but powerless to change his tone of voice, "I'm surprised at you, Katherine. Robbing the cradle."

She'd had no intention of answering. "You're one to talk," she said.

He laughed. "Atta girl." He wasn't looking at her. She watched him collect the various books he'd pulled out of her shelves and return them one by one to the exact places they'd occupied, although she didn't keep her books in any kind of order. She just let them accumulate, like her other household clutter, the volumes she bought settling on top of those that had always been here, a large pile displaced when it occurred to her to look for something in particular, and then those books dispersing gradually in various directions. There were scores of his books housed here, too. She could see he was uneasy. He never kept himself busy with pointless tidying otherwise. And then it was just an effort to hide his feelings from observers, not a way of finding comfort for himself. "Well," he said, slotting the last one in neatly. "Well, well. The very day I ask you to marry me you're off to dinner with somebody else. My own student. It's very surprising. But I like to be surprised. You're always surprising me." His thoughts only ever struggled on such a short leash when he was drunk. She dropped her coat on the floor and went to smell his teacup. It might have held tea recently, but now there was only warm, slightly watery bourbon. She took a long pull and set it down, feeling the paradoxical flood of utter calm mingled with violent capability that a stiff drink always gave her. "You didn't ask," she said.

"I did."

"You didn't. You said, 'I'm surprised you would want such a thing. Katherine. How pedestrian. How disappointing.'"

"I am prepared to give you what you want. I don't think you want this, but if you do, so be it. It makes no difference to me whether we are married or not and so we can just as easily be married."

"It makes all the difference in the world."

"I don't think so. I'm happy as we are."

"I am not happy as we are."

"I can see that. If anything you've made that clear, with your little expedition."

"Go away, Charles."

"You're so wonderfully unaware of how obvious you are," he said, quickly ducking the vase that she snatched up and hurled. It slammed into the wall and a small explosion of water bloomed forth as it shattered, all the water that had remarkably remained there throughout the vase's airborne journey, the arc of spray it had emitted clearly only a small portion of the whole. He came toward her and she stood waiting, thinking that she would sink into him, that she was ready, but when he slapped her she found herself landing a punch, her first, in his face. The pure shock that unfolded there somehow made love flare up within anger, for the first time that night. I've surprised him, she thought gratefully. He seized her arms to hold her still but then he simply held her against himself and she let him, feeling his shuddering breath, his erection. "What do you want?" he said, mimicking her. For years she had demanded this, attempting to articulate her own unhappiness by referring it to him, yet he had never seemed to want anything apart from what they had. *What do you want?*

"I've told you. I want to be married."

"Then we'll marry."

"It's not what you want."

"I want what you want. But I want you to be sure. You've always ridiculed marriage. You said it was bunk."

"I said what you wanted to hear."

"Don't turn it around."

"But it turns around," she said, "doesn't it." And then, because she wanted so much to be certain, even if it meant stepping off into a void, she said, "I am sure."

It was getting toward dawn when they were finally in bed but she remained sitting up, wide awake, with his head in her arms. She wanted to watch him without being seen. His eyes were closed. He kept verging on sleep but not quite getting there. She thought, This is the face of the first man I loved. She would never be that girl again.

"I knew you were unhappy," he murmured.

"Why didn't you do anything?"

"I hoped you would go away."

"Because you don't love me."

"I do. I adore you."

"And you wanted me to go away."

"Yes."

"Why didn't you make me?"

"I couldn't bear to," he said. She felt the sudden weight of him, sleeping. When he fell asleep he lay as if shot. He fell asleep sometimes in the middle of the day, in the middle of his work. She would come upon him, one arm flung out, cheek on his papers, his lips slightly parted, oblivious.

*T*he walk home was difficult. The clouds were solid overhead, blotting out the stars and any moon there might have been. He only saw the huge trees along the side of the road when he had almost slammed into them. Still, he plowed through the dark recklessly, almost liking the feeling that at any moment he might knock himself unconscious. He was out of breath. His haste made him overanticipate the distance to the ground, and he kept coming up hard against it. He concentrated all his mental powers on the nuances of this grating noise his feet made in the dirt. There was nothing to think of beyond it. Still, he drew up short when he finally reached Strake, completely unprepared for the black hulk that greeted him. Its darkness deepened in patches where the unlit window sockets must have been. The prospect of the stillness trapped inside there disturbed him far more than the still night outdoors. He finally felt his way into the door and took the stairs silently, as if there was a full house to wake, thinking that he would put all the lights on and leave them on permanently, but then he reached his room and fell asleep, not even taking off his shoes.

The next morning he awoke with a slight hangover and a sense of horror so acute that he might have committed a crime. While the whole of the previous evening was enveloped in a slight haze and many connecting moments were altogether missing from his memory, he retained the image of Charles Addison approaching him with perfect, even heightened clarity. He did not know precisely what boundary he had overstepped, only that there had been one, and that he'd forgotten himself. He tested a phrase he had learned. *"I carry away. I am carried away."* His voice sounded small and hoarse. Outside the pines were creaking, but everything else was deathly quiet. He missed Crane, although he knew that if Crane had been there he couldn't have talked to him. Then he thought of Mrs. Reston, and the ease with which she disclosed volumes concerning the intimate lives that she knew. He rose quickly and started to dress. He was afraid that she had also gone away, to some beloved person whose existence he'd never imagined. His calendar said it was four days to Christmas.

He hadn't seen Mrs. Reston since a chance encounter almost two months before, in the small, fastidiously kept flower and herb gardens near the botany department. He had been admiring the monomania of the bees, and she the magnificent flowers, what a fine example each was of its kind. She seemed to know them all. Their names had been pressed in someone's careful, straining cursive on small tags of soft copper, but as they went down the rows together, she named each without looking. "Bellflower," she told him. *"Campanula.* It's a fine one, isn't it? Do they have this sort of flower in your country?" He liked her easy assumption that his country would have flowers at all. He told her that Korea was on almost the same latitude as Sewanee; the familiar feeling of the cool, moisture-impregnated air was almost more jarring, so far was he from home, than if he had landed himself in a tropical zone, or a desert. They walked slowly along the rows and when they had studied everything more than once he found himself walking her across the quad and down the road toward the vice chancellor's house.

Mrs. Reston wasn't a lonely woman but she was always avid for conversation and she peculiarly enjoyed the intimacy of gossip, although she didn't consider herself a gossip at all, because she liked everyone. She often thought of her disclosures as a means to not only amuse but also reassure, in a warm, general way, whatever person she was talking to. "The vice chancellor's daughter Marilyn was jilted by her young man back in August," she told him. "I say it's better in the end because he was—how should I say this? He was pretty stiff. He didn't put out any warmth. You couldn't imagine it would be a very—" Mrs. Reston threw back her head and laughed. "I'm going to get myself in trouble, I'm going to corrupt your poor innocent ears. Well, I didn't like him. I thought to myself, She'll cry herself sick for a couple of months and then she'll mend up and maybe even be glad. The poor thing. But it hasn't been that way at all. Instead she's declared she renounces everything because it's all too late, and she's going to go to some Oriental country and be a nurse. That's why I'm telling you this, because I said to her—I'm the only one she talks to because she knows I won't give her away—I said, Why do you have to go all the way to some Oriental country? There are mountain people right up the road who live in just terrible shacks and eat squirrels and let their little children run around naked as jaybirds. I'll bet you didn't know that. So I said to Marilyn, If you have a Christian urge to help people that's all right, but couldn't you stay here and do it? It will kill her parents if she runs off to some Oriental country, it will just kill them. And she said, The people in the Orient are much more desperate. And I said"—here she squeezed his arm with humorous anticipation—"Mr. Ahn doesn't seem desperate at all, he's the calmest young man I ever saw!" Mrs. Reston patted him. "I love her to death but she does sometimes aggravate me. I know you'll never tell her I said it." Of course, he had never met any of these people. He might have slept in the vice chancellor's guest room his first night in

Sewanee, but he had only ever seen that man through a sea of combed heads from a great distance, when the vice chancellor sat with his family in their front pew at morning chapel, or exited in state down the aisle. "Why she says it's too late?"

"Her two little sisters are married already and she's taken that very hard. But Marilyn's also *dramatic*." For Mrs. Reston, being dramatic was almost as much of a disadvantage as being introverted, the one characteristic she thought truly hopeless. "She is on the wrong side of twenty-five. I'll give you that. And it is different for girls than it is for young men, especially young men who are doing their studies." Here she patted him again, but meditatively. The truth was that her husband had been killed in action in France and she didn't have much patience for young women who thought it was all too late and hopeless if they got disappointed at what now seemed to her a very young age. She'd lost Claude when she was older than that and had to remake her whole life root and branch, and she didn't lie down and die, did she? They had come to the base of the gravel drive, and she gave his cheek a dry peck good-bye.

Sewanee had one general store, with a post office in back and stacks of dry goods to the ceiling. He set out for there, arriving not long after it opened. A glass case near the cash register held a neglected collection of pens and faded notepads that no one ever bought. For scholarly equipment everyone went to the bookstore. There was also very little fresh food. The general store was a place for bachelor professors who cooked on hot plates in their rooms when they couldn't bring themselves to go to the dining hall, and servants who did not live outside town, as most of them did, in Monteagle, where they shopped for their employers. Most of Sewanee's residents considered the general store a place to look for afterthoughts, and so it stocked lemons and baking soda, and birthday candles and bottle openers, and the rudimentary supplies for sewing and first aid, as well as things that could be given

as gifts. When the proprietor caught sight of Chuck, he was nodded at. He was already a familiar figure here. He browsed the
shelves. As this phrase occurred to him he felt a pang and moved
forward hastily, as if he could outrun it.

He bought Mrs. Reston a small cup and saucer. There was only
one such cup in the store, and its singularity pleased him. He
went back to Strake and furtively looked through the jumble
drawers in Mrs. Wade's kitchen, and then, feeling less restrained,
threw open the hall closets, where the residue of generations had
accumulated and become compressed and damaged. He found a
small, well-made box, already lined with a pad of cotton that
might have dressed a wound; he found numerous half-used,
slightly tattered rolls of gift paper, and in the top of the closet
nearest Mrs. Wade's ground-floor set of rooms, a paper sack of
preserved fancy bows. The only trace that they had ever been
used were the faint clouds of paper dulling the gummy squares
on their undersides. Mrs. Wade oversaw any young man's opening of a gift with hesitant remonstrances to take care and much
greater anxiety than was voiced, so that she could add to this supply, which accumulated more quickly than it would ever be used
up. Mrs. Wade was a woman of providential and caretaking
habits, who lacked an object complex and demanding enough to
absorb all her efforts, even with a household of young men in her
charge. She and Mrs. Reston were of the same kind: women
suited most of all to be needed, who had been somehow left
alone.

"Oh, my Lord," Mrs. Reston said indignantly when she saw
him. "Have you been here by yourself this whole time? It's
Christmas! I thought you'd go home with one of your pals. Didn't
anybody think of you at all?" When she pulled his coat off his
shoulders he had to hand her the gift. "What is this? Oh, for
goodness' sake. Why didn't you come around here earlier? I think
I'm angry at you. The vice chancellor and his whole family are all

SUSAN CHOI

here and it's been so much fun." Her face changed abruptly. "You can meet Marilyn," she whispered, "and maybe wring some sense into her. Don't you let on I said anything." From down the hall a woman called, "Who is it, Charlotte?" and he gestured wildly as her mouth was swinging open. "No, no, I just visit you."

"Me?—Nobody," she hollered over her shoulder. "Don't you want to meet the vice chancellor?" She felt odd receiving a guest of her own. It seemed to represent the sort of liberty that for her was a private affair. When the vice chancellor was away she committed relaxations of the norm, but here was the house full of everyone. "Well, I'm sitting down to some tea in the kitchen." She waved away the package impatiently. "Oh, I think I'm angry with you. I really am. I didn't know you were here. Come on back. Let me go and make sure they don't need me."

Once they were sitting in the kitchen together she opened the gift with a great show of reluctance. "Oh, that is precious," she said seriously. She set the tiny cup in the saucer and studied it. "That is absolutely precious." She looked up at him blinking. "If I'd known you were here I would have got you something. Now you've embarrassed me. And being here all this time all by yourself."

"Not all the time. I see Katherine."

"Do you?" Her hands joined together uncertainly. "Are the two of you friends?"

"I think so."

"I'm glad of that." She stood up and busied herself with the tea. "She could use a friend. And so could you, though I suppose you get on all right. But you couldn't do better than Katherine. She's spent her whole life here and she's smart as a whip, and generous. Have you two had fun? Of course she sticks around all winter long. I'd forgot about that."

"And Professor Addison."

"Oh." She grimaced slightly and then said, when he looked at her curiously, "Don't mind me."

160

"He gives me English lessons."

"Well, good. That's what he ought to be doing. I never said he wasn't a brilliant man. I've said a lot of things but I've never said that." She laughed. "You always get me in trouble."

He smiled back at her steadily. "Why? What do you say?"

"I'm an old chatterbox, you know that. You landed in America and the first thing you saw is me chattering. I say he's a snake. But that doesn't mean he can't make you a fine English teacher. I can tell you've gotten better, do you know that? I noticed it even the last time I saw you."

"Yes? Really?"

"Oh yes. But I knew you'd be a quick study. Never mind what I said about the professor. You keep learning from him and soon you'll be spouting poetry and making the girls faint. Just don't take his example in everything. Has Katherine told you she used to think of being a missionary?"

"No. She told me once, when she is a little girl, she wants to be a nun."

"A nun!" She fell into a fit of merriment. "That's about the last thing that would suit her. Every little girl seems to go through that phase, though. They all want to be ballerinas and nuns. No, this wasn't such a long time ago. Katherine wants to see the world, she just can't get herself out of this town. But the thing she wants most is to go away. A cyclone could come along and carry her off and she'd be nothing but happy. She thought becoming a missionary would be something like that. It would take care of all the thinking and sweep her up and then she'd be gone. It's a woman's way of joining the army. But she lost her nerve. She said she wasn't sure about God. I told her that shouldn't have anything to do with it."

"A missionary is hard work."

"She could have done it. She doesn't know how lucky she is. I know she thinks certain chances passed her by, or she lost them.

That happened to me. But then you have different chances. The things I'd do if I had the kind of freedom she does. She was a bolder girl when she was younger."

"You knew her a long time?"

"As long as I've been here, and I came here in nineteen forty-four. Not to this house. First I cleaned in the upper-class halls. That was a trial. Katherine and her mother and daddy used to summer here. And then he fell ill, and they stopped coming, and then a while later she came back to look after their place. And she stayed."

"Why?"

She tilted her head slightly before answering. The gesture was pensive. It looked strange on her. "I'm sure you know that as well as I do, now."

"Maybe," he said carefully. He said nothing else, waiting.

"I don't feel right talking about it. I'm just help, I can be friendly with her and love her if I want to. That's my freedom." She fiddled her spoon in her teacup and watched the leaves swirl up. "It's a long time ago now. With so many years gone by it's easy to pretend things went differently. He's an important man here, and she's a grown woman. It's nobody's business. She loves him."

After this announcement she drank her tea a while, and he did too, lifting the cup to his lips easily even though he was plummeting. If she noticed the way in which he swallowed the tea a little too rapidly and in an unusually large quantity she did not remark on it, only filled his cup twice more from the pot while they sat in silence. At last she said, "But she was just a child when he started with her. And he ruined her."

seven

Curing himself of his attachment to Peterfield had not been so simple as realizing that it was what he had to do to keep himself alive. His loyalty to Peterfield had become indistinguishable from his loyalty to himself. In the years after the war ended plenty of people would revise their shock from the days just after it began, and tell him that it had all been utterly predictable, and that any idiot could have seen how it would go. Viewed that way, all his actions were just as inevitable as the circumstances that provoked them. At every juncture he'd done the right thing. "Smart boy," Langston had said. But he'd only been lucky. When the Americans had first arrived no one could have predicted how long they would stay, let alone how wise it would be to cast your lot with them. Dealing with them was one thing, and something that everyone did, but conspicuously trying to join them was entirely different. It hadn't been his initial intention, while he was working for Hodge. His intention had been to deal with them, to do business, because this was the surest way he knew to clarify he wasn't one of them. His father's decision to camouflage himself inside an occupation government had been his downfall. Chang turned a coldly analytic gaze on his family's catastrophe and declared it a strategic failure he intended to avoid.

It wasn't long, though, before he realized that his understanding of his situation was flawed. The Americans went to great lengths to establish that they were not an occupation government at all, but a facilitating presence. A favorite word of theirs was "transition." The Americans were to the brand-new republic as is the stake to which we tie the frail seedling, etc., etc. Sitting in the Ministry of Public Information devising puerile agricultural metaphors for the role of the U.S. toward South Korea he had realized that in avoiding an allegiance to the Americans he had overlooked his actual problem. No allegiance at all was an allegiance, by default, to the Republic of Korea, a government that only seemed to exist in order that it not be a Communist government, in the same way that his own recurrent desire to join the Communist party arose largely from his contempt for the republic's regime. His father had been jailed. His family's land north of the thirty-eighth parallel had been confiscated and redistributed by the Communists, but the land that fell south of the parallel, within the republic, had simply been confiscated for the sake of confiscation, and not put to any use. It occurred to him that his dislike of the southern government was a perfectly sufficient underpinning for whatever he might do. He could come up with philosophy later. His father had never been loyal to the Japanese, but he had recognized that they could be used. Chang felt that his recognition was the same: the Americans could be used, but the Republic of Korea was useless. He would be loyal to nobody but himself.

Then Peterfield had abandoned him in Seoul, and he knew that in spite of his resolve his loyalty had attached itself to Peterfield like an indiscriminate, compulsive tentacle, expecting loyalty and love in return. He regrouped, declared himself a small principality, and pledged his undivided allegiance again. The Committee for the Preservation and Welfare of Himself convened its first meeting and passed a resolution excising agitators from his heart, and these included Peterfield. The resolution might have been only the product of his injured feelings, but once it was made, he found it had the power to dictate each decision that followed, as if he'd come up with philosophy after all.

Returning from his visit to Mrs. Reston he felt similarly humiliated and similarly determined. He hadn't lived his life alone for nothing. His loneliness was a discipline aimed toward defeating itself. This idea had a clarifying force, like the shock of cold he'd met outside her house. It dictated a course of action. It made him almost happy, to imagine himself in the near future, consumed by his studies, and with the memory of Katherine Monroe shrunk down to size and confined to the past, pleasant but no longer relevant. He had been carried away. At Strake House he stood uncertainly in the silent lobby for some time before remembering that Mrs. Wade had arranged for him to take his meals with the dining hall kitchen staff. Of course; this was what he was supposed to be doing, having his meals with the kitchen staff and then returning to his rooms, studying himself to sleep, rising early and studying his way from breakfast to lunch, and from lunch to dinner, and from dinner to bedtime again. He had advanced calculus to achieve and when he wasn't systematically, single-mindedly pursuing this goal he had the Roget's thesaurus for amusement. This had been a gift from his friend, Charles Addison. A few new words a day, Charles Addison said. Slip them in sideways, when your mind isn't looking, and you'll be surprised how they stick. And he had been right. Charles Addison had examined his plodding, self-punishing method of studying English and then said, Forget about that. Get some light novels and leave them lying open in your room, and when you're bored, glance at them. Just glance. And don't sit hunched over a book in the dining hall, sit with your classmates, and listen to them talk, and if you feel shy about sitting with your classmates then come sit with me. Consider the thesaurus a collection of redundancies. Don't memorize it. Memorize poems if you have to memorize something, and meet me tomorrow for our walk and tell me something you haven't told me before. And he had done this, for months he'd walked with Charles Addison, thirty minutes a day on most days, and he hadn't known anything.

He went upstairs, put on a jacket and tie, and marched through the raw dusk to the main dining hall. The vaulted hall was dark and the long tables all obscured beneath upside-down chairs except for a small settlement at the furthest end, like a campsite in an austere wilderness, where one table was cleared and its chairs stood around at careless angles to each other, in the light coming out of the kitchen. A few candles were stuck to jar lids, or the tops of tin cans. A woman's voice languidly croaked from a small radio. He poked his head in at the kitchen doors and found the year-round dining staff there, a reticent and scrupulously polite group of negro bachelors which included Louis, standing around the industrial-sized oven tapping their feet and taking turns filling their plates from the pans on the stovetop. When they saw him they smiled uneasily.

"We're glad you're here, Mister Chuck," Louis said. "Let me make you a plate." They had cooked themselves a pan of baked chicken and mashed a pot of potatoes. He found a plate and tried to serve himself, as the others were doing, and Louis physically obstructed him. "Let me make you a plate," he said firmly.

The other men stood holding their plates until he'd seated himself, and then clustered at the opposite end of the table. Periodically Louis rose, with a pitcher of water, and refilled his glass. He sat with his gaze locked miserably to his food until at last the men began to talk and laugh among themselves. He had thought of the meal arrangement as the most adequate one for a solitary person but it, too, turned out to be an entanglement. For

Louis and his friends the desolate interval between the fall and spring terms was a time of simplicity and freedom, and he embodied the force of observation from which they'd expected a reprieve.

He decided that the desolate interval between the terms would be a time of simplicity and freedom for him, too. Where there was only emptiness and silence he would make a daily system, and his own meals, and when the semester resumed he would slide as effortlessly into that slipstream as a canoe into a broader, faster river and be carried so far and so quickly from this period of incompetent confusion he would hardly remember it. He established himself in the library with his thesaurus and his calculus texts, pulling the armchair close to the window from its ancient place, marked by four sharp holes in the carpet. This minor liberty briefly disturbed him, but soon such liberties multiplied. His room was impossibly cold and so he brought his bedding to the library and slept on the cracked leather sofa. He prepared his meals in the Strake House kitchen from the bland stock of imperishable goods, as if he were snowed in, or marooned on an island, or had a phobia of going outdoors. When a possible meal required some item which was only to be obtained from the general store, like a lemon, or a can of creamed corn, he ate something else. All his meals were white: rice, mashed potatoes, Bisquick. He began to wear Crane's bedroom slippers. When he grew tired of sitting still he wandered through the house, penetrating the rooms of students he had never spoken to, meticulously emptying pantries and drawers. Christmas came and went; he wasn't sure which day it had been. Each day was inexhaustible, full of heightened detail and blank space, and poorly set off from the next. The used biscuit pan growing rust as it soaked in the sink. The languorous sigh of the tap as it mined for hot water. One afternoon he went into Mrs. Wade's bedroom and perched on the end of her bed, smelling the sexless old woman's perfume that clung to everything, shyly, like an apology.

Once he realized he could leave the oven on all the time, he relocated to the kitchen. There was a fireplace in the library, but the idea of building a fire did not seem daunting so much as superfluous. He would consider building a fire—venturing onto the back steps for wood, spindling newspaper, transporting his kitchen matches (he thought of them as *his* now; no one else depleted the sturdy red drawer-sliding box, and he loved their fleeting, sulfurous stench; and he was accumulating a long row of them, lined up side by side like tiny corpses on the kitchen counter, because he feared a garbage fire) across the whole length of the house—and while he was considering it would occur to him that there was no fire now, and he was surviving. He was sitting in the armchair, in the hot overflow from the baking of another pan of Bisquick, eating a bowl of Cream of Wheat and strawberry jam, a combination he found completely gratifying. Then he heard Katherine's car arrive in front of the house like a hole torn in his perfect deprivation.

She rang at the front door and gave up on it immediately. He remained in his chair, slowly stirring his pink-streaked Cream of Wheat. When she came to the back door he glanced up and saw her seeing him through the window. She let herself in, meeting a sharp smell of skin and damp wool. He looked as if he hadn't bathed in days, and his face was sprinkled with stubble. He was folded up in an armchair with a blanket around his shoulders. Mrs. Wade's kitchen was in thorough disorder. A pile of textbooks wound toward the ceiling, and every drawer and cabinet stood open. The drawer nearest him, for napkins, had been filled with pencils. The baking smell was utilitarian and unappetizing. "I've found you in your monastery," she said. He looked around as if her analogy were something he might see. When he didn't rise she brought Mrs. Wade's kitchen stool from the pantry and leaned against it. She was wearing a pair of blue gloves and he watched her pull one glove off finger by finger and crumple it up in her hand. "I've wondered how you were, here by yourself."

The time without her had been such a delicate construction, a lengthening web which her presence destroyed. He might have left her house the night before. He reached beneath the chair and brought out a cold cup of tea which he sipped from, keeping his face bent toward the liquid and examining it thoroughly. At last he said, "Thank you for dinner."

"Please, don't. That's why I've come," she began, and flushed suddenly. He looked into his cup again.

"I can boil some," he said, still staring at it.

"That's all right."

He nodded absently. When the nods trailed off he didn't say anything else.

"You're working very hard here." She peered into one of his books. "This is like another language."

"It is."

"Do you understand it?"

"Yes." Speaking with her heightened the advantages of the language that filled up his books. Every meaning was absolute; it could be rendered in no other way. "I try to understand," he qualified himself. Each small advance spilled forth a fresh expanse of mystery, like turning a point inside-out to make infinite space.

"Could you tell me what you're doing?"

He wanted to refuse. Explaining his problem to her meant hauling himself out of an underground chamber the precise shape of his body. He remembered Peterfield once asking why he was taking so long with an article. "I can't find the word," he'd explained. Peterfield had flipped the dictionary shut in his face. "Just tell the story," he'd said.

"I determine groups. What law describes them. Which belongs with each other."

"Does everything belong in a group?"

"Yes. I think so."

"What will happen when you put everything in its group?"

"Then we see the structure. How it works."

"Of the world?"

"Of the universe," he said. After a moment he added, "I don't think this is interest for you."

"How do you know what I'm interested in?"

"I don't."

"Would you come outside for a walk with me? Just for a little while?" She pushed her hair behind her ears and then stood with her hands clasped in front of her, waiting. He did nothing for a long moment, casting his mind about and imagining several times that he had already said, No, thank you, I am busy in studying. When he stood up it was too abruptly, and the blanket fell off his narrow shoulders and slid to the floor. He kicked it aside and crouched down, looking for his shoes. His jacket was on the floor also. He buttoned it swiftly and clumsily and then stood giving her a wary look with the jacket misbuttoned.

Her hand rose unthinkingly. "Your jacket," she said. Her hand faltered before finding the first button and slowly undoing it. "I'm going to fix it," she announced. He didn't move. Her fingers skimmed down the rough wool until they found the second button, and eased it back through its hole, and then the third, and then the last. She found the edge of each lapel and carefully took hold, to make them straight, and he stood, paralyzed, until she suddenly finished the business, did his buttons up briskly, and turned for the door.

She walked so quickly he had to jog to keep up with her. She held her coat against herself, and bent into the wind. "I need to tell you something," she said. She nearly had to shout to be heard.

"Don't—you don't."

"What does that mean?"

"Nothing," he said anxiously. And then he added, because she was still looking at him with surprise, "You don't need to tell nothing to me."

She hovered in the middle of the road. One hand rose and pushed her hair behind one ear and right away the wind came and blew it loose again. "Please. If you know what I've come to tell you, let me know. Don't make a fool of me."

"I don't do this." Her hair was blowing across her face again and she winced in frustration. He reached toward it and stopped short. It could be held back. He could wind it carefully and hold it back. He put his hands in his pockets. She looked impatient.

"What do you know about me?"

"I don't know nothing," he insisted.

She started walking again and he followed her the rest of the way to the quad and down its length to the chapel. They went in, the noise of the wind dropping away behind them. He shuddered from the shock of warmth against his cold body. Inside the chapel candles burned on the altar and in the sconces, and although the light was dim there was profundity of color, blood-red plush and gold brocade and the oily chestnut gleam from the pews. His impulse was to linger at the edge of this chamber, but Katherine walked down the center aisle and slid into a forward pew, and he sat down beside her. He watched her profile, as precise as a pale mountain range. She was gazing at the quivering pools of the small altar candles. Their flames bent and turned in some draft he couldn't feel. He felt warm and unpained and utterly content. His resolve had so quickly transformed. Just minutes ago, she'd belonged to a previous life. Now the life without her was the distant one. For a long time the only fact that he knew was the nearness of her shoulder to his as they sat in the pew, with the many flames like a field of grass slowly shifting in front of them. Then she said, "I don't know why I'm having trouble saying it," and he remembered everything. But that remembrance still arranged itself around the central fact. Her shoulder near his.

"I don't want that you do," he said.

"You should know. It's not a secret, but your not knowing makes it seem like a secret."

"It is a secret," he said, "if I know it or if I don't know it. I want that you keep it. Not give it to me."

"I don't want to have secrets from you." Her cheeks grew hot again, a surge of heat that was separate from the glow that she felt sitting here, safely out of the wind. "But I just said it wasn't a secret."

"I don't explain this idea."

"Try again."

He closed his eyes. The words were there. He only had to listen for them. "What I know, this is everything. What happens here. What I see. There's no anything missing." After a moment he added, "It is how I would hope you know me."

"But it's not enough," she said.

"It is. Yes, it is."

"There are things that you can't know unless I tell you."

"No." His hand flew up to stop her and her heart caught. For a moment she had thought he was going to say, If you think I don't know what you're going to tell me, rest assured that I'm well aware of it. But that was something that Charles would say.

"I refuse it," he said.

"Even if I want to tell you?"

"Yes."

"That seems selfish."

He shook his head. "It's not for me."

"I don't see how it isn't for you."

"It's for you. Sometimes somebody tells too much. Later on they want to die instead of telling it, but it's no any good then. They tell it."

"Who is this?"

"Who is what?"

"This person who tells too much. It's not me, is it?"

"Yes. No. I don't want that it's you."

"Who is it?"

"It's nobody." He gazed ahead at the altar, suddenly angry at himself.

She watched him, but he didn't speak again. At last she stood and pulled her gloves on. "I have to go." He still didn't move. She left the pew by the other end and went down the side aisle. He heard the doors boom shut and kept sitting. Then the peculiar feeling of being alone and angry within the almost living warmth of the place overpowered him, and he rose and slowly made his way out. Leaving, he couldn't see her coat anywhere on the quad. It was darker outside now than it had been indoors. The only light left seemed to be trapped in the solid bank of clouds overhead. Behind that was a black sky. When he turned into the Strake drive her car was humming there, a thin line of exhaust trailing away. The headlights weren't on. He came near and saw the green glow from the dashboard, and when she rolled her window down he felt a rush of hot air. The car's small heater was roaring. "I am sorry," he said.

"It's all right." Her eyes rose to meet his and she seemed about to say something. Then he saw her change her mind, as clearly as if she had lifted the thing she was thinking, and set it aside. Instead she said, with no trace of reproach, "I do have to go." With dusk setting in, it had grown so cold he couldn't feel his feet. She had tugged her scarf loose and he could see the cool curve of her throat sinking into her collar. That expanse of skin was smooth as sand.

"Don't, you maybe don't," he ventured.

"I do." She leaned back and looked at him. "You don't want to know why, do you?"

"No."

She felt for the ignition and turned the car off. In the sudden silence they seemed to be too close. He stepped back from the car and looked irrelevantly at the sky. Katherine toyed with her gloves and her hair swung like a stage curtain over her face. He rubbed his hands together and pushed them into his pockets. "Come inside," he said, in a rush of decisiveness.

"I'll have to go. Soon."

"Come and have some little dinner with me. A fast dinner."

"The way you eat? Oh, no. You're eating out of cans with a spoon. Without even heating them up."

"I have some of very nice cans. I've been saving." He grinned foolishly.

"For me?" She laughed.

"Yes."

"Hoping I would come?"

"Yes."

"What have you saved for me?"

"A cranberry jelly. And something—a french-cut green beans."

"You've been denying yourself all this while you hoped I would come."

"Yes."

"What if I had never come?"

"I don't know."

"Shall I cook you dinner?"

"Yes."

"And then I have to leave."

In the blazing kitchen light her cheeks looked wind-burnt. She put a kettle on for tea and he turned up the oven and pulled its door open. Katherine remained standing, tapping a foot while she waited for the water to boil. "It's not as late as it seems," she announced to herself. She turned and looked at him. "Why are you here all alone? Don't you know what day this is?"

"What is it?"

"When I came today I half hoped I wouldn't find you. I was looking for something, but not necessarily you. I was looking to see if I'd find you."

"Why?"

"To throw myself in the path of things and see what came up. It's silly. I have superstitions. Would you like a drink? I think as long as I'm here I'd better have a drink."

"There's no anything here."

"Oh, yes there is. There's plenty." She went to the pantry and came back with a key chain. "I can't decide whether I'm deceiving you by not saying what's here or deceiving Mrs. Wade by giving up her secrets. But I do want a drink." He followed her through Mrs. Wade's bedroom into the small washroom and watched her kneel on the fluffy pink talcumy rug and unlock the cabinet beneath the sink. She took an unopened bottle of brandy from a box and locked the cabinet again. "Mrs. Wade doesn't drive. She has everything delivered from town and then once in a blue moon she needs something special and asks me to take her shopping, and once we're out it occurs to her we ought to drop by the liquor store while we're at it, just in case, say, she has to throw a party or entertain on short notice, which never happens. And so we go, and she buys a case of brandy, and I carry it in here and help her put it away for safekeeping from you boys." Katherine smiled sadly. "This is Mrs. Wade's fortress, where she protects herself from you. It has to be that way. She loves you all and she lives for you, she has nothing else, and so she must feel a little embattled by you. She must feel she's at war." They went back to the kitchen and she poured them two glasses. "I know all the sad secrets of all the lonely old ladies in this town. That's the advantage of being who I am. Everyone trusts me. They know I can't judge them and that I won't expose them because I don't have any credibility. I know that Mrs. Wade drinks. And you had better never tell a soul. I know why your friend Mrs. Reston wouldn't take another position for all the money in the world. She's in love with the vice chancellor. She might not even know that herself."

"Do you know why Marilyn is jilted?"

"That's funny. Mrs. Reston confides in you, too, doesn't she? I knew she would. She doesn't to everyone. She likes to gossip but she is very measured and deliberate. She likes you because you're an outsider. Certainly I know why Marilyn was jilted, but from Mrs. Reston, not from Marilyn. Marilyn is too fine a girl to ever talk to me. She was jilted because she's deadly dull. I was going to cook you dinner, wasn't I? Don't move. Sit there and drink your brandy and don't move."

"Don't go."

"I'm not going anywhere. I'm going to the basement." She took the key chain and came back with two steaks. He gaped and she laughed at him. "That's right," she said. "You don't think Mrs. Wade lives on Cream of Wheat, do you? And she stockpiles enough for an army. She's a hoarder. Poor thing. You're going to eat well for once."

"I don't care if I eat." He sank back blissfully in the armchair. The brandy had filled his limbs with warm lava, but it seemed to have invigorated her. She strode back and forth, finding onions and potatoes and ice cubes. She threw her head back, finished her glass, and poured another. She fried the steaks in a skillet and then she turned them onto plates and dumped his can of french-cut beans into the pan to soak up what was left of the grease.

"That's a beautiful meal," she said as they ate. They were ravenous. "You didn't think I could cook, did you?"

"I don't think," he shrugged. "Either way."

"What do you think of me?" She laughed. "That sounds vain. Tell me why you won't let me talk to you."

"I love you to talk to me." The drink made a wonderful easiness in his head. "I think, if it is something I need to know, I will know it. I don't want you to expose to me. In this way you say that Mrs. Wade, or these sad old ladies, expose to you."

"I am one of those sad old ladies."

He ignored this. "It is a principle," he said.

They finished their meal in silence. Then she looked at her watch and immediately twisted the face to lie under her wrist, as if the sight of it repulsed her. "Now I really must leave."

"Wait—" He lifted the brandy bottle and poured her another glassful, feeling the liquid's weight shift smoothly away as it fell toward the glass. The glass nearly spilled over. "A one more." He refilled his own glass. "We have a last one."

She took hers up and drank steadily, looking at him. She drained half of it before setting it down. "That won't work. I can drink you under in no time."

"Maybe."

"Careful. Do you know what night this is?"

"No."

"It's New Year's Eve."

"It is?" he said, truly amazed.

"I can't believe you didn't know. I'm very superstitious about it. It feels like choosing which door to enter a house, or where to start on a journey. Everything that follows, follows from it."

"What from this?"

"I don't know. I look for omens and I can never find them."

"What kinds?"

"Sometimes I think I'm surrounded by them." After a moment she said, "It's not a very happy tradition." She stood up quickly, embarrassed. "I'm sorry. I'd better get going." He watched her button the coat, pull on the gloves, wind the scarf. She took up her glass, knocked it against his, and emptied it. The glasses made a clumsy sound together. "I shouldn't have stayed so long."

He stared into the depths of his own drink. He had barely diminished it. It felt unbearable to be left alone with a full glass.

"Good night," she said.

He heard her hesitate a moment outside. The wind had died long ago and a deep hush had descended, like an endless exhalation. She crunched away, around the side of the house, and there was silence.

A moment later she was back. "It's snowed," she said flatly, throwing the door open, so that he could come stand beside her and look at it.

He drank with her for as long as he could and then he gave up and simply watched her drink. Her eyes grew deep and guarded, surveying complicated expanses within themselves. He had the feeling she knew how to lower herself, hand over hand, a very long way. She sat curled up in the armchair with her feet tucked beneath her, and he sat on the floor. His floor here was littered with things, small notes he'd written to himself in these past unhappy weeks, half-drained cups he'd pushed beneath the table with his toe so that he would not trip over them. After a while he moved across the floor to lean against her chair and she draped a hand around his neck. This moment didn't grope for the moment that followed. It spread outward from itself and filled the room. He couldn't remember the last time he had sat within a moment and given no thought to what would come after. He would have to have been very young. She drew her fingers through his hair, lifting it and letting it fall. "Your hair is terrible," she said. "It's so long." She sifted through it lock by lock. Her meticulous touch reminded him of a care he longed for. He had been a fastidiously maintained, strictly disciplined child, but there had always been hands turning him, whisking over his shoulders, pausing on his face. He closed his eyes and she touched the lids lightly. "You're tired."

He tipped his head back. "Are you?"

"Booze wakes me up after a while."

He fought against sleep. He tried to lift his head again and it lolled heavily. When he wasn't drunk it was always so difficult for him to fall asleep. He would listen to the pounding of his heart. All the way down, it would pound. He had difficulty falling asleep where there was noise and where there was silence and the most trouble of all in a large room with windows, like his room in this house. "Let's put you to bed," she said.

"Wait." He looked around and the room whirled.

She stood and took a long draught from her glass, and then she gave him her hand and he pulled himself up, weaving. She slipped her arms around his waist. "You can lean harder than that," she said. "I'm a strong girl."

"Wait," he said again, but then they'd climbed the stairs to his room, and he sank onto the bed and lost hold of her.

*T*he car took him as far as Inchon. He was left at the edge of a cliff overlooking the city. He could see the city's entire circumference, stretching from the waterfront, where the mouth of the river opened into a shallow harbor, marked off by a pair of black headlands, to the brief foothills far below him, where the city came up hard against the mountains. A cottony fog lay over the river, thinning where the banks gave way to steeply terraced rows of houses. Their scroll-edged roofs were orange and pink and gray. Then the river vanished inland, cutting a deep, narrow gorge through the rock. A shred of white cloud drifted in the void between where he stood and the rooftops. Haze lay over the water offshore, and he narrowed his eyes against the glare from it. In the far distance, between the black headlands, he could see a ship at anchor.

SUSAN CHOI

He should have come to Inchon long before this, he thought. He hadn't known how beautiful it was.

He found a rope ladder, lashed to a tree. He put his weight on the first tread and the ladder fell precipitately, several feet, and then caught and dangled, banging him against the rock face. The metallic taste of blood filled his mouth. He climbed backwards as quickly as he could, but his progress was clumsy. When he looked down his stomach reeled. Slowly, the city rose to meet him.

Then he heard a burst of gunfire and realized that he was hanging in the open air as conspicuously as if he'd been let down from the belly of a plane. Without thinking he jumped, recoiling in fright as he fell. The force of impact was strangely blunted. Lying outspread on the ground he felt the stampede of feet before he heard it. He tried to stand and his legs crumpled.

He tried again, and collapsed again. There was no blood. He seized his calf and felt nothing but his fingers pressing into dead flesh. A pair of KPA rounded the corner of the building he clung to and the mouth of a rifle swung into his face. The force of the blast carried him backwards and lent momentum to his legs. He ran, blindly. He could hear the soldiers gaining. Then he realized in a rush of disabling panic that he had lost his sense of direction. He didn't know where the waterfront was. He turned down an alley into a blank wall. When he spun back he was met by a hail of bullets. Jump! he thought. Jump! Jump!

Katherine bolted upright in bed. For a moment she didn't know where she was. Crane hadn't made any particular effort to clean his room before he went away. She saw heaps of boyish laundry, clean and dirty, a baseball trophy. She heard him cry out again, a despair-filled sound like *Ah! Ah!* She crossed the hall in her stocking feet and pushed his door open. That slight sound woke him and he twisted and stared at her.

"Don't," he gasped.

"You were dreaming. It's all right."

"Don't. Go away." He turned his face to the wall.

She went to him and he flung her off with such force she was frightened. She backed away, reaching behind herself for the door. "It's all right," she said again.

"Go!"

She took another step backwards and he shouted again. "Go! Go away! Go away!" He could still hear the sound of his own voice, whimpering. She hovered uncertainly in the doorway and he screamed, "Go!"

She vanished. He heard her swift steps cross the hall and descend the stairs, and after some minutes her car's engine straining through the fresh snow. Its pitch rose and sang out when it reached the plowed road. The sound made a line through the air, and for endless minutes he thought he could still hear it, growing thinner but not dying out.

He was bathed in sweat. His undershirt clung to his chest, and a stale alcohol taste filled his mouth. He tried to go to sleep again but he couldn't. Finally he rose and went downstairs.

White, bled-out dawn light was just filtering in through the windows. The kitchen was spotless: nervously, thoroughly clean. He found a scrap of paper taped to his Cream of Wheat box. *Happy 1956. I waited and watched it arrive for you.*

eight

After Inchon the front pushed north of Seoul and kept moving, encountering haphazard resistance or no resistance at all. Sometimes the KPA would fall back and simply disappear. Town after town was retaken and then the UN forces went crashing over the thirty-eighth parallel and began liberating towns that had been under KPA control all along. Once the army passed through, Rhee's National Police would arrive to hunt out Communists. Sometimes a village produced one or two vigilantes who claimed to have taken up arms against the Communist insurgents out of love for the motherland, but proving active resistance to what had been the status quo since 1945 was extremely difficult. Large numbers of villagers living north of the parallel and south of the advancing front were shot. Because the atrocities went unreported in the States, the mandate to expose them was taken up by the British press, and in early October Langston left for the front with no clear idea of when he'd be back. Chuck missed him sharply. In Langston's absence he and Peterfield were left uncomfortably alone with each other. They pursued their separate duties as automatically as they could, avoiding communication with each other, and were aided by the well-oiled, self-confident generosity of the army's information office. The numbers were so good that the numbers of the numbers multiplied; at the daily press briefing the army's information officers were now eager to provide numbers of enemy wounded, enemy dead, successful engagements, and even American casualties. In the terrible months before the Inchon turnaround, when the KPA had threatened to go all the way to the sea, the Eighth Army's numbers had often been "unavailable" or obviously manipulated, but these new numbers were robust and shameless, and very good press. Chuck had become the unofficial liaison between the Eighth Army's information office and Seoul's Korean-language papers, and he was lavished now with numbers, which he appended to his usual chunky pieces of translated wire-service prose, and passed along.

He came home one day and found Miki packing her things. Her sister had resurfaced, sidling cautiously up to the grand house, with its iron gate standing open and already showing the rust pimples of beginning decay, its waist-high weeds from the summer, its ruined garden, the petty violences done to its rooms. The two women had stared at each other as if they had stumbled upon their reflections in some unexpected place. He stood watching Miki whisk her small room clean and roll her sleeping mat up. He helped her tie it closed. He wanted to ask her to stay, but he couldn't. Since the end of the occupation their intimacy embarrassed them both, not because life had returned, to the extent that it could, to normal, but because there'd been no sign of Kim. Without him they were drawn too close together, and the insuperable disparity in their positions could no longer be ignored. Kim had always bridged that gap, even in his absence, until it was clear that he was not coming back. "If he was in the city during the occupation he would have gotten to us here, I'm sure of it," she said, thrashing the bedroll. Plumes of dust shot up, and melted away in the air.

"He left the city before the fighting started."

"How do you know?"

"He came to me. To borrow money."

She had straightened from her work and stood now as if nailed to the floor. At last she said, "You didn't tell me."

"I'm sorry."

"I would have stayed here with you. Even if I'd known he was gone."

"I never doubted that you would."

"Of course you did. You don't trust me."

"Yes, I do."

"There's no reason you should." She hefted her bag briefly onto her shoulder and dropped it again, looking for anything she had forgotten. But the room was a bare box.

"He never told me where he was going, or for how long. I thought he might come back here, too."

"If he didn't while the KPA had the city, he won't now."

"It's safe here now."

"For you it is. Kim's not working for the government. He could be in jail already. Or," she said, and didn't finish the sentence.

"I'm not working for the government. I'm working for the Americans."

"There's no difference."

"I think there is."

She shrugged and lifted her bag again. "Kim would say that working for the Americans you're still working for the divided Korea. He works against it."

"How?"

"You know."

"I don't."

She studied the floor. "He never told me his activities," she said finally.

"What made you think he would have told me?"

"He trusted you. More than he trusted me."

"I don't think that's true."

"He told you he was leaving. He never said good-bye to me."

"I'm sorry," he said again.

"Don't."

Although she was holding her bag she didn't move to go. They kept standing in the empty room, awkwardly. At last he said, "You could stay if you wanted to. I'd like it if you did."

"I know." He saw her flush slightly. Then the moment of shared sentiment annoyed her. "I wouldn't want to be here when the KPA come back. I was all right when it looked like I was in this house alone. They thought I was robbing the landlord. It would be different if I was seen here associating with the Young Master himself."

"You seem so certain they'll come back."

"I think they will."

"Hopeful, even," he said angrily.

"Whose side are you on?" She leveled him with a strange, snide gaze. Before the war she never would have spoken to him this way, not under any circumstances, and the instinct to reprimand her was irresistible.

"I reject both sides. I'm against this war. I can see that's not your feeling anymore."

"'I reject both sides,'" she aped him. "Oh, no you don't. That's the idealist's role. That's what Kim is doing, wherever he is. You're a pragmatist, like me."

"Meaning?"

"We're out for ourselves. Taking sides is the only way to do that."

"That's a contradiction."

"You're thinking too hard," she said, leaving.

ॐ

With Miki gone he drew one or two rooms close to himself the way he drew the blankets all the way around his body when he slept, cocoonlike, and never set foot in any of the others. In November MacArthur inaugurated a scorched-earth policy north of the front, razing the way for his army to march to the Yalu. He wanted a wasteland. Anything that could be located, within a generous margin of error, was intensively bombed. "Sinuiju," the information officer announced, "has been removed from the map." Towns and factories were bombed flat, burned out, plowed under, removed from the map. This phenomenon was also enumerated. Endless columns of refugees began to wind south toward Seoul, seeking the benefits of democracy; in Seoul they choked the streets with human waste, set fires to combat the increasing cold, starved to death in large numbers, and were easily recruited to become civilian spies. Striking stationary targets situated in clear, open spaces could be done entirely from the air, but moving targets had to be found on the ground, where they lurked in the trees. After the war Chuck would learn that the Communist forces had worn white on their daylight marches, and lain down in the snow when they heard a propeller. He would never forget this, and the extent to which everyone underestimated what the Communists could do. The Americans assumed the Communists were retreating so frantically that the fact that they broke contact with their enemy, making the determination of their position impossible, was only a matter of course. Northern refugees who were recruited, starving, sick, and often partially gangrenous, were flown back over enemy lines into the countryside they had just emerged from and air-dropped in the middle of the night, to walk back again. If the spy wasn't shot by the KPA while dangling in his parachute from a tree, or while making his way south, or by ROKA troops at the front, or by National Police patrols behind it; and if he didn't starve, or freeze, or become lost, or perish in some other way, but actually returned to Eighth Army Headquarters in Seoul and provided a coherent account of what he had seen, he was given a small payment and asked if he wanted to go again. Army Intelligence had officers sitting in jeeps across the front waiting to pluck these men out of the routinely harassed refugee columns and speed them back to Seoul. Ten or twenty were dropped every night, and of these, an average of one made it back. He was often injured and addled, acutely sleep-deprived, and so difficult to debrief, an inconvenience which was left to the translator to contend with, because the debriefing had to take place immediately. Any intelligence obtained in this way was likely to go stale within a few hours.

Chuck began debriefing civilian spies in the middle of November, days before Thanksgiving. The approach of that holiday, which had once formed part of a grandiose prediction of MacArthur's concerning the end of the war, was provoking general surliness. The optimism of October had begun to wear thin. The Army Intelligence officer in charge of debriefings quarreled violently with one of his ROKA translators and fired him. The first time Chuck filled in he extracted an elaborate account from his subject, largely, the observing officer thought, because he wasn't in uniform. When spies were debriefed by uniformed ROKA officers their loathing was visible. They would produce a modicum of information, and then demand payment. With Chuck the spy was somewhat conversational. From that time on Chuck was regularly pulled out of USIS. "There's always a fresh way to get fucked," Peterfield said. "Intelligence uses you and I get to pay you." But they were both relieved to spend less time together.

On Thanksgiving the American troops were given turkey drumsticks and photographed eating them on the banks of the Yalu River; copies of the picture were distributed at the daily press briefing. Three days later the Chinese entered the war and the front fell to pieces. Now it was the UN forces that broke contact, falling back as quickly as they could move. By the time the front was reestablished it had slid far south. The civilian spies that had been dropped just before the Chinese attack were written off and forgotten, but one of them, in obedience to the iron law of unvarying probabilities, came in. He was badly frostbitten. Three of the toes on his good leg had fallen off, and the bad leg was missing flesh from knee to ankle. The entire calf muscle was gone. He had ridden in an army truck from Kaesong and as the truck's heater thawed his flesh he had started to scream and not stopped until they reached Seoul, and fed him tranquilizers and whiskey. By the time Chuck saw him he was goggle-eyed but remarkably articulate. The man's trousers were knotted around his knees. Chuck looked at the leg and broke out in a sweat. The intelligence officer was angry. "Look at him. He's pumped full of booze." An army surgeon entered the room and said, "I want to cut that off. Now."

Chuck spoke to the man in Korean. "Hi," he said.

"Hi."

"Your leg looks bad."

The man looked at it impassively. "A dog did it," he said.

"A dog?"

"A wild dog. Tried to eat me." The man blinked hard and raised his eyebrows, trying to stay awake.

The man had come down, in part, by hopping a freight car. This was how he had made it so quickly. Chuck translated as the man talked. "He gets a freight car. He hop, hops-jumps it."

"A freight car!" the intelligence officer said. He gave the man an exasperated, threatening look. "Tell him that's impossible. We've bombed all their track."

Chuck spoke to the man and listened carefully to his reply. "They lay it down again," he told the information officer. They were laying down the track, picking it up and putting it on trucks when the train had moved over. This was extremely slow, but systematic. They were moving a great quantity of heavy things, matériel, this way. The man didn't know exactly what was on the train. No people. The man rode this freight train, hiding, to a town called Chaesong. This was the end of the line, and he slipped off unseen. He had not yet been attacked by the dog. He knew he was in Chaesong because there was a Christian church that said Chaesong on it. This Christian church was very beautiful, still standing because made out of stone. Chuck nodded wordlessly. "What is he saying?" snapped the intelligence officer.

"He ends in Chaesong. The train stops in Chaesong."

"Where's that?"

"It's pretty near to Seoul, maybe a half day by wagon," Chuck said. He paused and threw his head back, remembering. "Maybe two hours by car, if there is a flat road. A dry road." Someone brought a map and Chuck silently pointed to Chaesong, which wasn't marked. "It's a very small, a farm village." While Chuck spoke to the intelligence officer the man waited patiently.

The man had followed a road out of Chaesong that he hoped headed south. He walked for a long time, but he didn't know how long. Maybe it had been a short time. He had been very tired. The sun began to come up and he didn't want to walk alone in the daylight. He saw what looked like an old estate, an abandoned place, recognizing it by the useless kind of stone columns marking the entrance to an avenue, and he followed this avenue in the strengthening light. There were handsome old trees lining the avenue and to be less exposed he moved among their trunks. The place was very derelict; he could see that the great lawn sloping away from the avenue and back toward the road had been cut into plots and plowed. Their furrows were etched with old snow. At the top of the avenue was a big house, falling down. He did not want to go in here out of fear of finding other people. He went through the trees around the edge of this house and behind it discovered the trees gave out and a great exposed space descended a long way to a river, probably frozen over, but beyond this was an orchard, tightly packed globes of bare branches that looked like a dense mouse-colored carpet from where he stood, and he decided he wanted to be inside this shelter. He made a run for it down the great exposed space, crossed the river at a foot-bridge he found, and slipped into the trees. These trees were planted in perfect rows, which gave him the urge to continue. After some time he saw a hard shape ahead and growing near to it realized it was a tank, and that there were row upon row of tanks parked here among the trees, which frightened him, so he got out of there and walked all day and all night. The next night the dog had attacked him.

The rest of his story was of no interest to the officer. "Where was this?" he said. He handed the man a map but the man shook his head. "Christ!" the officer said.

"I think they were pear trees," the man said to Chuck hopefully. "They grow very neat." He made a shape with his hands.

"Yes, I think you're right."

"What the hell are they talking about?" the officer asked the surgeon.

He wanted to make no mistake. "When you went up the avenue, did it run steadily uphill, and curve to the left?"

"Yes."

"You couldn't see into the house because there is a stone wall running all the way around, high enough that only the very tops of the trees reach above it."

"Yes. Behind the house the open space isn't completely empty. There is one big tree standing there by itself, and a shrine."

Chuck turned to the army surgeon. "You should take him now."

"Have you got it?" the intelligence officer said.

"Yes, I got it."

After the army surgeon had taken the man away Chuck went into the hallway alone and sat down on the floor. With that place severed so cleanly from his life it had been easy to absorb the loss. He hadn't even felt it. But the sudden knowledge that the estate still existed filled him with longing. Tears flooded his eyes. He blinked wildly, trying to make them dissipate. The intelligence officer came out into the hall and looked at him. "I need your help," he said. "With the map."

"You are going to bomb it?"

"What?"

"You are going to bomb there? The orchard?"

"Not if you don't come in here, we're not. Come on."

"Oh, please!" he said. "Please!"

But the intelligence officer only pulled him upright by the elbow and steered him back into the room. "You're tired," the officer said kindly, after he'd made a neat X on the map.

The next day Langston returned from the front. It wasn't until Chuck came into the office and saw him, sitting with his heels on a desk, rolling one of his pencil-thin cigarettes, that he realized how afraid he'd been Langston would die. He felt his eyes flooding again, and he turned away in embarrassment. Now that he'd let himself cry he seemed ready to cry all the time. Langston pretended not to notice. "I've got stories," he said, cheerfully. "Bad stories. Let me buy you a drink." Peterfield waved them on and when they were standing outside alone Langston suddenly embraced him. He clutched his arms across Langston's narrow back, his bumpy spine, and let go hesitantly.

"Have you been all right?" Langston said.

"Yes." He accepted the cigarette Langston had finished and watched him roll a new one, with his wonderful, delicate adeptness, as they walked.

"This is the way it is," Langston said, when they were sitting in the Banto bar together. "The UN forces are in total rout. Your guys in particular are simply disintegrating, they're abandoning everything out there. There are shoulder launchers and radio units and wrecked jeeps and what have you, the wounded, everything, lying all over the roads. The desertion rate isn't being released anymore. I don't think they can calculate it. They're melting away."

"They are not any 'my guys.'"

"No, they're certainly not. I'm sorry. That was a filthy insult. But that's what else I want to talk about."

"Finish you were saying."

"I think the Chinese numbers are a lie. No way there are that many of them. I think it's smoke. The UN cannot hold the line, but it's not because of hordes of Chinese. The Chinese and KPA are attacking from the north, timed with guerrilla attacks in the east. They are synchronized and they span the entire peninsula. It's leagues beyond what anyone anticipated. Last week Truman said he thought he might drop the atom bomb. That was a terrible gaffe. Attlee flew to Washington and ripped hell out of everyone." Langston was grinning. He was always enlivened by the spectacle of British rationality confronting American stupidity. "That's neither here nor there. The point is that the Americans will not waste an atom bomb on Korea. They'll sooner leave."

"They can't leave it now."

"Perhaps not, but they can imagine leaving. Your army intelligence line is that the guerrilla activity in the South is wholly unrelated to the activity in the North. Two completely separate bands of misfits with no intention to coordinate their efforts, let alone the capacity to do so. This may not be true. I think it's not true at all. What is important is that your commanders are beginning to think it might not be true. They are being defeated by KPA-guerrilla coordination in the North, and the Communists are supposed to have a fraction of the UN's troop force. The rumor coming out of Britain is that the Americans are drafting plans for the evacuation of their troops from the peninsula. Cut their losses, bug out."

"I don't think they do it."

"They're very stupid, so you're probably right. But the bottom line is that at the moment there is no agreement how to stop the Communist advance and so nothing's being done. Units are scattered all over the place, trapped, and they're dying trying to get each other out. That's all that's going on. Your commanders are looking somewhere else, they're looking at digging in their heels at Pusan or getting out completely. As far as they're concerned, Seoul's already lost."

"You think Seoul falls again?"

"Certainly. I'll bet you. If it doesn't I'll buy you steak every night for the rest of your life. I hope I get to."

"But you do think."

"Yes. What are you going to do?"

"I don't know," he said honestly. "Peterfield tells me I should sign up with ROKA."

"Don't listen to him. ROKA is vile and corrupt, and worst of all, they're utterly incompetent. There's no safety for you there. They are killing everyone north of the parallel. They're rounding up whole villages of civilians, looping them up in rope as if they meant to take them prisoner, and shooting them."

"I can join KPA."

"I think that time is past. They will take you for rearguard ROKA if they find you here, or a spy."

"I don't really mean it." There was a time when he might have meant it, before the KPA had occupied Seoul. Now he never could have stomached it.

"I think you'd better get out of Seoul."

"When?"

"Soon. But you're going to have trouble moving. There are checkpoints on the roads south of here and they're picking up every male of age who isn't marching in a regiment. Do you have a way to get out?"

"I think so."

"Smart boy. I knew you would."

Langston always seemed to drink with bravado, but he got drunk quickly. His face would become rakish and sentimental. They walked to the elevator together and he felt distractedly through his pockets for his room key. "Don't disappear on me," Langston said. He gave Chuck a crooked smile. "Promise you'll leave but please don't disappear. Say a word before you go. I can't stand these disappearances. They wreck my sleep."

"I know," he said.

"You're such a young creature. When you get as old as I am you'll find people have dropped out of sight all around you. I lie awake at night thinking, What ever happened to so-and-so? and that face is as vivid to my mind as if a ghost had come into the room. I can never forget them."

"I have a lost friend."

"I'm sorry. You're too young for that."

"I have the feeling it's okay. I have dreams that seem he is here. A very plain dreams. Nothing special is happening."

"Mundane dreams."

"We are sitting on the ground, or walking, or eating."

"Ah, yes. Secret-agent dreams. They disguise themselves as memories and muddle up your thinking. How long has he been gone?"

"Since before fighting started."

"He's holed up somewhere."

"I hope so."

"I'm sure of it. Mind what I said."

"I will," he said.

He went home and curled up in his bed, pulling the blankets against his skin all the way around so that there was not even the smallest pocket of empty space beneath them. It was hard to keep warm. After some time he felt Kim pushing on his feet. "Wake up." He wrapped his head in his arms. Kim said, "I want to watch the sun rise. Sit up and move over." There was only one bench in the park with all its slats. The others were painful to lie on. Kim shook him. "Sit up or we'll miss it." They would drink in this park until Chang simply tipped over, snoring. When he woke again Kim was always clear-eyed, chatting, smoking his cigarette, as if their conversation had suffered no interruption. "Here's the sunrise," Kim said. First the shadow from the opposite hill would fall over them, and then start to shrink as the sun climbed above it, until at last it passed over and they were sitting in the light. The bench bounced violently. He caught his breath and shrank against the wall.

"You were dreaming," Miki said.

"How did you get in?"

"I still have my keys. Do you want them back?"

"No. You frightened me."

"I'm sorry. I didn't know how else to find you. Kim is on Cheju."

"How do you know?"

"There's a message chain. Part of it goes through the Farmers' Union in South Cholla Province and part of it goes through a priest at the Catholic mission on Cheju. All I know is the Seoul link. A man came to my sister's house looking for me. Kim was on Cheju at the beginning of November, in a cave."

"Where is it?"

"I don't know. You would have to go to the Catholic mission on Cheju, in the main village, and ask for Todaro, the priest. Tell him you're looking for Kim."

"What if Kim isn't there?"

"I don't know. Will you go?"

"I don't think so. It's dangerous to leave the city."

"But they're drafting everyone now."

"I'm not worried," he lied.

"You said you never wanted to take sides."

He laughed. "Now you believe me."

"My sister's husband was drafted last week. The NPs picked him up in the street. They drove him to the house to get his clothes, and then they put him in a truck. And he's old. He's at least forty."

"I'm sorry."

"Say you're sorry to my sister."

They were silent awhile. "If you went to Cheju you'd be safe from the draft."

"I'll be all right."

"I'm not sure you will."

He lit the lamp beside his bed and her face sprang into view for the first time, an intent moon. He could see the faint threads of the scar, like a scrap of lace sunk just beneath her skin. When his eyes met hers she looked away quickly.

"Just be careful."

"I will," he said.

"If you do go, I want you to take me there."

"I'll stay here. Traveling is too much of a risk."

"Staying here is a risk."

He nodded without speaking and she said again, "If you do go I want you to take me. Please." Now she looked at him.

"I don't think," he began.

"Promise me."

"I promise," he finally said.

She took up the edge of the blanket and smoothed it, repeating the gesture distractedly. "I trust you. Because he does."

"I don't think it will ever be so dangerous here that I'd decide to risk leaving."

"I know you don't. But you could always change your mind."

"It's possible."

"You've promised," she stated simply. Then she went.

❦

At the next morning's Army Information Office briefing he drew neat, empty boxes in his notebook. "The U.S. First Marines have been rescued from complete encirclement in a courageous effort," the information officer said. A Reuters correspondent asked about casualties. "We don't have a count at this time. That's unavailable." The number of engagements with the enemy was also unavailable. The number of yards that had been gained or lost was not yet calculated. The Chinese force was estimated, with vague stubbornness, at 500,000. Chuck paged backwards in his notebook and read, from three days before, "Chinese: some 150,000." He flipped the notebook shut. When the briefing broke up the officer approached him. "These numbers aren't for use, okay? I'll get you something tomorrow."

"What do I ought to say now?"

"Say the line is secure above Seoul. None of the departments are releasing troop movements to the local newspapers. Rhee doesn't want panic."

"Is there reasons for panic?"

"Not really. I'm going to level with you: I think the biggest danger right now is panicking civilians. We don't need that situation. I know you read the foreign press, but those accounts are exaggerated because the war isn't popular. Particularly *Time* magazine. I don't know why. Someone over there's got an ax to grind."

"I like *Time*."

"Yeah, I do too. Nice pictures. I'll have something for you tomorrow."

That night he called his uncle, the congressman, for the first time. After the Inchon landing his uncle had returned to Seoul from Pusan with the government and begun to rebuild his textile business. Chuck had seen him mentioned in the papers. Lee was an entrepreneur fifteen years younger than his half-brother,

Chuck's father; Chuck's father and Lee were the sons of the same woman, Chuck's grandmother, by two different men, Chuck's grandfather having died in the Doctor's boyhood. When Chuck was growing up, his uncle had never visited his home and had almost never been referred to. If he was mentioned, he was referred to only by his initials. He was a well-known philanderer and gambler. He had turned his failure to receive a university education to his advantage when he ran for public office, in 1948, and during that campaign he had also denounced Chuck's father in the press and questioned his recent acquittal. When Chuck called he simply said, "This is your nephew." There was no other person in that category. If his uncle was surprised he did not betray it.

"What can I do for you?"

"I need a favor."

"What sort of favor?"

"The tide is turning. I have it from Army Intelligence and it's all over the foreign news service. The offensive is cut to pieces and the talk is Seoul will fall."

"This isn't what I've been hearing. The government plans to stick it out."

"They're putting a good face on it. They're having the news from the front censored on its way to the Seoul papers."

"I guess if we decide to go, we'll go."

"Rhee won't put out the word until the last possible minute. It will make him look very bad to have to evacuate his government for the second time in six months. You won't have time to dump your stock or clear your business. I have access to more information than you. I know more than you do already."

There was a slight pause. Finally his uncle said, "How close do you think you can come?"

He thought about it. "I think I can peg it within about a week."

"What's your best guess right now?"

"Within a month."

"You have to be sure."

"I will be." In exchange he got a car, and a driver.

At the beginning of the third week of December all the Rhee administration's political prisoners were taken from the jails and shot. Langston and his photographer got two or three usable pictures of them, lashed together at the ankles and wrists and being shuffled through the streets wearing basketlike hoods on their heads. A few of them were carrying shovels that they would share when they got to the woods, to dig their own graves. The jails were empty now. The hush in them must have been like the hush in the streets. "Clean up, bug out. Leave nothing useful behind," Langston said. Langston and Peterfield had spent most of this day smoking wordlessly and playing gin on Peterfield's desk. A shallow pile lay between them, of nickels, dimes, quarters, candies, the butts from cigarettes, bottle caps, bullet casings, won, yen, shillings, shekels, small clods of wax. Langston lay his cards down on the desk, taking care not to mar the fan he'd made of them, and lit a cigarette. When he felt Chuck watching him he lit a second and handed it to him. "Did you ever find your friend?"

"I don't look."

"Smart boy."

"What friend?" Peterfield said.

"Friend of Chuck's," Langston said, taking up his cards again. He began rearranging them with thumb and forefinger outstretched, as if plucking hairs. From where he stood Chuck could see Langston's hand. He registered vaguely that Langston was losing. All afternoon he had been too restless to sit down with them. While they played he remained on his feet, ripping noisy reams of news off the wire, reading as he ripped, throwing much of it away.

Crumpled balls of news lay all over the floor, most nowhere close to the trash can at which he'd been aiming them.

"Oh, yeah. The friend of Chuck's who's Chuck's friend. See, that helps me. Now I know what we're talking about."

"A friend of Chuck's that went missing in May."

"I don't know if missing," Chuck said.

"You thought that he might be in jail?" demanded Peterfield. "Why?"

"He could have been picked up anywhere, like anyone," Langston said.

"Like Chuck here. Goddamned uncredentialed civilian."

"He's safer here than enlisted," said Langston mildly, but when Peterfield turned back to his cards Langston gave Chuck a sharp look.

"We're all fucked anyway."

"And his friend is probably free as a lark." Langston ignored Peterfield. "He's halfway to Timbuktu by now. Smarter than you, Chuck."

"This may be," Chuck said.

A few minutes later Langston flung his hand into the middle of the desk, scattering the loot. "I fold," he announced.

"Then fold, for Christ's sake, just put your goddamn cards down." Peterfield lay his own hand aside and began herding chips into separate piles. "What were shekels?"

"Fives. Your glow of satisfaction is blinding."

"You're a lousy loser."

"Nonsense. I'm buying." Langston stood and pulled his jacket on, shrugging his shoulders into place. "Chuck?" he said, expectantly.

He looked up. Langston stood there, in the mouth of a tunnel that endlessly ran from this moment. He would soon turn and enter it. "In a few days there may be no drinks to be drunk," Langston sang. Behind him Peterfield stood in the doorway, jacketed and impatient. "Or no bar to have the drinks in, or no city to have the bar in." This would be Langston, this image before him. He swore to remember it. "You know what they say, about sunshine and hay."

"Make the hay," Chuck said.

"That's the boy. On with your jacket."

"In a minute." His falseness made him dizzy. "I just do a little study."

"Come on," Peterfield said, irritated.

"At the Banto, then. Don't be long."

"Yes." It came out easily. But halfway to the door Langston turned back again. Their eyes met.

"I will see you," Chuck said.

After they were gone he started moving. He had thought they would knock off much sooner. He sorted through the deck of cards, removing the one without pips. The card was embellished at its borders, like a treasury note. It read *Genuine Bicycle Brand.* On its reverse were summarized the game rules for poker, hearts, and gin, in tiny, dense type. He took it to the Underwood on Peterfield's desk and spent several minutes adjusting the card against the platen. He wanted the added line of type to be flawlessly parallel with the line of print on the card. It was not what was said but the manner in which it was presented, the blackness of the type against the white field, the positioning of the letterhead emblem, the invisibility of the glue. He knew it wouldn't be convincing. The best he could hope for was to provoke a sufficient amount of uncertainty. After the typing he closed the card into the dictionary to flatten it again. In the desk he found a sheet of USIS letterhead and Peterfield's razor. He removed the blade, wiped it several times against his shirt, placed the letterhead on top of a folder and began to cut into it. His cuts were impossibly small and precise. He cut at the emblem, careful of every arrow and leaf. When he had finished this he telephoned his uncle.

"You're all set," his uncle said.

❧

He felt the car bob slowly over the Han River pontoon bridge. The Han was freezing over every night now, a clear skin forming on the black water after sunset that gradually grew opaque and stiff, creaked, snapped cracks in itself that resealed, and by morning was solid and still. Then ROKA mortared it again, to prevent people crossing undetected by the checkpoints. It was only an hour after sunset, and he could already hear the floes groaning against each other. The car stopped at the bridge entrance and the driver spoke with the sentry. The car had government plates, and the conversation was brief. The carpet pinioned him flat, filling his nostrils with dirt, hair, dust, a wet animal smell.

The car took him as far as Inchon, and then the driver uncovered him. He blinked uncomprehendingly. "My uncle said Pusan."

"Inchon," the driver said. "I can't take you all the way to Pusan."

He was dizzy from hunger and when he took a step his knees buckled. He could still taste the vomit in his mouth. "Don't you have a coat?" the driver said.

"No."

"Take this." The driver peeled a wool overcoat free from the loot in the back seat and gave it to him. "It's my extra. It'll be a little large."

"You're supposed to take me to Pusan."

"I'm supposed to move the congressman's things to Pusan. I was only supposed to get you out of the city. You can find a boat here."

"Please," he said. The driver pushed him, gently but firmly, away from the car. He reeled and almost fell over. "I'll tell my uncle."

"That won't matter. I'm only doing what he told me to do."

"I can pay you," he pleaded. But the driver got back into the car and pulled away.

He wrapped himself in the coat and stood quaking in the road, watching the taillights shrink and abruptly disappear. His hand found his heart. The card was still there, damp from his nervous sweat and perhaps from his vomit. The glued parts were peeling. He flung it away from himself and felt its maddening lack of momentum. It bumped up against the air's resistance and quickly fluttered to the ground. In a pointless act of fury he stamped on it. His attempt at cunning had been so inept. And so he had nothing, no homemade I.D., no useless American amulets, when he walked into the level, filthy, blasted, black streets of Inchon. Every streetlamp had been shot off its pole. He felt his way along the shapes of blind buildings to the waterfront, and spent the night curled in the belly of a boat with a greasy tarp over him. In the morning, reeking of fish gore, red-eyed, sweating from a sudden fever, drunk from hunger, and seeming even more diminished for the size of his coat, he discovered that a Japanese freighter was carrying displaced persons south to refugee camps on the coast. The Japanese had lent the Americans in Korea their navy, for evacuations and minesweeping, in the hopes of ameliorating the conditions of their 1945 surrender. He shuffled onto the freighter in the arms of the crowd, questioned by no one, and was lowered into an unlit, unventilated hold below deck with hundreds of unwashed and sick refugees. He lost consciousness, awakened briefly only by the terrible implorings of a woman in labor. A man beside him vomited into a hat. Children squatted in the tiniest of spaces, to urinate. The ship was three days at sea, two days in transit and a third full day sitting at anchor, although he didn't know this, and wouldn't know he was not at Pusan but on Cheju Island, fifty miles off the coast of the mainland, until he came onto the deck.

nine

On New Year's Eve afternoon Katherine had stepped into his study, wringing her gloves. "I need some air," she said. "I think I'll go out for a drive." He hardly looked up at her. "I'll be back before supper," she added, and then she left, very slowly, while he scratched his head and frowned down at his work.

When he was sure she had gone he went and pulled the cover off his own car, found the keys lying next to the brake pedal, and experimented with the engine. It started after several false tries, shuddered, and settled into an unhealthy-sounding idle. He generally hated to drive. He had always avoided it, walking wherever he could, even as far as Monteagle and in the worst kind of weather, and when Katherine had come back to Sewanee he gladly gave up driving entirely and let her take him everywhere, because she enjoyed it so much and because he enjoyed watching her. He loved watching her whenever she was completely absorbed and content, folded up with her chin in her hand, watching a bird or a rainstorm, driving, listening to another person talk. He loved watching her whenever she was disregarding him and the uneasy, searching look had left her eyes. Then she didn't seem to need him.

He got the car out of the garage and down to the road, fighting it the whole way, and drove with dangerously exaggerated caution to Chattanooga, where he bought a case of champagne. Carrying it out to the car he began to worry about having time to chill it, and on the way back to Sewanee he sped, careering wildly. He was a terrible, terrible driver. He wished that Katherine was sharing this errand with him. It would have been less nerve-racking, but then, of course, he couldn't have surprised her. He had never tried to surprise her before, although he had known her system of holidays for years. Valentine's: loathsome. July Fourth: an occasion for ironical fun. Halloween: irrelevant. Thanksgiving: painful. Christmas most loathsome of all and then New Year's Eve was absolutely crucial. She would be looking for her omen. He had never tried to surprise her before because he'd never fought to keep her. He had always wanted to believe that she was a casual visitor to his life and that his love meant very little to her. He remembered telling her years ago what a sophisticated girl she was, how jaded, how scornful of him. She graced his bed by virtue of her throaty sense of humor. She liked to believe in this fiction as much as he did, but it was grossly unfair to her. It left her no way to state her unhappiness. He did not want to shoulder the responsibility for making her happy. He knew he would fail.

He was briefly worried that she would already be home when he returned, but she wasn't. He filled the sink with chipped ice and cold water and submerged the whole case to make it chill quickly, and this was also accomplished before she got home. He uncorked a bottle, aiming it at a closed window, and cracked the glass. The small disaster pleased him. He dropped into a chair with a full flute—he had bought these, too; he'd been shocked to find he didn't own any—and began to drink, watching the western light slant through his windows. Soon he was drunk. He was halfway through his second bottle, and found it easy to imagine drinking the remaining ten without her. Champagne seemed to evaporate. It was the cotton candy of alcohol. It was not at all like Scotch; Scotch, he thought with a flash of boyish happiness, was the chewy caramel of alcohol. That was a perfect idea. It fit precisely. Good for you, darling, he thought. Here's your fucking omen. His throat swelled. The instant she came he would hand her a flute and fire another cork at the window. She had always loved him for his hard sheen. He never cried, he never begged, he never needed her. That was why she couldn't leave.

He knew something Katherine could not imagine he knew, although he had no proof, and had never demanded any from her. But he had never felt any tremor in his conviction, which had initially come to him with such ease, unbidden, in the first months of the resumption of their affair. She had never been with anyone but him. Until he realized this, it had never occurred to him that this was a condition to be wanted. Once he did realize it, it became a condition he could not imagine being altered. He had been certain of her faithfulness because he had his own version of it. While he had never suffered from an absence only she could satisfy, his desire somehow coincided with her. He was attracted to women in general, and felt the constant need to circle them, attend to them, be acknowledged and flattered by them, but in the same way that he never wanted to move house and in the same way that he ate, essentially, the same meal again and again, night after night, finding it gratifying as nothing else was, he wanted no other body beneath him but hers. It wasn't that he'd grown used to her. His own body was satisfying to him, not merely familiar. He knew what his own hand tightening around the base of his cock accomplished, he knew where to locate his orgasm, and the inevitable and untiring incremental escalations of his pleasure that marked the way through a narrowing space. His orgasms were more powerful when he was alone than when he was with her, because every cell of his body understood itself, but in the same way his pleasure was far more complete with her than it could be with anyone else, because he knew her, he had carved her out and no one had followed to alter his work. He had slept with many other women since becoming her lover, and they were distractions. Their demands, or their simple differences, diluted his own pleasure and opened what he felt as a slight, maddening space between his body and theirs. With her it was a precise, unalterable fit. He had never imagined that there could be yawning spaces opened in her by the very completeness of that fit, that the completeness in itself created space, like a miracle, created something by force of its power of exhaustion, and that it was in that space that she was marking out her distance from him, testing it, and testing her capacity to hurt him.

After leaving Strake in the morning she went home again, to pull another armful of clothing off the hangers in her closet. Her home had only grown more complicated, in part because of the many explicit difficulties it presented, but mostly because the greatest difficulty of all was not explicit but undefined and disturbing, a difficulty for which she suspected the house only stood as a symbol she could not even read. Going up the stairs she averted her eyes from the library, and in her bedroom she averted her eyes from the bed. She dropped her dirty clothing in her hamper and chose new things. She would have to have the laundry done soon, but she kept putting off calling the service. She had the irrational idea that the boy who picked up and delivered would somehow perceive that she hadn't been living here.

Charles had asked her what she wanted to do with her house. At first she'd felt relieved to have that problem to solve. It was a symptom of change, a way in which to bring this period of her life to a close. But soon she was uneasy. She had always had a fiercely proprietary attitude toward this house, even in her childhood, feeling that the small drama of her life was its sole occupant, and that it was her sole audience. She had taken for granted that it would one day be her property. Then her father had willed her the house and she'd been mortified, both by the fresh proof of his ignorance of her affair and by his inadvertent acknowledgment of it. The house had always seemed like a silent accomplice, enabling her liaison with Charles. But over time its significance changed. She began to associate her property with ideas of extenuation and independence, the slim space between disaster and survival. Although she knew Charles had asked her about her house to reassure her of his seriousness, she began to think that his assumptions about her would not accommodate the private hoard she felt she couldn't do without.

She considered selling the house and putting the money away for herself, but the fluidity this implied, at first inviting, soon seemed precarious. If she turned her house into money, what would keep the money from leaking away? She would clean it out and rent it as a summer house. Then the reality of having the house occupied by strangers, if only for three months of the year, presented itself. What if she were to want to go into the house, and sit in her room? What if she wanted to doze with a book on the screened-in porch, or dig ineptly, as she sometimes had, in the yard? What if she wanted to be alone and out of sight for some reason? There would be people in her house, moving the furniture, impregnating the curtains with unfamiliar cooking smells, discovering forgotten artifacts of her family's life in the attic. The idea became repellent to her, and her flirtation with it even more repellent. She didn't need the money; there was no reason to force the house, like a loyal old animal, to earn a living for the first time in its life. She would keep it as it was.

After she carried the fresh clothes to the car she went back inside, trying to understand this way in which the house now seemed to insist itself at her. What is it? she thought. The right thing to do—she didn't know where these arbitrary, overarching notions of right and wrong were coming from—the right thing to do, she suspected, involved gliding around in an elegiac way, touching things, settling into chairs not settled into for years so as to better bathe the house in her gazes. Some calm ritual of departure. Instead she had absconded from her own house in a fit of embarrassment. It was a strange, self-dividing condition to have returned to a childhood home as a grown woman, and to have stepped into that home both as if she had never left it and as if she had never been there before. She shouldn't have done it, she thought. How many things had she lost track of, plunged into this familiar murk? All around her were squandered opportunities for documentation, abandoned realizations, evidence of nothing consistent apart from her own inattention. Several years ago, after her father's death, she'd come across an old butane lighter of his in the back of a drawer. There was detritus like this sown all through the house, his abandoned sweat-stained workshirts and thumb-softened mildewing mystery novels, and she had been seized by the desire to gather this trashy legacy together and force the loss of her father through the disorderly workings of her understanding until it emerged in some distilled and eternal form that she could treasure, but she hadn't.

She finally went into the library. The vase lay in pieces on the rug, in the center of a tea-colored stain. She got down on all fours and tried various cleaning assailants, and the enormity of what had happened to her dissipated in the irritation of the chore. It seemed mundane, all mundane. She was always the one who threw something. Charles would only recede further and further within himself, watching her steadily. She could see the mark on the wall where the vase had struck and broken. How drunk had she been? She remembered the drive back from Nashville as fizzy with her own sense of indecision and the thrill of knowing that a weighty shifting and rearranging was taking place at the outer edge of her field of grasp. She thought love required the total absence of logic to be authentic. There could never be ulterior motives, justifications discernible to the impartial observer. To the outsider her chosen love must seem inconceivable or she couldn't value it highly enough. She was only drawn to choices that seemed to undermine her rationality. She had to aim this far from the agreed-upon center of things to find the real, utterly uninfluenced shape of her desire, and perhaps sometimes she went too far, seeking to define her love in terms of everything another thought it should not be, and mistaking this contrariness for a pure impulse of her own.

In her adulthood all these tendencies had become clear to her just as they seemed to have reached the point of being incurable. Twenty-eight felt like an ungraceful, unhappy age to be. It was overshadowed by the nearness of the subsequent decade, and the realization that, while she'd been finally lulled by the seeming youthfulness of any number in the twenties, a small death had crept up on her unawares. She felt now that daring and indifference to the social norms of her class were a function of age, and not character. She found herself wanting things she had never wanted before. Not necessarily marriage or the friendship of women her age or the thoughtless routine of a social life, but a sense of conclusiveness in whatever form it took. She had spent half her life immobilized by the fear she would lose Charles, and her unhappiness, she realized now, had been passive, and essentially hopeful. If he didn't love her, there was always the hope that he would. If he abandoned her, there was the hope he would return. So long as the power to withhold her happiness lay outside herself, she could wait, and stoke her despair with the intensity of imagining its opposite. But now she was suddenly sure of him, and for the first time free to wonder whether she was sure of herself. She looked into her heart and found a hall of mirrors instead of the simple chamber that contained the irreducible fact. Nothing singular yielded itself. There was the chasm her loneliness measured, or the fear of the chasm reopening, and there were comparisons between moments at which she had felt herself undoubtedly in love, and this moment. But plain certainty, if it had ever existed, was gone. Her investigation was inseparable from what she hoped to find, and so she ceased to trust any of her assessments of herself. It was only in moments of rare thoughtlessness, like pushing the door open with the heel of her hand and walking out of the house, that she would be visited by a flash of pure feeling: the pressure of her hand briefly printed by the texture of the door, the curtain's filigree of lace before her eyes, the sharp breeze, the brilliant glitter of the afternoon sun—a flood of mundane precision and hovering within this, like a momentary ghost, the real knowledge that she was unhappy. She had gained the one condition upon which she thought all her happiness hung, and found she was wrong. There had always been a distant, unlikely prospect, for which she lived, and this was gone.

When she arrived at his house the five champagne bottles were lined up side by side against the baseboard in the kitchen, labels facing out, as sober as if they'd held milk. She went quickly to the icebox and found the other seven. Her heart climbed into her throat and stayed there. The house was perfectly still, already losing the blaze from the morning light. It was nine o'clock, very late for him to not be awake. He rose every day at six, no matter when he'd gone to bed, and often went straight to his desk without washing. When she got up, hours later, she would find him there, humming to himself over Virgil, and bring him a poached egg sliding in a teacup, or a stack of dry toast he barely touched. He never ate anything substantial until late in the day. When his thoughts hit a snag he wandered through the house, unseeing,

mumbling lines from epic poems with no awareness he was
speaking aloud. She knew everything about him, she knew he
spoke seriously to the plants when he thought she was gone, she
knew he was secretly sentimental about dogs. No one had ever
studied her so closely, but sometimes his attention swept over her
and she felt it powerfully. "Tell me," he would say, his gaze settling
comfortably back into itself as if into an armchair. She would
have had a dream, or made some arbitrary decision, or spoken
with some irritating person. At these moments she had sometimes felt she was not being loved but consumed, idly, for his
pleasure. But she would see the pleasure in his eyes as she slid
further into chatty self-indulgence. "Tell me," he said. His taking
pleasure in her felt like love. She went upstairs and found him in
bed, gazing at the ceiling. His eyes were bloodshot. He swallowed
hard and smiled weakly at her. "This is your punishment," he
said. "Seeing me looking like this." She had imagined his accusations, her derision. As she crossed the room toward him, all that
slid off her like a daydream, forgotten. "What have you done
here?" she murmured, touching his forehead. "You've had women
here. There have been dancing and drinking."

"And song."

"Yes, song. I forgot about song." When she nudged him he
shifted and made room for her on the bed, wincing. She took his
head in her lap.

"I have a terrible hangover," he whispered.

"No, no, we'll scare it away." One fat tear fell before she could
catch it and struck his face.

"Katherine," he said, warningly, and then she began to cry in
earnest.

"I wasn't here," she said.

He craned to look at her. "You weren't required to be here."

"Of course I was." She pulled her wrist across her eyes, impatiently.

"It was a just a small surprise for you. Champagne."

"I don't know," she began. She pressed a pillow to her face and it came away wet. She took a ragged breath and sighed.

"Tell me."

"Can I?"

"I think you'd better." He pulled her down beside him and they lay face to face, sharing the dry pillow. She could smell the sweet stench from the alcohol, sweating off him.

"I went to visit Chang. I cooked him some supper. Then I showed him Mrs. Wade's brandy stash and we got tight. I had to sleep there. I slept in some boy's grimy dorm room."

He laughed. Then he said, too quickly, "Not his."

"I like him, Charles."

"I know you do." He touched her cheek. "Sweet Katherine."

"You're so sure of me."

"I'm not sure of you at all. I'm nervous." He imagined sleeping in a cold bed, knowing someone else was making love to her.

"I didn't mean to stay there. I never decided to stay."

"Perhaps that was your omen."

She was silent. She tried to stare past him, and sank one hand in his fine mane of hair. How often had she thanked God for this? Bald men made her clammy.

"Are you having second thoughts?"

"No."

"Did you make love to him?"

She sat up. "Is that all you care about?"

"That," he said crisply, "is what I care a great deal about."

"Sometimes I think you'd like me to go off with someone else."

"You're very wrong there."

"Have my nasty business with somebody else and then tell you about it."

"That would kill me." His calm gaze seemed sunk deep within him.

"Because I'm yours?"

"Don't you want to be?" he said.

She walked away and left him lying helplessly in bed. When he was this hung over he wouldn't even dare to sit up. It made him nauseated and he was terrified of vomiting. He would sooner faint from being poisoned than vomit. She sat down on the stairs outside his room and peeled off her dirty stockings. Their knees were torn through and the soles were gray. These were the stockings she'd driven to Strake in, and walked to the chapel, and sat in the kitchen without her shoes, and run across the hall when he was crying. She pulled them through her fingers. All that hapless travel was recorded here. She had gone to Strake to see him because she was frightened of what he thought of her. She didn't remember the last time she'd cared what a person thought of her. The preoccupation was painful and urgent, like a numb limb stirring. She didn't want him to think she was a careless, self-indulgent woman. She didn't want him to think that she was idly toying with him for her pleasure. But then she had to tell him about the engagement, and this very simple declaration, which she had rehearsed to herself in the car, giving it the inflection of flat statements of fact like "I have a new car" or "I come from New Orleans," began to snarl on itself. She couldn't tell him when this had happened without explaining what fourteen years of living through it hadn't helped her understand, but if she implied it was an engagement of long standing, would it be wrong that she had taken him to dinner? Every third thought she had was disgust with these labyrinthine proprieties. If she said she'd been engaged all along, would it seem strange that she hadn't told him sooner? Not having told him might appear like a presumption he would care. Every time she imagined that he would care she reproached herself for vanity, and returned to the original idea: I have a new car, I'm engaged, I was born in New Orleans. And then he had punished her, sensing the contorted weight of what she hadn't said, and not allowing her to say it at all.

When she looked into the bedroom again he was faking sleep. The way his arms lay by his sides on top of the blanket reminded her of an invalid's. She knew he wasn't really sleeping. When he slept his breaths seemed drawn from the furthest depths of his body like draughts of water from a well. He couldn't have imitated that sound even if he'd ever heard it. She went downstairs silently, in her bare feet, and began to make him a tray. Was this what it would be like, someday? When she turned forty he would be sixty-eight. But then, herself at forty was an inconceivable figure on the other side of an abyss. She loaded the tray with a poached egg, a stack of dry toast, a pitcher of tepid water, the Tabasco bottle, and the aspirin box and carried it upstairs. "I thought you'd left me," he said when she came in.

She spent the rest of the afternoon reading to him while he lay gulping and sighing uncomfortably. She only read him things he knew by heart, and wouldn't think too hard about. "I feel like Dorothea Brooke," she joked.

"That's nice for me. Dorothea Brooke felt like Milton's daughter."

"But she was an insufferable square."

"As I recall it, she was a noble young girl who made the mistake of marrying an old man she grew to loathe."

She kissed him. "It's lucky I loathe you already."

She thought there had to be a moment at which a decision was irrevocably made, and after that the worst was over. Now this moment kept receding. She could no longer believe she'd ever been a bold, thoughtless girl who had pursued a disastrous affair because she'd wanted to, who had accepted her mother's vilification as perfectly consistent with things she had done and not regretted, who had burned up her family's affection and walked away from her education and returned to this place, forsaking every other goal. Each of those decisions had been unsought and absolute and she had discharged them with an almost ruthless satisfaction, because no matter how damaging the result might be, to herself or someone else, the thing had to be done. But now she felt she could only arrive at a decision sideways, and by accident. She performed minor ceremonies of decisiveness in the hopes that she would exit the stage by a newly formed door and find the decision there, made. When Chang cried out in his sleep for a moment she'd thought he was crying for her. The thought belonged to half sleep, but even after she was fully awake, it didn't entirely leave her. Sometimes she was sure that the distance she felt between them wasn't difference, but a wariness they both turned toward the world. That they turned it toward each other was mistaken, the thing they shared camouflaging itself. She was oppressed by her inability to know what she wanted and say what she meant, but now she saw that he might be the same. He was only able to speak in the throes of his dream. And then she answered, and he made her go away.

Crane returned, in an explosion of new shorts and socks and other undervalued Christmas presents that effaced the slight trace that her body had left in his bed. He went and watched Crane unpack his luggage by the fistful. Shouts and greetings shook the floor below them. Everyone had returned on the same day, as if by common consent, although it was only Saturday. "One half-assed Christmas," Crane said. Mrs. Wade came and squeezed their faces between her palms. "I missed you!" she said. "Did your mother notice how bad you've been spoiled?" and then she turned to Chuck and said, "Louis tells me you came by for one meal and never again."

"I make meals here," he said.

"Out of what? Lint?"

"Count your cats, Mrs. Wade," Crane said, laughing.

"Why did you keep so scarce?"

"I study," he said. "I'm sorry."

"You thought you were trouble to them," and when he nodded she snapped, "I wish you hadn't thought that way. Everybody here wants to be kind to you, especially those boys. You won't find a better bunch of boys."

"I am glad."

"They won't know it unless you let them fuss over you. Receiving hospitality is hard work. It's harder than doling it out. Ask Mr. Crane. I'm sure his mother taught him right. Accept everything you're offered with grace."

Crane said, "And you won't get off either, Mrs. Wade, I have a box of broken pralines from Mother for you," and so his cross-examination was over. He went back to his room and moved Katherine's note again. It had been marking page fifty-six of his calculus book. The obviousness of this placement embarrassed him. He pushed his door shut, still hearing Mrs. Wade's voice. His room was no more safe than a sieve. Kneeling, he slid the scrap of paper between a bedframe slat and the underside of his mattress. And then he couldn't rise. He tipped his face into the bed. It had become a dreaded object. Since New Year's Eve he had slept only the way a night sentry would, stumbling into unconsciousness after a desperate struggle and immediately jerking awake again. The shame he felt when he thought of Katherine was violent, and ultimate. He did not even imagine that it would diminish. It was a final judgment, not resisted because it had been so expected. He had never wanted anyone to know that he was a madman, and a coward. And yet, because he'd feared this so intensely, he'd never doubted he would be exposed. He thought of Katherine's revulsion to punish himself. He cherished the small note she had left him but he couldn't look at it. He had folded it in half.

Crane came and sat on his bed and he thought with disgust of Crane's weight pressing down on the small piece of paper, that precise rendering of her voice in shapes drawn by her hand. "Tell me all about it, Ace," Crane said. Crane had a terrible habit, one of a constellation of terrible habits, Chuck reflected, of coming unbidden into a room and then looking around irritably at the upper corners, as if impatient to get away quickly.

"Tell about what?" Chuck asked.

"The break. What all did I miss?"

"Nothing happens here. It has been very quiet."

"You can't have been sitting with your books this whole time. You're tricky, aren't you. As soon as I'm gone I'll bet you're up to all sorts of high jinks."

"No."

Crane gave him a long, assessing look, to make it clear he wasn't being taken in, but he tired easily of questioning other people and returned to discussing himself. "Look at this," he said, derisively fingering the pricey cashmere scarf he still had slung around his neck, although the heat had come rumbling on again full force just in time for the return of the students, and the building was roasting. "From the minute I get home my mother's following me around poking at my neck and trying to look in my mouth because do you know what she says? I must have a cold. The woman is loony-tunes. She says, 'Does it ever frost on the mountain?' and I say, 'Liza'"—Crane called his mother by her first name to be particularly cruel— "'It snows,' and she shrinks up like I've said we all go around nude. Look at this," he repeated, and he lifted the scarf to Chuck's face. "It's always got to be the fanciest thing for her." Crane went on speaking at great length about the unique manias of his mother and Chuck listened, and responded periodically, but he heard almost nothing.

The semester resumed in all its stupid specificity and he hated it; he hated the walk to class, he hated sitting in class, he hated rising again and walking out of class, he hated propelling his pencil across the page. There were brief, sickening moments at which he realized he was even more unworthy of Katherine than he had ever thought, because she was gone, and he continued to live, like a monster. First-term grades were posted; he got an A in calculus, a surprising B in history, and the gentleman's C from Charles Addison. This last grade made him sneer. For history he had written an impassioned, grammatically reckless paper on the mistreatment of the American Indian which his professor had lavishly praised. Seeing it again he didn't recognize it. If he had been accused of plagiarism at that moment he would have surrendered. He had lost all interest in the English language and spoke less than ever, ate alone in the dining hall staring fiercely at a page of mathematics, the universal language that nobody spoke. He stopped browsing his thesaurus, and sank into monosyllables. His lust to master the language had never been abstract, no matter how fastidious and intellectual his approach might have seemed to observers like Peterfield, or Kim. It had always been utterly, ruthlessly pragmatic, driven by his faith in its power to transport him. It had gotten him into USIS, and across the ocean to Sewanee, and then, just as he was in danger of becoming apathetic from accomplishment, it had brought her within view. Every possibility of speech had been a possibility of speaking to her.

Now he lapsed into brutish inarticulateness. His walks with Charles Addison had ceased with no more incident than if they'd never occurred. He saw the professor on occasion in the dining hall, or walking to his lecture, but they weren't brought into the sort of proximity that would have required them to either speak or deliberately ignore each other. He did not see Katherine at all, although he looked for her everywhere, his heart pounding each time he left Strake's front door. His eyes swept compulsively over the knots of students smoking on the quad, now that the weather had begun to grow mild, and the snow had shrunk to a few dirty crescents in the shadows of buildings, and the daffodils were blooming and falling flat beneath poundings of rain. She would be a slender, solitary figure, an anomalous woman striding unself-consciously through the awkward crowds of black-robed or blue-jacketed young men, in a narrow gray suit or a bright green sundress, her car keys swinging in her hand. He never saw her. Walking alone, he would hear the steady tear of a small motor climbing the road behind him, and his head would snap around to watch the car pass, but it was never hers.

Crane had done so poorly the first term that his father threatened him with disinheritance and military service and he vanished, into a new, frightened seriousness, from which he only emerged when completely resourceless. These became the sole times Chuck saw him. The odd comfort Crane had derived from Chuck's presence in their first semester dissolved. Crane resented a foreigner's doing better than he did, and because Crane was doing his worst work in math he grew suspicious of math for the distasteful foreignness of its appearance, which he began to see as the root cause of Chuck's facility with it. Math was a pernicious, useless system controlled by pernicious, inscrutable persons, like his malevolent professors and his Oriental floormate. When Crane came to demand Chuck's help with algebra he flickered with resentment and impatience, and ascribed the difficulty Chuck subsequently had in helping him to Chuck's inability to communicate in the manner of a clear and normal person. Their friendship may have already died by the time Crane spoke his mind on a point which had been irritating him since the fall. "I see your friend doesn't come around here anymore," he said. They were bending tensely over a sheet of problems Crane refused to really look at. He had come in and thrown the paper down before Chuck and he'd be damned if Chuck wouldn't just do the work for him. He wasn't interested in clumsy explanations.

He stood and paced the room. Chuck had begun quietly working the page but when Crane spoke he stopped.

"What friend?" he said.

"You know. Your lady friend."

"You mean Miss Monroe," he said, stiffening.

"I don't care what you call her so long as you're not swooning anymore. You were starting to embarrass me, Junior."

"Miss Monroe is a good friend to me."

"Oh, horseshit. She wanted some sick business with you and you didn't have any of it or I'd be pretty sick of you. I would have said something about it, but it was none of my business."

"About what?"

"What she is."

"What is that?" he snapped.

"A whore. She's Addison's whore. Everybody knows that."

He sat staring at Crane, one hand lying flat on the algebra. Then he pushed the sheet forward.

"You're not going to work those?"

"I don't think so."

"Well, to hell with you. I'm not telling you anything you shouldn't have known." He slapped the door frame with the palm of his hand as he left. Chuck got up and slammed the door shut.

He and Crane had a system for cutting daily chapel services, the kind of arrangement only close friends and roommates consented to make with each other. Attendance at the service was enforced by a set of five lists containing all the students' names, nailed to the inside doors of the chapel like the articles of faith. Each student placed an X beside his name, beneath the watchful eye of God, as he entered every morning. Marking more than one name was a risky hassle and hardly possible on more than one list, and Bill Crane had considered it a magical dispensation of their friendship that they were both on the A through E list, "along with Jesus H. Christ," he had joked. As a result they had never gone to chapel together, or more than every other day. Now they each went every day, and marked their separate X's without speaking. Chuck sat in his pew, gripping the hard, smooth, palm-polished wood of the pew back in front of him, or cradling the soft leather hymnal, one finger following the music. He stood, sat, hummed quietly within the great shape of singing. Once he had bridled at the idea of an enforced faith, but now he lost himself in its upward-hurtling words, its bending flames, its instruments of martyrdom. He gazed across the glossy rows of water-combed heads and felt the hot glare of his Taskmaster's eye beating down. Outside it was April. The doors stood open, letting in the sliding breeze and the eager confidings of birds. The sunlight falling through the stained glass threw bright lozenges of color on the cool stone floor. Everyone stood, rippling upward, and he stood with them, his body easily obeying the complex rhythms of the service. The choirmistress raised her stick and slashed out the hymn's martial beat:

> I am living, on the mountain, underneath a cloudless sky (praise
> God)
> I am drinking, at the fountain, that never shall run dry

and when the singing was over and they sat down again he saw her, a glimpse of her back and bare shoulders in a blue summer dress, before she sank out of sight.

*H*e stood waiting for her on the far edge of the quad lawn. When the shadow from the spreading oak shifted slightly with the breeze she saw him, standing deep within it, leaning on the trunk. Charles had fallen into a conversation with a colleague and she hovered by him uncomfortably. She hugged her arms, although the morning had grown hot. When she looked again he was still there, waiting for her. She excused herself and Charles cupped his hand around her shoulder and held it as she moved away, as if he meant to restrain her. When she looked back the arm stretched absently after her, but he was still turned toward the man he was speaking to. She crossed the blazing lawn and when she stepped into the tree's shadow she was momentarily blinded. Then her vision cleared and he was there, watching her.

"I want to see you," he said.

"You could have come to see me."

"I don't think you would want me to."

"Of course I wanted you to."

"I am very stupid, then." His hands began a sentence and abandoned it. He had thought if she forgave him he would hate her. "I hoped you would come."

"I can't come anymore."

"Why?"

"I'm engaged to him."

He kept very still, looking at her. The line her arm made, descending from her shoulder. He wanted to put his mouth against the soft space in the shadow of her jaw. He would have to tilt her head back to see it. He caught his breath suddenly and she started toward him, but he had only forgotten to breathe. He hadn't moved at all. If he did he'd have to feel what she had said. "For how long?"

"Is that important?"

"No."

"I tried to tell you before. I didn't know if it mattered to you."

"It isn't." He touched his forehead, dizzy suddenly. He looked at the ground and then raised his head, gazing past her. She turned and saw Charles facing in their direction, one hand held up to block the glare.

"Not at all?"

"No." He placed his palm on the tree's trunk and closed his

eyes. The heat soaked his jacket and crawled against his skin. When he opened his eyes again mercury blotches exploded in his vision. Beyond them he saw Charles Addison crossing the lawn.

"Tell me quickly," she said, turning back to him. The color in her cheeks stood out as if she'd been slapped. "I've put it off and put it off. I want to see you, too. I think about you. But I don't have anything, I don't know anything." Past her shoulder he could see Addison growing larger, striding easily over the grass. "Could you imagine loving me?"

"Then what?"

"I could break it."

"Don't do nothing like this for me."

"But there's something," she said angrily. "Isn't there?"

"No."

"Don't look over there. Don't look at him, just tell me."

"Congratulation," he said evenly.

"Damn you!"

He put out his hand and Katherine wheeled away from him, covering her mouth. He was gone when the other man reached her.

t e n

He went to Bower and told him he wanted his summer to be a continuation of his education, not an interruption, and to that end he wanted to spend it somewhere else. A visitor's eagerness to see more than he has already seen is always pleasing, and Bower thought it was a wonderful idea. It was evidence of initiative, and offset his concern that Chuck had turned out to be somewhat withdrawn. Before ratifying the plan he interrogated Chuck very thoroughly, not only to clarify things for himself but to clarify things for the boy, as he always thought of him. "You will be on your own. Things are very easy for you here. I hope you realize that. You are surrounded by your friends. If you go off somewhere for the summer you'll have to watch out for yourself and keep your wits about you, and I'll expect you to be a credit to Sewanee wherever you are."

"I understand," he said.

"Do you think you can get along all right? I'll take your word."

"Yes."

Bower propped his fingertips together and tilted his head, awaiting some elaboration to this answer, and when none came he was momentarily thrown. Then he decided to be impressed by

Chuck's concision. "Well," he said grandly. "I'll start sniffing around, then. I'm sure I can come up with something."

A few days later, Bower called him back. "A great patron of Sewanee's, and an old classmate of mine, in fact. Tippett House '25." This man owned a publishing concern in Chicago, "complicated work," Bower said kindly, but there was also a bindery, which was always shorthanded. How did that sound? Chicago?

The Greyhound bus stopped in Monteagle on its way north from Chattanooga, Atlanta, Savannah, or on its way south to those places. Monteagle was a three-mile walk from Sewanee, all downhill, and as the road descended the trees thinned so that there was more and more tramped, dusty grass, and the sky opened wide. The town was small and straightforward: a gas station, a grocery store, and a small collection of houses he could see the beginning of, to the south, before the road took a turn. The grocery store's windows were crowded with advertisements for small sums. *Only 10 cents! Only 25 cents!* The houses came right to the road. He had always been southbound, heading for Chattanooga and a transfer that would take him to Alabama or Mississippi or Georgia, to whatever small church was awaiting him. The bus would slide around the bend and barely pause, and then as he weaved down the aisle he would lean to watch out the window as the front edge of Monteagle that he had gazed at exhaustingly, until it was no longer an impoverished sliver but the whole, intricate, unexpandable thing, suddenly rejoined the rest of itself. The entire town would flash by before he saw anything more than its tail as it slipped out of sight. The bus would pause only once more, in Jasper, before arriving at the Chattanooga station, where the noncommittal prelude was brought to an end and everyone leaped up and changed buses with new, narrow determination. Chattanooga was the aperture that seemed to give onto the whole of the South, and soon he would think of Evansville, Indiana, this way, as a gate to the North.

The northbound and southbound stops faced each other across the road, but he had never seen another person there. Now there was a man on the southbound side. Chuck perched self-consciously on his upended suitcase, which he had placed in the dust, where the heat wouldn't bounce off the stones back at him. The unprecedented traveler on the other side of the road had done the same thing. At first they only watched each other clandestinely, but after it was clear there was nowhere else to look they examined each other with obvious interest. The other man might have been older than him by ten or fifteen years. He was wearing a lopsided, curl-brimmed leather hat and a white cotton T-shirt, and his jacket hung over his knee. The road was too wide to speak across, but narrow enough that he could see the man's calm smile, and his eyes set in the shadow from his hat.

He tried to imagine where this man was going. When he pored over maps at the library he always strayed toward the coasts, analyzing the clues in the shape of an edge. The Louisiana coast looked like a splatter of ink. It had scattered islands everywhere. On the map New Orleans and everything near it was scored with blue lines, to indicate swampland. He imagined a lake of bright grass, the flash low in the stalks when the wind parted them and the sun struck the water. He missed the water, he thought, although beneath this thought his mind idly sorted the Louisiana names he had memorized, on the principle that memorization was always helpful in a general way—*10 cents! 25 cents!* was helpful, even if he had no more particular interest in these exclamations than he had in the names that fanned out from the hub of New Orleans. *Barataria, Lafitte, Meraux.* Out of nowhere the southbound bus slid around the bend and paused, and he saw the man reappear in its windows, moving down the aisle. As the bus pulled away the man bent down and waved to him, grinning. His own arm flew up and they waved energetically to each other for those few seconds as the bus plunged through Monteagle and left it behind.

His own bus came more than thirty minutes later, after his hair felt like hot metal to the touch and his vision was swimming with splotches. He had no hat. He climbed on board, unsteadily, and fell asleep. When he woke again he realized he'd been dreaming of being at sea. His heart beat quickly. But the bus swayed and pitched less like a ship than an ungainly, sturdy animal. The afternoon had grown long. Outside the bus windows the hills cast great, round shadows onto themselves, and beyond the reach of the shadows their color was a green-steeped gold, like a block of sun trapped in pondwater. All the trees were in full leaf now and the hillsides so densely forested that their substance seemed to be the leaves, unbroken but varying in color and texture from particle to particle. He saw a hawk wheeling over the road and strained his neck until it drifted out of sight. The land was so lush and the color of the light so palpable that at first he forgot that this was the same road he had driven up and down with Katherine, in the dark, the night she took him to dinner. When he remembered that he closed his eyes again. The sun was a bloated red ball as the bus pulled into Nashville, and he rose automatically, because Nashville was not so unlike Chattanooga. It was only a juncture, containing no significance. *Des Allemandes, Point à la Hache, Belle Chasse.* He had the thought, brief and irritating, that he was traveling in the wrong direction. He wanted to be going toward the ocean. The bus to Chicago was already crowded when he found it; he took a window seat and watched it fill completely. A ten- or twelve-year-old boy with thin blond hair cropped so short it looked pink climbed on board and, after a brief hesitation, took the seat beside him. "Where you from?" he asked, as the bus pulled away. It was dark now; he saw the bright dome of the capitol building as the bus turned onto the highway.

"Seoul, Korea."

"Oh, yeah."

"You know it?" In his surprise he sounded more eager than he'd meant to. He didn't want to talk to this boy.

"Oh, yeah. Seoul Poo-san Pyong-yang." He hit each consonant with relish. "My brother went in the war."

"He comes back all right?"

"Oh, yeah. You want some gum? My brother says gooks are nuts about gum."

He took the gum and they both chewed meditatively until the boy wondered whether he wanted the comic that came in the wrapper, and when he had surrendered it the boy asked with sudden, pouncing insight, "You going to Chi?"

"Chi?" he repeated.

"Chi-cago."

"Yes."

"Oh!" the boy said, as if he'd been whacked in the stomach. "I thought so! There's a big old Chinaman town in Chi where they've got a place where they've got sharks and giant snakes and monkeys hung in the windows to eat and you can go and they take the head off with an ax and cook it and then you can go and there's a wizard where he has lizards in jars and eyeballs, and there's a big assortment," he said with incongruous maturity, "of throwing knives and they've also got kung fu stuff and airplanes."

"You've been here?" he asked, when the boy paused.

"No," the boy said with unmistakable bitterness. "My brother goes and brings me stuff once in a while."

The boy was a resource of information on organized vice and Chicago's other miscellaneous depravities, Al Capone and restaurants where girls wore only feathers and other girls wore, as he said, "just a string"—which interested him solely as an example of the bizarre—and dull-looking places with hidden back rooms, perhaps behind a swinging wall, where there was gambling. Chi was his dream city. "I dream of going there," he said, very simply. "I sure envy you. I would make you take me with you if you swore you was going to go straight to the Chinaman town."

"I'm not a Chinese."

"That's okay," the boy told him kindly.

They lapsed into silence. The boy fell asleep for several hours, slumped crookedly in his seat, and woke up startled. He stared at Chuck in shock, and for a moment Chuck was afraid he would leap up and stand in the aisle, panting unhappily. "Where are we?" the boy whispered. He leaned carelessly across Chuck's seat and they peered into the darkness together. They were on an express bus. It had tunneled ceaselessly since they left Nashville. The boy sat back and sighed. They shared a weak, yellow pool of light. Everywhere else the bus lay in blackness, with the quiet roar of the engine and the outside air shearing past, like the sound of the ocean, and within this the shifting, sighing, breathing sounds of people. In the hours while the boy was asleep he had sat with his head turned toward the window, and the featureless night outside, dusted over with the reflection of his weak reading light, had eased its way behind his eyes and filled him with nothing but staring. He didn't know how much time had gone by. He hadn't thought of anything. The boy had also altered, with the hush inside the bus. "I have a comic, but I get motion sick reading," he said. "On a bus, I mean. Would you like to read it?"

At first he misunderstood. "Thank you, no," he said.

"It's a good one," the boy said hopefully.

He read the comic to the boy in a conspiratorial whisper. He had to describe the pictures, too, because even looking at them made the boy queasy. The boy put his head near Chuck and closed his eyes with pleasure as Chuck spoke. "The two guys now duck down, and third guy's feet we see coming to us, over their head. This third guy is a Chinese, jumping over the trench—"

"I know, I know," the boy whispered.

"American guy's eyes fill up the whole picture, stretched out big." The boy's eyes flew open briefly, in imitation. "'Ahhh!'" Chuck went on, in an undertone. "'They are coming too fast!' he says. Now we see Chinese coming, like a wall of them. They have bayonets raised up. 'Aieee!'"

They came to Evansville, Indiana, at midnight. The premature night, that had put the bus to sleep at nine o'clock, was suspended. Passengers woke, twisted in their seats, peered out the window. The bus bounced over a steel-girder bridge and its hum rose an octave. "Ohio River," the boy announced. They had left Kentucky, unseen and unthought-of. The great skeleton of the bridge poured past the windows and even there, hundreds of miles away from it, he felt the approach of a huge city and could never think of Evansville again—thrown there on the mud bank in the middle of flat land with one or two pale orange lights in the streets as the bus found the station—without it seeming continuous with that powerful center. There were people awake at the small station, alert and intelligent, with their bags in their hands. "Chi!" the boy said avidly, as they plunged into darkness again. Now the bus seemed to fly more quickly over the level land. He could pick out the horizon, where the wildly star-covered sky rose straight out of the ground. No one slept anymore, and the boy was reminded, with a fresh sense of urgency, of the rest of his brother's teachings. There were stuffed elephants! There was an aquarium with a tank as big as a lake, sitting in the middle of a room. His brother said if you went to a hotel they gave you anything, food and booze and *dames*, the boy noted emphatically. And the stuff they had in Chinatown, devil idols and a chicken that danced on a plate. The bus rumbled with conversation, and the tiny lights blinked on over the seats. "I don't want to go home!" said the boy with disgust. The bus was full of itinerants, people who slid through the night as a matter of course. "Where is your home?" he asked the boy, who seemed to feel compromised by the fact that he had one.

"Terre Haute," he spat. When asked to spell it he did so with convulsions and eye-rolling.

Terre Haute. He was startled, to think of such a name here. He had seen that word before. *Grand Terre Isle*.

"It means 'high land,'" said the boy, smirking. "Ha!"

They came into Terre Haute after two o'clock in the morning, an eerie hour for a boy to be arriving at home. "You got somebody who meets you?" he asked the boy, who had turned around backwards in his seat and now knelt on it, with his cheek flat against the seat's back, fixing Chuck with a steady gaze.

"Oh, yeah," he said. "My brother says you can't tell the difference between gooks and chinks so I'm getting a good look at you and when he takes me to Chinatown with him I'll bet I can tell. Can you tell?"

"Sometimes," he said.

"There's the river." The road ran next to it, hugging a hillside. The ground dropped away sharply to their right. The moon had risen and they could see the tops of trees and beyond them, far below, the silver sheet of the river reaching toward the opposite bank. "Wa-bash River," the boy said, and then the bus had swung into the Terre Haute station and he was gone, yelling, "I shouldn't even get off, I should just go right on up to Chi with you," and the bus was much quieter. He kept looking at the strangely empty seat beside him.

Terre Haute might have been named by a traveler on his way from the south to Chicago. That hill that rose up from the river was the last high land, or land of any shape at all, that he saw. After they left the town the land was level in every direction and the horizon made a vast circle with the bus at its center. For an hour or more the river remained alongside, although when the land had spread out the river slid a certain distance, sometimes as much as a mile, from the road, where it lay like a glittering stripe. Then it turned east, and stretched away. His eye could see it all the way to the horizon. The bus kept plowing north, and the whole eastern sky stood unobstructed. When the stars first began to seem weak he checked his watch. The dawn came by increments, always slightly outstripping his ability to notice it, and then all at once the stars were gone and the first unbelievably distinct ray of the sunrise had emerged. Farmland as perfectly flat as an ocean surrounded them. In the distance he saw an occasional tree, black and solitary. The combed fields turned past like the spokes of a wheel. When the sun was high a railroad line came to join the road, and filling stations and truck stops gave way to flat-topped brick houses and grain elevators and smokestacks and storefronts and traffic lights strung overhead, and then too many buildings to see anything but a flash in the distance, as if from the actual ocean.

He came out of the bus station into an early May morning just reaching the sidewalks on the west sides of the streets. The light was city light, stretching over the sides of buildings, blazing in windows. Businessmen still wearing their winter fedoras were walking to work. He had studied his map of downtown Chicago and memorized the way from the station to the bindery so that he wouldn't be seen standing helplessly on the street with a map in his hand: four blocks east and then fourteen blocks south along Michigan Avenue. But once on the street he didn't know which way was east. He stood there a moment, outwardly calm, feeling the cool that hadn't yet been evaporated by the concrete, seeing every particle of every building teem with color and roughness the way the hills outside Sewanee had teemed, because he hadn't slept at all. He stepped off the curb and looked down the canyon of buildings straight into a blinding glare. Sitting at the end of the crevice was a neat square of blue. He walked that way, east, toward the lake.

When he reached Michigan Avenue everything fell away between there and the water. Across the expanse of the park he could see the marina, with its forest of unrigged masts. Michigan Avenue was four lanes wide, and the sidewalks broad and level.

He passed the red carpets and taut awnings of luxury hotels; the colonnade of the library; gilty, scrolled theater-fronts. Then Michigan Avenue lost the park and, without changing direction, shifted inland, as the coastline of the lake curved away. The buildings diminished and cropped up on both sides of the narrower street. He found a cafeteria a block shy of his destination and ordered fried eggs at the counter, suddenly apprehensive. Yet when he presented himself at the bindery, a huge brick building on the lake side of the street, it was just nine o'clock in the morning, and he wasn't expected. The manager nodded at him and showed him the letter from Bower, lifting it briefly off a pile on his desk. "I expected you next week. Summer work, your guy said. We lay most people off in the summer. It's a bad time for bookbinding. The glue melts and the pages curl up. Not a lot of people want to work here in the summer anyway. But you'll have plenty to do. There's always backlog in the morgue." He looked up at Chuck for the first time. "So you're a Korean. We've got a lot of Chinese in this city and a lot of Japs but I don't know that we have much Koreans. How did you people like that war we had for you?"

"Very much," he said.

"I hope those aren't your only change of clothes. It's dirty work." He handed Chuck a card for a rooming house not far away. "Come back tomorrow. You'll work with Fran. She's in charge down there."

He had thought it would be an actual bindery, where books were made. He wasn't romantic about that idea, but he associated factories of any kind with mindless racket and a constant propulsion that kept just ahead of boredom, and people, grabbing things or throwing things or moving them around. But there were no people where he worked, down in the morgue. And it was a rebindery, for books that had already been made, used, and broken. The books came into his hands covered with grime and full of dust, printed in cheap ink that blackened his fingertips on porous yellowed paper that crumbled at the edges or broke if it was folded. He had to pick up every one, flipping through it carefully, his filthy, chapped thumb releasing a slow cascade of pages, each falling alone, and only when he was satisfied the book was empty could he perform the main task of tearing the old covers off, savagely, and flinging them away. This was the job as Fran explained it to him. Fran was haggard, straight-backed, perhaps seventy, with the stringy body of a boy and a halo of thinned hair the exact color of parchment paper. She gave him his instructions with the contemptuous resentment of a person who would rather do everything, no matter how degrading, herself. She called the work "cleaning." The unstripped books came heaped in a canvas sack stretched on a rolling metal frame which was so deep that the level of books would sink below his reach, even when he hung over the edge, and then he would have to fish clumsily in it with the dustpan stuck onto the end of the broom. At the end of his first day he asked Fran what he was looking for, exactly, when he flipped to make sure the book was empty. Sometimes a crushed beetle slid out, or crumbs.

"Money," she said angrily. He could see she didn't like him. Although she oversaw the work on every floor, the trimming and stitching and gluing, she had repeatedly come to his area, a great vaulted space like a garage at the bottom and back of the building, where the loading doors were, and stared at him.

"Money?" he asked.

"People stick money in books and forget. They do it all the time. And when you find it you give it to me, you don't keep it. That's stealing," she said, provocatively.

"I haven't found no any money."

"You've been doing this all day."

He shook his head helplessly.

"You're likely to find some every day. I've done every job in this place and when I did this job I found money in books every day," she said, and stalked out of the room.

He hated this work more than anything he'd ever done in his life. It was dirty and tedious, and he was always alone. The silence in the tall, hot room rang in his ears. He found a hooked pole and learned to cantilever the huge windows open, and on clear days a warm breeze wound around him while he worked and seemed to touch him with moist molecules from the nearby, invisible lake. He pretended to be a machine, flipping and ripping in time to an annoying tattoo that established itself in his head and began to coincide with his footsteps and the way he ate his eggs at the cafeteria counter. It beat within him all night while he lay in his sagging, prickly rooming-house bed, kept awake by the absence of sound, and it even reached him when he managed to sleep, so that he dreamed of work, and woke more exhausted than ever. He tried to skip the flipping but he couldn't. The one or two times he succeeded the transgression required such a summoning of will it slowed him down, and afterwards his eyes kept straying to the tainted book as it was slowly covered over, until, when it was nearly out of sight, he yanked it out and angrily searched it. Fran's surveillance was constant, petulant, and threatening. Because she was the only person he saw with any regularity she took on an inflated, morbid role in his thoughts. He tried to imagine her as a young woman, as a married woman, as a person with a home of her own, and each time her figure would rise up, unaltered and perfectly obscene against whatever backdrop he'd chosen. His eyes constantly ached. He looked at endless blurry fans of pages, roughly ten books every minute. Sometimes when he ripped he lost hold and the book went flapping through the air. Whenever Fran came she first stood behind him for an interminable minute as if she thought he couldn't sense that she was there. "I used to do this," she whined. "I used to find two-dollar bills. All the time." He rarely looked straight in her face because when he did he noticed an unhealthy wetness in her eyes, like the oozing from a poorly healed wound. He began to long to find money to give her. The things he did find he preserved carefully, signs of his perseverance. A bleached "Admit One" movie ticket. A yellow cash register tape whose purple numbers had bled, a piece of string, an empty envelope, the hairy hind leg of a bug. He found a crushed four-leaf clover the color of tea, eased it out with the tip of his finger and dropped it into his breast pocket. When he left the bindery at night he lay his findings on the sill of his rooming-house room. He was surprised by the things that could fit in the bodies of books. A scrap of paper that said, "Jean, I Love You." A greasy feather. A postcard of Portland, Oregon, written all over, even straight across the picture, in a feverish, illegible hand. He stopped dead and tried to decipher it and when Fran appeared he held it out toward her and she slapped it away. "Are you stealing from me?" she shrieked. "Slanty-eyed son of a bitch!"

The next day he took an old, soft dollar from his wallet and straightened it against the table edge. It felt buff and clingy. He sniffed it guiltily and smelled metal and powdery mold and a tang from the ink, or perhaps only dirt. Then he closed his eyes and put the bill in a book and put the book back in his bin and worked all morning calmly, unexpectantly, until the bill leaped out at him and he sighed with relief. He could never have missed such a thing. He lay the book open on the table, unstripped, exactly as he'd found it, and when Fran came she snatched the bill up. "It's usually more. It's usually a big bill, like someone wouldn't want to carry, but then they forget, or they die," she said, rushing away.

The flipping sent an endless plume of dust into his face. Black scum built up in his nostrils. His hands never came clean. When he drew breath he began to make a sound like a wet rag caught in a fan. His tuberculosis had battered his lungs and he had always smoked, with the sense that the acrid smoke burned his lungs clean. Now he smoked even more, to kill the musty taste that filled his mouth, although at the back of the taste there was something he relished. Completely separate, insignificant things became linked just by coinciding in time, and together they insisted on themselves and the moment that joined them. He had no reason to think of a cheap cut-glass bowl, just $3.95 not-available-in-any-store, every time a passing truck or the trains made the bindery shudder so slightly that perhaps just his heart noticed, quickening. But he had once sat in the USIS office paging idly, longingly, through a *Time* magazine, and though he'd hardly registered what lay before him on the page when he felt the impact of the bombing, miles north, touch the chair that he sat in, later the memory of his fear was always strangely presided over by that bowl, with its white blaze of light. The smell of dust that soaked into everything, turning his pores black, weighting his clothes, brought before him the cluster of dirty fake flowers that sat in a vase on the telephone table at Strake, and the sound of her voice.

*B*y the time his first weekend arrived he had a chronic cough. It roared up from the bottoms of his lungs as if it was bringing blood and tissue with it. He'd been at the job for four days. This was when the delusion of unchanging eternity left him and his awareness of the jerky motions of time returned with renewed intensity. He woke up early on Saturday morning, and bought coffee and cigarettes and a cellophane packet of cheap stationery with matching envelopes. He was living in an arid, treeless part of the city that was mostly storage warehouses and other windowless, unpeopled places. He longed for some noise made by humans, but the streets were deserted, and he'd grown afraid that his rooming house was perfectly empty apart from him. The desolation he felt was reflected by the building itself. It was only six stories high, yet it towered over everything around it. From his window he could see the tarred rooftops stretching away in every direction, and to the north the sudden wall of skyscrapers. The lake was a pale blue line. He stood still, remembering the thrill of arrival he'd felt when he'd first glimpsed that water. Then, inspired by his eagerness to get out of the room, he wrote two perfunctory letters. They came effortlessly, like letters to strangers he never expected to meet. He had nothing to say. The first was to Bower, reporting that he had arrived safely and taken up the job and that he found Chicago very nice. He wrote on every other line, as usual, although this time to take up space more than to ensure he could be read. His script still spread across the page with mathematical precision. He felt he hadn't seen it in a long time. "I don't feel any troubles at all," he concluded, and then, with an inch left, he thanked Bower again, and signed his name.

The letter to Katherine was even emptier. "I hope you are happy and well," he wrote. It was easy. "I am enjoying myself very much." He gazed down at this performance with some amazement. But he also knew, as he carefully printed his return address in the corner of the envelope, that this was something he might have not done. He had to go outside to make sure of the building number.

The El ran north–south above State Street a few blocks away, and after he'd mailed his letters he walked to the Roosevelt stop and climbed onto the northbound platform, walking as far north as it went. He knew from his map that Chinatown lay further to the south but he didn't care. He wanted to go back into the deep canyon of buildings. Looking down through the tracks and the steel fretwork to the street far below he remembered the

Evansville bridge. The day was hot and clear and quiet. The tracks stretched straight away like a floating road, and the approaching train was visible for a long time. When it arrived he got into the first car and sat in the first seat, in the forward-facing window. The tracks vanished beneath him and the distant wall of buildings grew steadily larger until he could see where the tracks would cut through them. The level plain of roofs to either side sprouted billboards and lone oversized buildings and then the solid mass of downtown was upon them and the tracks were enclosed. Windows of offices and sweatshops and warehouses were so close to the train that he could see deep within them. Every row of windows at train level was crowded with trash, plain paper to block the view or printed advertisements or home-made signs declaring love. He couldn't choose where to look. The train was crowded now and several children pushed past him to press their faces to the front window. He had gotten on board with no clear idea of where he would get off and no real desire to, but after the train passed out the far side of downtown and shuddered through a sharp turn inland he got off and walked east along Division. At Lake Shore Drive he had to cross through a tunnel because the traffic didn't stop, and as the tunnel's mouth widened he saw a mob, hot dog carts, girls in swimsuits and floppy straw hats, bicycles, and he was standing on the beach.

He walked north, carried along by the crowds. He stopped sometimes, to gaze over the lake. It was as vast as an ocean, blue and featureless until it drew close to the shore, where it swelled with small whitecaps. In the midst of this brightness he was a thin, dark, irregular figure. He was wearing the same cheap suit, his one preserved set of clothes. He could feel the heat of the day building up in his trousers and shoes. He took off his jacket and sat on top of a picnic table facing the water, smoking. At first he'd been self-conscious, feeling overdressed and funereal, but while the gaze of every person he saw roved constantly, hungrily, no one's gaze seemed to rest on him. He was surrounded and invisible. *Dear Katherine,* he thought. *There is an ocean here.*

He didn't know how long he had been sitting this way when he felt a tap on his shoulder, and turned to see an Oriental man, his age, in an open-necked shirt with his stiff hair forced into a pompadour, speaking Japanese to him. "It's pretty good," the man said, handing him a card, and before he understood what was happening he heard his own Japanese saying "Thank you," and the man had sauntered away, looking around, with a stack of the cards in his hand. The card was printed in Japanese but it was concise and he took it in quickly—exclusive massage house, only Japanese girls, rates according to type of room and length of time, from fifteen minutes to the night. To preserve exclusiveness interested persons should inquire with the manager of the Lakeview Hotel, North Clark Street, Little Tokyo.

He didn't question whether, sitting there hunched with a cigarette, from time to time doubled over from coughing, in a cheap, dark suit on a blazing summer day staring past acres of sunbathers, anything about him other than his being Oriental had compelled the man to give him such a card; he only took the card as a clue, fallen into his hands, and he followed it. He retraced his steps to the El and asked the token seller for directions. "Welcome to Chicago!" the man said excitedly. Riders crowded the platform, red-faced from the beach, hefting shopping bags, whistling. The train came quickly and he rode it to Belmont, descending the stairs from the platform straight into an entire vegetable market packed beneath the shade cast by the tracks, Japanese women yelling at vendors, Japanese children chewing hard caramels, glowing logs of pickled radish, bricks of tofu sunk in buckets. The Lakeview Hotel was a regular boardinghouse occupied entirely by Japanese men who lined the narrow stoop, smoking, and filled the broken armchairs in the lobby. No one blinked at him. Overflowing ashtrays stood everywhere. Signs in

Japanese tacked to the walls irritably barred from the premises all unapproved women, children, dogs, filth, and gambling. He had thrown the card away outside, not wanting to be misunderstood, but now he saw the same cards scattered everywhere, and piled on the ledge of the manager's window. The rooms were half as big as his room near the bindery, with lumpy Murphy beds, fraying lamp cords, stained carpets, and they were dark, loud, fouled with cigarette smoke and mildew, and they cost more, with extra charges for hot plates and garbage removal, and just one bathroom, with no lock, per floor. "If you want a woman, you have to talk to me," the manager told him. "I'll arrange it. Bringing your own woman here would be like bringing your own food to my restaurant." He moved the same night, packing his suitcase Crane-style, by the fistful. He left his artifacts of book trash on the sill, except for the postcard from Portland and the four-leaf clover, which he closed into his dictionary, and then he returned his key and marched away from that grim, lonely place; but just before he left he printed his new address on a sheet of notepaper and left it with the manager, in case he got mail.

Now he rode the El to work, a forty-minute trip the whole length of the city, rattling, sublime, the white morning light pouring in off the lake and the gold evening light from the west. He bought novels in the Japanese bookstore and read them on the train, or lay his head against the glass and watched the complicated inexhaustible city scroll by, a landscape he could never memorize although he lovingly tried. Every morning he chose to go down to the bindery, and because he felt he didn't have to, because he was certain, now, that there were so many ways he could slip into life, he didn't mind. His room was too dark and noisy to read and so he lived outside, in tea shops and restaurants or on the steps of his hotel, a member of the legion of do-nothing smokers. One night, while he was sitting in the Belmont Noodle House with a bowl of udon and his calculus open in front of him, the waiter leaned over his shoulder to look at his book. "Hey, Einstein," he said, raising his eyebrows. And from then on, in the noodle house, and then at his hotel, and even, sometimes, on the street, the neighborhood people grinned at him. "Sensei Einstein," they said. He'd been adopted.

*H*is Japanese was grammatically arcane, the Japanese he'd been taught as a child and had done absolutely nothing to remember, but it wasn't long before the constant effort with which he kept himself thinking and speaking in English collapsed. He was submerged in the other language and he couldn't resist it. It soaked into him, found his reservoir of schoolboy Japanese and completely corrupted it. When he was asleep he dreamed in Japanese. When he was awoken by mistaken drunken banging on his door he swore filthily in Japanese before he even knew where he was. It was strange that his homesickness was banished by a place that reminded him of the only other time he had been homesick. His childhood Japanese lessons had all been aimed toward the year he would be sent to boarding school in Osaka, and when that occasion arrived he'd been fluent in the stiff, terrorized Japanese that only a foreign child would speak. He'd done miserably, an early failure he wasn't allowed to forget. "Collaboration is outweighed by opportunity," his father would lecture him. "Take the police. They have the power now, but when the Japanese leave, what do they have? The hatred of the people, and ignorance. We'll have the knowledge." His father had always known the period of Japanese rule would end, and then the country would have to remake itself. The Japanese did almost everything to hobble native leadership but they enjoyed the practice of favoritism, and that was their weakness: someday they would leave, and leave in their wake, accidentally, some educated men. If it didn't happen in his own generation, his father reasoned, it would happen in the generation after. Chang was sent to boarding school bearing the frightening weight of that national duty, and the idea that this was an exalting flame that should make fuel of misery. But he'd only been eight years old. Obedience was a reflex but duty was abstract and quickly obliterated by his desperate, inexperienced unhappiness. His careful speech was scorned, his uniform stolen; he was beaten in the bathroom and falsely accused of small crimes. And then World War II came, like a godly intervention, and he was sent home.

In Little Tokyo he was treated like a shabby aristocrat. Doing his shopping at the street market under the El he would be offered cigarettes or bean cakes or cold cans of beer. When there was an eviction notice or a jury summons he was sought out to read it and comment. "You ought to be a lawyer and quit with these numbers. We need a lawyer, not an Einstein," they said. But they seemed proud of his unpragmatic erudition. "Einstein!" people called as he passed by, in his increasingly greasy suit coat. "Sit down here. Stop walking around like a cop." On Cub game days he and the men from his hotel walked up Clark to the stadium El stop and watched the game from the platform for the cost of a token, eating bento-box lunches, drinking beer, clambering onto each other's shoulders when the action moved inevitably to the right outfield, hidden from them by the stands. They brought a transistor radio with them, and he translated the play-by-play commentary into his awkward Japanese. If these people knew he was Korean, they didn't seem to care. Arriving Filipinos were eagerly courted by Japanese massage-house proprietors, and Japanese teenagers rode the El to Chinatown to work in the restaurants. Old prejudices were irrelevant and unprofitable. Many of the families in the neighborhood who weren't new immigrants had lived in California before being interned during World War II, and their only loyalty now was to the generous Midwest, where it seemed that anyone could do anything. He felt that way, too. Obedience might be a reflex, but he'd dodged it before. He thought of his father, experimentally, and then Peterfield. They seemed as remote as Dean Bower, or Bill Crane, or Katherine Monroe. He repeated her name to himself until it sounded empty and nonsensical, an unknown thing named by an unknown, unbeautiful language. It occurred to him, for the first time in his entire life, that he didn't have to be a student. There were endless other ways to live, endless other lives he could take, without waiting for church councils or Dean Bowers or a gracious invitation. He could stay here and get another job, in a restaurant, even at a casino. The men from his hotel had taught him poker and he wasn't just good at it, he was, he dared to think, occasionally brilliant. "You've never played poker before?" they asked, incredulously.

"No," he grinned. He was winning.

"Beginner's luck."

"I think he's faking."

"If he's faking he deserves to win your money, because he's faking so well."

"We're not playing for money," one said loudly, to be overheard by the manager. They were playing for rice crackers: plain broken, plain whole, and seaweed-wrapped, which stood in for nickel, dime, and quarter. After the game they were going to the Happi Sushi Restaurant and Bar, to settle mutual debts.

"You have a poker face, Einstein. I can't believe you've never put it to its most sacred use."

"A poker face?"

"It's impossible to tell what you're thinking." A few children had gathered around where the card table sat on the sidewalk, beside the steps to the hotel. One of them, a small boy, made the rounds, examining each player's cards with great seriousness, and then withdrawing to consult with his companions, whispering behind a hand. One of the players jerked his chin at the boy. "Like that kid. He knows if he gave away anything while he was looking at our cards, we'd spank him to pieces." The table was one of the hotel's several, which lived, when not in use, folded flat against the lobby walls, or upside down with their legs sticking up, like stricken animals, on inconvenient patches of the floor.

"Do I really have a poker face?" Chuck asked.

"Absolutely." Everyone nodded in unison, their eyes fixed on their cards.

He could no longer imagine the lack of imagination he'd arrived with. At the bindery he flipped sometimes and he skipped sometimes. He stood idly at the windows and watched the South Shore trains come and go. He planted another dollar, and briefly gained Fran's confidence; but then she returned the next day, narrow again with suspicion. "I think maybe you found a big one and took it and put this small one in its place," she said, waving the dollar accusingly. He almost laughed. Why give her anything at all? He still found forgotten artifacts in books, but they no longer held pathos for him, only varying interest. He found a love letter, still holding its scent, and pressed his face to it.

He kept studying, filling yellow legal pads with calculus. He worked in ink, to preserve his rare mistakes. The problems unfurled like chains, joined into webs, propagated through space. His enjoyment was as pure as he imagined making music must be. Once he'd loved to lose himself in the particularity of a language, among the strange names for long-known and intimate things, and the strange things he had not known at all, until their names found him. Now he swept all that arcana aside. The arcana of math trumped it all. Its crystalline structure reached into the heavens and down to invisible atoms, infinite with chances and yet absolutely true, and just by knowing this, in one way he had mastered it. No threshold loomed ahead, demanding to be crossed. Nothing measured and valued his progress. He thought of what Kim had said years ago about his destiny, and laughed with amazement. *How did you know that?* he wondered, as he gazed out of the El at the grid of the city, or into the glare on the noodle shop's window. He had the sense that, after having walked upwind so long that he'd grown used to the implacable resistance, the wind had changed direction and sailed him forward. He finished the book he'd brought with him and spent one Saturday riding all over Chicago looking for another one. Any day in which he worked problems was worthy, and complete. He could not see an accumulation of understanding but he could sense it, and it buoyed him up. He remembered the time he had felt that his future depended upon performing flawlessly at a succession of gates, and being judged, and allowed to advance. This idea was no longer his. He knew what he was meant to do, and wasn't he doing it? He was surrounded by people who struggled mightily and viciously and independently each day and they took him for the thing he dreamed of being, a scholar. "Ask Einstein," they said. "He should know." At the Belmont Noodle House he was allowed to sit for hours with his books, his empty bowl shoved aside, his teacup kept endlessly full, although the restaurant had just a handful of tables. His very presence transformed the place into a library. So he was a scholar, because that was what he did. He'd discovered the power to make himself, to throw away what he hated and say what he was. He didn't think he wanted anything more.

June turned into July. This was his first Independence Day in America and he woke with a sense of occasion. Sticks of TNT were exploding up and down North Clark Street by eight in the morning. He sat on the front steps of his hotel watching as one small picnic expedition after another assembled its equipment with a flurry of holiday urgency and waddled off toward the lake. The bindery was closed. He sat on the steps until the damp late-morning heat overpowered him and then he went upstairs again.

He tried to work on his calculus but the day stretched before him, and the contented hush that lay beneath its noises. He went to the zoo in Lincoln Park and lagged from cage to cage, hands jammed in his pockets, barely aware of the animals, the heat, the ripe smell. He wandered from there to the Oak Street Beach, and from the Oak Street Beach to the Navy Pier, but everywhere he went there were people together, leaning on each other's shoulders or crouching around picnic baskets. He returned to his hotel.

It was nearly evening now, and the miscellaneous habitués of the Lakeview had begun to pull the battered card tables and metal folding chairs and plastic buckets full of ice onto the sidewalk. He hurried forward gratefully. One of his neighbors handed him a beer in a sodden paper bag. "Ready to win big, Einstein?" He just shook his head and laughed. Even among them, he felt suddenly, incurably alone. The manager was standing at the top of the steps repeating "no gambling, no gambling inside, no gambling outside," while someone elbowed past him feeding an electrical cord onto the sidewalk, and plugged in a radio. Now they heard the tinny and exalted sound of the philharmonic orchestra playing live in the park. There would be fireworks after the sun went down. When the manager saw Chuck he motioned and Chuck followed him into the sudden darkness of the lobby. "Letter for you. It came yesterday but I didn't see you, always slipping in and out, Mr. Quiet." The envelope had a Sewanee postmark and no return address. From the date he could see it had languished at his old rooming house a long time before being forwarded. June 11, 1956. He turned it over and read, scrawled carelessly across the flap, *Addison.*

Dear Mr. Ahn,
 I didn't know you had arranged to spend your summer in Chicago, but now that I do I must congratulate you on your wisdom in getting

away from this sleepy mountain to someplace where there's a little life. Chicago is a terrific city, as I remember it, although I'm ashamed to admit I haven't been there in years.

I'm writing to thank you on Katherine's behalf for your letter. I assume you didn't know she's returned to New Orleans, where her mother is ill. I've sent your letter on to her there. It was thoughtful of you to write and I really do encourage you to continue. Any news from her friends cheers her up.

On a happier note, it occurs to me that Katherine and I might soon find ourselves indebted to you for solving a dilemma. So far we've had no luck agreeing on what city should have the honor of hosting our wedding. Now that you've brought up Chicago, though, I can't imagine a better place. Best,

At the bottom, her New Orleans address.

*T*he next day, Fran was waiting for him. "I came here yesterday and I cleaned books for an hour and you know what I found?" He was shaking his head, and when she snapped a ten-dollar bill before his face with both hands, he kept shaking it.

"You dirty shifty lying little punk," she said. "I'm going to get you."

All that afternoon he hardly saw what he did. With his mind so distracted his earliest habits returned, and he flipped through each volume languidly, hearing the distant flutter of the pages and the broad ripping sound as he pulled off the covers. He might not have even looked down, but out the east windows, into the blinding glare beneath which he knew was the field of tracks for the Illinois Central. The day was so still he thought he could hear the sounds of the bindery filtering down to him: the dirty edges of the books being shaved off, the rhythmic punctures from the stitching machines. For the rest of the day Fran left him in peace. She never once came to disturb him.

He had read Addison's letter so many times he'd memorized it inadvertently, and the sound of that man's voice was more present to him than the sounds of himself as he worked. He felt change impending. His life here was shrinking, relinquishing space to what had always lay around it. He had known, at the back of his intoxicating happiness here, that he would never really stay. He already saw this room as he would in the future, remembering it. The sun receded and then the rail yard was visible, gleaming like a river. South of the city its tributaries branched off, the South Shore Line clinging to the lakeshore, the other lines reaching everywhere like roots to the east, west, and south. He drifted back to the bin and fished a new book out of it with the dustpan stuck onto the end of the broom. He was working very slowly. He might not even reach the bottom of the sack. The pages softly riffled in his hands and sent a puff of dust upward. His face was turned toward the window and he didn't cough; still, he had seen something, and when he flipped back, a hundred-dollar bill stood in the crease. He took the bill out and examined it closely, never having seen one before. Ben Franklin was on the front: scientist, printer, inventor, a brash unruly person. On the back of the bill was a fastidious drawing of a building labeled Independence Hall. It was not yet five o'clock. The bill was stiff, but it was also wrinkled. It might have been there any length of time. He lifted his chin, trying to listen harder, but now he heard nothing. When he went to the door and looked behind it there was nobody there. He folded the bill, regretting marring it this way, and walked out the loading doors to the street and rode the El back north to Little Tokyo with the gold western light pouring on him. He used to think there was only one door, only one right answer to a problem. He hadn't understood how many solutions were possible, awaiting the equations that would bring them into being. And so he did this, without caring to know how things might have been different, if he had found the money a week before he got the letter, or a week after, or not at all; if he had found the money and never gotten the letter, or if the letter had been from a different person, or of a different kind, without that supremely self-confident tone, which seemed to betray something.

eleven

Katherine didn't have the things to do that a normal bride would. She was dismantling a life, not assembling one. She began to clean her house, trying to separate the impersonal, constant landscape from its intimate occupants. Bravely entering the house every morning she would think of what a simple task this was: papers would be packed, and clothing and books and knickknacks, while furniture could stay. The garden hose belonged to the house, but all the envelopes of unplanted seeds were her own legacy. The heavy armoire stayed but her little chest of drawers with the crudely painted morning glory trim was coming with her. Every day by lunchtime her belief in the simplicity of the task was defeated again. She wondered more and more often, always with a childish sense of the wrongness of the thought, why she couldn't just stay in her house. Either that or walk away and leave it holding its breath, preserving the warm spaces between things, in the hopes that she'd return. The pools of light from the library's lamps would reappear every night and fade away every morning, like moons. She put off packing and contented herself with emptying one room at a time, herding everything into a narrowing space. Downstairs it became difficult to walk. End tables and rocking chairs stood in the hallway, the library's books moved out of the shelves into boxes that stood everywhere stacked in twos and threes, their flaps unsealed, where she tripped over them. Charles came one afternoon and stood silently in the kitchen, amid nested saucepans and piles of plates and appliances that covered the counters and much of the floor. She had emptied all the cabinets, to see what there was. This house held a past version of himself he particularly cherished, to which no witnesses survived apart from these rooms. Whole decades of his life belonged to a time he could never discuss with her, not merely because she hadn't shared them but because the child she had been inevitably appeared at the periphery of his memory, as self-contained and solemn as an animal, dragging her doll across the room, sitting in the privacy of a shrub, and newly shocked him. He disliked what she was doing. Left alone, the house could contain the events of countless lifetimes invisibly, but now she'd kicked up all that sediment. And the house reminded them of something else that made them angry at each other. "Do you need any help here?" he asked when she came into the kitchen, wearing a huge old shirt he recognized instantly as having been her father's.

"No." She knew he didn't want to be here while she did this.

"Have you written your mother yet?"

All the while that she worked, she was afflicted with this letter to her mother. Her mind produced incessant variations and nothing that she thought of drowned them out. *I suppose this is the one thing you always feared most; I suppose this is the one thing I needed to do before you would forgive me; Dear Mother; Dear Mommy; Dear Glee.*

"No," she said. She wiped her hands on her shirt and left the room again.

❧

*T*he day she saw Chang at services she had finally stopped putting it off. Her mortification desperately needed some show of resolve to obscure it, and she marched back to her house in the afternoon, both ashamed of herself for what she'd said to him, and newly determined. She found her writing things sitting in the top of an unsealed box, her old blotter rolled up and her pen in its scratched metal case. She picked her way up the stairs through dust-filled cones of light to her bare, freshly dusted desk, in a room otherwise occupied now only by a stripped bed and an unwashed set of curtains floating gently in the breeze from the window, and wrote out the letter. It did not come as close as possible to expressing her actual feelings. She suspected it came nowhere near. She wrote what occurred to her, abandoning all her plans for eloquence, afraid that if she paused she'd lose her nerve. She abandoned "The art of the letter is not about expression, but persuasion." This was something her mother had taught her. Lead with your wrists when you dance. Never sound opinionated, only amused and indulgent. Carry your rib cage as high as you can and you'll look twice as slender. The loss of her mother rose up from where she tried to keep it, delimited but in no way diminished. She had been her mother's only daughter, and yet they had each failed to experience this bond. She wrote, "I'm not proud of my various failures. I have been a bad daughter, a bad student, a bad example of the independent woman. I have never been independent at all." What was more selfish, to struggle ineffectually against the tide, or to try and find a way to make it carry you forward, no matter how harmful a force it might seem? The cliché made her cringe but she didn't try to do better. Clichés were one of the worst sorts of truth and it was this category, the category of lousy, hackneyed truths, that she now occupied. The more she savaged herself as she wrote, the more confident she became that she was reporting plain facts. She was weak, she lacked courage, she lacked imagination. Her entire life exemplified the failure of imagination. Her situation was only redeemed by the fact that she had recognized it, and also recognized that truths could not be forced into existence out of hopes; they had to be found, scattered where they were, camouflaged to fit the background of the unremarkable. The truth was puny and disappointing but it was there. It didn't send you borrowing against the ungenerous future. She went back downstairs and pulled a bloom off the coral honeysuckle. "Here is one of your bright flowers," she finished, putting the flower in the envelope. She remembered her mother standing in the kitchen, wrists propped on her hips because her hands were still wet from the dishes, watching a hummingbird bounce through those flowers. "Look at this!" she'd cried. "Look at this cute little thing!"

It wasn't until after she'd mailed the letter that she imagined her mother receiving it. She would stride out to the postbox with a glass of iced tea for the mailman. Katherine remembered her embarrassment at this habit of her mother's, to lie in wait for the mailman and ambush him with talk and refreshment. Glee would prop an elbow between the spears of the black iron fence and toy with the hedge or tap her foot restlessly on the flagstones until the mailman had finished his drink, as if she were the one who'd been waylaid. Beyond this Katherine did not know what would happen. The letter now seemed vulgar, even insane. Each moment she had imagined as a final threshold had only complicated her emotions. She began to wait for the mailman herself, going repeatedly to the front windows all morning until she saw his car inching up to her house, and as soon as he'd passed out of sight she practically ran down the drive. She was disappointed every day that she found nothing, but also relieved. Perhaps her mother had thrown the letter away without opening it. Perhaps her mother was more offended by having been told than she would have been if Katherine had left her in peace. Katherine had always associated such maddening issues of protocol with her mother, and her mother's stringent, elaborate, always-disappointed expectations.

Then she received her reply. When she saw the envelope lying by itself in the shadows of the mailbox, the same pale blue engraved kind her mother had used ever since Katherine could remember, since she was a little girl and had thought her mother's writing table was an inexhaustibly interesting place to play, she started to cry. She stood at the end of her front walk, in her bare feet and the big man's shirt, which was thoroughly filthy, crying. She wiped her face on her sleeve and looked up the walk at her house, seeing it the way she might have seen it if she had gone away for decades and finally returned, to be amazed by the smallness of the closets she had once hidden in, and the shabbiness of everything. She had wanted Chang to say No, don't get married, don't be stupid, pack a bag and meet me later, when everybody is asleep. And how often did that happen? He had come from a distant land, and to her that was lighter than air. He always looked as if he'd briefly dropped out of an airplane, standing thin and transient in his dark suit, a glaring interruption in the background of the unremarkable. She had wanted to step inside that circle. And now here was the letter, ratifying her engagement. That sleek pastel square could not possibly contain anything but bland, unaffected acquiescence. She had wanted outrage, dispute, something that she had to fight against. She did not know how else to be sure of herself. She finally reached for the letter and realized she didn't recognize the hand.

Inside she mixed herself a drink. This was another imitation of her mother, complete with the haughty face which was supposed to conceal how eager she was to be drunk. Katherine sipped her drink haughtily, raising her eyebrows very slightly as it hit her. Then she slit open the envelope. There was the violet-pattern envelope lining, and the fussy notepaper. The letter was from a person named Mary Frances, who identified herself as the housekeeper, and it said, in a sloppy hand which Katherine immediately saw as evidence of carelessness, that Mrs. Monroe was much too sick right now to feel like bothering with composing a letter and wanted to know ("Mrs. Monroe is dictating this") if Katherine couldn't come down to New Orleans and talk about things face to face.

She lay the letter down and finished her drink. Then she poured herself a fresh one and went to the telephone. When the woman answered she said, "Who is this?"

"This is Mary Frances," the woman drawled carelessly. "Who is *this*?"

"How is Mrs. Monroe today?"

"She's sleeping. I don't think I heard your name."

"This is her daughter, Katherine."

"Oh," the woman said, in a tone that managed to be both obsequious and insinuating. "Shall I go tell her you're on the line?"

"Absolutely not. When she wakes up you tell her I'm coming down and that I'd like her to fire you. I'll be there tomorrow at lunchtime."

The woman laughed heartily. "Oh, she said you're a firebrand." She kept laughing.

"Will you tell her what I said?"

"Sure I will. She likes me, though." The woman's unconcerned laughter made Katherine bristle. She hung up and started to pack.

Mary Frances had positioned herself to be lavishly framed by the front porch wisteria, and had been there since the earliest limit of what could be interpreted as lunchtime, so that when Katherine arrived she was not even able to sit in the car for a while being shocked by the unchanged face of the house, serene beneath the murky yellow heat. During the drive the possibility that Glee was going to die had elevated Katherine into the realm of abstract catastrophe, but now that she had raced to this place, accomplishing her one clear imperative, the particularity of her situation overwhelmed her. After several seconds of intensely hating the person who must be Mary Frances, she decided she was glad for the distraction. As she came tottering up the walk with her bags Mary Frances called out, "I'm afraid I'm still here, Miss Monroe."

The house was full of newly cultivated prettiness that signified the departures of children, and widowhood. The rooms had new rugs on the floors that replicated real Victorian rugs from the collections of the Smithsonian Institution. Katherine was relieved to find at least the inside of the house this strange and standoffish. But the big bay window at the back of the parlor stood open, and the smell of honeysuckle came in, along with the more rancid scent of the magnolia petals that lay bruised and rotten all over the walkways like bleached banana peels. The garden smell overpowered her with its absolute sameness, which cut across everything. She stood behind Mary Frances, enduring the assault of Mary Frances's disquisition on the recent renovations only because Mary Frances was mostly addressing herself to the walls, which had been newly papered. She had not missed the implication in Mary Frances's exhaustive inventory, that this lovely project, which she, Mary Frances, had been thrilled to have a hand in, was the kind of thing a mother generally got help in from her daughter. Mary Frances had not offered to take her bags. Katherine put the bags down on the Smithsonian carpet and then she smelled a cigarette and heard her mother's voice say, "There you are, Kitty. Katherine." Her mother had come halfway downstairs and stood supporting herself on the banister with the heel of one hand, and holding her cigarette pinched between two fingers. Her hair was a fine, iridescent cloud around her head.

"I've been showing her the changes, Mrs. Monroe."

"I could hear you." Glee pulled carefully on her cigarette and released a thread of smoke. Her whole diminished figure was an otherworldly yellow, the shade of buttermilk. Her nails were unpainted and this made the hands look young and unfinished, except for the marblelike knuckles. "I thought over what you said, Katherine, but I can't let Mary Frances go because she remembers every word that I say. Isn't that a rare thing? I believe there are the makings of a cold lunch in the icebox which you could begin to assemble, Mary Frances. Unless Katherine has eaten in some colorful roadside café."

When Mary Frances was gone Katherine said, "She made me think you were very sick."

"Try not to look so disappointed. I knew you wouldn't come if I just asked."

"I certainly would have come, if you'd asked. You only ever needed to ask."

"That's very Katherine. I know you are completely reasonable so long as everybody else is. We only need to be reasonable, isn't that right? That's what you're waiting for. Reasonableness." This announcement exhausted her. "I thought I would appeal to your dramatic sensibility. Katherine Nightingale speeds to the rescue. I thought it was very sweet that you tried to fire Mary Frances. But she is my Boswell. I must have her follow me around or I wouldn't be sure I existed."

When they were sitting at lunch Glee said, "Shall I tell you how we live here, these days? I rise with the birds and Mary Frances and I take a turn in the garden before it gets hot. You are welcome to join in with us if you're up but you shouldn't feel bad if you're not. I hardly sleep anymore and Mary Frances must catch her rest when I don't need her. Then I rest until lunchtime. We usually eat lunch around noon. We waited this meal for you. After lunch we do the mail and then I take more rest. We eat supper whenever it gets dark because the heat kills my appetite. If that doesn't suit you Mary Frances can fix you something earlier, but you need to tell her after lunch because in the afternoons I generally let her go have her fun. You're in your old room. You ought to feel free to do as you please. Mary Frances will find you a map if you don't remember your way around town. They've put some new roads in but all the old ones are still there."

"I don't think I'll want to go out."

"That's fine."

"Don't you want to talk with me?"

"Yes I do, Katherine. I will speak to you tonight after supper."

"What are you doing until then?"

"I just told you, didn't I? We are busy all day until then." She watched her mother stalk slowly out of the dining room and back up the stairs, with her poker-stiff back and one hand squeezing dents in Mary Frances's upper arm.

Mary Frances had succeeded to the position of mailman-ambassadrix. After taking Glee upstairs she established herself in one of the grapevine rockers beneath the porch wisteria, and when the mailman arrived she advanced partway down the walk and let him meet her there. It seemed that he no longer got a refreshment. Katherine watched the transaction through the French window in her old room. When Mary Frances had released the mailman and come back indoors with her precious cargo Katherine pushed the window open and stepped onto the second-story porch. There were no chairs here. She could see in the fine clay-colored layer of dust on the boards the marks that a rainstorm had left. There were bits of acorn from the spreading oak that shadowed the front garden and reached over the iron-work fence to lock its branches with the trees that lined the street.

This porch did not seem to be used anymore. In her childhood it had been the children's porch, where they were allowed to sit up past their bedtime on party nights, with their radio playing very quietly, slurping important-looking drinks full of ice cubes and food dye. Glee would leave her guests to come and drop a sprig of mint in each of their glasses and kiss them goodnight, smelling strongly of lilac perfume and cosmetic powder, her eyes and lips standing out startlingly. Below them, on the lower porch, the laughter grew more riotous as the hush in the street deepened. From the upper porch there was a patch of sky visible between the trees where they could see the constellations turning by, and understand how late it really was. Katherine had been five or six then. She could remember the soft hiss of the radio, a universe of desolated space trapped inside that sturdy box.

She could hear Mary Frances reading the mail to her mother. If she had crawled quietly down the length of the porch she could have looked into her mother's curtained room. But her mother had turned her depletion into a regime, and this made the house a place of muffled chambers divided by impenetrable barriers, linked by very few gates that opened up only at designated hours. Everything breathed the grim determination to make privacy, and although Mary Frances's voice carried easily through the thin walls, emoting luncheon invitations, thank-you notes, appeals from genteel charities, Katherine felt the repellent force of her mother's room. This was a good sign, if it meant her own room would be treated with the same fanatical formality. Where her mother had once expressed herself with unrestrained intrusions into the world's business, she now expressed herself with empresslike indifference. As it turned out, Katherine was never called to dinner. She ventured downstairs as soon as it was dark enough to have to light the lamps, and the meal was being laid out, just as she'd been told.

Once they were seated Glee held her fork with the tines curving down and pushed her food into neat configurations on her plate. When she wasn't doing this she reached for her cigarette. "You're still looking pretty and thin," she said. "Although someone has laid siege to your hair."

"I cut it."

"What for? Were you in a renunciatory mood?"

"It's not that short."

"You always did veer unpredictably between hedonism and renunciation. Do you know what Mary Frances said to me yesterday after you called?"

"I don't see how I could."

"She said she thought you were drunk."

"I was."

"And I said, 'Oh, no, Katherine would never get drunk. She has been living like a Jesuit for years, denying herself all the pleasures of normal human intercourse. If she's drunk things are looking very up or very down.'"

"I was packing up the house and getting ready to move."

Glee ignored the obvious meaning of this statement. "That reminds me of some business I want to discuss with you." Glee spoke in a condescendingly indulgent tone, as if Katherine were a coed on vacation from her first term at college and afflicted with the false impression that she had grown up. "Daddy and I bought a house down on the coast after we stopped going up to Sewanee, but then we hardly used it at all. It was a very cute place, and the doctors thought the Gulf air would be good for your father but of course they were wrong about that." She reached for her cigarette and came back with nothing but the foul-smelling, smoldering filter. "Call Mary Frances."

"Why?"

"Because I need a cigarette."

"I can get your cigarette for you."

"No. Mary Frances will do it."

"Why do you need to bother Mary Frances when I'm perfectly able to stand up and get you your cigarette?"

"Don't start in with me, Katherine. I've invited you beneath my roof. Don't you start in with me."

"I need to talk to you," Katherine said, ignoring Mary Frances's grin when she entered the room.

"You'll talk when I'm finished. I told you I had business to discuss." Glee broke off as Mary Frances lit her a fresh cigarette. "Do you know what I think, Mary Frances? I think I've eaten about as much as I want. Now this little house, none of your brothers want it. They all have their own summer houses. I suppose this little house is too plain and inconspicuous for them. As I recall, it's just an unpainted place on the channel, with a fishing dock and a porch. You can hardly see it until you're practically on top of it. That's the sort of place I prefer, a natural-looking place that does not sit lording it over the beauty of its location, but your brothers are all married to women who find my simple tastes rather dowdy and laughable. Do you know your brothers' wives?"

"No, Mother. You've told them all I was cheap."

"I told them no such thing. You never did get very close with your brothers, did you? I would have thought that would be a girl's dream come true, to have so many handsome big brothers. But you never seemed to feel that way. I adore my boys but every single one of them has married the same sort of striving, showy, strong-headed girl."

"That's a strange coincidence."

"I think it's very sad, myself. But my concern is with this little house. Your brothers have all been out to see it because I offered to give it to them first, for a fishing camp or something fun like that, and they say it has grown derelict from the damp and the last hurricane and that I ought to tear it down and sell the lot."

"Maybe you ought to do that."

"I don't want to do that. I have a strong attachment to that house. After your father and I stopped going to Sewanee I felt as though the best part of my life had died. That was a terrible loss. And then we found this place and something about it fit around us like the shell around the egg. I think your brothers said it was in terrible shape so that I'd feel less bad they weren't taking it from me, but I want to see for myself."

"Why? What will that accomplish?"

"'Why?'" Glee repeated, derisively. "I have things I need to settle, and this is one of them. I'd like to see it settled right."

"What does this have to do with me?"

"Do you think we are all gathered here to devote ourselves to you? Do you think that your so-called engagement is at the center of my thoughts every minute? I have a world of concerns, Katherine. I will address your particular one when I'm able."

"Then what am I doing here? You lured me with a pile of nonsense about being so ill you couldn't pick up a pen."

"Do I look well to you?" Glee cried out.

"No," she said, after a moment.

"I'm going to die, Kitty. Katherine. I'm going to die and it's going to be pretty soon." She snatched her napkin out of her lap and wiped her eyes. "Oh, goddamn you to hell! You make me so angry."

"You are not going to die."

"Oh, yes I am."

"Don't let me hear things like this," Katherine said gently.

"Doctor will be here tomorrow for his weekly look-at-me-and-lie. You ask him when I'm in the next room. He'll level with you. I told him you were coming. I told him my daughter was coming to help out her mama."

"I will help you."

"I think I'll go to bed now." Glee wrapped her hand around the back of the chair and pulled herself rigidly upright. "Call Mary Frances for me." She was completely composed again.

"I thought you wanted to talk after supper."

"I didn't foresee we'd speak so much during supper," Glee said.

*D*octor came. He was young and handsome, animated right out of the bright new wallpaper-background of the renovated unremarkable. With one glance at him Katherine could see all the ways in which Glee would complain about him later. Glee became spirited and uncooperative—"Oh, no you don't!" she cried when he brought out the stethoscope. She batted a translucent hand at him. "He wants to put the cold thing on me," she told Katherine, "when I think it's plain to all of us standing here that my heart is still beating. Get that cold thing away." She made Katherine hold her hand while the doctor slid the instrument under her blouse and averted his eyes. "You had better not leave me alone with this child," she told Katherine. Katherine sensed that Mary Frances had once performed this function, but Mary Frances had been sent out of the room. "This boy is so young he retains the fraternity-house way of thinking. I'm going to send you away and ask for your father again," she warned the doctor, who grinned appreciatively. "My father is itching to get back on his rounds," the doctor said. "He's so senile he forgets he's retired. I'll send him right to you."

"If he knew you were talking that way about him he would whip you. Somebody ought to." The doctor laughed, and had to take her heart rate again. Then he said, "Question time," and Glee held up a hand.

"Kitty, go and tell Mary Frances to set up lunch in the garden. I feel like being outside."

Katherine waited downstairs for the doctor and when he emerged they shook hands. "How sick is she?" The doctor gave her a guarded, heroic look and Katherine said, "Don't do that, please."

"She's terminally ill. It's a cancer in the marrow of her bones."

"Will it kill her?"

"Yes. Maybe not this year."

"But maybe this year?"

"It's impossible to say right now. I'm not concealing anything from you. She's in what we call remission."

"I know what that means."

"Then you know it could go on for a year or more or it could give way next month. Remission's like a house of cards. You can never tell when it's going to collapse but you know that it will." He was packing his bag, and when he looked up again his gaze swept her. "It's a real pleasure to meet you. I didn't know Mrs. Monroe had a daughter."

"They don't talk about me since I went to prison."

The doctor laughed loudly. Imperfectly concealed in that sound she heard Glee's door creak open. "That's very funny."

"Good afternoon," she said.

They did not have lunch outside after all. Glee took a tray in her room. She lay back on her mountain of pillows and leveled the tray with a look of disgust. Katherine moved idly around the room, fingering the curtains and the handles on the dresser. The curtains were drawn. Sometimes a puff of air forced its way in and they rose slightly. "You asked him, didn't you?" Glee asked. "I heard him positively roaring with laughter."

"He wasn't laughing at that."

"What was he laughing at, then?"

"I said you'd never told him about me because ever since I'd gone to prison the family tried not to mention me."

"I never told him about you because my family relations are none of his business. His business is to make me get better."

"He doesn't seem to think he can do that."

"Stop pacing, Katherine."

"There are no chairs in here."

"There are no chairs because I can't stand people sitting in my bedroom and staring at me as if I were an invalid."

"I'll go, then."

"Come back here. When are you taking me to Kingfisher's Perch?"

"What in the world are you talking about?"

"The little coast house. Your daddy and I called it Kingfisher's Perch. When are we going there?"

"I can't take you there, Mother."

"Yes you can. You're going to."

"I have to go back to Sewanee."

"No you don't."

"What do you mean, 'No I don't'?"

"You may think you do, but you don't. You don't know anything. What do you need to go back to Sewanee for, when you've been there for ten years doing nothing? I could not believe your father willed you that house. I begged him not to. After he died I was going to turn that house upside down and shake it until you fell out, and then it turned out he willed it to you."

"I'm going back to Sewanee."

"Can I say something else? I know you must think making some joke about going to prison is very witty, but it isn't. It humiliates me. You don't talk about my family that way, in my house. You forget that the trash you say about yourself because you lack self-respect is going to reflect upon me. I won't have it. I won't have your flippancy. It's one of the ugliest things about you."

"I'm going." She pulled the door open and Glee said, "Kitty. I'm sorry. I know that nickname annoys you but it is carved on my heart."

She stood a while, just breathing steadily, and crushing the doorknob in her palm. Finally she said, "What is it?"

"He told you, didn't he?"

"Yes, he did."

"Will you please take me to Kingfisher's Perch? It is not much to ask."

"I can take you. I only wonder why no one else could do it."

"No one else could do it because I want you to do it."

"All right."

"When?"

"Soon. I can't stay here all summer."

"I'm certainly not asking you to. That's settled, then. We'll go soon."

But then they couldn't go soon, because Glee grew worse. The summer heat intensified, and she began to have trouble sleeping. Katherine ventured into town to shop for air conditioners. She was amazed by the sameness of New Orleans, and her own familiarity with it. At traffic lights her mind seemed to curl up behind her eyes like a cat in the sun. It could register warmth and nothing else. Then the light would turn and she would be gliding through the hostile city traffic, bumping over streetcar rails, squinting into the glare, seeing nothing. She didn't get lost. In the first store the owner was a man slightly older than herself, fleshy and tan, with tufts of black hair coming out of his collar at the nape of his neck. He was cutting keys. When she asked if he carried air conditioners he grinned first at her breasts and then at her unjeweled hands, holding her pocketbook, and kept screaming the new key against the saw blade.

"Did you hear me?" she asked.

"Sure."

"Do you have them?"

"Don't you like the heat?" he asked, and laughed protestingly as she left. But at the next store she found herself gamely flirting with the half circle of paunchy men who were seated talking there, on huge spools of garden hose or stacked car batteries. "Hi there, darlin'," they said, and she smiled.

"Whose darling am I?"

"Whose do you want to be?"

"Oh, I can't choose," she said.

Glee rejected the air conditioner because as far as she was concerned the air that came from those machines was like the breath of the dead, and so Katherine went back to the store and bought a pair of oscillating fans, and these sat on either side of Glee's bed like sentinels, humming night and day, endlessly scanning the room. To avoid the ubiquitous ears of Mary Frances, Katherine called Charles from the pay phone in the lobby of the Charles Hotel. "I'm in the Charles," she said, when he picked up. "I asked for you at the front desk but there is some kind of misunderstanding, because they haven't got a bit of you here."

"My sweetie," he said. "Do you want a bit of me?"

"Yes," she heard herself saying. She was thinking of something else. She was thinking of buying a box of éclairs, and wondering if Glee would eat one.

"How is Glee?"

"Very bad. I can't come back yet."

"How has it been to see her?"

"Do you know what? I'm in the only phone box. I'm going to write and tell you the whole story, but I can't now. I'll call again soon. I can't call from there, there's a housekeeper."

"Your voice sounds lovely. I miss you."

"I miss you, too," she said automatically.

The first few days that she'd spent in New Orleans she was so sensitive to time she thought she'd gone mad. Every minute that passed taxed her awareness with its swarms of detail and its cadaverousness. Every minute lay there and wouldn't yield to the next minute, and the hours went on for days. And then, without warning, the time began to sluice by in great featureless sheets. Her mind permanently curled into that warm New Orleans blankness. In the mornings she bought fresh brioches to bring back to the house, or sat alone in a café. She began to monitor the transformations going on in the garden. She helped Mary Frances stake the top-heavy peonies. "Before I worked for your mama I worked for this awful old woman," Mary Frances would commence, and Katherine no longer was impatient to escape her. She listened to the chronicles of Mary Frances's life in service, confirmed Mary Frances's opinions of the relative refinement of one lady, or household, or city, as opposed to another. She encouraged Mary Frances to exercise her full powers as a chef, and then spent days grocery shopping in attempts to acquire the ingredients Mary Frances demanded. Now that time was an indistinct force she could barely perceive, Katherine sank into a black, sexless sleep every night and in the mornings she stepped into the changeless regime of the house. She stood in Glee's room for hours with her, reading and interpreting the mail. *Mrs. Joseph Monroe's presence is desired.* "Oh, we've never liked those people!" Glee would cry. Each time Katherine assented, and then reread the invitation, so that the venue of the upcoming event could be extensively disparaged. She found she drew as much pleasure from playing the role of the dutiful daughter as anyone who has ever discovered they are more free to behave like themselves when they wear a disguise.

When Katherine came to see her one morning, Glee was anxious and distracted. The delicate skin beneath her eyes had turned as violet as a bruise. "I'm so tired, baby," she said. "I don't sleep at all."

"Yes, you do. You can't lie there all night wide awake. I came in early this morning and you were dozing."

"Was I? I don't think so. I heard you open the door."

"I must have wakened you then."

"I don't think so. You were wearing that strawberry-pattern wrap I gave you. You looked pretty in it."

"Thank you."

"There. That's a nice answer." From outside they heard Mary Frances calling out to the mailman. Glee sighed and looked at the ceiling. "I want to settle something with you."

"Don't you start talking that way," Katherine said chidingly.

"No lightness." Looking at her mother Katherine flushed suddenly and turned away. "You don't have to look at me but you have to listen."

"I am."

"I want you to know that your father hated me for the way I was with you. He never understood it, and that's what I wanted. He never knew about you. He thought I was vicious and he thought I was a terrible mother and I let him, because I never wanted him to know the fault was yours. If he had ever found out about it I planned to tell him Charles had raped you."

Katherine stared at her. "You wouldn't dare."

"I certainly would. And I kept us away from Sewanee. I didn't trust you to keep your own secret."

"Stop it, Mommy."

"You couldn't keep a secret if someone lifted the lid of your brain and dropped it in there without your even knowing. You would open your mouth and blurt it out. Or you would show it in your behavior. Your behavior always damned you."

She stood up, her face streaming. "Are you finished?"

"No, I'm not. If you're going to marry Charles Addison I'd prefer you do it after I'm dead."

"That's ridiculous."

"I said I'd prefer it. I'm well aware you'll do what you please."

She went down the stairs, over the fine carpet, out the back door and into the garden. The air seemed to vibrate with bees. The sun blazed distantly at the back of a perfectly clear, bleached noon sky. She didn't know why she had thought, sliding into a new normalness, that a moment like this wouldn't come. She walked up and down the narrowed pathways, bumping the overgrown plants, holding her ribs as she sobbed. The heat was so intense that the streets were deserted and the day almost silent, and she was determined to add no sound to it. Gradually the tranquil upper chamber of her mind began to notice how narrow the walk seemed, and how unmysterious its pattern was, compared to what she'd thought as a child. As a child she would sit here all day. She caught a glimpse of the way she'd seen then, a quick exposure like a camera's shutter opening, her brown child's legs against the rough red of the bricks. Then she heard footsteps behind her and Mary Frances saying, experimentally, "Miss Kitty?"

She turned around. "If you call me that again I'll murder you," she said, wiping her face.

"This ought to cheer you up. It's a letter."

The letter from Chang was nested inside the letter from Charles, unopened. "I'm sorry I didn't send this on sooner," Charles wrote, "but I kept thinking you would be back." Chang's letter was a month old, and postmarked Chicago. She tore it open and read four meticulous lines: "I am writing to you from Chicago, where I am enjoying myself very much. I will spend the summer here. I have the luck of an interesting job." She recognized that tone. A whole letter had been composed, assembled, and mailed to transmit to her that arctic, careless tone. She sat down in the arbor and smiled. Well, she thought. Well.

twelve

He left Chicago the way he'd arrived, sitting halfway down the length of a Greyhound bus with his single suitcase under his feet. This was his great American talent. The bus sailed southward. It had to stop constantly, but he knew by now that the bus was a humble way to travel and he loved its stops and its exhausted refuelings, the dramas of departure and reunion, the ragged end of someone else's travel trailing past him down the steps. He moved happily amid the ever-changing ranks of the brotherhood of smokers. They stopped in the buggy pools of light of small towns and in the antiseptic white glares of small cities. Wherever they were he bought a fresh pack of cigarettes and walked the small island that the bus spread beneath itself, its outer limit defined by the sound of the bus's motor idling. The gravel by the sides of roads was gray, veined, quartz; the people he saw were suspicious or distracted or, like him, they were exalted. He paced with his nose down, his cigarette unraveling, gazing. So many decisions that cannot be endured sink out of sight, but they persist, carving subterranean channels for themselves, dropping their silt, growing clear and defined. He had awakened one morning at the end of such a journey and now his body was repeating it, hungrily.

After seventy hours the bus—it was not the same bus, or the same driver, but it was, it was a segment of a vein of a system that embraced the world and to be inside the vein was to be all of it, an atom touching each part of the whole, like the oceans of the world, like the air—passed over the Lake Pontchartrain bridge and arrived in New Orleans. He had not slept more than a few accidental hours at a stretch. He didn't want to sleep, he didn't want to be robbed of his part in the whole. He hadn't bathed or shaved or eaten anything apart from the cellophane-wrapped confections in the bus station vending machines, the festively nomadic candied peanuts and marshmallow pies. He didn't know what he was going to do when he got off the bus. He trusted the subterranean movements to which he'd sacrificed all his prior thoughts and hesitations, like the great explorer who allows his discovery to remake him. He got off the bus and walked into the hot waiting room, full of flies, sticky pools of Coca-Cola, the taut beginnings and the ragged ends of travel, and sat down in one of the pews, sliding his suitcase beneath his feet. He was a fearless, invisible citizen of these places now. With no bus to climb onto again his mind relaxed its vigilance and he plunged into sleep, his head dropping onto his chest.

He was awakened by a man in shirtsleeves, who pressed his shoulder insistently. "Hey there. Hello." His voice was flat, northern. "Can you get up and come with me, please? Can you wake up now?"

He lifted his head with tremendous effort and peered at the man through a narrow fissure in the weight of his slumber. For a moment he had no idea where he was. He frowned.

"Speak English? Speakee English?" the man asked him loudly. Another man stood behind him, wearing a jacket, looking overheated and weary.

"Yes," he said.

"Can you come with me, please?"

He followed the men into a back office of the station, pulling a hand through his hair. He had cut it very short in Chicago because it was always filling with dust from the books. Now it stood off his head in greasy tufts. The office was hardly larger than a closet. A janitor's pail and mop leaned in a corner, giving off a sharp smell of mold. The jacketed man went to the one window, which was closed, and fought with it irritably, as if this was something he did often. The window was swollen shut. A ceiling fan stirred the air. The shirtsleeved man pointed to a chair and he sank into it, clutching his suitcase. "Where are you going?"

"Nowhere," he said. "I just come here. I have just come here."

"Where from?"

"Chicago."

"Chicago," the man repeated, flatly. "How did you travel?"

"On the Greyhound bus."

"Do you have your ticket?"

"No," he said. The ticket had been a thick accordion, Chicago–Champagne, Champagne–Cedar Rapids, Cedar Rapids –St. Louis, every leg commencing with the achievement of shedding one layer, and in Jackson, Mississippi, he had joyfully surrendered his last printed card—TO NEW ORLEANS—like tumbling over a cliff. "No, you give it in on the bus."

"Are you a Chinese national?" the man asked him. "Are you familiar with the Port Security Program? Are you an able-bodied seaman?"

"A what?"

"Are you an able-bodied seaman?"

He shook his head in bafflement. He thought he'd never been so hungry. The flies threw themselves against the closed window and fell stunned to the floor. "Are you a member of the Communist party?" the man asked him. "Are you or have you ever been associated with a known member of the Communist party? Do you have family or friends in New Orleans? Is someone expecting you here?"

She was sitting in her garden, toying with a string of columbine, pulling off the blossoms and eating them. They looked like jester's caps. And then a thin shadow blunted the daylight glare, and she saw that the clear sky had begun clouding over. A wind kicked up, shirring the surface of the birdbath. Within minutes the storm twilight was complete, the undersides of the clouds were dark as soot, and a thunderclap exploded overhead. She dropped her book and as she bent to lift it the dark stains from the first drops burst open all over the walk, as big as quarters. She heard Mary Frances running toward her as the load of rain fell, all at once, straight as harp strings, and a rock-splitting sound shook them; tucking the book under her arm she grabbed Mary Frances's wrist and they ran together back to the house. Mary Frances stood heaving and wide-eyed, rivulets of water streaming off her. "My Lord! I didn't want to shout for you because she's sleeping—she's finally sleeping!—but then I wouldn't have been heard anyway." Mary Frances wrung Katherine's hand so excitedly Katherine threw her arms around her. "The moment the sky started lowering I thought uh-oh, we're gonna have a crasher, and then she closed her eyes and nodded off so sweetly! When the phone rang I nearly screamed I was so mad, but she didn't wake up. It's the cool air. It's delicious." Katherine took the phone and it nearly slid out of her hand. "Yes," she said. Then she threw back her head as if she would shout at the ceiling, Mary Frances exaggeratedly hushing her. She recovered, found her sober tone of voice. "Yes he is," she said. "Yes. I can vouch for that." When she'd hung up she still had her arm hooked around Mary Frances's neck and she gave Mary Frances a great hard kiss on the forehead. "Whoa now. What has happened to you?" Outside the storm's noise repeatedly ebbed and then flared, with the sound of fat hitting a skillet. Katherine went and got her raincoat from the closet and struggled it over her wet clothes. "You must put on dry things," Mary Frances said, doubly indignant now. "Where are you going?"

"Run upstairs light as a feather and make sure she's still sleeping. Go on. Put a wiggle in it." Mary Frances went upstairs, blindly obeying the spirit of urgency, and reemerged signaling Yes.

She bloodied a finger pulling the top of the car up, cursing the stiff accordion of canvas, wrestling the hooks, and she came into the bus station still squeezing her fist around it. The blood was thinned with rainwater. He could see it welling up between her fingers. She had to wedge her way into the room, which was already barely able to contain the two men standing with their arms folded, looking beleaguered, misunderstood, underappreciated, their single cluttered desk and the chair in which he sat. She was afraid to look at him; driving there she had kept thinking, ridiculously, What if it isn't him at all? What if it's some other Oriental transient, assuming his name? She stepped around his chair carefully as she introduced herself to the two men, the two agents of the Federal Bureau of Investigation, and then there was nowhere else to go. The back hem of her damp coat touched his shin. Heat poured off his skull and stored itself in his shorn, greasy hair. The man in shirtsleeves offered her his hand but she didn't take it. She stood holding the hurt finger tightly, and the idea of that injury bore down on him. "It's just that I've cut my finger putting up the top on my car," she was explaining. She smiled dazzlingly at them.

"Do you need something?" said the jacketed man. "I have a hankie."

"Oh, I'm all right. Thank you so much. It's mending up fast."

"What's the car, British make?"

"As tiny as they come."

"Hope this storm doesn't float her away."

"I hope so, too!" she exclaimed.

"We won't keep you long," he grinned back at her.

"I can tell you this isn't the person you're looking for," she said. "He's a law-abiding gentleman."

"I have no doubt—" Jacket began, as his partner interrupted, annoyed.

"This is routine questioning, miss. We have a problem with Chinese Communist agents infiltrating American harbors. Ships from Communist China are barred from every port in the U.S. except New Orleans, this is their one point of entry, for their goods and their agents. Their agents recruit in this port. Among seamen. And then you've got mutinies. Communist seamen and Communist mutinies."

"But he isn't Chinese," she said.

He studied her a moment. "Are you familiar with the Port Security Program?"

"I'm afraid that I'm not."

"Are you a Communist yourself?"

"Me?" Katherine exclaimed, and then they all, even the irritable shirtsleeved man, burst out laughing, and laughed together a long time while he looked on amazed. She would have to give a guarantee, of his citizenship in a democratic nation, his occupation as a student, his anti-Communism, and the depth of her acquaintance with him. "This is something you're signing your name to, miss," Shirtsleeves said. "Please be sure."

"I understand," she said. "My finger's still bleeding. I guess I will need that hankie." The jacketed man crossed behind his partner and gave it to her, and as she turned to accept it he could finally see her face, amusement flashing beneath her polite smile, as she wound the handkerchief around her cut. Everything around him wove and faded and broke into coarse grain. The room was a bunker against the storm outside. Its air was stifling. Shirtsleeves had pulled the document out of a file folder and smoothed it on the desk in front of her; even so, its edges curled slightly from the dampness in the room. "Read, please," he said, as she bent over it. Her swaddled finger struggled with her thumb to hold the pen. "We'd rather question all of them and make a mistake than miss one of them. Err towards caution," the jacketed man was saying apologetically.

"That's very reassuring," Katherine said. She began to write and clumsily flipped the pen onto the floor. The jacketed man leaped to retrieve it. When she bent to try again he placed the pen in her hand and they signed her name together, in a large messy scrawl. Chuck felt the blood in his temples rising like the plume of a fountain, suspended in the air for a moment before crashing and spreading to his body's far reaches, so that he suddenly leaped to his feet, and at the same moment, she withdrew her hand from the man's grip and took up his suitcase, and he reached after it, trying to prevent her, and they collided and stared at each other with the wide-eyed panic of two people who had never met before. "Thank you very much," she called back, as they tripped over each other leaving the small room, and slid across the mud-streaked floor of the station, crashing through the doors into the pelting rain. "What have you done?" she shouted, as they ran, arms shielding their faces, across the swiftly flooding lot. "What happened to Chicago?" The car sat being battered, the water thrumming on the rag top and singing loudly off the hood. When they reached it she turned to him breathlessly, the color high on her cheeks, and he dropped his suitcase with a great splash onto the pavement and took hold of her hand, unwound the man's handkerchief and flung it into the gutter, although the cloth was pink with her blood. He put his lips to the cut. They both jumped with shock, feeling the warmth of his tongue meet the warm bead of blood.

The inside of the car was ruined with water. Crooked windings down the insides of the windows from where the top didn't fit had made a rising pool in each seat, marshy floorboards, every surface slippery and the windows thick with steam. They were hidden but the space was so small every contact was a struggle. They strained together, kissing hungrily until the cool tastelessness the rain had washed them with was gone, and they could taste each other's mouths. His hands touched her neck, the soft place beneath her jaw that might have never seen the sun, the cleft of her sternum where she was warm with sweat that hadn't rinsed away. He felt her inhaling the stink of his hair, pushing her tongue into his waxy, bitter ear. The storm's strength was dropping. As its noise subsided they heard their own quick breaths rising and falling, and the voices of recent bus station arrivals venturing out of the building at last and beginning to make their way across the lot toward the street. They broke apart and she found her keys. "Come on," she whispered, stamping on the gas pedal. The car started with a spluttering roar. She turned back to him triumphantly and he held her face again and kissed her even as he saw the people in the lot drawing closer, and the car's windows running with clear water, their brief shelter having dissolved.

They drove slowly along the flooded avenue, its surface chopping gently. The gutters were roaring with chocolate-colored water, tree-trash, colorful city debris. The engine gurgled as they moved, pushing a lip of water ahead of them and leaving a long V-shaped wake. They opened the windows all the way and a sultry breeze rolled across them. He smelled a rich odor of vegetable decay. When they turned onto a street lined with elevated sidewalks and storefronts, Katherine pulled to the curb. "Wait here," she said, kissing him quickly and leaping out of the car. The sun had emerged and a new day seemed to beat down on them, bright and unremitting. He looked around cautiously. The street was filling now with post-storm promenaders. A woman with a motley group of children stood talking with a man in a duster drenched black from the backs of his knees to the long hem, where it brushed his boot heels. "Our line is on the ground!" he heard her say. "A live wire laying right there in the water. Every one of these dumb kids was gonna get cooked." After she had vanished with her brood the man turned and walked up the street, splashing carelessly through the half foot of water that still ran through it. When he came level with Katherine's car he stopped and stared. Chuck's scalp prickled, and his armpits. He sat with his eyes trained ahead but feeling the man's gaze on him like a wash of unpleasant heat. Katherine came out of the store with a paper sack dangling from one hand and rushed back to the car, passing by where the man stood. Chuck felt the gaze harden further. His own heart was pounding. "Now where shall we go?" Katherine asked, smiling at him. Over her shoulder Chuck saw the man turn slowly and begin walking, frequently looking back. "Are you all right?" She touched his mouth gently. "Hungry?"

He pushed his hand into his pocket and felt the wad of money there, all his earnings in the world, plus the sharp-edged hundred-dollar bill, slightly damp. "What is a nice hotel here, where it's people from around the world stay?"

"The Charles," she said, without stopping to think.

They drove there, each of them for different reasons becoming more and more nervous, so that by the time they arrived they were wordlessly shy. The storm turned out to have been the outer arm of a hurricane brushing the city, and the hotel was full of well-heeled people who had just fled their estates near the coast, which were now flooded and had no electricity. They stood holding their cocktails in the lobby and swapping stories of adventure and deprivation. Chuck was given a room despite the circumstances, as he had gambled he would be. In the world of the rich, displeasure at the sight of a stranger was overruled by breeding and protocol. He paid for a week in advance, and felt a pang of excitement and terror. The desk clerk smiled a thin, artificial smile. The bellhop took his rotting, stained suitcase without the slightest flicker disturbing his inactive face, and led them to the room. When they were alone they ate the sandwiches and drank the cider she'd bought, sitting side by side on the bed in a state of near paralysis. "I can't believe it was a hurricane," Katherine said. She was talking rapidly and ceaselessly, a nervous habit he had learned to recognize. "I never see the papers anymore. I never even listen to the radio news." The afternoon was ending and the room had already grown dark. Katherine turned her watch around and around on her wrist, and he realized he had carried this gesture with him ever since the night he'd first seen her do it, when they sat together in the kitchen of Strake. "Isn't it amazing? To have come here to the city from Sewanee, and ended up even more, in a way—" He kissed her hard in the middle of her sentence and they fell backwards together across the bed, their mouths making a complicated language, like a semaphore they urged against each other. They inched themselves steadily, earnestly, undeterrably up the length of the bed, their shoes and the sandwich wrappings and the cider bottles with the last sloshing inches undrunk kicked onto the floor, the difficulty of their clothing where it clung, clammy and wretched, like a no-longer-useful skin that cannot bear to be discarded, and the difficulty of the tightly made bed. They wordlessly united their efforts, pulled the bedclothes from their tuckings and wrenched them aside. He had lain face down on his hard, slanting mattress in his North Clark Street room without moving, hardly breathing, as if an effort of his will could transport him. He'd had so little then, just the feel of her hand as it traveled his neck, or her arms around his waist as he reeled up the stairs, but those things had been singular, and total.

The evening was as long as Glee could make it. She was up from her nap, blinking keenly at everything. "We thought you'd been swept out to sea," she remarked, when Katherine came to the table. "Your hairstyle is unique, as usual. Very orphan-in-the-storm." Katherine bent to her soup bowl and emptied it by half while Glee watched, eyebrows elevated. "Have we dispensed with grace?"

Katherine sat back with an uneven sigh and took a long draught of her drink. "We never had grace."

"Well, maybe we ought to. Maybe it's time we had some kind of religion." Glee looked around for Mary Frances, who was audibly in the kitchen, lit herself a cigarette and almost immediately put it out. She picked with mild interest at her plate. "I have some ideas for tonight, Kitty. I have a magazine article I would like to hear, and I have some correspondence to do, and there is next week's menu and our trip to plan." Glee's face darkened. "Maybe you and your brothers have got your wish and my little house is gone."

"I doubt it," Katherine snapped, thinking of the evening and the trip and every other duty angrily.

She didn't get away until near midnight. At last there was no more to be done, not a magazine article Glee could stand to have read to her, no endurance for another cup of tea, Irish-style, as Glee said blandly, tipping the bottle. Inevitably Glee found her refusal to be left alone overridden by the unpleasant restlessness of Katherine's company, and she let Katherine go, down the hall in the nightgown and robe she'd put on to her bedroom, where she dressed again and waited. Glee's lamp blinked off. Katherine stole down the stairs, into the kitchen briefly, then out the back door, like a bad schoolgirl, running swiftly and noiselessly along her avenue's tunnel of trees in bare feet to the place she'd left her car.

When she turned the key in his door he shot upright and gasped. A rectangle of bald light stretching in and someone coming toward him. "Hah!" he yelped. *Where he was?* "You're all right," she said, grabbing hold of him, and at her touch he almost leaped off the bed. He waved his arm around behind him, groping for the lamp, and with that intuitive motion his memory returned. He saw her, intently looking at him. "You were dreaming," she said. "It's all right." She touched him again and he took the hand and held it too hard, trying to purge it of that electricity. The hand he held hers with was wet. He let go, and scrubbed his hair thoughtfully. "It's okay. I went in a deep sleep." His heart was still hammering: *toktoktoktoktok*. He wondered whether she could hear it.

He didn't sleep that night. For a long time he tried, turning his eyes to the ceiling and counting his own breaths, waiting for the numbers to climb to the point at which he had some difficulty keeping track of them. Doing this he often passed out cold in the three-digit range, his mind too preoccupied to stop him, and awoke in the morning thinking happily, *five hundred two*. From deep within the bowels of the hotel, he heard the hiss of a tap. He envisioned the riser moving through the suffocating tranquility of this hour, reaching the washroom sink, handling the water. He realized he did not want to let himself sleep. Carefully he brought the alarm clock that sat on the bedside table close to his face, turning it this way and that in the imperfect darkness. When he deciphered three A.M. his chest tightened. He hadn't passed one of those lost, black nights, from which he would awaken with the sense that the marrow had been sucked from his body, leaving him to wobble bonelessly and ecstatically from the bed in a state of true sedation, since before the day he'd read Addison's letter. That had been in yet another universe. Every muscular connection of his body, the bands holding his skull to his shoulders, and his shins to his kneecaps, and his eyes to their sockets, were stretched to their limits. He reached for the clock again, and saw three twenty-two. This night would never end. There was no certainty that he could sleep without dreaming, and no chance he could dream without betraying himself. Every dream, no matter how benign at the outset, eventually took the same turn. Katherine tossed sideways suddenly, violently, and he took her sadly in his arms and felt her sleeping weight, so much greater than the sum of her. Asleep she gave off waves of slumberous heat, and a sweet baking smell. She seemed to have yielded herself to alchemical changes. He knew suddenly, his shock dulled by the inevitability of the realization, that he would leave in the morning. He stared at the grip of his arms around her. His body seemed craven. He would take it, and hide it.

At last he could see a slight change in the space around him. He watched the bleak shapes of the furniture emerge. She stirred and lifted herself to look down at him, and his eyes flooded suddenly.

"Oh, my dear." She touched his lids gently. She could see he hadn't slept.

"Do you still get married?" he whispered.

"I don't know. I'm a bad, faithless woman."

"And I am a thief," he said.

He failed to leave that morning, and kept failing, in spite of knowing that there was no other right thing to do. He could give way to blind momentum, descend with her until he touched a subterranean current to which he might entrust himself heedlessly, but in the end it always fell away. He was left with the dearth of his prospects. In Chicago his attempt to will her from his thoughts had resulted in her immanence in everything, his sense that she was watching from afar, with a constant and transforming attention, as if his life were an American movie and she were his audience. He'd felt ennobled and remade. Yet he was full of immutable stuff. Holding her he could think only of the unseeable space his own body contained, like being slammed against a threshold, again and again. He might tear himself open and never see anything. The interval that began with her hesitant withdrawal from him, her fingers moving through his hair, her palms touching his jaw, the quick kiss because she was always late, and that ended, finally, with her face leaving him, obliterated by the closing door, after which he was alone in the hot room again, cast its shadow wider and wider. His heart began pounding as soon as she stirred against him, the outer edge of the tide of gray light just appearing at the top of the blinds, and gained speed all through their slow untangling, and over the course of days, not because he could not endure her leaving but because he was waiting for the morning he wouldn't endure it. After she was gone he would lie listening to the sounds of the hotel slowly coming to life. He found a little sign in his desk drawer that allowed him to decline housekeeping, and hung it on his door. Then he tracked the sad progress of the maids moving their linen carts down the hall. He would hear their gradual approach, room by room, sometimes the deep note of the vacuum cleaner, felt more than heard. One door would click shut and the one nearer him gently open. At last the cart whispered smoothly past his door. He carefully lifted the long, slightly curving hairs off the pillow, and dropped them in the desk drawer. He would find some kind of reliquary for them.

If she woke in the middle of the night he was sitting in his chair at the window, the small ember of his cigarette floating before him. His night vigilance never flagged, and it had gained such strength, like a motor burning infinite fuel, that he couldn't even sleep in the daytime, while he was alone. He would lie in a cool bath as the afternoon grew hot, watching the distortions his body made under the water, or he would lie in the bed, amazed by the fumes of her, held there. But when she was asleep in the bed he could not bear to lie down beside her. He would feel her vast distance from him, and think what he thought every night, that the next day he would go. He had nothing to give her. The things he had to hide weren't even things, he'd realized. They were a nothingness, but capable of damage. He felt already that so many people, people he had hardly known, who had done nothing but collide with his life in an effort to help him, had wound up his casualties. If he told her what pained him, she might care for his pain, and gain nothing. He did not know what happiness she could have with Addison. He felt sure she could not be happy with him at all. Yet he knew his own situation was not better than that man's, and he suspected it was very much worse. He was just a poor student. And not even that now, but a drifter.

She felt him leaving, and knew it was more and more urgent she make a decision. She had always sensed the transience that lay beneath his obedient Sewanee demeanor, and she'd always thought one day he might vanish. Her sense of him now was no different. Every night she braced herself for a stripped room, and no note. Then she saw him coming out of the chair to meet her halfway, carelessly crushing the package she held as they stood kissing slowly, like people reunited on a train platform, or on a pier beside a steamer. Even then she could feel a resistance in him, growing larger. "Why don't you sleep?" she asked. When he realized that she was awake he came and sat on the edge of the bed, and she lay her head in his lap and shared his cigarette with him.

"I worry on things," he said honestly.

"Are you afraid of your dreams?"

"Ah." He leaned his head against the wall and closed his eyes. "I am," he said.

"What do you dream about?"

He had never meant to tell her anything. But he wanted her so much to understand, to be happy somehow, when he left her. "I dream of the war in my country." Their voices were so quiet in that room, no louder than a dry hand brushing on cloth. And the nimbus of the streetlight, and the breeze pushing in. "I dream of being there."

"What happens?"

"Mostly I am running. Soldiers come behind me and I run, run, run." His hand moved slowly through the air. "Then I hear a shooting."

"This is when you wake up."

"No." He took the cigarette back from her, pinching it carefully. It was almost burned down. He examined the tip, its bright heart. "I feel the bullets come in me."

She was silent a long time. At last she said, "Did this happen to you?"

"No." He smiled into the dark suddenly. It was very strange, indeed. "No. This is never what happened to me."

Glee's health lapsed steeply again and she returned to her bed, weaker and more restless than before. She scowled at every meal brought to her, and greeted Katherine with a look of plain hatred one evening at dinnertime. Katherine set the tray down and touched her mother's shriveled eyelids, brushed her lips against the stiff, too-large ear, stroked the flannel of her mother's girlish nightgown. Her body was voracious for sensation and relief. She drove back from the hotel in the dawn twilight with one hand pressed between her legs; in the afternoons she locked herself in the washroom and ran baths so that she could open her legs under the pounding tap and be yanked into coming too quickly, muffling her scream with a wet fist in her mouth. When she bent to kiss Glee, her smell and her distracted, lazy gestures seemed so dissolute that Glee's tolerance snapped. "You reek," she said. "You reek of duplicity."

"You're tired, Mother."

"You're a liar. There isn't a true fiber in your body."

"It doesn't make you feel better to be ugly to me."

"Where are you going at night?"

"Nowhere."

"Liar. Is he here?"

"He is not here."

"Tell him to come and look me in the face. He can't. He's a coward who boosts himself up with weak people. He did it with your father. He patronized your father, he thought he was as stupid as a brick but he flattered him and kept him nearby to boost himself up and your father loved him. And it's the same with you, you stupid girl."

"He's not here and I'm not going anywhere."

"I lie awake all night and I can account for every minute. I know you leave. You could never keep a secret."

She walked out of the house without waiting for Glee to be done with her meal. When she arrived at the hotel an event was under way. The lobby was incandescent, as if the chandeliers' bulbs had been cleaned, or the missing ones replaced. Band music drifted in from the ballroom. A little overflow bar had been set up amid the potted palms and the deep chairs and a trim crowd of graying men in summer suits and wives in armless evening dresses trailed across the carpet in pairs toward it, or sat resting with their drinks. It had the look and sound of a charity ball, she thought. Her parents would have been at this party, if this had been another time. She might see them coming across the plush carpet, her father's easy, rolling gait and her mother's flawless angularity, her thin arm passed through the meaty bend of Joe's elbow and her step light even though she was wonderfully drunk. Katherine wondered if this event's invitation had been one of those she'd vetted, or if Glee had finally lost her place in the New Orleans social register of couples, and been quietly reclassified as "widow." Glee had always taken such pleasure in being part of a sought-after pair. Katherine suddenly understood what it must mean to her mother, to have lost that arena. She stood uncertainly at the lobby's edge, looking across the busy space which she had grown used to seeing sunk in a dawn twilight, its only occupant a night clerk asleep at the desk. Then she crossed to the telephone box, cutting straight through the palms and the milling partygoers, and pulled its door shut. "It's me," she said, when he answered. "It's Katherine."

"I was beginning to wonder."

"The phone lines were downed in the storm."

"Were they?"

"Everything was down for a while."

"I was a bit worried about you. Katherine in the tropics." She heard his voice lighten, that moment of deep irritation, coloring into suspicion, having already passed. Her heart raced with fear, and excitement. She'd had a deep intimation suddenly, when Glee had told her she could never keep a secret. *No,* she'd thought. *You're wrong about that.* From what seemed a great distance she heard him say, "What on earth have you been doing?"

"Nothing, really. It's dull. A good bit of reading." She remembered this. She remembered when deceit had been ecstatic. It was nothing to be proud of, but she'd felt so brave, plotting stratagems and telling lies, running risks and losing all the while, but only growing more determined, like a martyr. She had been testing her own powers for the first time, feeling herself presented with the first great abyss to leap across, and she'd leaped. And had never done it again. She had needed to believe that he loved her, but the thing that truly thrilled her was herself in love, determined to give as much of herself as she could force someone else to accept. And he'd always wanted less than she wanted to give.

He was cheerfully saying, "I don't think you miss me at all." *I love your lightness, I love that intelligence matched with such lightness, I love it when you tell me your stories, I love that about you.* He had never said he loved her. He had only ever told her what he loved, to impart the way he wanted her to be. Intelligent, but light. Never brooding or demanding. He had loved her independence so that she never could have needs, he had loved her stories because they meant that her real life lay elsewhere and in no way relied upon him. The loss she'd grieved for all these years wasn't that of some ideal Charles but of herself when she'd first striven toward him, shortsighted and rash but absolutely impelled by her love. A girl in that condition might lie, just to feel her secret. She might say, "I do miss you," and feel the words like a wedge dropped between them as she hung up the phone. And then there were all those ways to lie that bridged the gap and made it possible to move, brash shows of false confidence that muscled themselves forth and turned true, reckless bluffing, their lives as a confidence game. "We can stay here," she said, bursting into his room. "I'll tell Charles. I'll tell him everything, and we'll stay here. There's no reason not to. There's a house on the coast we can have, a little house with a dock and a porch."

"This isn't possible," he said. She knew it wasn't. That particular thing wouldn't ever be possible. But when they lay together in the room and he traced the curve at the small of her back, remembering her hair tumbling toward him, her head bent beneath the low tent-top of the car, her skin sealed to his with their sweat and the edges of the room rocking like a boat, or turning slowly like a wheel, because he was so tired that even the air around him had become a hallucination, they pretended it might be. There was no way of being in love without imagining that place, situated so near in the future that they were both exactly the same, but on the far side of a miraculous era of countless impossible changes. She held him in her arms, describing. The Gulf Coast was a great marsh of grass, with the sky lying unobstructed and hot blue everywhere above you. In the distance if you saw a small black cloud this was a lone tree, its trunk invisible from a distance, floating above the horizon. The long grass was furred silver on one side and exquisitely tuned to the wind. It endlessly rippled and parted and the sound it made cured sleeplessness. Below it was the sleepy tow of black water. You could sail anywhere through the grass, pushing your boat with a pole, although the grass broke into islands with glittering channels between them. Herons coasted the length of these, every beat of their wings like sails billowing. The severe little German-looking bird was a kingfisher, hunched on a bent bow of grass. The scholar bird, he murmured. He always looked so fastidious and so lonely.

"Our house is in the middle of the ocean," she said, and then she felt him falling, his hand slid from hers and dropped onto the sheets, and he was finally asleep.

thirteen

The freighter dropped anchor off an unsettled
strip of Cheju's coast and sent its refugees to shore in overloaded
rowboats. Chuck had come on deck looking frantically for what
he expected, the teeming disorder and climbing roofs of Pusan
harbor, and instead there had only been the waste of land creeping
out from the foot of the cliffs, and an unpaved road winding out of
sight around the bulk of a headland, the flat sky, and the screaming gulls. Once onshore people began making camp, digging pits
and building fires, feeding them with garbage and wet kindling
pulled out of the hills climbing up from the coast. A few U.S.
Army–ROKA joint patrols arrived from the far side of the island
with a small number of tents. After setting these up the soldiers got
back into their jeeps and bumped around the field, holding their
rifles ostentatiously over the sacks of rice they'd brought. They
started arguments with those refugees who had set up their own
tents and built fires inside them. The army-issue tents quickly
filled up with piles of clothing, chickens, cripples, children. There
hadn't been stakes to pin the flaps down and these lifted in the
cold wind, like blown skirts. It might have been warmer in the
open air, where every fire became the hub of a wheel of bodies.

The camp had sprung up out of only the contents of the ship, but he knew that the following morning, as soon as it was light, the army would arrive in greater force to solidify it. In spite of the government's efforts the guerrilla presence on Cheju had never completely disappeared. It persisted in small, isolated bands throughout 1949 and the first half of 1950, and after the war had broken out it was constantly enlarged, by people acting on the rumors that the network of caves sheltered army deserters and North Korean partisans who coordinated the guerrilla activity on the mainland, in the rear of the front line. National Police and ROKA units patrolled the island constantly, picking up young unenlisted men, older boys, surly trouser-wearing girls. All the risks he had run on the mainland were concentrated here. If he was still in the camp the next morning he would either be drafted or arrested. He saw no able-bodied men at all: only girls, women, cripples leaning on sticks, and sexless children, unattached to anyone, deeply self-absorbed and hungry, trotting on the lookout for food.

As the evening turned into night he kept picking his way in circles through the camp, wrapped in his great dark coat. Everywhere he went he was followed by eyes. His coat was expensive, conspicuous wool, and he was young, uninjured, and male, although he coughed incessantly, doubling over to spit clots of phlegm. He was running a fever, and the rich-looking cloak hid a swarm of lice. He had become infested on the boat. Walking, he pulled his arms out of the huge sleeves and his hands scrabbled inside his shirt, trying to claw the vermin off his body, but they seemed to have burrowed just beneath his skin to feed, like ticks. The itching was terrible but the constant awareness of infestation was worse. He flailed as he walked, like a lunatic. He paused briefly at one fire and was given a handful of undercooked rice. Eating it he tasted feces on his fingers. "What are you doing here?" a woman asked him. "How are you not in the army?" Gulls were wheeling overhead, inflamed by the ripe smell of garbage that was carried upward by the warm drafts from the fires, in spite of the cold air. He could see their pale, bulletlike shapes, lit up from below. "I have contagious tuberculosis," he said, hoping this would make a space of wordless loathing around him, but the eyes didn't waver.

He waited until sleep overtook the camp and then he slipped away from the field of prone bodies and walked into the woods. There he took off his coat and shirt, quaking from the cold, and banged the shirt with a rock. His panic erupted. He banged so hard he broke a sweat. He could hear his breath bursting out of him, like steam from a valve. When he was done the shirt was peppered with his own blood, smashed out of the insects, but when he put it back on, it still crawled. The lice were living in his coat, on his head, in the safe thatch of his pubic hair, under his arms. He didn't return to the camp. Instead, he stood leaning on the trunk of a large tree all night, sometimes grinding himself against it like a dog, to ease the itching, but mostly standing, letting it support him. His eyes had adjusted when he left the open slope, blazing with fires, for the dark trees. Now they grew even keener, and he could see the delicate tracery of the undergrowth, the bare interlocking canopy, the roosting shapes of birds. His breathing grew even and calm. His heart throbbed within him, firmly held, his flesh conveying the pulse to the soles of his feet, and out, into the ground. He heard the wind moving in the needles of pines, and beneath that irregular noise, the constant washing sound of the ocean.

When the sky grew pale he climbed the tree and tried to sleep, but his fear he might fall kept him awake. He sat in the tree all day, growing numb from the cold, and that night began walking. He walked for three nights, always keeping the sound of the ocean to his left so that he would not stray inland and become lost. During the day he slept in dead leaves or under low shrubs.

Although he saw no one, his vigilance never relaxed. It wouldn't have surprised him to stumble upon another filthy, starving, and paranoid person curled up in the mulch that he plowed through each morning to bury himself. He ate bark, and the lice from his body. His gums bled continuously; wiggling one of his teeth as he walked, it came out. It lay on his tongue, a little claw with a spongy root.

On the third day, crashing like a drunk through the trees, he heard a church bell striking discordantly. It was late morning. The bell gave him eleven baleful notes to follow and he rushed downhill toward it, seeing the scrolled shingles of rooftops before the sound died away. He entered the village clumsy with incompetent precaution, inching along the side of a building with his arms flung out for balance as if he teetered on a ledge, but the village was motionless. The weight of illness or stupor hung over it. Children lay asleep in the street. The church building stood at the head of a dusty square, anomalously European and solid, and ornamented by a pair of stone pillars that he might have wondered sarcastically about, imagining them ferried from the mainland by a platoon of missionaries, if he hadn't been mindless from hunger. Very slowly, trying to make no noise, he opened the door and immediately met a wall of bodies. It was a food line, winding back from the altar and bending past the entrance. He pushed his way in.

The line shuffled forward by inches. He was almost asleep when he reached the priest, a smooth-faced, hesitant-looking white man, perhaps no more than twenty. Chuck realized he had no bowl and cupped his hands, losing the water the potato had been boiled in. He hurried to a wall and wolfed the food, lapped his palms, sucked his fingers dry. Now the taste of his own filth on his hands made him dizzy with food-lust. He looked like a mad hermit, the coat crusted with mud, bark, bugs, the skeletons of leaves, his fingernails black with dirt, his mouth colorless.

He lingered hungrily at the edge of the room and watched the rest of the line labor past, his fingers playing desirously against his palms. It wouldn't have been so difficult to force his way past these people and take another potato. Each human in the line was a mindless segment, seemingly impassive, except for the barely perceptible, unyielding pressure by which first a tottering old man, and then a girl of about six, were squeezed out of the line by those behind them. If the priest was aware of what had happened he did not show it. The food dwindled and disappeared, but for some time the priest continued to dip his ladle into the pot, filling cups with the gray, starchy water. The pot looked like army issue: scratched aluminum with a pair of metal handles. When the ladle scraped bottom the people who had not yet been fed lingered uncertainly, tilting empty bowls as if something might fall from the ceiling. Finally they melted away. He stayed, watching the priest through the fringe of his hair. His hair had become streaked with gray. The whites of his eyes, he would see later, staring into the priest's small, flaking mirror, were yellow, the precise shade of phlegm. The priest's head and shoulders sloped forward even when he was not bent over the soup pot. His sad movements through the bare chamber, extinguishing candles, were led by his forehead. When the room was dark except for a tin-can oil lamp he was holding, the priest lifted the pot under one arm and forced himself to face the lingerer. "Go home?" the priest asked, in Korean.

Chuck answered in English. "Tell me your name."

The priest's eyes widened with fear. He had been guiding AWOL soldiers, leftist guerrilla farmers, teenaged boys who could very well have been Soviet agents for all he knew, from the gateway of this village into the island's hidden caves for almost fifteen months, since before the beginning of the war, and he had never been questioned before. In part, he thought, because he refused to know any more than he had to about the people he met. He had become a priest who refused to take confessions. "I'm Frank Todaro," he said. "I'm a Catholic priest from Cleveland, Ohio. I'm here to help these people, that's all. I don't know anything. I'm not on any side."

"I'm not on any side."

"What do you want?"

"Take me to the place," he said. "Hide me."

That evening Todaro deloused him. He stood naked in the washtub as Todaro carried water in and boiled it, using the same pot in which he'd boiled that day's ration of potatoes. The room they were in had a trapdoor to the cellar, where the grain and potatoes were stored. Todaro slept with a gun beside his bed which he had only fired once, taking it to the beach and shooting straight out to sea so he would not hit anyone, to be sure that he could. He added the steaming water to the washtub, thinning the black soup Chuck's body had made. Then Todaro gave him a pair of scissors and Chuck clipped his pubic hair, and scrubbed himself with kerosene until his genitals were red and the coarse stubble stood out hideously. Again he was riveted and saddened by the stuff of his flesh. After he had bathed, Todaro seated him in a chair and sheared him to the scalp. As the matted locks fell the priest said, "The hills above this village are just like your head. Swarming with creatures, and all of them perfectly hidden. There's no way to get them out apart from cutting down the trees."

"I'll be safe there?"

"There, yes. But you can't stay up there all the time or you'll starve."

They left the mission after midnight, in the dead hour. The wind stood still. The snap of a twig carried for miles like the report of a pistol. He followed Todaro, for a long time no more than a dark motion, until they entered a gorge and suddenly, where the rift in the trees allowed the moonlight to fall on them, he could see the other man again, moving with remarkable agility in his heavy skirts, his scalp glowing through his downy hair. They shrank against the rock face, into the margin of shadow, walking on the level, dry streambed. He heard the waterfall before they saw it, a thin, persistent stream dripping between long teeth of ice. Behind it the rock was eaten away in the shape of a small amphitheater; crouching in the total darkness of this shelter the curtain of ice and the open gorge beyond seemed to blaze with light. There was no natural cave here, but the mouth of a tunnel. They had to feel, crawling blindly on all fours, to find it. "Are you claustrophobic?" Todaro asked him. The opening felt about as wide as a barrel. Its walls were dry, powdery, as cold as metal to the touch.

"Tell me what it will be."

"This continues for a quarter of a mile, slightly uphill, and then joins with a natural cave. The tunnel widens very slightly sometimes, enough to crawl, but for most of it you'll need to wriggle on your stomach. It's tight."

"Okay."

"After this, as much as possible, you know nothing of me, and I know nothing of you. It's safest for us both that way. This is the only place I have ever been shown. If your friend has moved from here I don't know where he'll be."

As Todaro was turning to leave Chuck said, "Why do you do this?" expecting the answer to be, As a man of God I have a duty; All human life is a sacrament; War is a sin.

"You people don't touch my stores. Didn't I say that? My stores are off limits to you. My rice, my potatoes, my poultry. If I am ever robbed, I give this place up."

He watched Todaro slip past the gleaming teeth of ice. For some time after the other man had gone Chuck remained motionless, listening to the quick percussion of the thread of water striking down on the stones, like his butterfly pulse. Then he closed his eyes and pushed himself into the tunnel.

❦

*H*e had never meant to come to Cheju. The history of his actions over the course of the war consisted of lucky accidents and terrible blunders ameliorated by lucky accidents. He was still shocked by his own failure to leave Seoul, although he knew, at the back of his memory, in the place where he consciously sought to exclude humiliations and heartbreaks from thought, that he had stayed out of loyalty to Peterfield and selfish, naive excitement. He had imagined phones ringing, wires keening and sawing like a flock of locusts, pounding feet, the focused, angry, crucial work of urgent dispatches. He'd had boyish ideas of covering the war, enclosed in the American machine. He'd seen too many movies. His resolution of loyalty to himself had been a punishment. It cut hard against the grain of what he wanted, of what would give him comfort. The night that Miki brought him the message from Kim, he had tried to close his ears to the finer points of it. His first reaction, even before his stunned gratitude to learn that Kim was alive, had been disciplined scorn: joining Kim was a romantic, suicidal daydream that didn't even belong to the realm of ideas. He would go to Pusan, as he should have done in the first place. But he had decided to stay with Peterfield, and been abandoned by him, and he had decided to spurn Kim, and instead been thrust onto the island from which Kim had sent word. He was superstitious by nature, an optimistic propitiator of luck and a passive fatalist. He began to suspect he was at the mercy of a force of correction.

The cave was a great, cold lung, a space of utter darkness that throbbed, invisibly, with breathing. It was full of sleepers. When he pulled himself out of the tunnel, scraping desperately against its closeness and then suddenly falling unmoored into space, he heard a match strike. In the tunnel he had made himself a void, a nothing encased in a body, carried by the body's steady humping, writhing progress but in no other way touched by it. Simply carried. Then he felt the breath of the larger space curl down to him, and went mad with claustrophobia. Even when he reached that space, he would be buried in the ground. The yellow globe of light cast by the match struck every wall of the cave, and the three other men, awake now. The cave continued, narrowing again, into another chamber. Its natural mouth was a mile away, on the opposite side of the hill. The men raised themselves on elbows and watched him from beneath heavily lidded eyes. They were filthy, like him, but dressed in farmers' loose pajamas, and straw slippers. This cave was a haven for men who were wanted by the police or for desertion, but it was also a gateway; beyond it lay a network that encompassed the island. The physical connections between the underground chambers were few. If one was found, it could be cut off from the others and abandoned. The man holding the match could clearly see the quality of his coat, even through its grimy camouflage.

"Who are you?"

"I'm looking for someone named Kim. Kim Jaesong. He was here."

"He's not here anymore."

"He might be somewhere else?"

"I don't know." The other men were squinting at Chuck skeptically. The man with the match said, "Todaro brought you?"

"Yes."

"This Kim told you to look for Todaro."

"Yes."

"Well, this Kim isn't here."

"But he was."

After a moment the man said, "I think so. I never asked him his name."

"What did he look like?"

"Like you."

"How so?"

"He dressed like you." The man raised his chin, denoting Chuck's coat. "He wore fancy shoes. Good leather shoes, made with nails."

"Did they look like European shoes? They would have had a pattern in the leather, like little holes."

"They didn't have holes. They were nice shoes. Rich-looking."

"No, the holes would have been decorative. A pattern."

The man was shaking the match out. They all vanished into darkness again. "I never looked that close."

"Please. Light another match. Was there a piece at the toe, stitched like this?"

"Yes," the man said.

"There was?"

"Yes. Now I'm sure this was him."

"But what did he look like?"

The man shrugged dismissively. "It was him. He was like you. He talked like you."

"How long ago did he leave?"

"I don't know. In the fall. But you can stay here."

"Will you take me to the other caves?"

"You can stay here," the man said again, with finality. Knowledge propagated in relay, by inches, formed message chains, and crept everywhere. But no one knew what lay beyond his grasp.

He lasted two weeks, maybe more, maybe less. He would never be sure how long this period of preparation was, during which his body preoccupied him entirely, its needs swelling to eclipse the world, shrinking slightly to admit the world again, the return of which only brought his body fresh needs and embarrassments. In those intervals of clarity and terror he looked for Kim, but he'd begun to suspect Kim had sent him the message to lure him to safety, and that Kim had already moved on. Kim would never hide for longer than he had to. He would be organizing, and fighting. And so Chuck's vigil became as desperate and hopeless as it had been in the first months of the war, when he waited the whole occupation for Kim to appear. He slept curled in the cave, waiting, his coat coiled around him like a shroud, or he groped his way to the cave's real mouth and slipped into the woods. He sucked icicles, threw himself on rabbits which bounded lightly away. And then he was finally starving, and he became a beggar, loping coyote-style through the streets of the coastal villages, emerging only after dusk. The torn hem of his coat trailed. His ears were always pricked for the sounds of a patrol, his nose high in the air, leading him.

His senses weren't his anymore. They were exquisitely sharp now but he only carried them, like cold tools, in the same way that his body carried the cold void within it, which was nothing but emotionless awareness of itself, made by these senses which weren't his. His eyes scanned the streets for Kim, but they were a dog's eyes, indiscriminately interested in company. He lingered in kitchen doorways and stared at women until they were too frightened to refuse him food; there were no men left to protect them. As Langston had predicted, Seoul had fallen again, just days after Chuck had escaped. The Chinese and North Korean forces had advanced so far south that the only territories left from which the southern army could restock its forces were the peninsula's southernmost tip and the offshore islands. Cheju's villages were emptied of all their remaining boys, young men, older men who had no trouble walking, all of them rounded up by the American MPs and the National Police and gathered into blinking, silent crowds, straw sleeping mats or wool army-issue blankets rolled up and tied to their backs. Small children and women and the very old gathered in a crowd opposite and also stood wordlessly, a strange reflection, to watch them walk away in motley columns, without looking back. No one expected them to return. Their departure was a funeral, every man wearing or carrying his most cherished item of clothing, the thing he was willing to enter the next world attired in. Their best clothes: some owned real wool coats, aviator-style sunglasses, hats with bills or ear flaps, felt fedoras. Some had leather bags slung across their chests, fragile wire-rimmed glasses, American-made combat boots. Others wore only loose pajama-style shirts and pants, dark vests, canvas slippers, with lengths of cotton tied around their heads to warm their ears. If you were a man walking through one of these villages from which every man had been taken, then you were a ghost, or a beast. Women dropped bowls of rice on the ground and withdrew quickly, slamming their doors, as he leaped on the food. Thinking of finding Kim had been a way to mark time, but time stopped for him. He only wanted to gorge his body on hot food, slake his thirst, fall asleep overcome with the drunken sensation of having been fed. He excreted solid waste with tremendous pleasure and regret. When he was not dizzy and amnesiac from hunger he moved through the village streets deliriously, enthralled with his body's continuance, forgetting more and more often to withdraw to the woods until twilight, falling asleep curled like a lover against the warm flank of a building, his hands squeezed between his legs, dreaming of food, shit, flesh, liquid. Preparing. At last he woke howling in pain; his hand had been yanked from its ardent embrace with his body and stamped into meat. There was still the boot on his hand, still stamping its heel, his flesh shredded back to the cool blue knuckle. When a second officer stepped forward and doused the wound with gasoline he fainted. He had been arrested by the National Police on suspicion of espionage. He woke up in the back of a bouncing jeep, screamed, and was clocked in the side of the head with the butt of a rifle.

ॐ

*H*e was put on a boat and sent to Pusan, to a detention center that had been made from a converted school building. While he was conscious he argued so strenuously for his release that he was repeatedly knocked out again. When he came to he would resume the litany, listing every superior he had ever had during his employment by the United States Army, naming Police Chief Ho, his uncle Lee, his father. "My father is in Pusan," he sobbed, as his head snapped back. And then, the black mist moving aside again, he lunged forward, trying to butt the driver of the jeep. "Minister Su is a friend of my family," he gibbered, "My father is a famous professor, my uncle is Congressman Lee," rushing the words out before he was struck. He threatened his captors with jail. A used bandage was stuffed into his mouth, gooey with fluids. By the time he arrived at the school building both his eyes were swollen to slits. He wove when he walked. The ground seemed to be bucking up toward him. Inside the school building there were still maps on the walls, but scrolled up, and the windows were covered with tar paper. He was taken into a classroom that had been cut in half with a thin wood partition. At first he thought the classroom would be his cell. Later he understood that this never could have been the case, because the classroom had to be periodically withdrawn from him, so that he would live in fear of seeing it again.

On his first day he was beaten with a sawed-off length of wood left from the construction of the partition, and a baseball bat found leaning in a closet. Two soldiers beat him while an officer watched. The officer said, "Avoid his head." When he fell to his knees he was kicked in the stomach, ribs, and buttocks. He bent his face into the cage of his forearms and went sliding back and forth across the floor. A boot tip hit his scrotum and he vomited a clear splash of liquid. "You're a spy," the officer said. "No," he gasped. "First the lies come out," the officer said, as if he were a doctor calmly talking his patient through a procedure. "Stand him up."

The two soldiers stood him up and he crumpled. They stood him up again and one pushed the end of a rifle into the soft pocket of flesh beneath his jaw. Unknown reservoirs of strength opened in him and he continued to stand.

Now his body would fail him by enduring, to be damaged further, and by failing to endure, for which he would be damaged further. There was an exposed pipe bending into the room near the ceiling, covered with blisters of rust, steadily leaking dark rust-thickened water that looked like clotting blood. "Do you see that pipe?" the officer asked him. He nodded. "Point to it." His arm lifted, jerking violently. "Salute the pipe," suggested the officer. "Say, I salute you, pipe." He said it, gurgling. A fire spread from the center of his back up the ropes of his arm, and down the backs of his legs. His kneecaps popped. One of the soldiers was dismissed. The other came and punched him in the sternum with his gun. He doubled over but did not fall. "Louder," said the officer. He shouted again. He was made to stand perfectly still with his arm extended, shouting his salute to the pipe. He did not know how many times he shouted. He could not adjust his body, accommodate its pangs which quickly turned to blinding, unrememberable, voiding black pain. He fainted, waking as he struck the floor.

The officer stood over him. "Are you a spy?"

"No," he said.

He was made to stand up again, immobile, with the arm extended, shouting his salute at the pipe. He could not endure the posture for more than a few minutes at a time without collapsing. Each time he did the officer told him he could remain lying down if he admitted that he was a spy. The soldier kicked him idly. He rose again, stood, saluted, fell, was questioned, kicked idly, made to stand. At the end of the day he was taken to a cell in the basement of the school building, on an empty hallway. The cell might have once been a cement shower stall, a few feet square, with a drain in the center of the floor and a stub of pipe extending out of the wall just beyond his reach, about a foot below the ceiling, with a threaded bolt set like a bar across its mouth. His right arm was handcuffed to this. He had to stand on his toes to keep the cuff from dislocating his wrist, but in spite of this he plunged into a deep sleep, and broke his wrist with the weight of his body.

The next morning he tried again. His wrist had swollen so astonishingly that the guard who retrieved him called a doctor. "My father is here in Pusan, my uncle is a congressman, I'm not a spy," he told the doctor. His face was washing itself with tears, but these tears were like the tears the eye always produces to roll in its socket, they meant nothing to him. His purpose was to communicate his point to this doctor, who was a good man, an educated man, and must have taken some kind of oath to protect human life. The doctor said, gazing past him with mild surprise, "I think that is your father coming now," and when he whirled to look the doctor squeezed the wrist, snapping the bone into place. His voice tore out of him unbelievingly. *"Haaaaaaaaaaah . . . "*

He was taken back to the classroom, with the wrist bound. He begged the officer to call Eighth Army headquarters, USIS, his father, the government. "What?" the officer said. "Are you talking? All I hear is blah blah blah blah!" Nothing he said was ever audible. "What?" the officer shouted, striking him across the face. He hadn't been heard. He saluted the pipe until his voice was so strained he was nauseous. He was stood beneath the pipe, and made to throw his head all the way back, so that it screamed on its hinge, and then to swallow the rust-thickened drip. When he fell backwards he was punched in the sternum with the butt of the rifle, or the baseball bat, which stood in the corner when not in use, at an impudent angle, observing him. He would be allowed to stop swallowing if he admitted that he was a spy. When he screamed his own name, the name of his father, the

name of his uncle, the two soldiers kicked his scrotum and buttocks, slapped him across the face with their gloves, stood him
up, and pulled his head backwards by his hair until he thought
his neck would break, while the officer said, "What? I don't
understand you. What language is this?" He was stood beneath
the drip again and made to swallow, with his head thrown all the
way back. The rusty water filled his mouth and ran in streams
down his neck. He vomited again, like his gut being withdrawn
through his throat. The officer strolled the perimeter of the room,
dangling the baseball bat thoughtfully. "Are you a spy?" he asked.
He wanted to know where the Communists were hiding on
Cheju. The soldier's rifle was resting against the soft pocket of
flesh under his jaw and he was made to swallow his vomit, and
the rust-thickened water. The sound the pipe made as it dripped
was like a kind of incontinence.

That night he was given a piece of putrefying meat to eat; the
next morning, when the guard found a pool of feces quivering on
the floor of his cell he said, "Make that disappear," and stood over
him with his gun cocked while he pushed the waste through the
grate of the drain. He was shackled by his left hand now. He
learned to haul himself up by it, to gash the inside of his right
forearm against the sharp end of the bolt. He made a new gash
every night. The marks spread across his arm, crisscrossing sometimes, but still readable, like the lines on his palm. He did not
know how else to keep track of time, and he was determined to
control at least the passage of his body through time. He could
not control anything else. He could not control what his body
expelled, or even what it ingested. He was given cattle feed, and
ridiculed as he wolfed it down. He was so hungry he ate whatever
was given to him, no matter how rotten or inorganic. His body
suffered from the lack of everything, and it convulsively took in
material, in the same way it convulsively vomited. Five marks on
his arm, then eight. Looking at them, he did not experience the

duration they represented. He only felt the pain in his body and even this became a dome he lived inside of.

On the ninth day his jaws were held open, and the officer took a straight razor and made small cuts all over his tongue; then he was given a bowl of salt. He ate it, weeping. "Are you a spy?" the officer asked. He said he was. He could have said, so long ago, I am a spy. The officer unfolded a piece of paper in front of his face. There were words coursing across it. He was only watching them, not trying to read them. Words came from a world which did not exist. His face washed itself with tears that were made in the same unfeeling place where his urine was made, and his blood. It meant nothing to him. The officer gave him a pen but his hand couldn't grasp it. His swollen wrist was numb and bound, and his fingers were broken. The officer placed the pen carefully between his fingers and it fell out again. The soldiers laughed. Although they couldn't have said why, this seemed very funny. The officer had to hold his hand, with the pen in it, so that he could sign. They performed the maneuver together, painstakingly. When they had finished, the officer sat down across from him, without releasing the hand. He held it lightly, with a regard for its injuries. "Thank you," the officer said. He nodded gratefully. He was so glad to have done it at last. His hopes kindled. He was being spoken to. The officer watched him with interest and he watched back, enraptured, his breathing quick from his exertion. Then the officer asked, "Where are the caves on Cheju?" He was returned to his cell.

After this there was very little left of him. He mimicked his torturers, making himself deaf to his body's cries for help. His knowledge of his body propagated in chains, telephone lines, bridges between a limb and his love for it, coursing braids of communication wire. He sliced through lines and wires, exploded bridges, excised his mouth and his groin, amputated his limbs. He no longer knew when he urinated. Cast outside the boundary of itself, his body had ceased to obey any boundary between itself and the world. He was always damp and acrid with urine, trickling out of him the way blood trickled out of his various wounds. His terror at the mangling of his fingers had evaporated, and the memory of that terror was as unrecognizable as any of his other possessions. He watched his hand being mangled from a great distance. He had already sawed it off. He had thrown away his body as if it were ballast, not to speed his death, but to survive. It was his body that would kill him.

He stopped keeping track of the days, and his torturers grew tired of him. Truckloads of captured guerrillas and other prisoners of war from all across the peninsula were arriving at the school, naked from the waist up, roped together at the ankles. They filled the school yard, squatting on their stringy haunches in the cold, falling asleep on top of each other. They were too unwieldy with their arms bound behind them, unable to pick themselves up when they fell over, and bringing the whole column down, and so they were allowed to keep their hands and arms, holding them clasped against their chests as if in prayer. Their shaved heads and bare shoulders shingled together like the scales of a single, ailing creature. In the classroom he was made to stand on a wooden chair that was set on top of a desk, beneath the pipe, with his hands cuffed behind him. The cuffs were attached to the pipe with a short length of chain; he had to double over as his arms were pulled up. He dropped his head and swayed dangerously on the chair, his toes grabbing ineffectually. He was left alone.

He fell, finally, tumbling off the chair, and dislocating both his shoulders as the chain snapped taut. Then he hung, his toes brushing the desk, swaying slightly. This was how the officer found him. The upset chair lay on the floor. The baseball bat leaned in the corner. The officer cut him down and stretched him on the desk, knees bent, arms stuck out behind him. "Can you tell me anything?" the officer asked.

He was desperate to be useful. He didn't want to disappoint. He didn't want to be discarded. "I went to church," he whispered. His voice crawled out of him.

"Where? What church did you go to?"

"Moon," he rasped. He saw the bright moon. He remembered the way from the cave's natural mouth to the village where he had been captured more clearly than the way from the mission to the tunnel, but even this memory was flattened and distorted, like the globe of the world unpeeled and forced onto a map. Ravines were very deep and particular landmark trees very large, but he could no longer assess the distance between any two points on his route. He struggled to feel the short trip again, but he needed his body around him. "Moon," he repeated. To betray the world he'd stopped believing in it. He no longer saw it clearly to describe it. Something in him kept dragging that memory to safety and he could not save himself.

The officer sighed. "Where are the guerrillas on Cheju," he said. His voice did not inflect this as a question. He intoned it, soothingly. "Give me a name."

Chuck reached and only felt a void, the silty, lightless bottom of an ocean. Within it he brushed against things that darted from him in the instant that he sensed them. He was sweating profusely, a cold, coursing sweat he was not aware of. The officer wondered if he was in shock. "Todaro," Chuck said suddenly. He remembered that man's gentle hands on his head, shaving the lice from his scalp, and the intense relief of his skin coming clean.

The doctor was brought to him and he was untied. He could not raise himself up. The doctor lifted him into a sitting position and then embraced him, wrenching the shoulders back into their sockets with the tightness of his clasp. He collapsed in the doctor's arms and did not move until the doctor pushed him away. "Hold yourself," the doctor said. "Like this." The doctor took hold of his arms for him and folded them across his chest, and closed his fingers around his elbows, so that the weight of his arms did not hang from the joints. "Can you?" the doctor asked. He nodded mutely, cradling himself. He began to cry. "Yes," he said, in the high, thin hiccup of a child. He held himself. The doctor walked him outside and the cold spray of wind struck him, carrying its atoms of the sea. He saw the prisoners squatting, their faces downturned.

Later he would realize that they had been there for days, but at that moment they seemed to have materialized as a result of his confession. Their posture remained frozen but their eyes rotated swiftly and found him. His heart accelerated, hammering so hard his ribs bounced as they tried to contain it. He was following the wall of the yard, the steady pressure of the doctor's arm across his back. His feet spun forward, paddling the ground. Gulls burst out of the storm clouds. Even in that twilight, his vision was stunned. The prisoners' gaze rippled after him, the perfect repetition of heads with their close fur of stubble, the large, delicate ears, the quick shift again and again of the eyes. Then he saw him. A pair of outsize eyes met his, stared. He stumbled hard and the doctor shoved him forward. The other face passed out of sight. He twisted and tried to look back but there was only the ocean of bowed heads, bare napes, humped shoulders, rolling away. The doctor walked him through the gate and steered him out into the street. He sank down where he was but the doctor prodded him. "Not here. Go away. Disappear."

fourteen

When he was brave enough he prayed, more often than he liked to admit, although he hesitated at calling these prayers. They were motivated not by certainty, by belief in a power, but by total, irresolvable uncertainty. He prayed to Kim. And it was only conversation. Was that you? he asked. You were there, facing death. And you looked up. And saw me.

He wondered what had shaped him more, his guilt toward Kim, or the chance it was mistaken. And he wondered what he feared more: to be guilty, or to know that if that face had not been Kim's, he would feel absolved. Perhaps he didn't want to be certain. Still, he returned and returned to that moment, frustrated each time by his inability to lengthen his glimpse, or to sharpen its focus. But he felt what he'd felt no less powerfully: a shock of recognition that bound him to someone he might not have known. He had longed so much to feel something, even loss. The feeling might have been misplaced.

And so he didn't know if this was Kim, or even if, by confessing, he'd saved himself. After the cease-fire Dr. Su, the former Minister for Social Affairs in the republic's prewar government, encountered Chuck's father, Dr. Ahn, in Seoul, on the lawn of

Yonsei University. Both men had returned to teaching. Dr. Ahn was reinvigorated by his gigantic lectures, the swollen student population being one effect of American funding for the reconstruction effort. The Doctor regarded these raw, overage, unruly students with excitement, poorly masked by contempt. They had no patience, no work ethic, no appreciation for the nonpragmatic arts. They wanted money. Glittering buildings would soon climb from the foundations at that moment being poured. The noise of construction shook every street. The two men stood talking for a long time, comparing notes on the university's administration, catching up.

At last, Su brought himself to mention a particular incident during the war. Early in 1951, after the government evacuated to Pusan for the second time, he was contacted by an official of ROKA's intelligence office who asked him if he knew a professor named Ahn, with a son. Ahn's brother was supposed to be Congressman Lee. Su had said yes. He'd given a description of Chang, doing the best that he could, not having seen the boy for almost three years. Slight, well-spoken, fairly fluent in English. He was not enlisted as a soldier. Su understood he worked as an army translator. "Why?" Su had asked the official. "Do you know where he is?" At this point the official had seemed eager to get off the phone. No, no, he had said. Intelligence had picked up a boy, a no-name, with amnesia, but his claim to be Dr. Ahn's son must be false, because he was very poorly educated, and did not speak any English at all. "That would be the tip-off," Su said. Su recalled Chang's English as having been very good. It did not occur to Su until much later that the story made no sense. How would an amnesiac remember his father, and uncle?

At the time, Su had offered to come and take a look at the person in question. His offer was refused. "It is not the same boy," the official said firmly. The exchange had disturbed Su, but it soon left his mind. One of Su's own sons was dead.

"How is Chang?" Su asked the Doctor hesitatingly.

The Doctor nodded, reassuring him. "Alive," he said.

The cease-fire was made in the late summer of 1953. The following spring he returned with his parents to Seoul. Their house was still there, derelict. They closed most of its rooms: the attic, where the Doctor had been interrupted in his attempt to take his life by never taking action again; Miki's room, the libraries, the third and second floors. The staircase was sealed. Squirrels filled those upper rooms, their frenetic activity making a sound like balls rolling. Doves and pigeons roosted in the eaves, and their ardent moans filtered down through the house. He loosened the panel of the staircase chamber, and placed his hand in the hot, dark space. He did not think to walk around the grounds. He might have deliberately forgotten. He was busy with his letter-writing campaign, which his father alternately ridiculed and grieved. His father did not want to believe he would really leave the country when his opportunity, and his duty, were both here. "Harvard, maybe," his father said. "Certainly. That would be an honor." But Chuck meant to go anywhere. His whole purpose, beyond getting to the U.S., was to leave South Korea. He sent the letter to every address he obtained, recopying it endlessly in his precise, blocky print, only changing the university's name. *You will not regret supporting me.*

He could never have said he trusted fate in that blithe, blind way which sees fate as a simple instrument to bring about well-being, but he acknowledged its absolute power, and this meant he trusted the announcements it made. He took to doing his reading on the high terrace of his family's home, so that he could watch for the mailman's approach through the tops of the trees. The warmth of the summer was beginning to make itself felt. He would hear the chirring of insects, and feel the still-cool breeze.

The trees would sway together like boats at their moorings. Around three the miniature figure appeared at the base of the hill, just the top of his head and the bulge of his bag, passing out of sight and returning, slightly larger each time, until he had come through the street gate, left ajar now that there was no servant to answer the bell. And after two months during which Chuck waited with no expectations, no real hope that he would ever get an answer, the mailman came trudging through the gate clutching an unusually large envelope. Chuck threw his book to the ground and went running down the path. He wasn't sure how he'd known this was it. The letter held an offer, of full financial support, including airfare, from the University of the South, in Sewanee, Tennessee. He hadn't known where Tennessee was. When he found it on the map, he was frightened. It was so far from the ocean. He'd sent out seventy-four letters in all.

And then he did walk around the grounds, which were waist-high with weeds, rutted from trucks that had driven across them, dotted with islands of wildflowers he'd never seen there before. Little saplings had grown up, and waved like switches. The old tree was still there, a time traveler, in a landscape that was strangely transformed. When he entered the shelter made by its branches he immediately saw the pair of shoes, their laces tied together, slung over a branch eight or ten feet off the ground. He could never have missed them, the night he sat for hours beneath this tree, after the war began, waiting for Kim to appear. They had been hung there since then; they turned slightly, as if still reverberating from the hands that had positioned them. He climbed up, reaching with one arm, and knocked them down: fine, European-made shoes, wing tips, real nails. They were badly scuffed, a hole worn in each sole, the leather faded, dull, and stiff as wood from the rain, but overall they had stood up very well through the war. He could see the way a second pair of feet had worn them down differently, the way Kim's gait told itself, laid over his own. He held them against his chest. They smelled clean, of the outdoors and the elements. He would never know how they had come to be here, but he knew that they were meant to say good-bye. If Kim was alive, he would never return. He remembered Kim saying, "Do you know what I think makes a great man? It's not what he does, but whether or not he has passion, the kind we have now, when he's old. And I will. I shall." He imagined that Kim had left Cheju long before he arrived, to rejoin the fighting. He would have traveled with the current of the Communist retreat, back through Seoul, stopping here before he went across the parallel. In the years to come he would think of Kim in the North, in what was now the other country.

He himself never saw the North again, or his family's country estate, for as long as he lived. The estate could not possibly exist anymore. But that memory, of that place, was sealed like a globe within him. The trees, and the rise of the land as you walked toward the shrine, the precise moment at which the twinge in your calves announced that you would be renewed, that the strain of the climb would rush your blood through you, now, that perspiration would begin to dew out on your skin, and the breath in your lungs grow hot and regular, as the line of trees slowly rose over the crest and became visible. A boulder sat halfway up the hill and was a perfect place to look back from, over the valley, at the wide flashing river, but you never rested on the way up, you did not want to stop. All of that was within him, the feel of his body when he walked there was within him, in the way that the other memory was not; that was a full place, it expanded him, where the other thing diminished him. It obliterated itself and took part of him with it, like the injured tissue surrounding a wound, fusing together where it shouldn't, and shrinking the body. He could not remember the pain he had felt, as if all that had happened to him had been enacted on another. Although he had witnessed every detail, the pain was as distant from him as the distance between two bodies; the other may be there, in your arms, their length matched against yours, but whatever they feel is darkness. It could be another universe, it could not exist at all. He could not imagine what the other body felt, and so he became another to himself; and after this happened, how could he be close to someone, when he was two people?

But one morning, in the Charles Hotel in New Orleans, he bathed, dressed in his suit, and drove with Katherine to her home. He rose up the stairs, through the languor of those rooms and the scent from the garden. This was the house she had lived in. As a child she'd split her head on this banister; the small scar, just a tiny movement of skin, like a whitecap far out on the ocean, lay almost hidden in her eyebrow. He had touched it and touched it. He followed her into her mother's room and Glee looked up and smiled; a beautiful woman, the fine armature of her bones too evident beneath her skin. "Is this your friend?" Glee asked. "Yes," Katherine said, and he moved forward shyly. Glee studied him. The light in her eyes was like Katherine's. Metallic or warm, sometimes lethal. But there. Always there. She lay taking her time, taking it all in, this very thin, brown, tentative young man sweating in a shiny black suit. He did not do what an American young man of his age would have done—stand too close to her with a familiar, overconfident air, and pretend she wasn't sick, and joke around to hide his nervousness. This young man didn't do that. At last she said, "I never in my life imagined I'd find myself in such a situation. Did you?"

"No, ma'am," he said.

It was a hot day, humid and blue, but outside the city the air was cool as it coursed over them, and through it they could feel the plain warmth of the sun and not be oppressed by it. The car's shadow was stark and detailed. When they looked at it riding alongside them they saw their elongated figures stretching out of the top, Glee's great straw hat flopping like a bloom in the wind, Katherine's gossamer scarf, almost translucent to look at but thrown down on the ground in black outline and streaming behind, and between them, his unadorned head. They drove through wild, rich, flat country, with only the foliage of trees, like dark cumulus clouds, and the telephone poles rising up from it. The furrows of unplanted fields spun past, red with clay or the color of coffee, and the car's shadow bumped wildly over them. He was perched in the high space behind the front seats, with the car's collapsed top to lean back against. He would have to hunch to feel the shelter of the windscreen, but he didn't. He let the air roar against him. Glee sat with her eyes closed and her cheek turned against the seat, resting. Katherine reached back, and he caught the hand and held it. He could feel the water coming. The earth changed so subtly beneath them that, although they watched carefully for it, they missed the threshold where the water started conquering the land. They only knew when they had passed it. Marsh grass rippled away from the road. The sky's color was diluted with light and it seemed to recede even further above them. They turned onto a narrow track, white from crushed shells, and the ground broke apart, water standing low in the grass, the road rising to run like a dike, and then a channel taking shape to one side, deepening, and showing current on its surface. Beyond them was the pale brown line of the Gulf, where the channel was bound. And then they glimpsed the small house, floating in the air, and as they grew nearer saw its legs, one pair on land and one pair in the water, and the porch that jutted over the channel, with wooden steps descending to a short, sturdy dock. The water was still high from the storm, and it kicked lazily through the dock's slats. Nothing else about the house seemed affected. It stood serenely, bleached silver and tinged green with mildew, from years in the sun and the wet. Katherine turned off the engine and they sat in the vast quiet of the bright day, feeling the heat settle onto them again, and listening to Glee's reedy breath. At last Katherine touched her. "We're here, Mommy."

They went into the house together, carrying Glee between them like an armload of tinder, so light, and so brittle. When they were inside they encountered a sweet mushroom smell. Mold bloomed delicately on the couch cushions, but the cushions were oilcloth, made for an outdoor life, and they dusted them off with their palms. When they pressed their faces to the stripped beds they smelled nothing worse than skin. A bare bulb hung down over a rough wooden table that stank faintly, eternally, of crab. An old murder mystery paperback of her father's sat on the window ledge, yellow and swollen with water. They found one of the deck chairs, its faded canvas still secured to the frame with gray cord run through grommets, and pulled it onto the deck. Chuck threw himself down heavily, and the old gray cord held. Then they lowered Glee into it. She lay squinting out over the waterway, at the shifting grass, and the brown stripe of Gulf, and the sky. "Well, Kitty," she said. "Do you think we can do it?"

"There's a grocery twenty miles back. Your doctor won't come out here, though."

"That is the idea." Glee closed her eyes and smiled.

"I think we can. If it is what you truly want."

"It is."

"And no complaining about heat and damp and bugs."

"You forget how much time I've spent here. I used to get in that water wearing your father's old sneakers and a pair of his old saggy pants I cut short."

"What on earth were you doing?"

"I was catching our supper. Your father had a horrible broken-down outboard that he went off in every day, and if this water wasn't four feet deep all the way to Mexico I would have been a widow that much sooner. But he never caught anything. He just liked to get out in that boat and then he fell asleep. Do you believe I could catch a fish with a net, Mr. Ahn?"

"I do," he said, imagining her standing stock-still with the net held out, severely patient. Her image would be doubled by the water. "Like a bird."

"That's right," she said, pleased. "Will you wait for her?" she wondered suddenly, as Katherine said, "Don't," and batted her arm. Glee ignored this. "Will you wait for Kitty, while she's here with me? Are you that kind of young man?"

"Yes," he said. Glee returned his gaze, interested. They studied each other.

"It won't be long," she said at last, without sadness.

When Katherine called Charles she said simply, "I'm staying here, until it's over. And I've thought about things."

"What things?" he asked, unnecessarily. He knew. Bower had telephoned him, remembering his early kindnesses to Chuck. Bower thought Addison might have some idea of where Chuck had gone. The manager of the bindery had called Bower claiming Chuck had robbed her of a one-hundred-dollar bill, and of some imprecise sum of money which she surmised he had taken on the basis of his snapping at her bait. That Chuck had absconded from the job without leaving a trace corroborated what would have otherwise been a preposterous accusation. Bower spoke with awkward extravagance. He was mortified and sad. He didn't want to believe this was so. The worst of it was that the boy had gotten such an easy ride. He'd had everything handed to him. Perhaps this was what to expect.

"He's with you, isn't he?" Addison said. And something in her answer, the hesitant, guttural tone of her voice when she said, after a moment, only "Yes," struck him so finally, with such actual love for her, that he hung up the telephone that instant, not out of anger, but because that rough sound in her voice was the thing that he wanted to keep. He found himself walking to her house.

He hesitated a long moment before he let himself in. It was half packed, suspended in the midst of its disturbance, like the ruins of Pompeii. A cup sitting too close to the edge of the table, awaiting its saucer. An open box of awful children's gifts that had been given, over decades, to her mother. He sat among these things, with a lump in his throat, amazed that she had gotten this far in her belief that she could stay with him. Then he called Bower, and persuaded him to dignify Sewanee not with vengeance, but justice and mercy. "We've all done things, George. The mistakes of young men. We've all made them."

"I suppose we have," Bower said. It cheered him to be placed in the youthful category, even if retrospectively.

In the end, Bower expelled Chuck, with this offer: a job in the dining hall kitchen for the duration of the summer, to pay off the theft and the bindery's cost in replacing him. He would have to relinquish his room in Strake House. If he fulfilled his debts, he would be permitted to apply for readmission. And if admitted, in the future he would work. His scholarship he gave up forever. "I accept it," Chuck said, and Bower cried out, "Splendid! My boy, I'm relieved."

"I am," he swallowed hard. "I am very, very glad. Yes, I am."

Bower heard the slight quaver and hastened to get them past this awkward moment. "We've all done things," Bower said kindly.

She drove him to the bus station and they stood there again, in that provisional place. They searched each other for small details they might have missed. But he already knew how to see her. On the porch of the coast house with Glee, as if they rode at the front of a ship, their gaze fixed on the same point ahead. The house had so few rooms, was so bare, yet held so many things. The tin lid of Glee's cigarette filters, each one stained by lipstick. The cheap transistor radio, through which music only drifted, as if in transit between galaxies. Glee would lift a finger in the air, and grow perfectly still, always hoping to hear the whole song. The sheets from the beds folded up into squares. The dishes, the sun hats, the fish net. He will see her, gathering what's left into a box. Not yet, but soon. Pressing the windows shut, and leaving last night's new mold undisturbed. Rinsing her glass, setting it in the box, standing in the open door holding the box tightly, taking a last look around. Then she pulls the door to.

And she sees him, back in Sewanee. Walking with his head down and a letter of hers in his hands. Reading her prophecy. *This is what I imagine.* She knows his landscape so well, better than he'll ever know it. She can tell him where the shadow lies on the quad lawn, when he steps into it; how the colors around him emerge, as his gaze readjusts; when the branch will brush him, as he ducks beneath the tree. There he stops. Her presence accompanies him everywhere, gliding at his shoulder, needing nothing to make itself felt, but sometimes, even so, she lays a hand on him. He waits, leans against it a moment. He had thought he would always have two things, the great space within him where his home had to live, and that diminishment, when his body had imploded. Between the two, the excess of memory and its absence, was left a story he couldn't describe. But the story had begun to circumvent these difficulties. It grew shorter, and simpler. It would close around that event as his memory had closed around the torture and his body around the wound, and, constricting, leave no absence behind. She waits with him, patiently. It always takes such a strange summoning of himself, not reluctance, but the need to be poised, every thread of him knit. He breathes deeply, and whirls to face her. She sees him looking, through the tree's shifting shade, across the empty quad. He hears the sound of a lawnmower. Senses five forty-five in the slant of the light. And then he folds the letter carefully, and slides it into his pocket, and feels it there beneath his hand as he walks back out, into the glare.

For the rest of that summer he worked in the kitchen with

Louis, and the rest of Louis's bachelor crew. There was a terrace that hung off the back of the president's house, a wide, shady surface overlooking the lawn, and beyond that, the mossy and delicate woods falling toward a ravine. The summer people came here, for cocktails at six, and barbecue. He became a barbecuer, garbed in a stiff, full-length chef's apron as he turned and basted meat, waved the smoke from his face, solemnly served off the grill. It was summertime, and 1956. There had been a great relaxation of protocol, but the atmosphere remained genteel, and forgiving. He saw Charles Addison sometimes, squiring the niece of a Sewanee dowager, or standing at the center of an outburst of laughter, or standing alone. Addison would nod to him, a single tilt of his head and a momentary fixity of his eyes, and he would bow in return. Dance music wafted off the phonograph. One of Sewanee's many resident dogs trotted up to menace his grill, or a woman strode over the terrace and said, "I've been looking for you, Charles, here's your drink," and their connection was broken. He turned back to his work.

After dinner was over, the kitchen crew took what was left of the food, carrying their plates down the stone stairs that led to the lawn. They ate sitting there, gripping sweaty bottles of beer that the president set aside for them. They put off cleaning up for quite a while, lingering to smoke, gaze, exchange well-worn comments on the beauty of the day. The kind of talk that carried nothing but their feeling for each other, which was reflexive, and affirming. Yes, I'm here, it said. I see it, too. He got along well with these men. They never peered into his thoughtful silences, but they accepted him with humor, and their company sheltered him. He rode the bus with them, back to his small rented room in Monteagle, and even at the end of their workday, eight o'clock in the evening, the sun was still with them, guttering through the trees. He turns his face toward it. There are moments like this, rare instances of certainty and self-possession. When he found his family in Pusan his mother shooed him away from the door, because she thought he was a beggar. He had recoiled from her rebuke, gone down the street, and sat against a wall for hours before he went and knocked again. And yet he hadn't been angry or frightened, but only relieved. His cowardice, his weakness and sickness, were all swept away. In his mother's failure to recognize him, his duty to his family was done; and the suspicion that he had, despite shame and uncertainty, secretly harbored all along— that this could not be his life, that this war would never define him—finally proved to be right. And although his mother had wept that night, endlessly, and found food to give him, and washed his clothes, and sat clinging to his hands until he simply fell asleep in front of her, and although he went the next day to the USIS offices in Pusan and got a job, and spent the next two years, until the cease-fire, translating wire—consuming it, as if it could give him a new frame for thinking, a new lexicon—he was already gone, at that moment. He was already free.

❦ Perennial

Books by Susan Choi:

AMERICAN WOMAN
A Novel
ISBN 0-06-054222-5 (paperback)

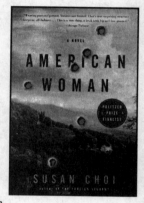

Fugitive Jenny Shimada, on the lam for an act of violence against the government, agrees to care for three younger fugitives who were smuggled out of California. One of her charges, the kidnapped daughter of a wealthy newspaper magnate, has become a national sensation due to her embracing of the philosophies of her captors.

"Weaving past and present, hunters and hunted, Choi's taut surprising structure keeps us off-balance. . . . This is a rare thing, a book both big and fine-grained."
—*Chicago Tribune*

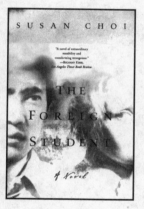

THE FOREIGN STUDENT
A Novel
ISBN 0-06-092927-8 (paperback)

In 1955, a new student arrives at a small college in the Tennessee mountains. Chuck is shy, speaks English haltingly, and on the subject of his earlier life in Korea will not speak at all. Katherine is a beautiful and solitary young woman who, like Chuck, is haunted by some dark episode in her past. Without knowing why, these two outsiders are drawn together, sensing in the other the possibility of salvation.

"A novel of extraordinary sensibility and transforming strangeness."
—*Los Angeles Times Book Review*